A *Baby* FOR HANNAH

JERRY S. EICHER

HARVEST HOUSE PUBLISHERS

EUGENE, OREGON

All Scripture quotations are taken from the King James Version of the Bible.

Cover photos © Chris Garborg; Bigstock / golfkatze

Cover design by Garborg Design Works, Savage, Minnesota

This is a work of fiction. Names, characters, places, and incidents are products of the author's imagination or are used fictitiously. Any resemblance to actual persons, living or dead, or to events or locales, is entirely coincidental.

A BABY FOR HANNAH
Copyright © 2011 by Jerry Eicher
Published by Harvest House Publishers
Eugene, Oregon 97402
www.harvesthousepublishers.com

Library of Congress Cataloging-in-Publication Data
Eicher, Jerry S.
A baby for Hannah / Jerry Eicher.
    p. cm. — (Hannah's heart ; bk. 3)
ISBN 978-0-7369-4336-9 (pbk.)
ISBN 978-0-7369-4337-6 (eBook)
1. Amish—Fiction. I. Title.
PS3605.I34B33 2011
813'.6—dc22

2010046521

Printed in the United States of America

11 12 13 14 15 16 17 18 19 / BP-SK / 10 9 8 7 6 5 4 3 2 1

One

Hannah Byler walked up the graveled lane toward the cabin, her right hand clutching the mail. She glanced down briefly at the letter on top of the small stack. Her mom had written, no doubt to rejoice with her and perhaps to tell her she was praying for her.

As Hannah slowed down to catch her breath, a shadow crossed her face as the dark memories of her miscarriage ran quickly through her mind. It had been only recently that she had known she was with child again, and this time she would make it through the nine months. She *must*. Miscarrying again would be too painful. Jake hadn't said much, but she knew he watched her in the evenings when he didn't think she'd notice. He'd glance away when she turned toward him, shadows from the gas lantern playing on his young bearded face. He loved her, Jake did, but Jake was also a preacher now. And for that reason—in addition to all the others—she must carry this child to full term.

Jake would still love her if she lost another of his children. They would sorrow together, comforting each other, but pity would be stirred in the eyes of the people. "He can preach," they would whisper when she wasn't around. "But why has God chosen to leave him childless?"

Jake had been ordained so suddenly last year, and just as quickly their lives were changed. They were no longer Jake and Hannah Byler, lost in their love for each other, living in their own world under the shadow of the Cabinet Mountains. They were now Jake Byler, the minister, and the minister's wife, Hannah.

Hannah paused, allowing her gaze to follow the mountain peaks disappearing toward the south. Hadn't Jake quoted the words of King David this past Sunday while he preached the main sermon? "I will lift up mine eyes unto the hills, from whence cometh my help." Only he had quoted the words in High German, in which he was now becoming quite fluent. Jake was like that—*gut* in a lot of things. Although the community didn't compliment him on his preaching—that just wasn't done—Betty, Hannah's aunt, was one of the few who dared whisper things after church like "My, that Jake of yours sure can preach."

But Betty dared to do and say a lot of things the others didn't. She was that way, and even on occasion was known to press the line on the *ordnung.* Her laugh and jolly spirit covered many sins, as Jake would say. Of course Jake liked her, as did everyone in the community. But would Jake's liking her be sufficient to cover for Betty if he knew she had hired an *English* girl to run her horse riding business last summer, even allowing the girl to wear very *English* clothing while working? Likely not. And so Hannah kept her mouth shut. Jake was kind, but he also had responsibilities that could override his heart.

Hannah studied the mountain range, following the familiar ridges and valleys. This was her home now, her beloved home. Here she and Jake had found each other that long-ago summer and then nearly lost their love while it was still in its infancy, only to find it again by the grace of God. Hannah glanced down, running her hand over the front of her dress. Her pregnancy didn't show much yet, but that would change soon.

What would it be like to walk into church on Sunday morning when everyone could see that she carried Jake's child? A thrill ran through her at the thought. It was too wonderful to comprehend. And surely she wasn't taking pride in the yet unborn child? Was this not what *Da Hah* wanted? Children born to carry on the human race and the *faith* her people believed in? *Jah*, and she was blessed to carry Jake's child. Surely this time *Da Hah* would have mercy on her. Surely this time, in His great wisdom, she would be permitted to see the baby's face.

"Please let it be, dear Lord," she whispered, picking up her steps again. "I want to give Jake a child. His and mine. Jake might be a great preacher, but he is also a man. And a man needs children."

The soft sound of a truck came over the hill moments before it came into view. Mr. Brunson was driving slowly. Hannah pushed her thoughts aside and stepped off the lane. Mr. Brunson slowed even more, rolled down his window, and came to a stop.

"Good afternoon there, Hannah," he said, smiling broadly.

"Good afternoon," Hannah said. "And how are you?"

He laughed. "As good as can be expected for an old man."

"You're not that old. Come on, now."

"That's easy for you young people to say. Jake works like a man on fire in the furniture shop."

"I know. He comes home so tired at night."

"Don't blame me," Mr. Brunson said with a grin. "The furniture is selling well enough, but Jake still won't slow down. In fact, it seems to make him work even harder."

"He's probably thinking of his family," she said, a warm blush spreading over her face.

"Can't say I was any different in my day," he said. "Oh, to be young again."

"Would you like to come down for supper?" she asked. "Perhaps next week some night? We would love to have you again. It seems quite a while since you visited, and I could make cherry pie."

"Cherry pie? Now how can I turn that down? But really, you don't have to bother."

"Is my cherry pie that awful?"

He laughed, "You know better than that. It's enough to reduce a man to tears, if that were possible with an old codger like me."

"It's not that *gut*," she said, laughing. "But please come. We could make it suit most any night."

"Most any night is good for me too. You know I don't have much to do."

"Jake tells me you help a lot in the furniture shop, so you shouldn't undersell yourself. You've been a great blessing to Jake and me, and we're very thankful. There wouldn't be much of a shop without your help in starting it up."

"I was glad to do it. And it took more than me. Jake makes beautiful log furniture. I simply came along behind him."

"We're still thankful," she said.

He laughed. "I'd better be going, Hannah. You take care of yourself. I'll let Jake know which night works next week, and I will expect an extra pie to take along home with me."

"You will have it," she said, waving as he drove off.

Mr. Brunson was a wonderful man, sent by *Da Hah* when they so needed help starting up Jake's business. He was not only a *gut* neighbor, but a *gut* friend.

At the front walk, the roses were trying to bloom, opening halfheartedly in the chilly air. Hannah stopped to admire them, the letter from her mother forgotten for a moment.

"It'll be warm soon," she said, bending over to brush their soft petals with the back of her hand. "Then you can really bloom. Just like me with Jake's child."

She laughed but it was the truth. How like a blooming it felt to be with child, and surely this time there would be a cry of a baby in the house by winter.

"Please, dear God," she whispered, standing up to walk toward the cabin. "I know You will help us."

Pushing open the front cabin door and listening to it creak, she stepped inside. After latching the door she walked over to Jake's little log desk. Holding the letter from her mother up to the light from the front window, Hannah studied the familiar handwriting before pulling the letter out.

> *Dear Hannah,*
>
> *Greetings in the name of the Lord. This finds us all well, and your dad is busy in the factory as usual. I think summer is coming early around here. We had a really warm day today, which was a surprise since the trees only recently got all their leaves.*
>
> *Your dad plowed the garden last night after work, and I see the neighbors have also done theirs today. I have half a notion to hitch the Belgian to the disk and work the ground, since I can't wait to get the early things in the ground. I think your dad would appreciate the job being done, but he wouldn't appreciate it if I wrecked something, so perhaps I'd better wait.*
>
> *I am so thrilled with the news in your last letter. I'm sure you and Jake are very happy, and if you are careful this time, everything will be fine. We will pray for you and for the health of the baby. Don't worry too much, as the Lord is merciful and does not give us greater burdens than we are able to bear.*

I know you don't want the news spread around yet, so I've been keeping my lips sealed with your sisters, even when they dug around for news at the last sewing. You know how they can be, but I think I kept a pretty straight face.

I suppose you haven't told Betty either, which brings me to the point I need to ask you about. Miriam has been pestering us for some time, saying she wants to visit you, perhaps for an extended time. I know how small your cabin is, and so I've not agreed to ask you, but your news brings up an interesting idea.

With the baby coming in late November, why couldn't we have Miriam come out for the summer to work at Betty's with the riding stable like you did those two summers? I guess the first question is, does Betty still run the stable? Perhaps her oldest daughter Kendra is involved?

I suppose I might as well tell you, Miriam has been really discouraged with her romantic options around here. I don't know why, as there are a lot of nice boys, but then what do I know? It's not like I'm going to marry them, as Miriam is quick to remind me.

Anyway, she has now turned twenty-one and has dated a few times, but nothing ever comes of it. I think her wish to visit you has more to do with that than anything. Miriam thinks that since you found a good husband in Montana, she might also be able to. I've told her things don't work like that, but she's not convinced. I've never been quite as close to her as I have been with you, but neither has she been as much trouble as you were. So I guess it all works out even in the end.

Anyway, maybe you can ask Betty, if you like the idea, or I can write her. Either way would be fine, but please let me know. Oh, and you could then break the news to Miriam later in the summer about the baby. You know—once you begin showing. You could ask her then about staying and taking care of you and the baby after the birth. I think that would work out great for all of us.

Think about it, and I'm so happy with the news. We will pray for a very nice, healthy baby.

With love,
Your mom, Kathy

"Mom," Hannah said, wiping her eyes as she folded the letter, "I love you so much." Sighing, she stared out the window, remembering. Wouldn't it be wonderful if her parents could visit again like they had last year? But no, that wasn't possible. A visit from Miriam would be second best but greatly appreciated once the baby came. *Jah*, she would ask Betty. And the sooner the better. Miriam might have wrong motives for the trip, but there were wonderful people in the community who would welcome her with open arms. They wouldn't know what her reasons for coming were, and there might indeed be someone special here who would satisfy her sister's requirements.

Perhaps, but who? And wouldn't that be something if there really was? They could both live in Montana, and she would have not only a baby, but a sister nearby.

Two

Hannah stood on the porch, her hands in her apron pockets, glancing down the graveled lane. Jake should be home soon, his driving horse prancing up to the driveway, anxious to get in the barn for the night. What a wonderful man Jake was. *Da Hah* had favored her with a *gut* husband to love. And here he came now, the buggy a black speck out on the main road.

Walking to the split-rail fence, Hannah waited by the rose bushes, idly running her fingers over the green leaves, gently touching the sharp thorns. How much like a rosebush life was turning out to be. So full of sweetness and beauty, with things mixed in the greenery to pierce one's heart at the most unexpected of times. But she must not think of them now. Life was growing green again. The winter was past, and spring had really come. Ahead lay summer—and then fall when she would have a *bobli* in her arms.

Hannah shivered. Even then there would surely be more thorns. There were always thorns of some sort—but there would also be the grace of God to carry one along. Her people believed in the one as surely as the other. It was *Da Hah*'s way of doing things, blessings and sufferings, both to mature the soul and keep one from becoming too attached to this world.

Jake's buggy came up over the last rise, the horse holding his head high, turning his face toward the barn with a loud whinny. When they got to the barn, Jake pulled up, the buggy door opened, and he leaned out with a smiling face.

"Howdy," he hollered as she ran toward the barn.

"Jake!" she said, leaping into his arms when he stepped down.

"My, what a welcome," Jake said, still holding the reins. The horse turned his head to look at them, giving another loud whinny.

"I'll help you unhitch Joel," she said.

"You came rushing out to help me unhitch?" he asked, tilting his head at her. "There must be more to it than that. You must have news."

"Oh, Jake," she said, wrapping her arms around his neck again. "I'm just happy to see you."

He laughed, "I think it's more than that."

"Jake," she said in mock reprimand. "Okay, there *is* news...but I do love you." She hugged him again and then said, "I got a letter from Mom. Miriam would like to come for a visit this summer to help Betty, and then stay to help me once the baby comes. We need to ask Betty though. Can we ask her this evening so I can write back? Can we, please? Can we go over and visit after supper?"

"Did I hear you mention supper?" he asked. "So you will at least feed me before this evening trip?"

"Of course I have supper ready," she said. "I wouldn't think of starving you."

"That's *gut* to hear. Let me tie Joel, and I'll be right in."

"I'll help you," she said, taking the tie rope out from behind the seat. Attaching the snap to the horse's bridle, she led him to the hitching post, where he dropped his head, looking longingly toward the barn.

"Looks like he doesn't want to visit anyone tonight," Jake commented.

"He's not that tired, and Betty isn't too far away. He'll get over his disappointment."

"If I feed him, he'll take it better," Jake said with a smile. "Just like a man does."

"You spoil him." Hannah laughed as she moved the tie rope to Joel's neck and fastened the rope again. She slid off the bridle while Jake went into the barn and returned with a bucket partially filled with oats.

Hannah stroked the horse's neck while he lowered his head, chomping greedily. Jake left for the barn again, returning quickly with another bucket filled with water. Setting it down within Joel's reach, he took Hannah's hand, leading her toward the house.

"So you want your supper too?" she asked, glancing back at Joel busily chewing the oats. "Didn't I pack a large enough lunch?"

"You packed a fine lunch," he said, pulling back on her hand, and stopping to look toward the mountains.

Hannah turned with him, following his gaze to where her eyes had gone earlier in the day. The last of the sun's rays had set the clouds hanging on the ridges on fire with a blaze of golden light. Stretches of dark gray and brown ran into the valleys, with the dark blue of the sky above them. A three-quarter-sized moon hung over the wooded tree line of the highest peak toward the south.

"It's so beautiful," she said.

"Yes, it is," he said, his fingers tightening on hers.

"I was looking at the mountains earlier," she said stepping closer to him. "I was thinking about our child. Do you think everything will be okay this time? I still feel like last time was my fault. Eating the infected meat surely was the reason. But this time, I'll try not to do anything wrong. Do you think *Da Hah* will bless us with His grace?"

"He already has," Jake said, pulling her close to him, his arm slipping around her shoulder. "He gave me you, and that's already enough. And it wasn't your fault. It could have happened to anyone."

"But it happened to me—to us. I so want this child to be born. He's yours Jake, yours and mine. I don't think I could stand it if something went wrong again."

"We can bear what *Da Hah* wishes to place on our shoulders," he said, his grip on her shoulder still tight.

"But Jake," she said, drawing far enough away to see his face. "You don't think that something *will* happen?"

"No, I don't," he said, kissing her gently on the forehead. "I think everything will go very well. And you will be an absolutely wonderful mother."

She ran her fingers through his beard, and he kissed her again.

"You're just saying so," she said. "To make me feel good."

"No," he said, his face growing serious. "I really do think everything will be okay this time."

"Thank you," she whispered, running her fingers down the length of his beard again. "When are you going to trim this again?"

"Why?" he asked, laughing. "Is it getting too long?"

"It makes you look so wise. I don't want a husband who's too wise. Not while I'm still so…unwise."

"Then I will clip some of it off," he said, laughing again. "It helps me feel—well, not quite so young and inexperienced—especially with the preaching and all. It's been so sudden."

"I know," she said. "And please don't trim your beard. I like it just the way it is."

He laughed. "We will see, and now, where is that supper before I starve completely and faint dead away from hunger?"

"Warming in the oven," she said, leaning against him, soaking in his strength. She stood looking at the mountain range again. He was so strong, so steady, and so sure of himself. He never wavered regardless of the storms they faced. How blessed she was to have such a husband. He would not falter in the months ahead, regardless of how things turned out.

"What are you thinking?" he asked, lifting her chin with his fingers. They smelled of hickory wood and varnish and felt calloused yet gentle on her skin.

"How wonderful you are," she said, meeting his eyes.

He laughed again. "Now, now, you'll have my head swelling soon, and my hat won't fit anymore."

"You are still wonderful," she repeated, walking toward the house, pulling him behind her.

He didn't resist, following her willingly to the wash basin, where she poured in warm water from the woodstove, waiting while he washed his hands and face.

"There!" he said, drying with the towel Hannah handed him. "Now I'm ready to eat."

"Come," she said, taking him by the hand again.

"My, I am getting special treatment tonight."

"You will soon be a father, and you deserve it."

"I think mothers deserve the praise," he said, kissing her on the cheek. "They are the ones who have the babies."

Hannah pushed him away, motioning with her hand. "Sit down."

Jake sat down as Hannah removed the chicken and fried beans from the oven. The bread she sliced quickly, and took the cover off the salad. With the butter and blackberry jam taken down from the lower cupboard, Hannah sat down across from him.

"Ready," she said.

Jake nodded, bowing his head, and speaking in German, led out in prayer. Hannah lifted her head when he was done, passing him the mashed potatoes before filling her own plate.

"I have been thinking about something," he said, pouring on the gravy.

"*Jah*? About us?"

"Sort of. It concerns us."

"The baby perhaps?"

He spoke slowly as he said, "I think we ought to build a new cabin further up on the hill."

For a moment, Hannah couldn't speak. "A new cabin? But we have a cabin—a nice one."

"I know. But it will become crowded with the baby and has only one spare bedroom. What happens when we have visitors?"

"But we hardly get any visitors. My parents came last year, but yours have never visited. When they do come, surely they will understand. Young people don't have a lot of money, and you are a preacher now."

"That should have nothing to do with it," he said. "I want to take care of my family."

"But you are," Hannah said, pausing to butter her bread. "I'm perfectly happy with what we have. This is a wonderful cabin and so full of memories. Of us, and of the time we have had together."

"That's exactly why you deserve better. Just look at you. You're still cooking on a woodstove when hardly anyone else in the community is. And we still don't have a refrigerator."

"But the money? Where's the money coming from?"

"I'm making some good money now—with Mr. Brunson's help, of course. I never could do it without him."

"Enough to build a brand-new cabin?"

"Maybe not yet," he admitted, staring at his food. "But I would like to. Especially with the baby coming."

"Maybe then we should wait until the baby comes to decide," she said, searching his face.

"Dear heart," he said, stroking her arm. "The baby will be okay."

"I don't mean that," she said. "It's just that I can make do for a little while yet. That way you don't have to spend money unnecessarily with the business starting up the way it is."

He thought it over for a moment and then said with a sigh, "It might be for the best. But maybe I can buy you a refrigerator at least. That doesn't cost that much."

Hannah laughed at the look on his face, reaching across the table to touch his face. "The springhouse is fine. It's good and strong, and it suits me. I get to walk outside in all kinds of weather, which is good for one's health. Besides, where would I put a refrigerator?"

"I don't know," he said. "See, you need a new cabin with a larger kitchen."

"It can't be fancy now, you know that."

"Log cabins aren't fancy," he said. "That's what I like about them. They are just nice."

"Anyplace would be nice with you," she said, touching his face again. She rose to bring a cherry pie back from the plastic pie container on the counter.

Setting the pie on the table she said, "I hope you don't mind, but I invited Mr. Brunson for supper next week."

"Of course not. I would love to have Mr. Brunson down."

Hannah caught a look of concern on his face as he spoke. "You seemed to become so sober looking when you mentioned his name. Is something wrong?"

"I guess it's because of the other news he mentioned."

"Bad news?" Hannah asked, passing him a piece of pie.

"I'm afraid so. Ben Stoll is setting up a tent in Libby this summer and bringing in a Mennonite Evangelist. I would guess it's the same one who ensnared him and Sylvia last year over in Kalispell."

"Surely not, Jake. Are you sure Mr. Brunson has his facts straight?"

"I'm afraid so. Apparently Ben has no plans to leave us in peace."

"But that won't affect us," Hannah said over her own piece of cherry pie.

"No," he said. "But I'm worried about the other people in the community. Who knows how many of them will fall for this revival wave that's sweeping the area. Bishop John has been worried about it ever since we lost Ben and Sylvia."

"I know, but as long as it doesn't reach us, we'll be okay...won't we?"

"I hope so," he said, smiling thinly. "At least we have a *gut* bishop to guide us through the rough waters. For that we can be very thankful."

Three

Jake slipped the bridle over the horse's ears in the glow of the dim buggy lights as Hannah climbed up on the seat. She held the reins, while Jake threw the tie rope in back and then stepped up to sit beside her.

"Get-up," Jake called to the horse after taking the lines.

The horse jerked his head, protesting the trip, and turned to walk slowly out of the driveway. Jake slapped the lines again, and Joel took up a slow trot toward the main road. At the blacktop, Jake pulled him to a stop and looked for traffic before turning east toward Libby.

Hannah settled back into the seat, pulling the buggy blanket over her knees.

"It's a little chilly tonight," she said as Jake lowered the storm front.

"There's nothing quite like Montana though," he said. "Even if the spring and fall are a lot shorter than back East."

"I like it," she said, snuggling up against him. "And I like you."

He snapped the reins, and the horse moved into a trot.

"You sure are sweet tonight," he said.

"I'm always sweet, but maybe it's the spring weather, or perhaps it's just being with you. We ought to take drives more often in the nighttime. I miss them from our dating days."

"Like driving home from the singings," Jake said with a laugh. "Like taking you home and staying till midnight. I think we're a little beyond that, don't you?"

"I suppose," she said, her head on his shoulder.

The silence of the night wrapped around them as the sound of the horse's hooves beat steadily on the pavement.

"Do you think Bishop John can do anything about Ben setting up that tent in Libby?" Hannah asked.

"I don't think so. There's not much we can do. If Ben sets it up, then he does."

"But surely Bishop John can speak with the Mennonites. They ought to respect our church and not have their meetings so close to us. There are lots of other places to have meetings if they want to save souls."

"I'm afraid they're trying to save *our* souls," Jake said. "That's why they're setting up so close."

Hannah jerked her head upright and sat up straight. "*Us*? They are trying to save us?"

"Something like that."

"But we don't need saving."

"Remember what Ben and Sylvia said at the meeting we had with them last fall? They both said they felt like sinners for the first time and now felt cleansed. It has something to do with that."

"But we are saved. Aren't we?" Hannah asked, searching his face in the dim light of the passing *Englisha* yard lights.

"We have our hope set on God's grace," Jake said. "No one can be saved without God's grace."

"Then I'm saved," Hannah said, nestling back against him. "But I wish Ben and Sylvia would leave us alone. I don't think it's nice of them to set up this tent in Libby, right on our back doorstep."

Jake didn't say anything, and when Hannah glanced up, his beard was a dark shadow in the darkness. His hands tightened on the reins as he pulled back, guiding Joel into Steve and Betty's driveway.

"There's no one in the barn," he said. "We'd better go straight to the house."

"Are you saved, Jake?" Hannah asked softly, climbing down the buggy step in the darkness.

"I hope so," he said, not turning around from tying the horse to the hitching post.

"But Jake," she said, grabbing his arm, "the way you preach and the way you pray and how you talk with God. I know you're saved because I know your life. I'm your wife. You surely don't doubt, do you?"

"No," he said, shaking his head in the shadows. "But I guess I grew up in a different community than you did. We believed a man's relationship with God was a private matter. That you didn't go talking about it with everyone, like it didn't mean anything, and like you could tell God what He was and wasn't supposed to be doing."

"You are a *gut* man," she said, still holding to his arm. "If I love you so much, God must love you a whole lot more."

He bent over slowly to kiss her cheek. "We really should talk about something else, Hannah. What if Betty looks out her window and sees us kissing in her yard?"

Hannah giggled. "Then she'll think we're really in love."

"She also will think we're losing it. We've been married long enough to have two pregnancies."

"All the more reason to have you kiss me," she said, letting go of his arm as they approached the front door.

Jake rapped gently with his knuckle. Soft footsteps followed, with Betty's oldest daughter, Kendra, opening the door. She squinted for a moment and then broke into a broad smile.

"It's Jake and Hannah," she shouted back into the living room, turning to hold the door wide open. "Do come in. What brings you out tonight?"

"Hannah wanted to speak with your mom," Jake said, stepping inside.

"About what?" Kendra asked Hannah as she walked past.

"Secrets," Hannah whispered back and Kendra gasped.

"Really?"

"No, not really," Hannah said. "Miriam wants to come out for the summer, and we need to see if that might work into your mom's plans."

"I would *love* to have Miriam here," Kendra said. "So *my* answer is definitely yes."

Hannah smiled. "I also think it would be great, but we'll have to see what your mom says."

"Jake and Hannah," Betty said, entering from the kitchen, "what a surprise! And we have no popcorn made at all."

"There's still time," Steve hollered from his chair, observing the scene.

"I think I will," Betty said. "Are you staying long enough for that? Surely you are. You can't just drive all the way over here and not stay for popcorn."

"We can't stay long," Jake said. "But a little popcorn would be great."

"Then Kendra," Betty said, "get some made up right away. It won't take long at all."

"I'll get right to it," Kendra said, disappearing into the kitchen.

"I can help," Hannah offered.

"No you won't," Betty said, taking her arm and leading her after Jake. "You are visitors tonight and will be treated as such."

"Visitors do work," Hannah said with a grin.

"Not tonight they don't," Betty said, letting go of Hannah's elbow as they walked into the living room. Jake was already seated on the couch next to Steve in his rocker.

"I had to talk with Betty," Hannah said, explaining the visit to Steve as she sat beside Jake.

"Women's secrets?" Steve said. "I suppose Betty will be glad to get in on the new gossip."

"Now, Steve," Betty said with a glare, "Hannah is a minister's wife, and she doesn't gossip."

"Oh, I suppose minister's wives still have a few faults," Steve said with a smile, glancing at Hannah. "Don't they, Jake?"

"She doesn't have very many," Jake said, patting Hannah on the arm.

"Now see there," Betty said. "You've hurt the poor girl's feelings for no good reason at all."

"I'm not perfect, Betty," Hannah said, getting a word in edgewise. "Now, let's talk about something else besides me."

"Do I get in on the secret?" Steve asked.

"Really, it's nothing much of a secret," Hannah began. "Well, maybe it is, but Mom wanted me to look into this right away so they can make plans."

In the background the sound of popcorn popping came from the kitchen, and Hannah paused to listen.

"Go out and help your sister," Betty said to twelve-year-old Nancy. "Maybe you could get the apples from the basement."

Nancy closed her book and headed for the kitchen.

Hannah followed the young girl with her eyes. "Your children are growing up so fast."

"Yes, we all are getting older. I suppose it won't be long now before Steve and I are grandparents."

"Hey, don't be rushing things," Steve said. "He just brought Kendra home on Sunday night for the first time."

"It was Mary Keim's boy, the youngest—Henry," Betty explained. "He's so handsome, I couldn't believe it when Kendra told me he asked her. I always wanted good-looking boys for my girls, but this was such a surprise. It's as if *Da Hah*'s actually seeing eye-to-eye with me on the subject!"

"They're not married yet," Steve cautioned.

"But they will be…in a few years," Betty said knowingly. "Kendra won't let this one slip away."

"So, I still haven't heard the juicy gossip," Steve said, rocking steadily.

"Steve, there are children around, and there is no gossip," Betty said. "So please quit saying so."

He laughed, "Well, I'm waiting all the same."

"Popcorn!" Kendra announced, coming into the room with a heaping plastic bowl, carrying smaller bowls with her other hand.

"Popcorn," Steve said. "Help yourself there, Jake. You're sure not saying much tonight."

"Well, it's Hannah who wants to talk with Betty," he said.

"Jake uses up all his words preaching," Betty said. "Don't you know that, Steve? You shouldn't tease the man like that."

Jake grinned. "I'd talk if I had something to say, but eating popcorn looks like a better idea."

"That's the man for me," Steve said, heaping high one of the smaller bowls. He handed it to Jake, who took it, settling back on the couch. Steve filled his own bowl, while Betty stood up to prepare one for Hannah.

"Just a little popcorn," Hannah said with a wave of her hand.

"So start from the beginning," Betty said, sitting down again.

"Mom wrote a letter," Hannah said before chewing some popcorn slowly. "She wonders whether Miriam could come out for the summer and perhaps on into the fall. Miriam has been wanting to travel for some time, I guess, and this would be the year for it since she turned twenty-one last summer."

"Oh," Betty said. "Well, of course she would be welcome."

"Mom is wondering if she could work at the riding stable like I did those two summers."

"Hey, that's a great idea!" Steve said. "I could use all that money like you made for us those two years."

"Steve," Betty said, "watch what you're saying."

Steve laughed and Jake joined in.

"Well, I guess it did help," Betty said. "So maybe it would be an idea to consider, as I'm certainly not hiring that *English* girl again. But we don't have but two horses this year. Although I don't imagine Miriam would care."

"She shouldn't," Hannah said. "It might leave her more time for other things, as I remember us being pretty busy with four horses the year I worked."

"I think it's a great idea," Steve said. "So let's consider the matter settled. I'll even get two more horses if Miriam's as good with them as Hannah was."

"They're sisters," Betty said. "She ought to be."

"I think Miriam will do fine," Steve said.

"Well then, there's your answer," Betty said. "If Steve has no objections, then neither do I."

"I have no objections," Steve said.

"Then I'll write Mom right away," Hannah said, "and see when Miriam can come. I have a feeling it will be fairly quickly."

"Oh, it will be a great summer then," Betty said, smiling from ear to ear. "I can feel it in my bones."

Jake cleared his throat on the couch, and Steve glanced sharply at him.

"Is something wrong with this plan?" Steve asked. "Are there ministerial objections?"

"No," Jake said. "It's just that Betty's comments about a good summer just reminded me that Ben Stoll is setting up a tent in Libby for Mennonite revival meetings."

"Oh no," Betty groaned. "Not the Mennonites in Libby. What is this world coming to, anyway?"

"I'm afraid it's true," Jake said.

"Do you think they'll give us much trouble?" Steve asked.

"I hope not," Jake said. "Bishop John has things fairly well under control, I think."

"That's good," Steve said, scooping up another bowl of popcorn.

Betty groaned again, "I think I changed my mind. It's going to be a perfectly awful summer. I can feel it in my bones."

Four

Hannah sat writing at the kitchen table, the cabin silent around her. Signing her name with a flourish, she paused to read what she had written.

Dear Mom,

It was so good to hear from you yesterday, and thank you so much for your concern. We are doing well, and the baby is fine as far as I know. I hope and pray things will stay that way.

Jake is doing well at the furniture shop. Mr. Brunson is such a blessing to us and has become a good friend. He is coming down for supper tomorrow night. He wants cherry pie for dessert and one to take home with him. I'd better get busy soon with the food making.

Jake took me over to Betty's last night so I could ask her about Miriam's visit. Betty agreed at once. They were all very excited, including Steve. I think Steve wants the extra income this summer again. I don't think Betty planned to do much with the riding stable this year since they had trouble with the English girl they hired last year. Kendra could manage, I suppose, but she doesn't like horses that much. Plus she's dating Mary Keim's boy and likely has her mind on other things.

So Miriam is welcome to come. I say the sooner the better. If she wants to stay at the cabin for a while, I would love to have her. Long term of course, she could stay at Betty's place. Jake is talking of building a larger house higher up on the ridge, but I don't think it will happen anytime soon. Such things take money, and even if Jake is doing well, I'd hate to spend his hard-earned money on a new house unless it's absolutely necessary. He works so hard already, and then there's the church work yet.

Which reminds me to tell you—Jake said the Mennonites are setting up a tent revival this summer here in Libby. That's our closest town. Jake thinks they are definitely targeting the Amish community, which seems like an awful thing to me. We only have one district and not that many people. Last year we lost Ben and Sylvia Stoll, the young couple you met on your visit, and it's not like we can afford to lose any more.

I know each loss would hurt Jake and Bishop John terribly. Jake has a lot of faith in Bishop John. He thinks John's steady hand will guide us through this time. But the reason I'm telling you this is in case it has any effect on Miriam coming to Montana. I don't think it should, but I wanted to warn you. Jake and I certainly have no intentions of being drawn into this new thing, and I can't imagine there being much danger to Miriam either.

Well, I have a house to clean and plans to make for Mr. Brunson's supper, so I'd better get busy.

With much love,
Hannah

Hannah sealed the envelope and walked quickly out the front door. She glanced briefly at the mountain range shrouded in low-hanging clouds before walking down the graveled lane toward the main road. A gentle breeze from the south pushed gently at her back. Hannah spread her arms, throwing her head back and laughing softly. Summer really was just around the corner, and Miriam was coming to visit.

"It will surely be a *gut* year. Won't it?" she said, looking over her shoulder and pausing as the sun broke through the clouds, flooding the distant valley in sunlight.

"It sure will be," she whispered, still watching as the sunlight grew until the whole mountain range was filled with light. As Hannah waited, the growing light paused, and began to slowly fade away as clouds moved in.

A smile trembled on her lips before Hannah turned to walk on. At the blacktop road she placed the letter in the mailbox and raised the flag. Turning to walk back up the hill, the wind was in her face now and she spread her arms again, closing her eyes.

"Go ahead, world," she whispered. "Make your trouble. Because I'm safe with God and with Jake. They love me."

The gravel crunched beneath her black shoes. Hannah opened her eyes, looking toward the mountains. All was cloudy now with no sign of the earlier breakthrough of sunlight. Approaching the cabin, Hannah paused at the split-rail fence.

"Good morning, roses," she said. "Are you happy this morning? It looks like there might be rain later for you. That's better than my water, isn't it?"

The roses swayed gently in the soft breeze and she laughed. Flowers couldn't talk back, of course, but it sure would be *gut* to have someone in the house soon who could. A little *bobli,* perhaps a boy, who could coo as well as cry. He would be Jake's boy, and a part of Jake would have come into the world to carry on his name. Or perhaps the child would be a little girl, a cute little girl, because Jake could only have cute little girls. Either way, the *bobli* would come to bless them with sweetness and love.

"I hope you don't die from too much attention," she said to the roses with one last backward glance.

Going into the cabin through the kitchen door, Hannah laid her recipe book out on the table. It was time for serious planning for Mr. Brunson's special night. He had done so much for them and deserved the best.

Flipping through the pages, her mom's recipe for underground ham caught her attention. Would that be the thing to make for Mr. Brunson? It tasted *gut*, but might it be a little fancy? Perhaps he was expecting something more Amish. More simple. Even something like mashed potatoes, gravy, and chicken.

Jah, Mr. Brunson would like the basics. With a smile, Hannah closed the book. The gravy and fried chicken could be made without recipes. Yet there needed to be more or Mr. Brunson might think she'd simply slapped something together.

There was the cherry pie of course, but something even more was needed. Hannah thought for a long moment and then found the tab for salads in her recipe book. Opening the page, her eye caught the recipe for a seven-layer salad. *Jah*, that was the very thing. This would add a touch of fancy, and then perhaps homemade ice cream for dessert. Mr. Brunson would be so impressed his eyes would sparkle with joy.

Hannah laughed at the thought. Homemade ice cream would be just the thing and would go perfectly with the cherry pie. When he came for supper, Mr. Brunson would have something to eat that fully expressed Jake's and her gratitude.

Walking into the living room to the hickory desk, Hannah came back with a pen and paper and sat down at the table. Looking over the recipes, she began her grocery shopping list. There was no way she had all these items in the house. Carefully she wrote down a bag of potatoes and cream cheese to add a little extra taste to the mashed potatoes. There was enough flour and seasoning in the house for gravy, but no cherry pie filling. This summer she really would have to can cherries instead of relying on store-bought. Betty said there was an orchard north of Libby that sold cherries for a reasonable price.

Scribbling on the list, Hannah added the vegetables for the seven-layer salad, extra lettuce, and buttermilk for her chicken batter. Two bags of chicken should be enough—if she remembered correctly the bag sizes the grocery store carried. Now, did she have enough bacon for the green beans?

Stepping outside through the kitchen door, Hannah walked to the springhouse above the presently budding garden. The long rows of corn had sprouted last week already, holding their green shoots skyward this morning, apparently eager for the rain that now threatened over the mountains. One long row was devoted to tomatoes and beside it, the potatoes. Shorter rows went for green beans, carrots, and lettuce. Now that Miriam was coming, she could help with the weeding and harvesting.

Opening the springhouse door, Hannah stepped inside the cool darkness. The spring waters bubbled out of the ground here, and Jake had built the shack over the spot. Shelves lined the walls, with an open, graveled pit for vegetables and potatoes. Hannah squinted, finding a single package of bacon on the lower shelf.

So it had been *gut* that she checked. She also would need ice to make the ice cream…or should she cheat and bring back store-bought ice cream? It would keep in a plastic bag lowered into the cool water.

Nee…it must be homemade. Mr. Brunson deserved the best. So she needed cream. They really needed a cow. Perhaps someday when Jake could put up a larger fence since the two horses didn't fully use the present pasture. But that could all come after the *bobli*.

Carefully Hannah closed the springhouse door and walked back across the lawn. Back inside the cabin, Hannah finished her list and retrieved her billfold and checkbook from above the cabinet and her bonnet and shawl from the utility room. Out in the barn she pushed open the door with both hands. Mosey wandered over at the sound, and she quickly snapped the tie rope on his halter. "That a boy," she said, rubbing his neck. "You're a nice horse, aren't you?"

He whinnied and bobbed his head.

Leading him out of the stall, Hannah threw the harness over his back in two big heaves. Laughing, she tightened the chest straps while he turned his neck and head to look at her.

"I'm going to make them good and tight," she said. "I don't want things coming off while I'm driving alone."

He turned his head back, and Hannah jerked on the strap, bringing it up another notch.

"There," she said. "That's good enough. Now we're ready for the bridle."

Mosey opened his mouth without any resistance as she slid in the bit, tightening the throatlatch. He could be a pain, clamping his teeth shut if he was in a bad mood.

"You're in good spirits this morning," she said. "Which is *gut* because I'm bringing back an awful lot of groceries."

Hannah pulled on the reins, and Mosey followed her out to the buggy, swinging under the shafts by himself when she held them up.

"Good boy," she said. "That's the way to act. Now hold still while I fasten things."

Slipping the tugs on, and walking completely around him one last time, Hannah threw the lines through the open storm front. Placing her hand on his bridle, she held Mosey for a few seconds before making a dash for the buggy steps. He didn't move until she was inside and picked up the lines.

Driving to the main road, Hannah pulled Mosey to a complete stop, checking for traffic both ways before she let out the lines. Mosey quickly settled into a steady pace, eating up the miles, as she allowed the peace of the drive to settle over her.

Englisha cars slowed down, pulling out before they zoomed past her, but she paid them no mind. Everyone seemed to drive faster around here than back East, but there had never been any Amish buggy accidents in the small community yet, so maybe the *English* people here in Montana were more careful.

At the edge of Libby, she tightened up on the reins. The grocery store parking lot only had a few cars near the building, and Hannah pulled up to the nearest light pole, climbing down to tie Mosey securely to the metal pipe. Walking toward the grocery store, her eye caught a large advertisement posted on the glass doors. Such posters were common on the grocery store doors, but this one brought her to a complete halt. A large picture of a tent was plastered over the pane with words in black above it: *Old-Fashioned Tent Revival. Everyone welcome.*

Hannah caught her breath and stared for a long moment. The Mennonites really were coming to Libby.

Five

Hannah rushed about the kitchen stirring up the last of the ice cream ingredients. Jake had come home early with the ice wrapped with blankets in the back of the buggy. He was outside now setting up the hand freezer on the walk.

"I'm ready," Jake hollered, his voice carrying faintly through the log walls.

There was no use shouting back; her voice wouldn't carry. Opening the kitchen door she stepped around the corner of the cabin.

"It's almost ready," she said. "I just have to stir in the cream."

"The ice is melting," Jake said, leaning against the rail fence, two bags of ice at his feet.

"I'll be right back," she said, turning back inside.

Carefully she measured the cream, poured it in, and stirred slowly until the mixture turned an even color. Mr. Brunson must have the best homemade ice cream possible, and it all started with preparing the base correctly.

"That should do it," Hannah said, giving one last stir before tossing in handfuls of pecans. Butter pecan ice cream was a little risky, a last-minute decision at the grocery store, but she could do this. Her mom had made butter pecan ice cream many times—but then she wasn't her mom. Still, Mr. Brunson was worth the chance.

Emptying the bowl into the metal ice cream canister, she wiped the edges clean and replaced the lid. Carrying the canister with both hands, she opened the kitchen door with her foot and squeezed through.

"You should've called for help," Jake said when she came around the corner.

"I know," she said, gasping. "This thing is slipping out of my hands."

"Then I'll take it," he said, running over and grabbing the bottom. With a flourish he carried the canister forward, lowering it into the wooden outer shell of the ice cream maker.

"Make sure the crank's on tight before you add any ice," Hannah said, watching Jake struggle with the alignment. He grunted and started over by latching in the crank on one side, lowering it down and turning the canister with the other hand until it snapped into place.

"There," he said. "I think that's it. Now for the ice and salt."

"I can help you turn the crank for awhile."

"Not with all your work in the kitchen," Jake said. "I can manage."

"I have some time, and the chicken is still in the oven."

"But you don't have to. I've made ice cream by myself before."

"I want to help," she said, tilting her head. "I want to be with you. You don't come home early that often anymore. This is a real treat for me."

"I hope it turns out to be a real treat for Mr. Brunson," Jake said. "It sure is a lot of work you've gone to."

"He's worth it. We owe Mr. Brunson a lot for what he did for us with the furniture shop."

"*Jah*, I sure couldn't have done it without him," Jake said, pouring the ice around the canister.

"Just think how this ice cream will taste when it's done. It seems like years since we've made homemade ice cream."

"We haven't made any since last year," Jake said, sprinkling on a thin stream of rock salt. "I do miss it a lot."

"Some things are like that. You forget how much you like them if you don't do it once in awhile."

"Like kissing you," he said, touching her cheek with his finger.

"Oh, you do that often enough!" she said. "Now keep your salty hands off me."

He laughed softly, kissing the back of her hair where her *kapp* didn't reach.

Hannah giggled and took the ice cream handle, motioning with her other hand, "We have to get some work done around here. You hold down the freezer, and I'll take the first turn."

"This is going to be *gut*," he said, pressing down on the crank with both hands.

"Oh, it will be," she said, spinning the handle until she was breathless.

"You don't have to turn so fast. It won't get done any quicker."

"I know that. It's just for fun, that's all," she said, slowing down.

Jake stretched his back and, motioning up the gravel lane with his beard, said, "Mr. Brunson is coming. Let me take my turn."

"Afraid he'll see the woman doing all the work?"

"*Jah*," he said. "Now quick before he sees you."

Hannah laughed and stood up, "He wouldn't care. I know he wouldn't."

"There's no sense in taking chances," he said, grabbing the handle and twirling it rapidly.

Hannah held down the ice cream freezer as Mr. Brunson pulled in and parked by the barn.

"Well, well, what have we here?" he asked getting out of his truck. "The Mr. and the Mrs. making homemade ice cream?"

"Butter pecan at that," Jake said, pausing in his twirling. "I was taking my first turn."

"Then let me take my turn," Mr. Brunson said. "Since I will no doubt be eating a large portion of this."

"Just leave plenty for me too!" Jake said with a laugh.

"Good evening, Hannah," Mr. Brunson said.

"Good evening," Hannah said. "I'm so glad you could come."

"I think I'm the one who will be glad," Mr. Brunson said, rubbing his stomach. "I still have pleasant memories from my last visit."

"We'll need to have you down more often," Jake said. "I'm glad Hannah thought of inviting you."

"Leave it to a woman's touch," Mr. Brunson said. "I had a wonderful wife myself once. But we will not go there tonight on such a joyous occasion as supper at the Byler house. I sure hope you didn't work yourself too hard, Hannah."

"I didn't at all," Hannah said. "And you have been such a help to Jake with his furniture business, we can never properly repay you."

"Oh, but Jake already has," Mr. Brunson said. "He has made me quite a lot of money, so you shouldn't feel bad at all."

"Then supper will be for our friendship's sake," Hannah said.

"Fine with me," he said, pulling down on the bill of his John Deere cap. "Now what can I do to help? I've never made homemade ice cream before."

"Hold the freezer so it doesn't tip while I crank," Jake said. After a few minutes he paused to add more ice and rock salt. "Things are starting to move along. It's turning harder."

"I'm going back to the house," Hannah said as Mr. Brunson placed both hands on the crank.

Hannah turned the corner of the house, catching her last glimpse of the two men. Jake was saying something and laughing heartily as Mr. Brunson took a turn cranking the handle. In the kitchen she quickly cleaned off the table and set it.

Then she attended to the last of the supper preparations. Opening the oven, Hannah tested the chicken. Satisfied, she closed the damper on the woodstove, and transferred the chicken to hot pads on the table. Retrieving more hot pads from the drawer, she did the same with the mashed potatoes and gravy.

After slicing the bread and setting out the butter and jam, she removed the cover on the bowl of salad and transferred it to the table. The green beans still were on the back of the stove—in a warm spot—since there wasn't room left on the table. She had an extra table leaf in storage in the bedroom closet. The problem was the kitchen was too small for its use. Even when her parents had been here last year, they had made do with the way things were. Maybe Jake was right in saying they needed a larger home.

Walking outside, she called around the corner of the house, "Supper's ready anytime."

"Almost done," Jake said, looking up, his face intent as he strained to turn the handle.

"How do you know when it's done?" Mr. Brunson asked.

"When you can't turn anymore." Jake groaned, stopping his efforts. "I think we just arrived at that point." He picked up the icy freezer and headed for the kitchen, "Mr. Brunson, maybe you could get the door for me."

The older man squeezed around Jake and swung open the door as Jake hurried through. Jake slid the freezer onto the kitchen counter and sighed. "Heavier than I thought it would be."

"The food's hot, so we should eat," Hannah said.

"Have a seat," Jake said to their guest, waving toward a chair. "I declare Hannah has worked me harder since I got home than I did at the shop."

"But it's worth it," Hannah said. "You'll think so too when you taste the ice cream."

"I think so already," Mr. Brunson said. "Look at all the food you've made. Mashed potatoes, gravy, green beans, fried chicken, salad—and that doesn't even cover the dessert. You really shouldn't have, Hannah."

"I hope you like it," she said.

"I already *more* than like it," he said, shaking his head. "But all this food is a little much."

"If we don't pray soon, the food will be cold," Jake said. "Would you please ask the blessing, Mr. Brunson?"

"I would be glad to," he said, bowing his head. Hannah followed, closing her eyes. It was strange that Jake would ask an *English* man to lead in prayer in their house, but she trusted his judgment. Plus he was a *gut* friend—not like the Mennonites who sought to lead them astray.

"Dear Father in heaven," Mr. Brunson prayed. "I thank You tonight for these, my two friends Jake and Hannah. I thank You that they have invited me into their home. I thank You for this wonderful food Hannah has worked so hard to prepare. I pray that You bless Jake and Hannah's efforts and their kindness, both to me and to so many others.

"I thank You for Jake and the hardworking man that he is, for the honesty he shows in his business dealings, for the quality of his work, and that he cares about the people who buy the furniture he makes.

"Bless now this wonderful food that is before us, and give us Your blessing for the rest of our evening together. Amen."

Jake lifted his head, and Hannah avoided Mr. Brunson's eyes. She was sure there were tears in her own, and it might be best if Mr. Brunson didn't see them. He had said some wonderful things about Jake in his prayer—which were all true, but still, her people didn't just go around saying things like the *Englisha* people apparently did. And certainly not in speaking to *Da Hah*.

"Mashed potatoes first," Jake said, passing the bowl to Mr. Brunson. He heaped his plate high, and then poured on the gravy Jake handed him.

Mr. Brunson is planning to eat his fill tonight, which is gut, Hannah thought. Jake too piled on the mashed potatoes. Both men already loved her food, she could tell.

After a few minutes of casual conversation, there was a lull. Mr. Brunson cleared his throat, and Hannah glanced at his face. It had sobered, as if he had something important to say. She held her breath as he laid his fork on the table.

"Perhaps this is not the time to say it," Mr. Brunson said. "But I don't know when a good time would be."

Hannah was glad when Jake said, "Speak what's on your mind, Mr. Brunson. We'll make it the right time if it isn't already."

"Well," Mr. Brunson said, clearing his throat again. "You are a minister, aren't you, Jake?"

"*Jah*," Jake said. "I am. The youngest one around here, but a minister."

"Then can you tell me what happens if I wish to date one of your women?"

Six

Jake paused, his spoon halfway to his mouth, as Hannah gasped.

"I hope I haven't been too forward," Mr. Brunson said. "I didn't mean any disrespect. But how do you deal with outside people who wish to marry one of the Amish women?"

"I do assume you have someone in mind?" Jake asked, clearing his throat. "Or you probably wouldn't be asking. Have you spoken with the woman in question about this matter?"

"Not in the way you mean," Mr. Brunson said. "But I buy the occasional dozen eggs from her stand along Highway Two, and I have spoken with her when we met once in the grocery store in Libby. I didn't want to pursue the matter any further until I knew what the proper steps would be."

"Then you mean Mary Keim," Jake said. "She's the only one who has a stand along Highway Two."

"She is a widow?" Mr. Brunson asked, glancing at Jake's fallen face.

"She is," Jake said more stiffly than he intended. An awkwardness fell over the room.

A shadow crossed Mr. Brunson's face. "I'm sorry about this. I had no intention of disturbing you with my question. I wouldn't want anything to affect my friendship with you and Hannah or with your people. I have a very high regard for your faith."

"Yes, we know you do," Jake said, taking a deep breath and attempting a smile. "And I apologize for my reaction. I had no idea you were thinking of such things."

"Why? Is it because I'm old? Jake, old men get lonely. Am I to be denied love even though I'm up in years?"

35

Hannah held her breath. What was Jake going to say? Would he offend Mr. Brunson?

"But you have your own people," Jake said, meeting Mr. Brunson's eyes.

"That I do," Mr. Brunson said. "But good women at my age are hard to find. At least good women with the values I admire."

"Surely there would be someone," Jake said. "Have you any idea how hard it will be to marry into our faith? And that's if Mary would even accept your offer."

"Now, now," Mr. Brunson said, laughing softly. "You underestimate me, Jake. What woman would turn down a great catch like me?"

Jake laughed as Mr. Brunson's words broke the tension.

"It's not that simple," Hannah spoke up. "There would be the matter of becoming part of us. Do you know what taking on our ways means? It's very hard."

"I would think it would be worth the sacrifice," Mr. Brunson said. "Especially to win the heart of a woman like Mary."

"I take it then that you are well into thinking about this," Jake said. "Is there anything we can say to persuade you otherwise?"

"I've thought long and hard about it," Mr. Brunson said. "I didn't ask to have you tell me I couldn't pursue the woman. I want to know how to do it legally. So I don't run afoul of traditions, religious beliefs, and that sort of thing."

"And do you think Mary will be agreeable to this, ah, pursuit?"

"I don't know. But an old man must try again when he sees another chance at love. I don't have many years left, Jake."

"This is a hard thing you ask."

"But don't you see?" Mr. Brunson continued. "I am what I am today because of you and Hannah. Because of you two I have a renewed relationship with my son, Eldon. I came back from my self-imposed exile after the accident that killed my wife and daughter. I could never have come back from all that without your friendship, without the kind of Christian example your people gave me. I've received hope from watching your lives, and I was given a reason to try again. I know it's hard to explain, but I want what you people have."

"And you think marrying one of our women would give you what we have?"

"No, not entirely," Mr. Brunson said. "I mean, it's not something I intentionally did or set out to do. It just happened between us. I would call it one of the most improbable things imaginable. Who would have thought that buying a dozen eggs would open such a door?"

When Jake and Hannah had no reply, Mr. Brunson spoke again. "I've upset you both and I'm sorry for that. I don't like to upset my friends."

"Jake's a minister," Hannah said, leaning across the table toward Mr. Brunson. "He can't tell you what to do in a case like this. There are others to think of. Other opinions that could be different from his. Jake will be okay. He's got a really *gut* heart. So why don't you tell us about Mary and yourself?"

"Is that correct?" Mr. Brunson asked, glancing at Jake.

Jake smiled, "I don't know about my *gut* heart, but the rest is correct. I can tell you what the rules are, but I don't have the power to decide anything. That is done in counsel with the other ministers first, and then with all the church members."

"I see," Mr. Brunson said, toying with his fork.

Hannah stood up from the table and said, "The ice cream is melting, and the cherry pie needs to be eaten. We can talk further while we eat dessert."

"That's sounds good to me," Mr. Brunson said. "What better time to speak of love than over cherry pie and butter pecan ice cream?"

Jake laughed. "None that I know of."

"Do you think if I tell my story it will help my case any?" Mr. Brunson asked.

"I don't think so," Hannah said, dishing out the ice cream. "But I want to hear it anyway. A love story is always worth telling."

"You are really encouraging," Mr. Brunson said, taking the bowl of ice cream offered him. He tasted a spoonful, a look of delight spreading over his face.

"I'm sure Mary can also make ice cream like this," Hannah said.

"Hannah," Jake said, "Mr. Brunson wouldn't marry for such reasons."

"I know," Hannah laughed. "I'm being bad."

"Maybe I would," Mr. Brunson said. "Now that I think about it, I haven't tasted ice cream like this in years. Perhaps never."

"You'll get all the cherry pie and homemade ice cream you could possibly want if you marry Mary Keim," Hannah said, placing the pie on the table. "I hear she loves to bake." She sat back down, a bowl of ice cream in front of her.

"So you're really serious about this?" Jake asked, glancing at Mr. Brunson.

"As serious as I have been in a long time."

"Tell me the story then," Hannah said. "I want to hear."

A smile crept across their guest's face. "Well, I pulled in for a carton of fresh eggs one day, on a whim since I usually buy them at the grocery store. I knew the woman was Amish. I mean, that was obvious. I told her good morning, and made my purchase, and then I left, thinking no more about it."

"Did she sell you rotten eggs?" Hannah asked, giggling.

"No," Mr. Brunson said. "They were perfect eggs, and they fried much better than the watery store-bought ones, so I stopped in again. This time the conversation went a little further—about the weather and such things. She told me she knew who I was—that I was your neighbor and the man who had shot the grizzly bear last year. Funny to be known that way, but I didn't mind.

"Her eyes were what got me first—their kindness, their alertness, their look of life, as if she loved living. I wondered about that. Here was a woman who had so little of the modern things of life and yet she looked so happy. Excuse me for thinking this, Hannah, since I know you are the same way, but to see it in someone my age made it feel different. She was so alive and in so many ways. Perhaps in ways I'm no longer alive myself. I wanted to speak longer with her, to understand her life, to see how she lived.

"Anyway, my first thought was that she was married and that her husband had something to do with her obvious happiness. I felt embarrassed for my interest in her but overcame it enough to ask about her in town. They told me she was a widow."

Mr. Brunson paused from eating his ice cream, a gentle smile on his face.

"I'm waiting," Hannah said. "I want to hear the rest of the story."

"Let the man eat his ice cream," Jake said. "Then we can move to the living room. It's much more comfortable in there."

Mr. Brunson laughed. "I think I'd rather finish the story here over homemade ice cream and cherry pie. It seems fitting."

"Whatever you wish," Jake said, taking another bite.

"It's too bad Hannah isn't the minister," Mr. Brunson said. "I think she'd let me marry the woman on the basis of my story alone."

"You have always been a charmer," Jake said. "But I'm listening."

"I'm not trying to convince you," Mr. Brunson said. "This story is for Hannah's benefit, and for the sake of a wonderful woman named Mary Keim. I mean, how many women can sweep an old man like me off my feet?"

"I'm not sure that's a good thing," Jake said.

"Don't listen to him," Hannah said. "That's the preacher in him talking. He's a romantic at heart."

Mr. Brunson sighed. "I'm afraid it will take more than a romantic heart to solve this one. Anyway, I started thinking about Mary after I found out she was a widow. You know how it goes. I told myself, 'No, it isn't possible.' That we lived in two different worlds, that it would never work, that she would tell me no on the spot if she even thought I was romantically interested in her. After a week or so, I stopped by again and spoke with her for as long as it was comfortable. I asked her about her canned goods she had set out that day. I ended up buying a jar of peaches, since I do like peaches.

"The following week we ran into each other in the grocery store in Libby. We exchanged the usual greetings, chatted for a few minutes, and moved on. My interest was growing greater even as I saw more and more the impossibility of it all. I went back the next day to her stand, hoping to catch her alone. When there were two cars parked along the road, I waved and kept going. An hour later I tried again, and there was no one there. I was as nervous as a youngster, Jake. I haven't had a woman shake me up like this since I met Bernice when we were both in our teens.

"Anyway, Mary said she was all out of eggs, that she had just sold the last carton and was about ready to close up the stand for the day. I said that was fine and some other things which I can't remember. Nothing that I shouldn't have said, just fumbling around. I know she saw through me, Jake. I don't have any question about that. She could have gotten all cold and embarrassed, like women do when they want to send a *not interested message*. Instead, she smiled the sweetest smile and engaged me in small talk until I gathered myself up enough to leave. So there you have it, and I have no idea what to do from here."

"That's a beautiful story," Hannah said.

"Perhaps," Mr. Brunson said. "But that only makes it worse. Am I to elope with her?"

"You're too old for that," Hannah said.

Mr. Brunson laughed, "You can say that again."

"And it's not honorable," Jake said. "At least I hope you won't consider that option. I don't think that would be the right approach at all."

"Is that as a minister or your personal opinion?" Mr. Brunson asked.

"Both," Jake said, finishing his ice cream.

"So where does that leave me?"

Seven

Hannah stood on the porch, her arm around Jake's waist, watching the taillights of Mr. Brunson's truck bounce up the gravel driveway toward his house. The soft chirp of night creatures in the garden could be heard in the background.

"You gave him *gut* advice on a very hard question," Hannah commented.

"You think so?" Jake muttered. "I don't know sometimes. I'm just a young man, and this has all been so sudden. This thing of people coming to us for advice."

"Us? He came to ask *your* advice, Jake."

Jake pulled Hannah close to him, "Perhaps, but he also wanted yours. And you did really well."

"Thanks," she whispered, snuggling up to him. "It's chilly out here."

"Yes, it is. I think we'd better get back inside," he said, opening the front door for her.

Hannah stepped over the threshold and waited while Jake latched the heavy wooden door behind them.

"Do you think he'll take your advice?" she asked, sitting down on the couch.

"I don't know," he said. "What do you think?"

"I don't think he will. He might want to forget about her, and even try by not stopping in at the egg stand again, but I don't think it will work. I think he really loves her."

"But he's *English*. Not that he can't fall in love with Mary because he's *English*, but they are both older, and how would they ever adjust to each other? I mean, we're Amish, and marriage was a big adjustment for us. How will it be for him? And if Mary went *English*, that would be even worse."

"You'd have to excommunicate her, wouldn't you?"

"I wouldn't," Jake said. "You know that."

"But you'd have to agree to it, wouldn't you?"

"*Jah*," Jake said, sitting down beside her and stroking her hand. "Are you going to hold that against me? You seemed really taken in with his story."

"I know you can't help it, but it's still awful. How can something so beautiful as love between two people cause such terrible trouble? And not just any people, but two older people. Surely there's got to be some way in which they can be together, Jake. It just doesn't seem right."

"The world is what it is. I don't mean to sound harsh, but it's true. We can't just have things happen because we want them that way."

"I know," Hannah said. "Look at the trouble my dreaming got me into those many years ago."

"With 'old Sam.'" Jake chuckled slightly. "You did almost mess up— and big time. Don't you wish you were a farmer's wife now instead of a preacher's wife worrying about all these things? Think of how much simpler life would be."

"Don't even suggest such a thing, Jake! I wouldn't trade you for any farmer, not even if he were the best farmer in the world."

"You do know how to warm a man's heart," he said, tracing her face with his fingers.

"And I wouldn't trade having your child for a farmer's life either," she said, kissing his cheek.

"There are still the dishes to do," Jake whispered, in her ear. "Why don't I help you?"

Hannah laughed, "Well, that's not very romantic…but it's true. There are lots of dirty dishes tonight."

"You made way too big a supper," Jake said, taking her by the hand and helping her stand. "Next time we have visitors, a little less would be just fine."

"Oh no! I forgot to give Mr. Brunson his cherry pie to take along home. It completely slipped my mind."

"He had things on his mind other than cherry pie tonight. I think Mr. Brunson will be okay."

"I'll take it up tomorrow. I need the walk anyway. He needs his cherry pie," Hannah insisted. "If nothing else—to comfort his broken heart."

"You're something else," Jake said, shaking his head. "Come, we have dishes to do."

Hannah followed him to the kitchen, her fingers still wrapped around his. She let go, and lifted the lid on the firebox, slipping in two more pieces of wood.

"We'll need more hot water," she said. "It should be warm by the time we finish the first batch of dishes."

"You have every dish dirty in your kitchen," Jake said, looking around.

"Almost." Hannah smiled. "But it was a good supper. You have to admit that."

Jake smiled, pouring water from the kettle into the sink and adding a dash of soap. He began washing the plates he could reach. While Jake washed, rinsed, and placed them on the drainer, Hannah cleared the table and scraped the dishes before stacking them for Jake to wash. The soft hiss of the gas lantern above their heads filled the kitchen as they worked.

"I have something to confess," Hannah said softly.

"I don't know if I can take any more confessions tonight. I was just trying to get my brain back together after learning that Mr. Brunson is in love with one of our women. I still can't believe it."

"That's what I'm worried about. Do you think it will end up as awful as my dreaming used to?"

"You didn't marry Sam, so that turned out okay."

"I don't mean that," she said. "I meant Peter."

"Is that your confession? If it is, you already told me about Peter. How you snuck out of the window with him that night against your parents' wishes. How he wanted to kiss you in the car. How you didn't let him but made him bring you back home. How he had an accident that night and lost his life. Is that what you mean?"

"You're not angry with me, are you, Jake?"

"No," Jake said, washing the dishes slowly. "I never was angry with you about Peter."

"Are you sure?" she said, touching his arm.

Jake stopped his task and turned toward her. "There really was nothing to forgive, Hannah. I wasn't there, and we all do things that mess up our lives. That's what God's grace is about."

"But what I did was bad. Would you have married me if you knew you would be a preacher someday? I mean, I don't really make good preacher's wife material with that kind of background."

"I would have married you even if I had already been a preacher. That has nothing to do with it."

"Are you sure, Jake?"

He turned and kissed her on the cheek, his beard damp with water sprinkles. She grabbed his towel, rubbing her face.

"Do you believe me now?" he asked.

She nodded slowly.

"*Gut.*"

"So can I tell you something else then? And you won't get mad?"

He glanced quickly at her. "Something more about Peter? Was it more than an ordinary kiss?"

"Jake," she said, "I never would have done something like that. I've never known anyone but you."

"Then how come one little kiss would make a boy so mad that he crashes his car?"

"I wondered that too," she whispered. "I even wondered if maybe it was because he thought he might love me. That maybe under all that bravado he had real feelings for me, and it cut his heart deeply when I turned him down. I mean, Peter didn't have to take me back home when I asked him to. Lots of boys in *rumspringa* don't. And what could I have said in my own defense? I did sneak out of the window to be with him. No one would have believed me. Not even Mom and Dad would have."

"That's what you wanted to tell me?"

"There's more. Something I've never told anyone. Not even Mom and Dad." She paused. Jake was quiet and then nodded her on, his beard moving slightly in the pulsating light of the lantern, his eyes on the water in the sink.

"The night after the accident, I went down to the crash site, Jake. I snuck out of the window, climbing down the same way we had gone the night before. I walked down there in the darkness, using a flashlight so I could find my way. I hid in the ditch every time a car came along, scared to death someone would see me and report back to Mom and Dad. I never could have explained it to them, what I was doing. They would have thought me mad, and perhaps I was mad, Jake."

"You went down by yourself? But you should have taken someone with you."

"I know I should have, but I didn't. And besides, who would I take?"

Jake rinsed a plate, lifting it carefully into place on the drainer, moving with deliberate motions.

"It was awful, Jake. The night was dark, and I found the spot where the grass was all burned away—and the bark halfway up a tree. It still smelled of gasoline, and tires, and horrible things I couldn't even imagine. I shone my little flashlight around and found a piece of cloth they must have missed when they cleaned up. It was from the seat where I had been sitting only hours before. I looked at that cloth and thought how it could have been me in the car with him. Peter didn't deserve to die, and I didn't deserve to live. But I think he was sorry before he died, Jake. He *had* to have been. It was just too horrible to die there alone without the angels to carry him to heaven. The tree was all burned black, and the ground was all black too. I'll never forget it, Jake."

A tear formed and Jake reached up to brush it away from her cheek.

"Do you think he was sorry, Jake. Before he died?"

"I don't know," Jake said. "No one can know. Only God."

"The minister at the funeral said it was possible."

"It *is* possible," Jake said as he nodded. "God would give Peter the time to repent if he wanted to."

"I think he must have repented, Jake, because I think Peter wanted what was right."

"It would be better if we didn't live like Peter though," Jake said. "Repenting so you can live right is better than repenting so you can die right. I want to teach my children that lesson."

"I'm sure you will," she said. "You will be a wonderful father."

"What did you do with the piece of cloth? You didn't keep it did you?"

She shook her head, "I buried it underneath the tree using a big stick I found. I got my hands all dirty, but it felt better. Anything that has to do with that awful night had best be buried in the ground."

"I think so too," he said. "And now you had better bury your memories by giving them to God."

"I want to—I really do. But first I had to tell you. You are my husband."

"That was a nice thing to do," Jake said, drying his hands on the dish towel.

"And now, you scat off to the living room and let me finish my work," Hannah said. "You've done enough and plenty."

"I'll take the ice cream freezer to the barn, and then I'm done for the night," Jake said with a sigh. "And what a night it has been."

Hannah held the door open as Jake went out with the ice cream canister in both hands. Five minutes later he was back and settled down in the living room to read. Finishing in the kitchen, Hannah made two trips out to the springhouse with the extra food, taking care that Jake didn't hear her open and close the kitchen door. He would have been up in a flash to offer his help, and he had already done enough for one night.

The poor man. First Mr. Brunson spilled his story on him, and then she had to add to his load. Turning on the flashlight only when she came close to the springhouse, she stored the items, making sure the latch was securely in place. There had been no bear problems since Mr. Brunson had killed the grizzly all those months ago, but neither she nor Jake wanted to take any chances. When she was finished in the kitchen, she moved toward the bedroom, asking Jake if he was ready to retire for the night.

Jake yawned and followed her readily into the bedroom. As she prepared slowly for sleeping, Jake quickly changed out of his clothes and climbed into bed. By the time she joined him, he appeared to be asleep, his even breathing a comfort to her.

"So why did Mr. Brunson make you think of Peter?" Jake asked suddenly, and Hannah jumped under the covers.

"Because so many things can go wrong when you think you love someone. We need to pray for Mr. Brunson."

Eight

Hannah sat on the hard bench without moving. Bishop John's wife, Elizabeth, sat beside her, but Hannah's eyes were on Jake's face. He looked tired—and had ever since he came down from the morning ministers' conference upstairs. She could read the signs in the tenseness of his jaw and in the deepening lines on his face. Jake was much too young for the heavy responsibilities laid on his shoulders. He should be sitting on a bench across the room, seated among the men his own age, instead of standing up front by the kitchen doorway, closing out the main Sunday sermon.

Did *Da Hah* always know what He was doing? Jake didn't complain, so why should she? But then he didn't have to watch himself suffer as she did.

Bishop John's eyes were also on Jake's face, watching him from the ministers' bench set up against the kitchen wall. He looked pleased, nodding from time to time, so Jake must be doing okay. Of course Jake always did okay, regardless of what was required of him. So perhaps *Da Hah* had known what He was doing.

"The Scripture says," Jake said, his hands hanging by his side, pacing slowly in front of the doorway, "that 'man shall not live by bread alone, but by every word that proceedeth out of the mouth of God.' Jesus Himself quoted those lines from the Old Testament, applying it to Himself. If Jesus needed those words, then we need them even more urgently."

Jake paused in his pacing and seemed to be thinking, his eyes looking down. He looked up and continued. "We, as the people of God, can get so busy with our work, with our jobs, with our farms, that we forget there is more to life than what we can see. Just as the physical body needs food, so too our spiritual man must also be fed the spiritual Word of God. And this is true today even more than ever before.

"Trouble gathers in the world. The devil goes about not only as a roaring lion seeking whom he may devour, but as an angel of light seeking to deceive even the best of us. We must humble ourselves as we never have done before and listen to the Word of God. Not only must we read it for ourselves, but we must listen to the voices of our brothers and sisters, who sometimes can see the dangers to our souls better than we ourselves can.

"I want to close now with one final Scripture from the letter to the Roman church. Paul wrote to tell them they were not to be conformed to this world, but transformed by the renewing of their minds that they might prove what was the good, the acceptable, and the perfect will of God. I believe those words are still true today and can be applied to many situations in our lives."

Hannah moved on the bench, feeling goose bumps running up her arms. Jake and the other ministers must be very concerned about something. Likely it was the Mennonite revival meetings heralded by the posters on the grocery store door or perhaps it was some news Jake had learned this morning. But surely not. Or had Mr. Brunson ignored Jake's advice and spoken to Mary Keim about his interest in her? And even worse, had Mary accepted?

Hannah turned her head slightly, finding Mary's face on the other side of the room. She looked calm and untroubled, so it must be the Mennonite meetings.

"I will now bring what I have to say to a close," Jake said, sitting down. "Would both of the other ministers give testimony to what has been said—and perhaps Will Riley also?"

Hannah listened while Bishop John spoke. He seemed to like what Jake had said, but she had already known that. This meant Minister Mose Chupp wouldn't object either unless he broke the tradition. Glancing at him quickly, Mose looked calm enough, so nothing negative must be coming. That left Will Riley, but what could he say against what Jake said? He liked Jake.

The bishop closed his remarks, wishing the blessing of God on His Word, and then he glanced toward Mose. Mose nodded and began speaking. He didn't have much to say though, only quoting one of the verses Jake had recited and closing with his blessing.

Hannah moved slightly on the bench as a long silence hung over the room. Several of the men cleared their throats, but none of them sounded like Will. *He must be really nervous at having been asked for testimony and is having a hard time finding his voice,* she thought.

Bishop John raised his head to look in Will's direction, and Will started speaking with a sudden burst of sound. Hannah couldn't understand what he was saying, even when he ran out of breath and slowed down.

No one was looking at Will, but Hannah glanced at him. Still unable to understand the rush of words, she listened more closely.

Bishop John shook his head in Will's direction, but the layman continued talking. Slowly comprehension came over her. Jake's jaw was even tighter than it had been while he was preaching. Bishop John looked ready to stand and say something.

Faintly Hannah caught some of the words. "I can't agree with the implications of what was said here today…I do appreciate Minister Jake… his testimony that he has, but today I cannot help but think he is guilty of twisting the Word of God to fit his own purposes. Why don't we all be honest and admit that we all know what is happening around us?

"If we would open our eyes we would see that the world is changing… We have to move along with it. This is all about the Mennonite revival meetings…We all know they are coming to town this summer. And I don't think we should be speaking against what other Christians are doing.

"And don't say that I'm immature…that I don't know what I'm saying. I'm married and have two young children whom I desire to raise in the fear of the Lord. But this is not the way to do it. We don't have to make Scripture fit our purposes to try and accomplish the will of God."

Will paused, taking a deep breath, "So I don't give my blessing to Minister Jake's sermon…I wish he would speak more plainly if he wishes to instruct us, without hiding behind the true Word of God."

Silence hung heavy over the room as Jake got slowly to his feet, his eyes watching the floor.

"I regret that our brother does not give his blessing, and it was not my intention to hide behind the Word of God. Rather I thought I was using the Word of God to open our eyes to what is going on around us. I will take counsel with the other ministers and see if they have any further words of correction for me."

Jake raised his eyes to look in Will's direction, nodding once. "I hope that is satisfactory with the brother. If not, he is welcome to speak further with the bishop about the matter. Let us pray now."

A soft rustle filled the room, and Hannah knelt with the rest of the people. What in the world had come over Will to cause such an outburst—and in public at that? Soft sobs came from across the room as Hannah covered her face with her hands. There was no need to look around to know who was crying. The voice of Will's wife, Rebecca, was clearly recognizable.

Jake read the prayer, his voice rising and falling like usual. He must be handling things very well, but then he always did. She was the one who wasn't. Her heart was pounding so hard it hurt. Why did those Mennonites have to come into the community and make trouble for all of them? Didn't they know life caused enough trouble already?

Jake closed his prayer with a strong voice, "In the name of the Father, the Son, and the Holy Spirit. Amen."

Hannah rose slowly, sitting back on the bench. Elizabeth was looking sideways at her. She reached over to squeeze Hannah's hand, which didn't help much. It just made the threatening tears that much closer to falling. She wiped her eyes with her handkerchief as Bishop John announced the close of the service, and the smaller boys made a dash for the outside.

Will's oldest boy, Andrew, followed behind them, already too old to walk fast at six years of age. He was the spitting image of his father, walking erect, and grabbing his black hat by the front door. How his mom loved her children, and now Will was acting up again. Apparently Will's desire to leave the Amish hadn't been fully resolved last year, even with Jake's best efforts.

Bishop John couldn't blame Jake for that, could he? Jake had tried his best and had come away from a difficult task with excellent results. It was those Mennonites who were stirring things up. They were the ones to blame, but she must not be bitter about it. *Da Hah* gave grace to all, and He wished His people to love even those who did them wrong.

Hannah watched the short line of older boys get up and walk toward the front door. Not that long ago Jake would have been in that line, and her heart would have been pounding with joy instead of wrenched in pain.

Will's brother, Dennis Riley, was the last one in the line, stooping low to pick up his hat before stepping outside. He was tall, even taller than his brother, and good looking. Why had he never married? Surely he could find a girl if he wished to? Sylvia's sister Susie had been looking at him at the last Sunday evening hymn sing, smiling in his direction in between songs. Apparently he wasn't interested in her attentions or was taking his *gut* time about it.

But then perhaps he shared Will's desire to leave the Amish and wasn't interested in an Amish girl? Wouldn't that be an awful thing? Yes, but surely not as awful as the situation Rebecca was in—married with two small children and her husband disagreeing with one of the ministers in public. Bishop John wouldn't let Will's outburst pass, but Jake would likely speak on Will's behalf for patience. Jake was that kind of man.

Why didn't Dennis date? Perhaps he had, and she didn't know about it. It wasn't likely that any girl would have dumped him though. He wasn't the kind of boy a girl would do that to. Miriam was coming soon, and cold chills ran up Hannah's spine at the thought. Miriam was looking for a relationship. *This is too horrible to even contemplate! If Miriam falls for Dennis, and he for her, what will happen? Surely Miriam wouldn't join the Mennonites—but then Rebecca hadn't wished to either. It was her man who did.*

Was there time yet to warn Miriam? She would arrive soon. Even a rushed phone call would not reach her in time. And would she believe her anyway? What would she tell her mom? Something like, "I noticed again how handsome one of our young unmarried boys is, and I'm suspicious of him because his brother criticized Jake's preaching today." What sense did that make, except that she might be sore at him because his brother spoke against Jake? And Miriam would laugh anyway. She had yet to meet a boy who impressed her, and she had seen lots of them in Indiana. The young folk gatherings were crawling with Amish boys, and there were always plenty of visitors. Certainly not like Montana, which saw Amish visitors only once in a blue moon.

No, there was no use in warning Miriam. She wouldn't listen anyway. Regardless, their mom had given her blessing to the trip, and that was that. Perhaps Miriam would have enough sense not to fall for Dennis once she arrived. She was a sensible sister most of the time, but love did seem to bring out the strangest qualities in people.

Elizabeth squeezed her hand again, and Hannah got to her feet. Behind them the benches had already emptied out, the women heading toward the kitchen. Hannah followed them, pausing when Betty grabbed her arm and pulled her into the bedroom. Several young children lay sleeping on the bed, with two babies lying on the floor, one with his eyes open, staring at them while he sucked his thumb.

Betty shut the door behind her.

"I can't believe Will would do something like that," Betty whispered. "That was another of Jake's wonderful sermons, and Will was completely out of line. The man ought to be rebuked and called out in front of the church for his transgression."

"Jake asked him for his testimony," Hannah said. "And I guess he gave it."

Betty jerked her arm, "Don't be trying to butter things up, and don't you go counseling Jake to be soft on Will when Bishop John wants to deal with the man. I saw your face afterward. And did you hear Rebecca sobbing? The poor woman. Will broke her heart in pieces, and this after we thought their problems from last year were over with."

"It's the Mennonite meetings that are causing the problem," Hannah said.

"I think so too," Betty said. "It's disturbing the life of the community."

"That's not the worst thing," Hannah said. "I just had the most horrible thought after church. I was thinking, what would happen if Miriam falls for Will's brother, Dennis? She's coming here hoping to find someone."

Betty's eyes widened and she clucked her tongue. "Yes, it's going to be a hard time ahead. I do indeed feel it in my bones, child."

Nine

Jake drove silently, his eyes on the road ahead. Hannah glanced briefly at him as she rubbed her forehead. A pounding headache was forming and promised to burst into full bloom.

"I'm sorry it went so late," he said. "But the ministry needed to talk."

"How are you doing?" she asked, touching his arm.

"Okay," he said, not looking at her.

"What does Bishop John think should be done about Will?"

"He's going over to visit him tonight."

"That's better than sending you like he did last year."

"I guess I failed in my mission."

"You didn't, Jake. It's those Mennonites. They are the problem."

"Don't say that," Jake said, turning to look at her. "We shouldn't blame other people for our own failures."

"But you didn't fail." Hannah squeezed his arm. "You gave Will excellent advice that night. I was there and I heard it and Will listened. You can't carry all the weight of the world's burdens, Jake."

"I have to carry the ones that are my fault."

"This wasn't your fault, Jake. Believe me, it wasn't."

"I wish it were that easy. Bishop John wants to discipline Will, maybe make him do a church confession. He said we can't have people disrespecting the ministry like that."

"It was disrespectful. But I don't know about discipline. That could make things worse. And poor Rebecca. She already took it hard enough the way it is."

"I know," Jake said. "And there are their two children to think of. I don't think it's good for young boys to see their fathers in trouble with the church."

"Maybe Bishop John will accept a private apology—if you ask him to?"

"I already said that, but I guess we will have to see. Will might not even back down that far. And with that Mennonite revival coming, well, it could just pick off any of our discontented members."

"They are the only reason Will is acting up," Hannah said.

"Do you really think so?"

"I do. And isn't there something that can be done about that? Can't you go to the Mennonite leaders, whoever they are, and speak with them? Surely Ben Stoll would know who they are. You could ask them to call this meeting off."

Jake laughed dryly. "I don't think that would work from what I've heard. There's this movement sweeping across the Mennonite communities right now, and a lot of them are into this kind of thing. I don't think they'll stop just because the people they want to convert object."

"Convert? That's sounds awful. What are we supposed to convert to?"

Jake shrugged, "It's a good word—if what you are converting to is good."

"You wouldn't ever convert, would you, Jake?"

He laughed, slapping the reins. "Now, why do you ask that?"

"Well, you're a really *gut* preacher. My guess is they'd put you right to work preaching all over the country in a fancy new car they might even buy for you themselves!"

Jake shook his head, laughing again. "You are full of strange ideas, Hannah. But don't worry, I'm not converting to their way of doing things."

"Are you going to attend the meetings? You said once you wanted to see what goes on."

"I was teasing," Jake said, turning up their driveway. "I have no plans to go."

"What does Bishop John say about people going? Is he going to forbid it?"

"We talked about that," Jake said, allowing Mosey to walk up the hill toward the cabin. "He wants a rule against any attendance, and Mose feels the same way."

"And you?"

"I don't know. I'm afraid it will be perceived as too harsh and it might backfire."

"But what if people go? From the talk today, I'd say Will is going to drag Rebecca there whether she wants to go or not."

"It's the end result we have to keep in mind. The summer will be over in a few months, the Mennonites will be gone, and we will have to live with ourselves."

"So you will defy Bishop John's opinion?" Hannah asked, her hand shaking a bit on Jake's arm.

He turned, a weak smile on his face. "I just gave my opinion. Bishop John can do what he wants."

"You know he wouldn't want to go against your opinion. Can't you tell him you've changed your mind? Betty thinks it's time for harsh measures with all the trouble we're having."

"It's always time to do what's right," Jake said, pulling to a stop in front of the barn.

Hannah climbed down and took the tugs off of her side of the buggy, holding the shafts while Jake led Mosey forward. She watched him disappear into the barn before she walked toward the house. Jake was always right and had a way of saying things that made one shut one's mouth. Still, Betty wouldn't be convinced, but Hannah had done her duty. She had advised Jake not to be soft on Will.

Jake was taking an awful risk in holding to a different stand than Bishop John. He could say what he wanted to, but that was what it was. If things went wrong this summer, and the worst happened with several or even a few of their members being lost to the Mennonite revival, Jake would take a lot of the blame. Word would leak out that Jake had been the one who stood in the way of dealing harshly with the ones who chose to attend the tent meetings.

She rubbed her forehead again. Thankfully her threatening headache had subsided. It must have been the conversation with Jake. He could do that for her, and soon they would be able to comfort each other as a family. Wouldn't that be wonderfully *gut*? They could sit around the gas lantern at night, the baby playing in the crib, and be a happy and complete family regardless of what people thought of Jake.

Hannah opened the cabin door, and walked in, hanging her shawl on the rocker before taking off her bonnet. She needed to start supper soon. At this hour it would need to be warmed-over casserole from last night and the blueberry pie she had made yesterday. That would still leave enough pie for Jake's lunch tomorrow. She would do additional baking then.

While starting the fire in the stove, the cabin door opened and she glanced into the living room. Jake tossed his hat on the floor and lowered himself on the couch, his face streaked with weariness.

"I'll have supper soon," Hannah said. "It's already quite late."

"That would be *gut* as I'm starving."

While the casserole warmed, she made a batch of popcorn and brought it to Jake. A smile spread over his face as he took the bowl Hannah gave him.

"Don't eat too much," she said, "or you won't have room for supper."

"I can always find room for your delicious food," he said.

"Thanks, and I'm glad you like my food. But you haven't gotten fat yet."

"Am I supposed to get fat?" he asked, laughing.

"Well, some men do once they get married. But I guess you work too hard. And then there's the church work."

He smiled halfheartedly. "It would keep anyone thin."

"I don't want you fat anyway," Hannah said, nibbling from her own bowl of popcorn.

Jake sat upright suddenly, listening. "There's a buggy coming up the lane."

"Oh no," Hannah gasped, standing up so fast her bowl tipped over, spilling the white kernels across the floor. "I hope it's not trouble. We can't stand any more of that tonight."

His face shadowed, Jake gave her a quick look. "I'm sorry this is so hard on you. But I don't know what to do about it."

"You can't do anything. It's not your fault."

He ran his fingers gently down her cheek. He stood up, went to the cabin door, opened it, and stepped out onto the porch.

Hannah quickly swept the spilled popcorn into a pile with her hands and deposited it into the wastebasket. She could at least present a clean house to whomever was coming.

Voices reached her from the front porch—muffled sounds of laughter. *Who would be laughing when the visit has to be a serious one?* Hannah wondered.

She watched as the door swung open and Jake held it while Betty and Steve walked inside.

"Hannah!" Betty said, coming toward her with open arms. "We had to come over and comfort you poor people. I can't imagine how hard this has been on both of you."

"You came to visit us?" Hannah asked, tears forming again.

Betty wrapped her in a big hug.

"You poor things," Betty said. "And to think I gave you all that advice after church when I should have been comforting you. Thank *Da Hah* that Steve got me straightened out. He insisted we come over right away and spend the evening with both of you."

"You are such dears," Hannah said, wiping her eyes. "But I don't even have supper for all of us. I only have enough casserole for Jake and me."

"Don't worry," Betty said, a smile flooding her face. "I brought supper along. Well, meatballs and baked beans. No dessert though, but perhaps we can live without dessert tonight."

"I have some pie. Maybe we can cut it into small pieces," Hannah said, smiling through her tears. "I'd like to save one piece for Jake's lunch tomorrow."

"I'm sorry for what happened today," Steve said, nodding toward Hannah. "I was just telling Jake that I think everything will be handled correctly. I have a lot of confidence in Bishop John."

"I hope so," Hannah said, her smile shaky. Steve obviously hadn't been told about Jake's advice to Bishop John, and she wasn't about to tell him. Steve would only say something that would likely contribute to Jake's unease.

"Let's get this warmed up a bit," Betty said, taking the covers off her pan of meatballs and leading the way into Hannah's kitchen. "It shouldn't take much."

"My casserole should be about done," Hannah said, opening the oven door to check and then placing the casserole on the top rack. "It'll stay warm here until yours is done."

Betty set the table while Hannah sliced the bread.

Fifteen minutes later Betty called into the living room, "Come and get it!"

Jake and Steve came at once, Jake motioning for Steve to sit down first. When they were seated, Jake led out in prayer, his voice strong. It sounded *gut* to hear him pray like that, especially after what he had been through in church.

"Now for a solution to our big problem," Betty said, passing her meatballs around.

"Like what?" Jake said. "We already talked about the church problems we're having."

"That's not what I meant," Betty said. "I'm talking about Miriam coming. It's next week, isn't it? How are we going to keep her away from Will's brother? The more I think about what Hannah told me, the more certain I am that she will fall head over heels in love with him. I can feel it deep in my bones. We can't just stand by and do nothing."

"Hannah told you?" Jake asked, raising his eyebrows.

"I just thought of the possibility," Hannah said, meeting his eyes. "Maybe it will never happen."

"Like you two are going to stop love," Steve said with a laugh.

"That's what I was thinking," Jake said.

"That's not a very good thing for a preacher to be saying," Betty said. "And Miriam's your sister-in-law."

"I faintly remember that," Jake said, and Steve laughed again.

"This is not a laughing matter," Betty said. "It's very serious."

"I agree," Hannah said. "And what can we do about it?"

"We have to come up with a plan," Betty said. "Some way of keeping Miriam away from Dennis."

Jake cleared his throat and glanced at Hannah.

"What?" Hannah asked him. "Did I say something wrong?"

"No," Jake shook his head. "I was just thinking about how Betty's plans for you went awry when we were dating."

"Jake," Hannah said, "Betty was trying to help. And I didn't do much to help her either. We all did things wrong."

"That's right," Betty said. "And this time we must be smarter in our planning."

"I think you'd better not do *any* planning," Steve said. "Things can get a little out of control when you women start planning. I expect the more you tell Miriam not to notice Dennis, the more she's going to notice him."

"I agree," Jake said.

"Of course you would," Betty said. "You're thinking like men."

"That's the best way, isn't it?" Jake said. Steve laughed heartily.

"You are a smart aleck, you know that?" Betty asked, joining in the laughter. "But something has to be done about this situation. We can't have Hannah's sister falling in love with someone as unstable as Dennis Riley."

Jake and Steve shook their heads as Hannah brought the pie over from the counter.

Ten

Hannah drove the buggy toward Libby, urging Mosey to move faster as he plodded along. She shouldn't have spent those last twenty minutes weeding in the garden, but it had simply been too tempting, the weeds coming out easily in her hands after the shower last night. The bus was due at ten thirty, but Jake said the arrival time could vary due to how the bus managed the mountain roads. It simply wouldn't do to be late and have Miriam wait alone at the depot in a strange town. Traveling was frightening enough for a girl without having anyone to greet you at your destination.

Passing an open field at the outskirts of Libby, Hannah glanced sideways. Who were those three men and what were they doing? Two of them were obviously *Englisha*, and the third looked very familiar, his huge form standing with his back turned toward her. When he glanced in the direction of the buggy, Hannah caught her breath. It was Ben Stoll in his Mennonite clothing.

He waved, smiling broadly, and then turned back to the two *Englisha* men. She clutched the lines, her heart pounding. So that was it. The men were obviously staking out the ground for where the Mennonite tent revival would be held. How did Ben dare do such a thing in broad daylight, coming to lure people away from the faith he once was a part of and obviously feeling no shame at all.

Oh, if Miriam only wasn't coming this summer. Last summer would have been so much better—or perhaps even next year. Now she was walking into the jaws of a church storm…and looking for love on top of it all. Betty had agreed that they must do something, but there really was nothing that could be done. Some things were out of their hands.

Ahead on Main Street, the tall Greyhound bus came climbing up the hill. Hannah pulled into the gas station parking lot where the bus would stop. She climbed out of the buggy and tied Mosey to the fence. Behind her the roar of the bus filled her ears as it lumbered into the parking lot. Miriam was here, and she had best forget the community's troubles for the moment and gather herself together to properly welcome her sister to the West.

The door swung open and two *Englisha* women came out followed by a young boy holding his suitcase. He looked around, shading his eyes from the sun, before heading toward the gas station. Slowly the door of the bus moved in the slight breeze, but no Miriam appeared. Was Miriam not on the bus? Had she perhaps missed a connection and been unable to let her know?

Hannah walked forward quickly. Perhaps she could ask the bus driver. Clutching her bonnet she approached the open door, catching the words in her mouth just as Miriam appeared on the top step.

"Welcome!" Hannah shouted above the din of the bus motor.

"Oh, it's so beautiful!" Miriam said, stepping down. "I can't believe you live in such a lovely place."

Hannah wrapped her arms around Miriam, pulling her into a tight hug. "It's so good to see you."

"And you too," Miriam said. "Has Betty come along?"

"No, she's busy at the house, plus we need all the room in the buggy for your luggage."

"I don't have much," Miriam said, walking over to retrieve a single suitcase from the bus driver who was still unloading luggage.

Hannah took it from her hand and motioned toward the buggy. "I'm over there."

Miriam was staring at the mountain range, moving around to catch a better look between the storefronts. "The mountains are so beautiful. I don't remember noticing just how lovely they are when I came out for your wedding."

"Come," Hannah said, pulling on her arm. "You can see the mountains outside the town. People will soon be staring at us."

"I guess that's true," Miriam said, pulling her bonnet forward and hurrying after Hannah. "I got caught up in the moment is all."

"I still remember the first time I saw them when we came in with the van," Hannah said, sliding the suitcase beneath the buggy seat. "I was hurting pretty badly from Peter's funeral, but they lifted my spirits even then."

"Talking about Peter…" Miriam said, climbing into the buggy as Hannah untied Mosey.

"What about Peter?" Hannah asked, swinging the reins to head Mosey toward Main Street.

"I saw Alice in the fabric store in Nappanee. She's married now and has two children."

"Well, she was his girlfriend. I'm glad she's been able to move on with her life."

Miriam continued, "She was friendly. I don't think she knew about you and Peter—or that you were out with him on the night of his accident."

"I would hope not. I have enough sins on my account without everyone knowing about it."

"With people not knowing—that did make it easier, but then you've always had things easier."

"Miriam!" Hannah exclaimed. "How can you say that? After all I went through. I mean, I was partly to blame that Peter had his accident. How can that be easier? Look at you. You've never done the things I have."

"I know I haven't," Miriam said. "And look at the boring life I'm living. You take risks. Sure you make mistakes, but look at where you are. You had all kinds of chances for love. Sam was falling over his farmer's feet, taking you right to the marriage altar, and Jake sure didn't waste much time. And now your husband is a preacher. How much better can it get? But me? Look at me. I'm the older, ugly sister who can't even get a date, let alone a husband."

"Miriam," Hannah said, snapping the reins sharply. "You could get all kinds of boys back home if you wanted to. You know that."

"Perhaps," Miriam said with a short laugh. "But I've been waiting for the perfect man, which I'm beginning to think doesn't exist. So I'm ready to settle for the next decent boy that comes along, even if he drives a broken-down horse and doesn't have two pennies to rub together."

"Does Mom know all this?"

"Most of it. I think that's why she agreed to allow me to come out here again. I think she hopes some of your good sense will sort of slide over onto me."

"But you are a wonderful girl, Miriam. I'm sure the right man is out there for you. You don't have to settle for second best. I thought I had to, but it's not that way. *Da Hah* led me straight to Jake once I got my eyes opened."

"I think some of your good sense is already trickling down over me," Miriam said, watching the passing mountains out of the open buggy door. "And your beautiful mountains will completely set me on the right path. My, but what would it be like to find love here like you did, Hannah? It must be the most wonderful feeling in the world. The air here is clearer, the sky bluer, the people more dashing and brave, and the heart must be larger to take it all in."

"I think you've been reading romance stories," Hannah said with a laugh as she slapped the reins again, startling Mosey out of his plod.

"I don't think so," Miriam said. "The only romance story I've read was watching my sister and her husband. I still haven't forgotten your little wedding out here, and I think I want to get married in Montana too."

Hannah glanced at Miriam. "You can only do what *Da Hah* allows, and maybe He has other plans for you."

"That's what I'm afraid of," Miriam said, shaking her head.

"Betty wants us to stop in and say hi," Hannah said, giving the lines another shake. "You'll be staying at our place for the weekend, and then come back to Betty's on Sunday night. Betty won't open the stable for business until next week."

"Sounds fine with me," Miriam said, watching the passing fields.

"I would keep you at our place all summer and fall if we had room. But it will still be wonderful to have you so close by. I get lonesome for family, even with Betty around."

"I can imagine. Now if only I can find love out here, you might have me around forever."

Hannah laughed. "Can't you think of anything else?"

"Not at the moment," Miriam said. "Tell me something. You were so good at finding Jake. Pick out a boy for me. I'm sure he'd be perfect and adorable, and I might not have to settle for second best."

"Miriam, you know I can't go picking out husbands for other people."

"But you could. Come on and tell me. My guess is you already know the perfect boy for me, don't you? One that I would fall head over heels in love for, and with whom I could live for the rest of my life in these beautiful mountains."

"Miriam! I can do no such thing."

Studying her face, Miriam let out a yelp of joy. "I knew it! I knew it! You already *have* picked someone for me. And he's the perfect Montana boy who will delight my heart. Oh, I can't believe this. *Da Hah* has finally decided to have mercy upon my poor aching heart. Hannah, you're so wonderful. Oh, Hannah, will I have to wait till Sunday to see him or will there be a young folks gathering sooner than that?"

"Would you calm yourself?" Hannah asked, giggling. "You will have to pick your own boyfriend. The only boy on my mind is one who is *not* right for you."

"Oh, this is so sweet," Miriam said, pushing her bonnet back. "I knew it. I just knew it."

"But I said he's *not* right for you."

"That's why I know he *is*. If you said he was, I'd doubt you, but you said he isn't."

"How convoluted is that?"

"That's how you think, Hannah. You may not know it, but that's how you picked Jake. You liked him, but you didn't think he was the right one at first. And then it turned out he was. This is the same thing."

Hannah stared straight ahead, pulling back on the reins, and turning Mosey into Betty's lane. Before she came to a stop by the front door, Betty was already running down the steps, her apron flapping.

"Oh, you've come back to Montana!" Betty hollered, grabbing Miriam in a hug before she barely touched the ground. "I'm so glad to see you. And how is your mom?"

"Quite well and she sends her greetings."

"Of course, of course," Betty said. "Can you come inside for a few minutes before you go on to Hannah's place? We're in the middle of the morning's work, but we can chat for a little bit."

"Oh, I wouldn't keep you from your work," Miriam said. "But there is one thing I would love. Could Hannah take me on a ride with the horses and show me around? Sort of where she used to ride while she was here and where I'm supposed to take the riders."

"I suppose that would be a great idea if Hannah has the time," Betty said. "Steve just opened the trail along the river a few days ago."

"I'd be glad to," Hannah said, walking around the buggy, as the house door opened again and Kendra waved a greeting to Miriam.

"Come and give your cousin a hug," Betty told Kendra. She ran across the lawn and gave Miriam a hug.

"Let me know if you need something in the barn, Hannah," Betty said. "I'd better get busy. We look forward to having you with us this summer, Miriam. You don't know what a blessing that will be."

"I'll be the one being blessed," Miriam said, smiling broadly. "Especially with the news that Hannah has already told me."

"News?" Betty asked.

"That she already has a boy picked out for me. And the perfect boy."

"Hannah! You didn't tell her?" Betty gasped. "That's exactly what you were not supposed to do."

Eleven

Hannah adjusted the stirrup on her horse's saddle, while Miriam, still laughing, threw a saddle onto hers and cinched it down.

"It's not one bit funny," Hannah said. "Betty and I were trying to solve a very serious problem."

"I think it's funny that I caught you in the act, like two old women planning my future. And the look on Betty's face. That was priceless."

"Well, you could take this a little more seriously."

"You know I'm not likely to fall in love with a boy you don't like. I was teasing you. If I was the falling in love type at all, I would have done so a long time ago."

"I guess I should have known that," Hannah said, smiling a little. "We're a little on edge around here with the Mennonite revival meetings coming to Libby. I guess I worry about it too much."

"I wouldn't worry a bit," Miriam said. "We have Mennonites all around us in Indiana, and they don't bother anybody."

"They already took one of our young couples last year—Ben and Sylvia Stoll, and that was when the meetings were in Kalispell."

"Where's Kalispell?" Miriam asked, swinging up on the horse.

"Over the mountains an hour or so," Hannah said, leading her horse outside before she climbed on. They rode together down the trail behind the barn, Hannah leading the way. At the river she pulled her horse to a stop, motioning with her hand at the swift-flowing water.

"It's a good-sized river," Miriam said. "And dangerous looking."

"That's what this country is like," Hannah said, looking across to the other side. "And we have bears, mountain lions, that sort of thing."

"And dangerous boys that I'm not supposed to fall in love with."

"Stop teasing!" Hannah said. "It's not funny. And it *is* dangerous country out here."

"I see that," Miriam said, as Hannah urged her horse forward again, following the river north. At the top of the next rise, Hannah pulled to a stop and turned around. "This is the plateau," she said, her face brightening. "The trail runs level for almost a half mile. What do you say? Do you want to run the horses?"

"Why not?" Miriam said, bending forward over the saddle horn. "Lead the way!"

Hannah let out the reins, pressing her knees against the mare's ribs. "Let's go," she whispered. "But be careful, I haven't done this in a long time."

Moving quickly to a gallop, Hannah rode with her weight resting on the stirrups, pushing upward with her feet. Behind her came the pounding of Miriam's horse. Hannah kept the reins tight, throwing her head back and laughing as the wind blew her head covering off, the strings snapping tight around her throat.

The trees went by in blurs, the feel of the horse's footing solid, the strength of the mare's body flowing through Hannah until she felt as if it were her own. This was the way she used to feel in those long-ago summer days while riding her pony in the pastures at home. Then there was only the wind, the joy of the ride, and the freedom of the open skies that flooded her heart. Those were the glorious days before Jake, and the baby, and the weight of church problems hanging over their heads.

"Whee!" Miriam said when Hannah pulled to a halt, the horses breathing heavily. "I can see you've done this before."

Hannah didn't say anything as she pressed her eyelids together, resisting the urge to wipe her eyes. Hopefully Miriam thought the tears came only from the wind.

"There are a lot of memories out here for you, aren't there?" Miriam said softly. "It looks like a place where only good things would happen. With the mountains on all sides, and the river. It brings God close, doesn't it?"

"Sort of," Hannah said.

Miriam didn't seem to notice the catch in her voice.

How was Hannah to explain all that had happened here? Her rides alone on Prince, reading her letters from home, wrestling with what to do about Sam, and then that fateful last ride with Jake when she thought they would confess their forbidden love for each other, only to have it end so tragically. Only the grace of God could ever have put all that mess back together again.

Perhaps Betty and she should keep their fingers out of Miriam's relationships, regardless of what will happen. Betty's interference with Jake and her relationship certainly hadn't turned out well. In fact, it had done more harm than good.

"Perhaps I can find love out here," Miriam said, gazing off into the distance toward the towering mountains. "I was only half serious before, but you're making a believer out of me. I had forgotten how deeply moving this country is. Anything can happen out here."

"The road of love is not always easy," Hannah sighed. "I suppose you'll find that out soon enough."

"You think I'm setting myself up for a broken heart, don't you?" Miriam teased.

Hannah wiped her eyes, and said, "I think I'm going to stay out of this from now on."

"I don't suppose Betty will do likewise. I'm expecting a summer full of advice about boys, and who I should and shouldn't date."

"Then I'll try not to join her. Really...I'll try really hard."

"No, don't try," Miriam said, reaching across to pat her sister's shoulder. "You're a wonderful sister, and I value what you have to say."

"You shouldn't tease me with sugary words," Hannah said, turning her mare back toward the barn.

"I wasn't, Hannah. I wasn't."

"Thanks for the compliment then."

"So tell me about this boy who has Betty and you so worried."

"Miriam, I said I wanted to stay out of it."

"It's already too late for that, so tell me. What am I going to see that will be so awful?"

"Something you've never seen before."

"Hannah, now you're teasing. Quit it! You're not good at it."

"What if I'm not teasing?"

"But you are."

"No, I'm not."

"Then please tell me more. My heart is already pounding."

"He's a little older than you are, tall, very handsome, a little dark and moody, and he will give you shivers down your spine."

"Hannah," Miriam said. "Now you're scaring me. Tell me you're just making this up."

Hannah laughed. "His name is Dennis Riley. And his parents weren't raised Amish. He and his brother live here. His brother Will is married to Rebecca, who is a very good friend of mine. They have two children, Andrew and Edith."

Miriam took a deep breath. "Well, to be honest, I do like the part about him not being from the Amish. Maybe that's what I've been missing all my life. Amish boys are boring."

"That attitude is what I'm afraid of," Hannah said. "When you meet the right Amish boy, he won't be boring. Jake's not boring. At least not to me."

"Still, this Dennis sounds interesting."

"Miriam, he's trouble."

"Does Jake think so too?"

"No. Jake says he's a solid, upstanding member of the church."

"And you don't believe him?"

"His brother Will isn't stable, and doesn't instability run in a family? We've seen that a lot."

"Hannah, you've been Amish too long. That's your problem."

"Talk like that scares me, Miriam. Surely you'd never leave the Amish? Is this what the trip is about? If it is, it was most dishonest to leave Mom and Dad under a false impression, and I won't have anything to do with it. If you're planning to leave the Amish, I think you should turn around right now and go back home. Jake and I can't have this on our hands. Mom and Dad would never forget it if you left the Amish while you were visiting us."

"Oh, Hannah, you *do* worry too much. I'm not leaving, I promise," Miriam said, urging her horse forward. "Come on. Let's take another run. This time you follow me. We've had enough of this serious talk. I want to enjoy Montana."

Hannah followed her, feeling the wind in her face again and allowing her worries to fly off her shoulders. Miriam was right. There had been enough serious talk for awhile.

"I love it!" Miriam shouted from ahead of her, throwing her hands in the air. "Hello, Montana!"

"You're as wild as I am," Hannah said, laughing heartily when they slowed down at the turn toward the barn. "Doesn't this remind you of our growing up years, of riding our ponies in the pasture?"

"I didn't have my pony for very long," Miriam said. "But you had Honey for most of your growing up years. It's a miracle he didn't break his leg the day Sam came by to moon over you."

"*I* did break my collarbone, but Honey was okay. That was the important thing."

"You should take better care of yourself. You have accidents, bash your head in, break your collarbone, date boys who die in car wrecks. But maybe that's my problem. I've been taking such good care of myself nothing has ever happened, good or bad."

"It's the grace of God, Miriam. It's not anything I've done."

"Then I think it's time to get a little of that grace for myself, Hannah."

"You're scaring me again."

Miriam laughed and pulled her horse up in front of the barn. She swung down and loosened the saddle cinch.

Kendra came running across the yard waving her arms at them. She arrived breathless and stood still for a moment to catch her breath.

"Is something wrong?" Hannah quickly asked.

"No, no," Kendra said, between breaths. "Mom wonders if you'd come inside and help her move a piece of furniture to the basement. Dad told her he would help her some evening, but Mom said she might as well seize the moment with both of you here."

"Of course," Miriam said. "As soon as we get these horses put away."

Hannah led her horse to the barn and pulled his saddle off. Beside her Miriam did the same, swinging the saddle to its place on the rack.

"Your hands will get tired doing this all summer," Hannah said. "But I got used to it and really enjoyed the job."

"You'll have to come over and help me sometimes."

"I might come to ride since you're here, but I don't know about helping."

"Then I'll look forward to riding some more with you," Miriam said with a smile. "It's been a long time since I've had so much fun."

"Same here," Hannah said as they walked toward the house.

Kendra held the door open for them, and Betty came rushing down from upstairs.

"Oh, thank you two so much for helping out. If I can get this old desk down to the basement, I will feel so much better. The thing needed to be out of the living room for I don't know how long, but we've been putting it off."

"Then a heave and a ho," Miriam said, taking one corner with Kendra, while Betty and Hannah took the other. Together they managed to slide it over to the basement stairs. Betty had rugs ready, and they slid it down, placing rugs in front of the desk as it moved.

"There, that's done!" Betty said, when she was satisfied with the new location. "And thank you so much. I will see both of you on Sunday then, if not before."

"I'm already enjoying my visit so much," Miriam said, turning to follow Hannah up the outside basement steps.

"To a happy summer!" Betty hollered after them.

"And to a happy meeting with this handsome Dennis fellow," Miriam said over her shoulder.

The two young women heard Betty gasp.

Twelve

Mr. Brunson drove out of the grocery store parking lot and turned northwest on Highway Two, his weekly grocery bags on the floorboard. The single carton of eggs sat on the seat, sliding sideways as he accelerated. Now he had no excuse to stop in at Mary Keim's stand on his way home. It was better this way, as Jake had said. The distance between the two cultures was simply too wide for even love to bridge. *If* it was love. Perhaps he was experiencing just another crush, mirroring his youth. Didn't old people enter a second childhood somewhere around his age? But then he knew the real thing when it happened. He had experienced the real thing with Bernice those many years ago. Wasn't this like that?

Accelerating, he pulled out of town, approaching the speed limit before he slowed down. Jake's friendship was an issue in his decision, but of greater concern were Mary's feelings on the matter. How was he to find out how she felt about him if he couldn't ask her out to dinner? Apparently from what Jake said, trouble would begin for Mary if the Amish community even heard of her interest in an *Englisha* man. But *did* she have an interest? Or was he simply imagining his own feelings were hers?

Ahead of him the framed box stand with the blue tarp covering the top came into view. Beside the stand Mary's horse stood tied to the fence, switching its tail at flies. Mr. Brunson had no reason to stop, but even so he found his foot easing off the gas pedal. He turned slowly into the small parking area under an oak tree. His face felt flushed and his hands were sweaty. What was he to say to her, and what was he to do with another carton of eggs?

Climbing out of his truck, he walked toward the stand, meeting Mary's peaceful eyes as he approached. This woman was obviously happy in her world, content to submit to what God had sent her way. Could he fit into that will, or was he the interloper come to disturb and ruffle that peace? His heart pounded as he greeted her.

"Good morning, Mrs. Keim," he said. "It certainly is beautiful weather this morning."

"That it is, Mr. Brunson," she said, laughing softly, the sound like country church bells on a Sunday morning. "I just sold my last carton of eggs, and here I saw your truck coming down the road. But I'll have more eggs tomorrow if that isn't too much of a problem."

"Oh, that's perfectly fine," he said. "Do you have any more canned goods?"

"I have peaches," she said. "Although these are from a batch I canned two years ago. I don't know if that makes any difference to you. It'll be a few months before the new crop of peaches comes in."

"I'll take a jar," he said, reaching into his pocket for his billfold. "I'm sure they'll be delicious."

She took his money as she handed him the jar. "I hope you enjoy them."

"I know I will," he said, clearing his throat.

Did he dare? But what could he say that wouldn't produce an automatic rift in their current comfortable relationship?

"Is there anything else?" she asked, waiting, her bonnet pushed back on her head, revealing her white *kapp* and the dark hair stretched tight across her forehead.

"You have a good day," he said, looking away and turning back to the pickup. He pulled out of the driveway and headed back toward town. His groceries needed to be home in the refrigerator, but they could wait. He needed to speak with Jake.

Careful to maintain his speed, Mr. Brunson drove into Libby and pulled into the small parking lot in front of Jake's furniture store. A small display room in front had a rocker, a log bed frame, and a dresser in the window. Mr. Brunson exited the truck, walked to the door, and entered. He stepped past the empty front desk and almost slammed into Jake when he went through the door to the workshop in the back.

"Oh, it's you," Jake said. "What's the rush?"

"I've got to speak to you," Mr. Brunson said. "Can we go to the front office?"

"Sure," Jake said. "I hope nothing is wrong."

"Not unless you count my feeling like a bogeyman," Mr. Brunson said, taking the chair behind the desk. Jake dusted off his apron and sat on the rocker.

"You look distraught," Jake said. "Is everything okay?"

"No, everything is not okay," Mr. Brunson said. "And you're going to have to help me."

"All right. What can I do?"

"This matter of my feelings for Mary Keim, that's what. I know you told me to stay away from her, but I can't. At least not until I know how she feels. And I can't ask her myself lest I get her into trouble with your people. Besides, she'd probably die from shock if an *Englisha* man asked her out for dinner."

"She would be surprised, that's for sure, and, yes, troubled," Jake said. "Regardless of what her feelings might be on the matter. She would think she's to blame for giving you ideas."

"But how can it be wrong? I love the woman, Jake."

"You *think* you love her," Jake said. "Love to the Amish is much more than romantic feelings. It's commitment, respect, and a willingness to place the good of the other first."

"And what would be best for Mary? That I disappear?"

"I don't know," Jake said. "This situation is a new one on me."

"And you think it's not for me?" Mr. Brunson said, laughing grimly.

"Would you be willing to join the Amish?" Jake asked.

"Join the Amish? But why can't she join me?"

"I don't think she would. Mary's been Amish all of her life. Do you want her to leave the faith now and face a separation from her family? That's what she would experience if she marries an *Englisha* man."

"No," Mr. Brunson said. "She's a sweet woman, and I wouldn't wish any hardship on her, even for my own benefit. But still—if I at least knew how she felt that would help."

"And if she expressed feelings for you, you'd really join our faith?"

"What would that involve? Do the Amish have any weird doctrines hidden under the surface that would come out to haunt me?"

"No." Jake laughed. "I don't think so, anyway. We are very similar to Protestant churches in matters of doctrine. Where we differ is in our belief that the church needs to be separate from the world. And you can see for yourself how that takes shape. We don't drive cars, have electricity in our homes, and so on."

"And would you take me in as a member? I mean, what could an old man like me lose from joining the Amish? And for a woman like Mary I would be more than glad to."

"I don't think you should rush into a decision," Jake said. "It's a lot harder than what it may look like to you."

"I can imagine," Mr. Brunson said. "Is there any way I can talk with Mary, perhaps with you or Hannah present? I could let her know that my feelings for her would prompt me to become Amish. That would prove I was serious."

Jake shook his head. "I don't think that would be fair. She'd think you were joining just because of her."

"But I would be."

"But that's not good," Jake said. "I think you're going to have to take the risk beforehand. She'll respect you for that. That is, *if* she has feelings for you, which I don't know. If you attempt to secure her affections beforehand, it will never be quite the same. I think she'd want to know you had become Amish because you were convinced it was the right thing for you to do...not just to please her and win her heart."

"I don't know," Mr. Brunson said. "Are you sure that's not the preacher in you talking?"

"It could be," Jake said, smiling. "But I'm responsible for her as a church member, as are the other ministers."

"Still, I think the eloping idea is better," Mr. Brunson said, getting up. "I'd sweep her off her feet with my offer of marriage. What could the poor woman say to the life I have to offer her? There's the money. I could take her on cruises to Alaska, to the Bahamas, to Europe, to the Mediterranean, and that's just the beginning. Plus, she'd be getting me," he added with a wink.

"You would be a good catch," Jake said. "You're a good man, but we value our faith above anything this world has to offer. That's part of who we are. Would you wish to take that away from Mary?"

"I declare you could outtalk a Princeton graduate in rhetoric, Jake. Let alone being a master at making me feel guilty. No, I wouldn't want Mary to give up her principles."

"Then you don't have much choice, do you?"

"Look, Jake," Mr. Brunson said, placing both of his hands on the desk. "At least tell her that I wish to speak with her. Do that for me, and I will take it from there. You don't have to tell her why, just make it legitimate, let it be someplace where she doesn't get in trouble for it and can give me a fair hearing."

"So you want to get *me* in trouble?"

"No, but I have no other choice. I have to talk to her. Do you want me to go down and do so on my own?"

"No," Jake said. "I like both of you too much to let that happen."

"I'll go to your bishop if you want me to."

Jake laughed. "And what makes you think he'll tell you anything different from what I say?"

"It'll probably be worse."

"Probably."

"Then you won't help me?"

"I didn't say I wouldn't."

"But you didn't say you would either."

"Tell you what I'll do," Jake said. "I'll send Hannah down tonight to speak with her. I don't think it's the best way, but coming from a woman, it might be better received."

"That'll be fine," Mr. Brunson said, a broad smile on his face. "But let's be sure about this. I won't be getting you or Hannah in trouble, will I?"

"Not if you behave yourself," Jake said. "Hannah will speak to Mary tonight, and I'll let you know her response next week."

"I knew you'd come through for an old friend." Mr. Brunson beamed. "I can never thank you enough for this, Jake."

"Just remember you said that—when and if you begin learning how to be Amish," Jake said with a smile.

"It will be worth it," Mr. Brunson said. "Trust me."

Jake shook his head, turning back to his shop as Mr. Brunson went out the front door.

Mr. Brunson got into his truck and headed home. As he drove past

Mary's now empty roadside stand he smiled confidently. Jake had agreed to his proposal, and he would soon know what Mary's feelings were for him. That would make things so much easier.

Turning onto the gravel lane toward home, he drove past Jake and Hannah's cabin, slowing his truck to cut down on the dust. Then it occurred to him. Why couldn't he make his own case to Hannah instead of having the words go through Jake's mouth? He knew Hannah well enough, and she had always treated him with the utmost respect. The other night she had been very sympathetic to his story. Surely that all figured in his favor.

But it might not be wise. Better to let Jake tell her, as they had decided. The Amish faith was still a mystery, and there was no sense in stepping into any hidden traps along the way.

Continuing to his place, the truck bounced up to his house. He unloaded the groceries and hurried on his aching legs to get the now warm eggs into the refrigerator. If they spoiled before he finished the carton, the stop to see Mary had still been worth it. Finishing the last trip he walked back outside, standing on the front porch to look at the mountains in the east, his eyes following the long rise and fall of the majestic ridges.

What would it be like to join the Amish? Surely it would be fun, if nothing else. He had already experienced a life of seclusion in these mountains in the years after Bernice and Elsie's deaths. Going Amish shouldn't be that much different. And as close as the Amish community seemed, he would certainly no longer be so alone. It might be a good thing, this Amish conversion.

With Bernice he had dreamed of cruises and travel to exotic places. They had never gone, except for the trip to Guam on their honeymoon, always pushing the dates back until the day they would retire. Now Bernice was gone. Could another woman ever take her place?

No, but Mary was a different woman. She wouldn't be taking Bernice's place at all. In fact, with Mary it was obvious there still would be no cruises ahead or travel to exotic places. Perhaps it was just as well. He sighed and turned to go back inside.

Thirteen

Hannah turned Mosey into the gravel lane and drove up the hill toward the cabin. Miriam, impatient, pulled the storm front open and leaned out of the buggy front to look eagerly around her.

"You'll fall out if you're not careful," Hannah warned, hanging onto the lines as Mosey lifted his feet high, almost prancing at the sight of the barn.

"I have to look around," Miriam said. "This is such beautiful country. And look at your adorable little cabin."

"It's small," Hannah said, "but we like it."

"I can see why," Miriam said. "I never dreamed it would be this nice—not even with all the descriptions Mom gave from her trip out here."

"I suppose you have to see things before they're real to you," Hannah said, guiding Mosey up to the barn. Miriam was already on the ground before Hannah pulled to a stop, jumping out over the buggy wheels.

"This is where I will find love, and I will always remember this as the moment when I first knew for sure. The sight of your little cabin will be forever burned in my mind as the place I finally knew that love had come knocking on my door."

"Don't you think that's a little silly?" Hannah asked, climbing down from the buggy and loosening the tugs.

"And this statement comes from the girl who used to dream herself!" Miriam said, turning to loosen the tugs on her side of the buggy.

"You don't sound like it's a dream," Hannah said, leading Mosey forward while Miriam held the shafts. "You sound certain of it."

"I *am* certain of it," Miriam said. "And you will let me use the cabin on Sunday nights, won't you? I don't think I can risk having him take me over to Betty's place. She would be up to her usual sabotage, like she was with you and Jake."

"Don't be hard on Betty. She had her reasons."

"But you *will* let me use the living room, won't you, Hannah? Please? Do I have to get down on my knees and beg?"

Hannah laughed, "He has to ask you first. Have you thought of that?"

"This Dennis will *swoon* at my charms," Miriam said, rolling her eyes skyward.

"I'm glad Mom's not around to hear you talk like this. She would scold you to no end—and rightly so."

"Ah, but she's not here."

"No, but don't forget that *I'm* here to watch over you on her behalf," Hannah said leading Mosey into the barn. "You can go on inside if you want."

Pulling the harness off the horse, Hannah turned Mosey into his stall. Making sure his door to the field was open, she left the barn. Jake would see to the horse's feed and hay when he arrived home from work and took care of Joel, his driving horse.

Hannah entered the cabin to find Miriam standing in the middle of the living room, her suitcase beside her.

"This is where it will happen," Miriam said, swinging her arms wide. "My future husband and I will have our first long talk right here."

"I still haven't said you could use the living room."

"Come on, Hannah," Miriam said. "*Please* let me."

"But I don't approve of the boy—if you're still thinking of Dennis. I'm sorry now I even mentioned him."

"Hannah, Dennis is a church member in good standing, isn't he?"

"*Jah*, but I still don't like it," Hannah said and then quickly changed the subject. "We'd better get you unpacked. Let me show you where the spare bedroom is."

"This is *so* wonderful," Miriam said, following with her suitcase. "And this is where Mom and Dad stayed when they visited last year. It's exactly like Mom described it."

"It was a great blessing that they were here over Jake's ordination," Hannah said. "None of us could have timed it any better."

"A log bed! Oh, Hannah!" Miriam shrieked. "Did Jake make this?"

"*Jah*, a month or so ago."

"So it wasn't here when Mom and Dad visited?"

"No, we just had an old mattress frame then, since money was kind of tight."

"I remember Mom saying that," Miriam said, lifting her suitcase up on the bed. She turned and gave Hannah another hug. "I am so happy, Hannah. Happier than I've been in years. And to think my little sister had so much to do with it."

"I'm glad," Hannah said, returning the hug. "I'll let you unpack while I start supper. Take as much time as you need."

Hannah went into the kitchen and placed wood in the stove. It caught fire easily on the embers from the morning, the flame leaping to life, the smoke curling toward the back of the firebox and then up the chimney.

Supper would be simple tonight, even with Miriam here. There would be time later for more elaborate meal making. For tonight Miriam needed time to relax and get used to her surroundings after all the exuberance she was expending. Perhaps especially because of all the exuberance...

Starting work on a meat casserole, Hannah went out to the springhouse and, upon returning, found Miriam in the kitchen.

"Are you unpacked already?"

"Not quite," Miriam said. "But I can't stay cooped up in there while the sun is shining. I can finish unpacking after supper."

"Then why don't you go outside and look around? I can handle the supper preparations."

"I have a better idea," Miriam said. "Why don't I help you get your casserole in the oven, and then we both can go outside. You can give me a guided tour."

"I'm afraid there's not much to give a tour of," Hannah said with a laugh. "But it does sound like a good idea."

"Decided then," Miriam said, glancing at the recipe. Hannah showed her where the bowls were under the counter, and together they quickly finished the casserole.

"We'll have to time the oven," Hannah said, sliding the dish in. "What does the recipe say?"

"An hour and a half at three-fifty."

"Then we have plenty of time," Hannah said, shutting the oven door. "Come, we'll start with the garden."

"So you don't have problems with deer?" Miriam asked as Hannah pointed out the sprouting rows of vegetables and corn.

"Not really," Hannah said. "The deer stay mostly in the mountains. I guess they must have plenty of other things to eat. We did have a bear problem. Did Mom tell you about that?"

Miriam laughed. "They talked about it for months. That and this neighbor of yours who shot the grizzly. Mom and Dad seemed to think he was quite the decent man."

"That's Mr. Brunson. You'll get to meet him while you're here."

"I think I'd rather meet this Dennis fellow you don't want me to meet," Miriam teased.

"If you do meet him, don't ever say I didn't warn you."

"I won't," Miriam said as she bent over to pick a tiny flower from the edge of the pasture. "Now isn't this cute?"

"It's a purple geranium. I've noticed them in the pasture before."

"Take a long sniff," Miriam said, holding the flower up to Hannah's face. "Isn't that just the best perfume anyone could buy? I think I'll rub my face with them on Sunday night when Dennis brings me here for our first date."

"Don't be silly," Hannah said.

Both women glanced back toward the house at the sound of rattling buggy wheels.

"Is that Jake coming up the lane?" Miriam asked.

"That's him!" Hannah said, a big smile spreading over her face.

"Oh my, he's a minister now," Miriam said with a shiver. "I haven't seen him since he's a minister. And here I was making plans to have my dates in a minister's house. Maybe I'll have to rethink that."

"I think Jake approves of Dennis," Hannah said, leading the way toward the barn. "At least a lot more than I do."

"Then bless his shirt buttons," Miriam said. "He'll be a good minister then."

"Stop your prattling and come tell Jake hello," Hannah said.

As the two approached Jake, he spoke first as he pulled the horse to a stop by the barn. "Howdy! I see you've made it, Miriam. Has Hannah been keeping you entertained?"

"More than entertained I would say," Miriam said. "She took me on a horseback ride at Betty's place and showed me around your place. It's so lovely here, and the countryside is absolutely awesome."

"That's *gut*," Jake said, as Hannah helped him unhitch. "Is supper ready?"

"Almost," Hannah said. "Are you hungry?"

"No more than normal," Jake said with a laugh. "Let me get Joel into the barn and taken care of and I'll explain."

Hannah turned toward the house to see that Miriam had gone ahead of her and was already entering the kitchen door. When she arrived inside, Miriam had the casserole out on top of the stove, a slightly worried look on her face.

"Did we miss the time by that much?" Hannah asked. "Did I burn it to a crisp?"

Miriam shook her head, "I don't think so. It might be browned a little extra, but nothing serious." Her smile returned. "These woodstoves have got to be hard to regulate."

"They are," Hannah said. "But I usually succeed in not burning anything."

"Well, your record is still intact, so you can breathe a sigh of relief."

"That's *gut* because Jake wants supper early for some reason."

"Then let's get it on the table for him," Miriam said, as the front door of the cabin opened.

"Hannah, may I talk with you for a minute?" Jake called from the living room.

"Go!" Miriam said, motioning with her hand. "I'll get supper on the table."

"I'll be right back to help with the salad," Hannah said over her shoulder. "The bread, butter, and jam are in the lower cupboard."

Jake was sitting on the couch, his face deep in thought when she came up to him.

"Please sit down," he said. "I have something to ask of you. Mr. Brunson stopped by today, and I told him you'd pay a visit to Mary Keim tonight."

"Why?" Hannah asked, sitting down beside him.

"Because Mr. Brunson talked me into this. He wants to speak with Mary about their possible future relationship."

"But Jake, you can't do that. You know you can't. It's not fitting."

He laughed nervously, "Perhaps I made this sound worse than what it is. Mr. Brunson seems to think he wants to join the Amish, but he'd like to speak with Mary first. To know her feelings...if she has any for him."

"If any of this comes back to Bishop John—and it surely will—think of how it will sound. You giving an *Englisha* man permission to speak of marriage to one of our women. That will get you in so much trouble— more trouble than you've ever been in before."

"But I promised Mr. Brunson."

"I'm sorry, dear," Hannah said, stroking his face. "But you have a very soft heart, and I think Mr. Brunson took advantage of you. Come, we have supper almost ready, and you can still eat early."

"So you won't go?" he asked, getting to his feet.

"I don't think that would be for the best," Hannah said. "Not for your sake, or my sake, or for the sake of the baby."

"The baby," he said, taking her gently in his arms. "I had forgotten about the baby."

"We must think of him...or her. Your reputation—and mine and the baby's—is at stake here."

"I suppose you're right," he said, kissing her gently on top of the head.

Fourteen

Jake walked up the gravel lane toward Mr. Brunson's place, squinting from the early morning sun in his eyes. The matter could have waited until Monday morning when Mr. Brunson came by the furniture shop, but he wanted it off his mind. He had promised the man something he couldn't deliver, and he needed to make it right.

Hannah was correct in her objection. He did need to protect his family as much as possible from any fallout his actions might produce. And this could have been avoided if he had simply held his ground. He had no right to give Mr. Brunson access to Mary Keim. Bishop John would be the first one to tell him so. Thankfully Hannah had caught his mistake before it had borne any bitter fruit. She was a *gut* wife for him, and truly the kind of helpmeet the Scriptures spoke of.

He stroked his beard, quickening his pace. If he hurried he might be able to get into town this afternoon and work a few hours in the shop. Not that he had to, but it might settle his restless nerves. Bishop John had the main sermon tomorrow, and Mose would likely preach the beginning sermon, so he would have no responsibilities other than reading the Scriptures. Those could be read through this evening to make sure he knew how to pronounce the German words.

A lazy stream of smoke came out of Mr. Brunson's chimney, so he must have lit a fire to take off the early morning chill. Hannah had their stove going around six, which was early for them on a Saturday morning, but she had wanted to surprise Miriam. The two had talked in the living room last night until long after he had gone to bed. They were both sleepy-eyed over breakfast, but it didn't slow down their plans for the day. Something about a trip over to Betty's and then a trek further back into the mountains on Betty's horses.

Stepping up on the porch, Jake knocked, waiting for sounds of footsteps before he knocked again.

"Coming!" Mr. Brunson hollered from the back of the house.

"I didn't get you up, did I?" Jake asked when the door opened.

"Nope," Mr. Brunson said with a big smile on his face. "I see you couldn't wait though. You had to come up with the good news this morning. So what did she say?"

"Ah," Jake said, clearing his throat. "I have to make something right, Mr. Brunson. I shouldn't have made that promise to you regarding Hannah visiting Mary."

"Oh," Mr. Brunson said, his face falling. "And why not?"

Jake cleared his throat again, "Hannah pointed out to me that it will make trouble for our family if I allow you to talk with Mary Keim. Bishop John won't appreciate that at all. So I'm sorry, but Hannah didn't go down last night."

"I see," Mr. Brunson said. "So Hannah told you she wouldn't go?"

"*Jah*," Jake said.

"Then I'll have to think of some other way, young man," Mr. Brunson said, slapping Jake gently on the shoulder. "We wouldn't want the missus upset now, would we? When mama's not happy, nobody's happy."

"It's more than that," Jake said. "Hannah was right. I shouldn't have agreed to your request in the first place. I knew better."

"Jake, you and Hannah are a fine young couple," Mr. Brunson said. "I wouldn't want to make any trouble for you, so there are no hard feelings on my part."

"Thank you," Jake said, turning to go. "You have a good weekend."

"And you too," Mr. Brunson said.

Jake was in the driveway before he heard the door close behind him. So what was Mr. Brunson going to do now? The situation hadn't seemed to damage their friendship. Mr. Brunson hadn't acted like he was overly upset, and the man was honest. Still, Jake knew he had done the right thing. Hannah and the baby came first, and he couldn't intentionally do anything that might make life more difficult for them.

His church work already placed enough of a strain on Hannah, and it was nothing but the grace of God that he was married to a woman who could handle the pressure. How many young Amish women were asked to go through what she had already been through? Not many. And Hannah had stood up well through the unexpected ordination, the miscarriage, and now carrying their child again.

"It's going to be a boy," Hannah had whispered to him again last night when she had finally come to bed. She had been so sleepy and so happy, and he was part of the reason. She loved him.

Jake arrived at the cabin door, pausing on the porch to listen to the silence of the house. Hannah and Miriam must have already left for Betty's house. He pushed open the door and called inside, "Are you still here, Hannah?"

He heard only silence. Walking out to the barn, he pushed open the door. The buggy Hannah drove and Mosey were missing, so the two had gone to Betty's. That left him with the day on his hands and little to do. He would go to town and return before it was late. Hannah hadn't packed a lunch, but it was Saturday, and he could splurge on a sandwich at the diner.

Catching Joel, he hitched him to the open buggy and drove out the graveled drive toward the main road. Turning toward Libby, he let the horse have its head. He had driven Joel each day this week and still he was full of energy. Hannah was afraid of him driving the horse on Sunday. Hanging onto the reins, Jake smiled. It was *gut* to be on the road on a Saturday morning, knowing that he was heading into town where he had work that needed to be done.

Not that long ago he had struggled to find a job and keep money in their checking account for bills. Hannah had carried that stress well. Now he could think of building her a new cabin—a larger one to fit their growing family. Of course that depended on the furniture business continuing to do well, which hinged on Mr. Brunson's continued friendship.

Jake's face darkened. Had he endangered their future this morning? That was not likely, but even if he had, Hannah had still been right. He had needed to take back his promise to Mr. Brunson.

Near the edge of town a blue pickup truck was parked along the edge of the road. Jake caught a glimpse of the driver's face as he went by and then craned his neck for another look. It was Ben Stoll all dressed up in his new Mennonite clothing. But what was he doing parked along the field outside Libby? Hadn't Hannah mentioned he was here the other day, walking around this field with two *Englisha* men? Hannah had been sure Ben was staking out the lot where the Mennonite tent revival would be held.

Jake almost pulled back on the reins, but quickly relaxed. It was none of his business what Ben was doing nor was it his place to confront him. The Mennonite revival meetings would have to be dealt with in their own good time. Behind him, Jake heard the truck start up. When he turned to look, he noticed Ben was following him. Down the streets of Libby Jake drove, the blue pickup truck close behind. When he turned into the furniture shop lot, the truck did too. Parking in his usual spot, Jake jumped down from the buggy to tie Joel. There was no sense in unhitching since he wouldn't be here but a few hours.

Ben Stoll also parked. He got out of his rig and walked toward Jake. Jake waited. Whatever Ben wanted could be discussed outside. He had no intention of welcoming him into the office and making him feel comfortable.

"Good morning," Ben said, stopping a few feet away. He stroked his freshly shaved chin, still pale from his recent full beard.

"Good morning," Jake said. "I see you've wasted no time getting rid of your beard, and you're all decked out in new clothing. I thought you left the Amish for spiritual reasons?"

Ben chuckled. "You don't have to get testy about it, do you, Jake? I just stopped by for a friendly chat about what we're doing in town this summer."

"*Jah,*" Jake said. "Hannah saw your sign at the grocery store. I'm sorry about being snappy with you. I guess you know you have us all on edge with this tent revival you're planning. Is that really necessary in this community?"

"Hey," Ben said, "the Bible tells us to preach the gospel to the whole world, and I guess Libby is included in the whole world."

"It was the last time I looked," Jake said. "But you know good and well what you're doing. This is all about capturing Amish church members. Do you and your preacher friend have plans to start a Mennonite church around here?"

"What if we do?" Ben asked, shrugging. "The Mennonites are everywhere the Amish are. You don't expect that you can avoid the real world forever, do you, Jake? You know you can't. And rather than just criticize what we're doing, why don't you come on down to the meetings and see for yourself?"

"I'm not interested in supporting something I don't believe you should be doing," Jake said, kicking a little stone across the parking lot. "Why don't you call off this meeting of yours and set your tent up someplace where there aren't any Amish people?"

"I can't do that," Ben said, shaking his head. "We've received a call from God to come to Libby, and I don't think the Lord would appreciate it if we were unfaithful to the call."

"Oh," Jake said. "And what Scripture told you to come to Libby?"

"It wasn't Scripture exactly," Ben said, scratching his face. "It came through the brethren at our church. They felt like God wanted meetings in Libby this summer."

"I see," Jake said. "Well, I don't think they're right. I think you should reconsider. It's going to cause a lot of problems for us, and we are already part of the church of God. Or don't you believe that anymore?"

"The Amish church doesn't care a whole lot about God's will," Ben said. "It's all about tradition—not having electricity and not driving automobiles. Salvation is a free gift, Jake. It's available to anyone, including the Amish."

"*Jah*, it is, and how else could we live the way we do if we didn't think it was the will of God? Do you think being separate from the world and living a godly lifestyle is easy? It's a lot of work, Ben. Something you apparently weren't very willing to do."

"Salvation is free, Jake. And no man has to work for it. That's all the Amish are doing. They're working for their salvation, trying to please an angry God. I'm tired of that, Jake. I'm tired of living in fear, wondering whether I will get to heaven or not. I'm free now from all those rules we used to live under, and that's the gospel I'm going to preach in Libby, Jake. Freedom from fear and the bondage of what man thinks."

"You're going to preach?" Jake asked, raising his eyebrows. "I thought you had some minister preaching."

"Oh," Ben said, "there is an evangelist coming, but I've also been called to preach and might do so for a few nights. It depends on how long the meetings go on."

"I see," Jake said. "So you have been ordained?"

"Not by a church," Ben said. "At least not yet, but I have a higher calling from the Lord Himself. He has called me to preach wherever I have a chance. That's what our forefathers used to do, Jake. Many of them weren't ordained men. Most were common folks like us who went out preaching and baptizing everyone who listened to the gospel and believed."

"Yes, but that was different. If the authorities were looking for me and planning to throw me in prison and burning me at the stake, I probably wouldn't worry about being ordained either."

"You shouldn't make fun of this," Ben said. "The calling of God is a serious matter."

"And you don't think I know that?"

"Well, I don't see you going out and preaching the gospel. I know your sermons in church were always decent, but it's not the same as going into all the world and spreading the good news. That's what I'm called to do."

"Well, that's fine," Jake said. "But maybe you could take Libby off the list. I think there are thousands of towns out there who would welcome a good tent revival."

"I can't do that," Ben said, shaking his head. "It would be disobeying the Lord's command."

Fifteen

Hannah paused on the plateau by the riverbank as Miriam rode on past her toward the wood line. Her sister was in high spirits this morning and taking in the full taste and feel of the countryside. Of course, she had done the same that summer a few years ago, only not quite as energetically.

"This is as far as I've ever gone," Hannah yelled. "I don't know about going any further into the foothills."

"Why? Are you scared?" Miriam asked, turning in the saddle to look back. "Betty gave us good directions, and we have all the time in the world on this beautiful Saturday morning."

"I don't think Betty has been up this far either," Hannah said. "So how would she know where the trail leads?"

"Steve probably told her, and he would know."

"Well, we shouldn't go far," Hannah said, nudging her horse in the ribs to catch up. "I certainly don't want to get lost."

"We won't," Miriam said, leading the way up out of the plateau.

"You don't exactly inspire confidence," Hannah said as she followed her sister's lead.

When they broke out into an open meadow, Miriam spread out her arms in a wide arc and threw her head back, laughing. "Have you ever seen anything so beautiful, Hannah? Look at the flowers, there are thousands of them at these higher elevations. Just think how much more wonderful it must be higher up!"

"It is a wonderful sight," Hannah acknowledged, pulling her horse to a halt. "And to think that I've never been up here before."

"That's what you've been missing out on without me here to spur you on. I think I'll be coming up here every chance I get this summer while I work for Betty."

"As long as you don't get lost."

"I'll be like the Indians and mark my trail," Miriam said, leading the way back into the woods.

They rode in silence, listening to the soft rush of the wind in the pines. They spooked a herd of white-tailed deer at the next meadow. Hannah watched as the graceful animals bounced toward the far side, their white tails standing erect and waving like small flags. Before entering the trees, the deer paused, looked back at them, and then vanished like ghosts.

"We should turn back," Hannah said.

"Not yet." Miriam had a catch in her voice. "This is so beautiful. I want to see all of it at once."

"You can't do that, silly," Hannah said, but she followed Miriam as she turned her mount up the gentle incline in the direction the deer had gone.

Higher and higher they rode, stopping at a small opening in the trees. Hannah caught a glimpse of a road winding below them.

"Who lives down there?" Miriam asked, pointing toward the road.

"I don't know all of them, but a few of the homes belong to Amish people. That's Will and Rebecca's place in the distance. John and Elizabeth's house is another mile up the road, but not too far. Maybe we can see it if we climb higher."

"I want to see your cabin," Miriam said, leaning over the horn of the saddle. "It's got to be around somewhere."

"I think it's further north and out of sight. We'd probably have to go really high to see it."

"Then let's!" Miriam said, urging her horse on again.

They climbed until the trees opened up again to reveal a broad vista of a meadow. Above and off into the distance towered the higher peaks. The path continued at an increased incline. Hannah stopped. *Dennis Riley's cabin is up here somewhere, isn't it? It's hard to tell, but if it is, what if we run into Dennis himself?*

Miriam was already disappearing into the trees, so Hannah encouraged her horse forward.

"I think we should turn back," Hannah shouted.

Miriam looked over her shoulder and called back, "Not yet. I'm having too much fun."

"But it's getting late," Hannah said, catching up.

"Don't be silly, it's early yet," Miriam said as they broke out into the open again. Immediately below them a little cabin nestled above another meadow, and a herd of deer was standing at the tree line looking at them.

"Look, it's probably the same deer we saw earlier," Miriam said. "We've been chasing them all this time."

"There are lots of deer up here. They're probably different ones," Hannah said, glancing around desperately. Was this Dennis's cabin below them? It certainly didn't look like it, but she had been to Dennis's place only once with Jake on a Sunday evening.

"Let's go see if anyone's home," Miriam said. "They're probably lonesome and would welcome visitors."

"I don't know about that," Hannah said, but Miriam was already walking her horse toward the cabin. Giving up, Hannah followed. They crossed a little ravine, the horses jumping smoothly. Hannah slowed down, her eyes going back and forth over the cabin and the barn set in behind the trees. Suddenly she was sure. She urged her horse forward and caught up with Miriam.

"Stop, Miriam. I know whose place this is."

"You do? Then that's so much the better. Perhaps they'll offer us something to eat. I'm starving."

"It's Dennis Riley's place. Jake and I were here once in the evening."

"Dennis Riley?" Miriam said, her eyes growing large. "Really? I wonder if he's home?"

"How do I know? And I don't want to find out. What will he think if we come riding in on him?"

"But I want to see him."

"He'll think we've come on purpose to introduce you. Boys think that way. And he'll think Jake had something to do with it."

"Probably," Miriam said. "But I still want to see him."

"Oh no," Hannah groaned. "He's coming out on the porch. Start riding toward the woods. Maybe we can get out of this yet."

Miriam was staring across the short distance to the house as Dennis leaned against the rail. His fingers were hooked in his suspenders and he was hatless as he looked across the meadow at them.

"I want to see him up close," Miriam whispered.

"You're going to follow me," Hannah said, turning her horse back the way they had come.

"Howdy there!" Dennis yelled. "Is that you, Hannah?"

"He's recognized you," Miriam said. "We have to go up now."

"Then let me do the talking," Hannah commanded, turning her horse around. "Maybe we can move on quickly."

"I don't want to move on quickly," Miriam muttered as she followed Hannah.

"Hi, Dennis. We're just out riding this morning," Hannah said as they approached. "This is my sister Miriam. We saw some of the other Amish places further down, but I forgot exactly where your cabin was."

"Nice to meet you, Miriam," Dennis said. "Yes, my place is kind of up out of the way...but it's nice here, and I like it."

After a moment of awkward silence, Dennis said, "Say, have you had lunch?"

"No, we haven't," Miriam said quickly before Hannah could answer.

"Would you like to stay?" Dennis asked, tilting his head. "Nothing fancy, but I've got sandwich makings."

"I don't know," Hannah said, glancing at Miriam. Her face had turned shades of white and red, and this from a girl who had always handled herself around boys. Obviously Betty and her fears had not been groundless. She turned back toward Dennis.

"I mean, you're welcome," Dennis said, a wide grin on his face.

"We'd better not," Hannah replied, glancing again at Miriam's blushing face. "We need to keep moving if we plan to get home soon."

"Aw, come on," Dennis urged. "I know the bachelor life doesn't produce good cooking, but maybe you two can make sandwiches for me. I mean, better than I would make them. I'm pretty clumsy in the kitchen."

"Oh, of course we can!" Miriam blurted. "It must be hard looking out for yourself all the time."

Dennis laughed again. "Perhaps, but I don't think Jake would think well of me if I let the two of you wander the woods weak with hunger."

"I think we can surely fix sandwiches," Miriam said, her voice now a high squeak.

"Of course you can," Dennis said, walking off the porch. "Let me tie your horses to the rail. Come on in."

Hannah dismounted and handed him the reins. Dennis tied them quickly to a post. Miriam was already on the ground when Dennis turned toward her.

"Here," Miriam said, holding out the reins, her eyes fixed on his face.

Hannah watched as Dennis took the reins, a soft smile on his face, his eyes lingering for a moment on Miriam's hands before guiding the horse to the next post. Dennis finished the knot with a quick twist and turned to walk up the steps toward the cabin without a backward glance. Hannah reached over to shake Miriam's arm before turning to follow him. Had her sister lost all her good sense so soon? How had they gotten into this situation anyway?

Inside, Dennis opened the gas-powered refrigerator door, waving his hand over the stocked supplies inside.

"I'd offer to make the sandwiches myself," Dennis said, "but like I said, I'm not much good in the kitchen. They wouldn't be good enough for womenfolk."

"Oh, I'm sure you'd make a *super* sandwich," Miriam said, her voice still a squeak.

Hannah glanced at Miriam's bright-red face and shuddered. For all her fears of what Miriam's reaction would be, this was not what she had imagined. Her tough sister was falling apart in front of Dennis's piercing blue eyes. *This would be funny…if it were anyone else but Dennis that Miriam was swooning over,* Hannah thought. "Well," she said, not looking at either of them, "I see you have everything here we need: tomatoes, salad dressing, lettuce, ham slices, and cheese. I must say that's pretty good for a bachelor. I never got to see the inside of Jake's cabin before we were married, but I doubt if it was this well stocked."

"I like to eat well," Dennis said, still looking at Miriam's scarlet face.

"Let me help you, Hannah," Miriam said, gasping suddenly, and rushing over to stand by Hannah's side.

Hannah suppressed a laugh at Miriam's shaking hands as her sister took the tomatoes and lettuce out of the refrigerator.

Behind them Dennis settled into a kitchen table chair, obviously happy to watch them fix his lunch. "It's not every day I have two such wonderful cooks preparing a meal for me," he said, his grin spreading over his face again. "Rebecca does a really good job when I visit their house, but this is even better. This must be what the *Englisha* mean by in-house service."

"You haven't even tasted our sandwiches yet," Miriam said, her voice closer to normal. "So don't be crowing too soon."

"We might put in tomato stems," Hannah quipped, quickly slicing a tomato into five pieces.

He laughed heartily. "I doubt that. Jake looks pretty healthy. And by the way, what's he doing today?"

"He went up to Mr. Brunson's before we left this morning, and he's planning on being in town till after lunch."

"He's pretty busy with that furniture business, isn't he?"

"*Jah*," Hannah said, laying two of the tomato pieces aside, and keeping the three larger ones for the bread Miriam was spreading with salad dressing.

"I think I'll be hired on for a log cutting job from Mr. Wesley this spring. At least that's what some of his help told me."

"Well, you can have it," Hannah said, laying the meat and tomatoes on the sandwiches. "I never liked it when Jake used to work on the crew. It sounded like awful dangerous work driving the machinery around the mountainside."

"Ah, but it's fun," Dennis said, smiling broadly. "But I guess each to his own taste. I love logging."

"So you log?" Miriam asked, her voice squeaky again.

Hannah glanced at her sister, resigned to the situation. At least Miriam looked normal now without those splotchy red-and-white patterns on her face. There was really nothing Hannah could do about this anyway. Fate…or was it love…or perhaps *Da Hah* Himself…seemed to be against her. But then perhaps she shouldn't be so dead-set against this if Miriam was really finding love with Dennis. She hadn't appreciated it when Betty had interfered with her and Jake—and look how that had turned out.

"Yes, I do," Dennis said. "And what brings you out to the great and wild West?"

"Oh, nothing," Miriam said. "I'm just visiting for the summer."

"For all summer?" he asked. "That's a long time to just visit."

"She'll be working at Betty's place for the summer," Hannah said. Miriam would also be taking care of her baby, but that wasn't something Dennis needed to know.

"Hannah helped Betty for two summers with her riding stable," Miriam said. "Before she was married to Jake."

"That was before Will and I moved here," Dennis said. "Well, I'm glad you'll be here all summer. I expect we'll get to see more of each other at the young folk gatherings."

"I think so," Miriam agreed, dreamy-eyed, as she sliced the tomatoes.

"The sandwiches are ready," Hannah said. "We should pray and eat. Betty will be wondering where we have gotten to."

"Betty will be okay," Miriam said, smiling for the first time.

Dennis nodded and they sat down, bowing their heads. Dennis didn't pray out loud, but then he wasn't expected to. Jake hadn't either for the longest time.

"So you come from Indiana?" Dennis asked after the prayer as he glanced at Miriam.

"*Jah*," Miriam said, keeping her eyes on her sandwich. "From around the Nappanee area."

"I've never been there," Dennis said, chewing slowly. "I guess I ought to visit sometime."

"With country like this," Miriam said, "I can see why you don't visit anywhere else."

"Oh, I've been around," Dennis said. "My parents live in Idaho, but most of my travels have been in the mountain states. They kind of grow on you, I guess."

"I can see why they would," Miriam said. "I absolutely love it out here."

"Then you should come and live here permanently," he said, flashing a smile.

"Maybe I will," Miriam said as the red streaked across her face again.

Hannah swallowed the last bite of her sandwich and stood up. She grabbed a washcloth in the sink.

"No you don't!" Dennis said, holding up his hand. "You girls made lunch, and I clean up. And that's the final word on the matter."

"Okay," Hannah said. "Then we had better be on our way."

Dennis nodded and led the way outside. Hannah and Miriam mounted their horses as he untied them. A good distance from the cabin, Miriam turned to look back over her shoulder.

"He's still on the front porch," Miriam whispered. "What did I tell you about him? Didn't I say it would be love at first sight?"

"Quit looking back," Hannah commanded. "You're making a spectacle of yourself."

"No, I'm not," Miriam said, turning around at the edge of the clearing.

"You know, it's amazing that of all the cabins we should discover on our ride, it would be Dennis Riley's," Hannah remarked as they made their way toward Betty's.

"Hannah," Miriam said with a laugh, "I have a confession to make. I didn't mean to trick you, but I knew you wouldn't come if I told you. See, after you brought up Dennis Riley's name, I asked Kendra if she knew where he lived. She told me, and I figured if we kept heading far enough in that direction we'd arrive there. And there it was, just like Kendra said. Now what's so awful about being in love?"

"What's awful is not telling me."

"Well, sometimes a little leading along doesn't hurt."

"I just hope you know what you're doing," Hannah replied with a sigh.

Sixteen

The Sunday morning sun blazed through the hall window as Jake followed Minister Mose Chupp's broad back up the house stairs, pausing on the landing as Bishop John opened a bedroom door, peaking inside before he pushed it wide open. *Menno Yoder's whispered instructions before the service must have been garbled or the bishop forgot which bedroom wasn't being used for sleeping babies,* Jake thought. He kept his eyes on the floor as the sun went behind the clouds and the window darkened. He followed Mose inside.

Bishop John's face had been sober all morning as he stood in line by the barn, greeting the men as they walked past him. Something was troubling him, and it didn't take too many guesses to figure out what it was. News of the coming Mennonite revival meetings had buzzed all along the line of men this morning. Ben Stoll must have paid other Amish friends visits in addition to the one at Jake's furniture shop.

Where was this matter going to end? Obviously Bishop John intended to tackle the problem head-on this morning. Jake tried to still the racing of his heart as he took a chair against the wall.

Outside the sun was breaking through the clouds again, and rays of sunlight pierced through the window. Jake squinted and scooted his chair sideways, but the width of the beam still reached him. Shading his eyes, he glanced at Bishop John, who was staring at the floor.

Jake stood, his legs weak, and walked to the window and pulled the shade. He glanced back where shadows now lay across his chair. In the silence his shoes echoed loudly on the hardwood floor as he walked back to his chair.

Bishop John cleared his throat.

"I suppose both of you have heard of the goings on in the community. I didn't receive a visit from Ben Stoll, which doesn't surprise me at all, but many of our men did. Elizabeth told me she thinks that well over half the church members were personally visited and given brochures and invitations to the upcoming Mennonite revival meetings. Have either of you received a visit?"

"I didn't," Mose said. "And Clara didn't mention anything. I'm sure she would have if Ben had stopped by while I was away from the farm."

"I see," Bishop John said, clearing his throat again. Silence settled on the room, and Jake's heart pounded in his chest. This was not going to look good for him, as Ben was obviously only stopping in at the homes of those he considered easy targets. Protesting and repeating what he had told Ben would do little good.

"Ben stopped by the shop on Saturday," Jake said, not looking up.

"I see," Bishop John said. "And what did he have to say?"

"He said he stopped by for a friendly visit and to invite Hannah and me to the meetings."

"And you told him what?" Bishop John asked.

"That I thought he was wrong in what he was doing, and that he should take his tent revival somewhere else."

Mose laughed. "There's not much chance of that, I don't think."

"It doesn't sound like it," Jake said. "Ben says he has a call from God, whatever that means. I think he's even planning to do some of the preaching himself."

"I hope you were firm with him, Jake. He needs someone to bring correction to him. He's a confused young man. It's hard for me to imagine what these Mennonite preachers put into their members' heads, but they do produce radicals is all I can say. I mean, who would send a young man out to do meetings and let him preach on some flimsy feeling that he has? It's reckless, if you ask me."

"I thought I might have been a little hard on him," Jake said, shifting on his chair.

"Well, that's also possible," Bishop John said, nodding. "We have to be careful about both extremes, but it is *gut* to hear that you sought to correct the man. Ben needs it."

Jake relaxed a bit. Perhaps he had done okay after all.

"What are we going to do about this within the community?" Mose asked, rubbing his hands together. "I'm afraid some of the church members might have given Ben a greater welcome than what Jake did."

"I'm thinking the same thing," Bishop John said. "And I think we ought to take some further steps with the congregation."

"Perhaps we should call a special meeting specifically to warn them of the dangers Ben and those people pose," Mose said. "We could call such a meeting today after church while this is still fresh in everyone's mind."

"We could do that," Bishop John said. "In fact, I think that's the least of what we can do. My feelings are that even further steps should be taken."

"Like what?" Mose asked.

Bishop John clasped his hands in front of him, "Of course we would need unity in whatever decision we make, but we *must* act. I'm thinking Ben and Sylvia might need to be warned that excommunication will be used against them. That is, if they continue pushing these meetings, which are clearly targeted at us, his former church. Our understanding with Ben when he left the community was that he and Sylvia would join a decent church, and this doesn't sound like a decent one, even if they call themselves Mennonites."

"From what I hear, it's a new church conference of some sort, and they really push these revival meetings," Mose said. "That's what Clara told me, and she heard it from her relatives back East. They said this conference has its main church in Pennsylvania somewhere."

"It doesn't matter what they say," Bishop John said. "It's how they're acting out here in Montana that matters to me. Do you think there's a chance we could reason with their leaders?"

"I don't think so," Mose said. "It sounds as if they allow their people to work without a lot of oversight. I doubt if they will feel responsible for what's going on."

"That's what I was afraid of," Bishop John said. "Then we may have to deal with Ben and Sylvia ourselves. What is your opinion on asking the church for an excommunication?"

"There might be some objections," Mose said. "But I would be in favor of it."

"I don't think there will be objections among the members we can't overcome," Bishop John said. "Not if we're in unity on this decision."

They both turned to look at Jake, silence settling on the room again.

"I don't know," Jake said. "I hate to be the one who disagrees, but maybe we ought to ride this thing out. Bringing down an excommunication on Ben and Sylvia may only make things worse."

The men were silent. And then Bishop John spoke. "I'm surprised at you, Jake. I thought you were opposed to what Ben is doing."

"I am," Jake said. "But we have to be careful not to inflame the situation."

"But what if we lose members?" Mose asked. "With things being what they are, I'm fully expecting we might. Remember how Will Riley spouted off the other Sunday? He should apologize to you and to the church, but we let him get away with what he said."

"Jake, weren't you the one who objected to excommunicating Ben and Sylvia when they left the church last year?" Bishop John asked, turning to look toward the window. "It seems to me that you were."

"I still think I was right," Jake said. "We normally don't excommunicate our members for joining the Mennonites, and I don't really want an apology from Will about the testimony he gave. He was only expressing his opinion."

"This problem would be much easier to handle now if Ben had already been warned about excommunication, is all I can say. I doubt if he would even think about holding these meetings with that hanging over his head," Bishop John said.

"I tend to agree," Mose said. "Jake, I think you need to give on this before it's too late."

"So what do you say, Jake?" Bishop John asked, turning toward him. "Are you ready to give your word to the excommunication?"

Jake stared at the curtains of the window. It would be the easiest thing in the world to agree with them, and no one would blame him. In fact, it might be the best thing to do. This would certainly deliver a jolt to Ben and his plans, if no Amish member could attend the tent meetings without facing excommunication. Hadn't Hannah said he wasn't supposed to bring trouble on the family from his church work? This would be trouble if he dared stand up to Bishop John and Mose. Yet how could he not?

"I'm not ready yet to give my word," Jake finally said. "I'm sorry, but this is all so sudden."

"I can see that," Bishop John said. "And in a way I can understand it, but we must not allow this to drag on much longer. Perhaps we can wait awhile and see where we're at, but we have to do something. Our forefathers warned us what happens when our hearts become weak in the face of threats to the church. When that happens, sin gains a foothold and many are led astray.

"I hope you'll consider the matter long and thoughtfully, Jake, and come to the right decision. Our people have long held to the belief that excommunication needs to have an active and present role in our churches. They believed it needs to be exercised whenever church members leave or threaten the faith." He paused and then added, "So I suppose we will leave the matter there for now."

Mose cleared his throat, "I sure hope you don't stand up for Ben Stoll, Jake. The young man is completely out of control from what I have heard. He's talking about having a calling from God to preach himself, and he has never even been ordained. I hope you can see how wrong-minded that is, Jake. We need your support on this."

Jake nodded. What else was there to say? He knew he would need to speak with Hannah, but he also knew that might make matters worse. He opened his dry mouth, but no sound came out.

"Well," Bishop John said, "let's get back to the church. I will have the main sermon, and Mose, it's your turn to do the opening. Jake will read the Scriptures."

Bishop John opened the bedroom door, leading the way downstairs. Jake kept his eyes on each step, steadying his hands by his side. Beads of sweat were popping out under his collar. Once seated on the ministers' bench between the men and women's sides of the house, he leaned against the wall and slowly raised his head to watch Mose get up to open the sermon.

Had he gone too far this time? Hannah would be shocked when she learned that he was even thinking of disagreeing with Bishop John on such an important subject. Worst of all, Bishop John would think he had secret sympathies for Ben and his cause. *Did* he have secret sympathies? Was there perhaps somewhere in his heart a longing to leave the faith and flirt with the world?

His dad, Uriah, hadn't been a preacher, but he used to warn his sons of such things when they gathered around the living room for prayer on cold winter nights. Under the hiss of the gas lantern, with the weight of the long, dark evenings on them, Uriah would say, "A man's heart is full of iniquity. Never place your trust in your own heart or in any man, but only in the Word of God and in the protection of the church. Remember that in each of us there is a secret longing for the ways of the world. It is only by the ever-present counsel of the brethren and sisters, and by applying their interpretation of the Word of God, that anyone is safe."

Had Bishop John's own fears after Jake's ordination been correct? Had his ability to preach well gone to his head? Jake kept his eyes on Mose, pushing the questions away. He soon would need to get up before the congregation to read.

"'Man shall not live by bread alone,'" Mose said, "'but by every word that proceedeth out of the mouth of God.' Please take warning, everyone, to what this Scripture is saying. Satan came to tempt the Lord God Himself, and surely he is not afraid of us. Satan will offer us all the temptations of the world if he can convince us to follow after him."

Jake swallowed hard. Mose might not be talking to him, but then again perhaps he was. It would be hard for Mose to preach and not allow something from what had just happened upstairs to slip into his sermon.

"And now I will bring my words to an end," Mose said, backing up to the bench and sitting down. "Let us pray, and then the Scriptures will be read."

The rustle of kneeling bodies filled the room, and Mose's voice filled the house, reading the prayer in German.

> Now unto God, the great God of our fathers, full of wisdom, and knowledge, in whom dwelleth no darkness at all, shine upon the humble and broken spirits of Your followers today, and lighten our hearts.
>
> So will You, O Lord in heaven, send us grace and help us walk justly before You. Know our hearts, as You alone, oh Lord, know the hearts of men, their thoughts, their sins, their council, yea all things are open to the light of Your face.
>
> So give us, O Lord, wisdom from above, lead us to fear You above all things. We ask You, O Lord, the Lord of all lords, and the Kings of all kings, for the sake of Thy kingdom, and

for the sake of all the righteous, give men Your fear in their hearts, that they may obey You.

We ask this in the name of the Father, the Son, and the Holy Spirit. Amen.

Jake slowly got to his feet, keeping a tight grip on his Bible as the words spun in front of his eyes. He cleared his throat and began to read.

Seventeen

Hannah changed her position on the hard bench, glancing at Jake's face as Bishop John brought his sermon to a close. Jake looked more relaxed now, but the stress lines were still there. They had been there on the way to church and had seemed worse when he came back downstairs with the other two ministers.

Something was troubling Jake. His run-in with Ben at the furniture store on Saturday had been hard on him, but meeting with the ministers upstairs and sharing his burden should have improved his mood, not soured it more. Apparently something had gone wrong.

"I will now ask for testimony of the word that was preached," Bishop John said, assigning Mose and two other of the older married men to speak before he sat down. Hannah caught her breath. Why had the bishop not asked Jake? He always did before, but then perhaps that was why he didn't this morning. Perhaps it was a harmless break in the normal schedule.

She slowly turned to look at Jake's face. His head was down and he was stroking his beard gently. Dennis Riley sat on the boys' bench staring at Jake, a slight smile on his face. Did Dennis know something she didn't? Had some awful news about Jake spread around the community, and was Dennis happy over it? But how could that be? Dennis liked Jake, didn't he?

Her heart pounding, Hannah turned sideways and her eye caught sight of Miriam seated in the girls' section behind Jake. She took a deep breath as relief flooded through her. Her fears were groundless. Dennis wasn't gloating over Jake's suspected setdown by the bishop. He was making eyes at Miriam. And Miriam's face was redder than a beet. Before long others would notice.

The voices from the men's testimonies droned on as Hannah turned back to study Jake's face. He looked so troubled, so deeply forlorn, as if his life had taken a sudden spiral downward. After church she would comfort him, whatever his problem was, and tell him what a wonderful man he was and how much she loved him. She would place her arm around his shoulder the minute she was in the buggy, and it couldn't come a moment too soon. With a sigh, she settled back down on the bench as the bishop got back on his feet.

"I'm glad the preaching has been testified to as the word of God," Bishop John said. "We can be thankful for the unity of the brethren, and must always pray that *Da Hah* will continue to grant us that grace."

The bishop sat down after glancing briefly toward Jake. Hannah caught the look and the pain in Jake's face. So what could Jake be doing that caused disunity among the brethren? Surely he hadn't spoken up in defense of the revival meetings. She knew him better than that.

From the back of the men's section the song leader called out the song number and then immediately launched into singing. He expertly twirled the notes up and down for long moments until the congregation joined in on the second syllable.

Hannah sang along, allowing the joy of the singing to fill her. This was where Jake and she belonged. So would their soon-to-be-born *bobli*, and the many other children she hoped would follow. With one last burst of sound the song leader led out, and as they finished the final line, silence settled on the room for only a moment before the young boys popped off their benches for the race outdoors.

Hannah smiled. This was the ritual she had watched all her growing-up years on so many Sunday mornings. Who would want to leave this tradition for whatever the Mennonites had to offer? How could anything be better than this peace she held in her heart? The Mennonites didn't have anything to replace this, and if only the others in the congregation could see that, so much trouble could be avoided.

"So is Miriam settling in?" a woman's voice whispered from behind Hannah.

Hannah turned to see Rebecca Riley leaning over the bench toward her, her baby asleep in her arms.

"*Jah*, and quite quickly," Hannah said. "It seems to me she loves Montana as much, if not more, than I do."

"That's *gut*," Rebecca said, breaking into a broad smile. "Will wouldn't want to live anywhere else, unless it would be Idaho, but Montana suits me just fine."

Did Rebecca know about the stop she and Miriam had made at Dennis's cabin yesterday? If she did, she likely also knew about Miriam's open display of her affections. Hannah felt her neck grow hot at the thought. Who would have thought that her always-in-control older sister would be making such a show of herself?

"How's Edith coming along?" Hannah asked, forcing herself to smile. "Betty said you had flu in the family last week."

"Oh, she's doing fine. Edith was over most of it by Friday, so I told Will there shouldn't be any problem with coming to church today. Andrew and the baby might still get it, but we'll hope for the best."

"That's *gut* to hear," Hannah said. "May I hold the baby?"

"Sure," Rebecca said, handing over the infant. "Little Jake is such a *gut* baby."

"Oh, he's so sweet," Hannah said, tickling the baby's chin. He broke out into a laugh and waved his arms around.

"He likes you already," Rebecca said, laughing. "And I'm so glad Will insisted on naming him after your Jake. I think he's going to grow up to be an honorable man like him."

"You shouldn't have though," Hannah said, shaking her head as little Jake laughed softly. "Babies should only be named after old people who have lived a long and *gut* life."

Rebecca smiled. "Will really wanted to, and I can see more each day how right he was. Jake is a real inspiration to everyone."

"Well, I hope we don't disappoint you," Hannah said, handing the baby back. "I think I'd better go help in the kitchen."

"I'll put Jake in the bedroom and join you," Rebecca said as Hannah rose. Stepping across the bench, Hannah walked toward the kitchen where the young girls were scurrying about carrying peanut butter bowls and pickles to the tables.

Miriam came by, her eyes shining.

"He's going to ask me soon," she whispered. "Can I still use your place tonight after the singing?"

Hannah nodded but Miriam was already gone, disappearing into the living room. The girl had obviously taken leave of her senses. What was going to happen to Miriam if Dennis didn't ask to take her home? The fall could well be devastating.

"Let me help with something," Hannah offered, stepping into the kitchen.

"You will do nothing of the sort," Betty said, coming up to grab her arm. "I'm taking you right out to the first table to eat."

"But I'm not one of the older women," Hannah whispered.

"You are today," Betty said. "I saw how troubled Jake looked, and the least I can do is take care of his wife."

"You noticed too," Hannah whispered. "What do you think is wrong?"

"I don't know, but you take good care of him tonight," Betty said. "It's probably got something to do with those horrible Mennonite meetings."

Hannah said nothing. They were already at the women's table, and Betty let go of her arm and retreated to the kitchen.

"I'm glad Betty brought you out," Bishop John's wife, Elizabeth, said, making room beside her. Hannah sat at the table, feeling an ache in her stomach. What would Elizabeth think once she arrived home and John told her about whatever was troubling Jake? Would Elizabeth still be friendly next Sunday? If not, that was more pain than she would be able to bear.

"Thanks," Hannah whispered, trying to keep a smile on her face.

Bishop John's clear voice floated out across the room, "If we have gathered to eat, let us now pray."

Hannah bowed, waiting just a moment longer than the others when the prayer was done. She still wasn't used to sitting with the older women—and wouldn't have if Betty hadn't taken matters into her own hands. So much had changed with Jake's ordination, but she must not complain. Jake's ordination was *Da Hah*'s will, and He would give the grace she needed.

"So have you been to the doctor yet?" Elizabeth asked, her voice a tease.

Hannah gasped, her hand halfway across the table to get a piece of bread.

"It's nothing to be ashamed of," Elizabeth said, laughing softly as the hum of voices rose higher around them.

"But I don't show yet," Hannah said, whispering even if no one could hear her. "How did you know?"

"Oh, it was just a guess," Elizabeth said. "I thought *Da Hah* would be blessing the two of you again, and that right soon I figured."

"I hope all goes well this time," Hannah said, spreading butter on her bread.

"Oh, I'm sure it will," Elizabeth said. "Just stay relaxed. You'll be okay."

"I'll try to," Hannah said, as Elizabeth turned to speak to the woman on the other side.

"Do you need any more bread?" a young girl asked at Hannah's shoulder.

"I think we do," Hannah said, turning to the girl.

"I'll bring back some peanut butter too. Your bowl is almost empty," the girl said, disappearing in the direction of the kitchen.

Hannah ate her sandwich, leaning aside when the girl returned to replace the bread and bowl of peanut butter. All around her the buzz of conversation rose and fell, but thankfully no one paid much attention to her. Elizabeth was still talking to the woman on the other side of her, which was *gut*. At the moment, being left alone was just fine.

When they finished, Bishop John led in prayer again, and the women moved away from the table. Hannah grabbed a washcloth over the young girl's objections and helped clean the utensils for the second round of tables.

Out of the corner of her eye she saw Jake leave for the barn and surmised that he must surely be troubled to be leaving so early. Hurrying out to the washroom she found her bonnet and shawl. Jake was coming out of the barn with Mosey when she reached the buggy. She waited for him, holding up the shafts as he swung the horse in. He didn't say anything as they fastened the tugs.

Driving out the lane, she leaned over to slip her arm around his shoulders.

"I'm so sorry," she said, "for whatever is troubling you. But I want you to know that I love you, and that you are the best man *Da Hah* ever made."

Jake smiled weakly. "That's a mouthful. And you haven't even heard the story yet."

"It doesn't matter what the story is," Hannah said, nestling against him as Jake turned onto the blacktop.

"Did it show that much?" he asked. "I was trying to hide my troubled mind."

"It showed. Even Betty noticed. She made me go to the first table in an effort to comfort you by comforting me."

Jake smiled. "That sounds like Betty."

"So what did you do, Jake?"

"Bishop John wants to excommunicate Ben and Sylvia over the Mennonite revival meetings, and I haven't consented."

"Does Mose agree with John?"

"*Jah.*"

"Then why doesn't Bishop John go on without you? You're just a young preacher, and he doesn't need your consent."

"No, but he needs unity," Jake said. "And I understand that."

"I think he must be afraid of what will happen when people find out he's done something you disagree with."

"You shouldn't say something like that," Jake said with a glance in her direction. "Pride is an awful sin before *Da Hah.*"

"It's not pride, Jake. You're a very wonderful and trusted man."

"So you don't think I should give in and agree with Bishop John? I thought you would think he was right."

"I don't know what is right," Hannah said, leaning against him. "I'm too tired to think right now, and I don't want to think about it. I just know you are usually right, and that's *gut* enough for me."

"But I'm not the bishop," Jake said. "And I never want to be one."

"I know that. So you'll just have to do what you think is right."

After a moment of silence, Hannah changed the subject. "Just so you know, I think Miriam is bringing someone home after the singing tonight. I told her it was all right."

"Dennis?" he said with a short laugh.

"Yes, I guess it's a bit obvious then. I suppose I should try not to worry… even though I think my sister has fallen for someone who is quite unstable. And I sure hope Mom doesn't worry herself sick when she finds out."

"Dennis is stable," Jake said, pulling Hannah tight against his shoulder. "More so than his brother, Will."

"I sure hope you're right," Hannah said, as Jake turned Mosey into the graveled lane toward home.

Eighteen

Miriam sat on the front bench between two girls younger than herself. The sounds of young people singing filled the room. The volume was lower than it would have been back in Indiana, but still *gut* for the small number of young people this community had. She leaned toward the clock for what seemed like the one hundredth time. Finally the hands were creeping toward nine o'clock.

Soon the hymn singing would be over, and she would be climbing into Dennis Riley's buggy. How had all this happened so fast? Teasing Hannah about finding the perfect love of her life was fun, but what had happened wasn't as she had expected after all. Dennis was doing strange things to her. Other girls had always turned red when their boyfriends came around and spoke with them. Some of them had started blushing even when the boyfriends weren't around, but she never had. And she hadn't wanted to or ever planned to. Not even when the perfect one came along.

Now she was doing all of that—and even more. She was allowing a boy whom she had just barely met to take her home. Had she taken leave of her senses? Was this handsome boy seated across the room bewitching her with his rugged good looks and the way he held his head so confidently?

Have you had lunch? he had asked on Saturday. As if any girl wouldn't love to stay for lunch at his cabin.

It must be the Montana air and the majestic mountain range. She would come back to her senses once she saw the *gut* and decent plains of Indiana again. The enticement of this man would likely cease, and everything would be common, sensible, and full of reasonableness again.

The only problem was, Indiana wouldn't come again until late this fall, and Dennis Riley was taking her home tonight in his buggy.

Now her heart was pounding in anticipation. She would have to get control of herself. Perhaps this would all pass once she saw him up really close, like sitting beside her in the buggy or on Hannah's couch. Surely that would change the way she was feeling.

Miriam listened to the rise and fall of the singing and to the beating of her heart. No, it wasn't going to get better soon...unless she wanted to give Dennis a *no*. Miriam's hand on the songbook jerked at the thought, causing the girl holding the other side to glance at her. Finally the closing song number was called out. She took a breath and launched into the first line of "God Be with You Till We Meet Again," with everyone joining in. Miriam sang with goose bumps on her arms. What would it really be like to sit so close to Dennis in the buggy? Sitting across the table from him on Saturday had been bad enough. Would he like her or would she say or do something that would make this be the last time he asked to drive her home?

With the last line sung, Miriam kept her head down and her eyes away from where Dennis was sitting. Why did she have to be so nervous? Surely he would notice. And all the while she wanted desperately to make a smashing impression on him.

Dennis stood, still laughing with a boy on the bench behind him. He walked toward the door without glancing in Miriam's direction. The girl beside her followed Dennis with her eyes until he stepped outside into the darkness. So there were other girls who were after him, and here she had walked right in, snapping him up on her first Sunday night in Montana.

A thin smile spread across Miriam's face. What would the other girls say about that? Oh, if only she could control her pounding heart!

"So how long are you staying in Montana?" the girl next to her asked as she turned toward Miriam.

"For the summer at least, and likely into the fall. I guess it depends how long Betty keeps the riding stable open."

"Didn't Hannah work for Betty before she married Jake?"

"*Jah*, she did," Miriam said.

"Hannah enjoyed it, if I remember correctly. Of course, I was much younger then."

"I think I'll enjoy it a lot too," Miriam said. "You have such wonderful country out here. Hannah took me riding on Saturday."

"Oh, I love our mountains," the girl said, with another look toward the door where more boys were leaving. "But then I grew up around here."

"Well, I guess I'd better be going," Miriam said, getting up. "Thanks for sitting with me at my first hymn sing in Montana."

"So who's taking you back to Hannah's place?" the girl asked, glancing around the room. "Neither Betty nor Hannah are here. Do you need a ride? My brother Nelson and I have room in our buggy. We go right past Betty and Steve's place."

"Oh, I've got a ride," Miriam said.

"I didn't know you had any other relatives in the area," the girl said, laughing nervously.

"I don't," Miriam whispered, trying to smile, heat rushing up to her face.

"Oh," the girl said, realizing Miriam's meaning. "I see. So you knew him before you visited here?"

Miriam shook her head and left. The girl would think what she wanted. She had meant no harm nor had she intended to steal another girl's dreams, but the world was what it was. By tomorrow morning the whole community would know Dennis Riley had taken her home. Hopefully they wouldn't say much else, unless Dennis had been playing with some poor girl's heart. But surely he wasn't that kind of boy.

Finding her bonnet by the light of the kerosene lamp, Miriam stepped outside into the night air. The sky was clear with the stars ablaze, twinkling with great vigor. Her eyes searched the darkness for signs of buggies. There was one out by the end of the walks, but it was a double surrey, and Dennis wouldn't drive a double buggy.

Out by the barn two boys were still hitching up, but Dennis had left some time ago and should have been ready by this time. Should she wait or walk out toward the barn?

She would walk. That was easier than waiting like some lost puppy at the end of the walks.

Approaching the two buggies, she recognized Dennis's broad back beside one of the horses. He was fastening the last tug when she cleared her throat behind him.

"Oh," Dennis said, turning. "I'm sorry I'm late, but James and I got to talking in the barn, and I ran a little behind."

"Howdy," James called from the other buggy. "Take good care of Dennis there. He is as fragile as hot chimney glass."

"He's just kidding," Dennis said, shrugging. "If you get into the buggy I'll throw you the lines to hold. My horse is a little skittish starting out, and I don't want you getting to my place alone instead of Jake and Hannah's with me."

"Maybe I should hold the bridle," Miriam said, looking at the now rearing horse. "I don't think I want to be dashing down these mountain roads by myself with a wild horse I don't know."

"You can hold him," Dennis said, the faint buggy light playing off his face. "He's got a tender mouth. All you have to do is pull back tightly on the lines."

"Okay," Miriam said, turning to wait until the horse stood still for a moment. She pulled herself up the buggy steps. Dennis tossed her the reins, all the while hanging on to the horse's bridle. The animal lunged into the air again, and Dennis stood in front of him until the horse landed. He made a dash for the buggy.

Holding tightly onto the reins, Miriam watched the horse rear again. Dennis came up the buggy step in one clean jump, grabbing the lines from her hands, his arm brushing against hers as he pulled back.

"Whoa there, Molly," he said, letting the lines out before the horse reared again. They dashed out the lane, swinging out to miss James's buggy sitting at the end of the walks.

"Molly," Miriam said, laughing nervously. "You call this wild horse Molly? Blitzen would be more like it. Is she always like this?"

"Yep. That's the way she's been since I've owned her, although someone else came up with the name."

"You'll have to get a calmer horse if you ever plan to settle down."

He grunted, glancing sideways at her.

"I didn't mean that the way it sounded," Miriam said, feeling blood rushing to her face. Thankfully it was dark, and he couldn't see too well in the dim buggy lights.

"No," Dennis said, "you're right. I do need to settle down someday, but it hasn't seemed right so far. I know I'm a little older than most unmarrieds. My brother Will married young and has several children already."

"That's what Hannah told me. She's good friends with Rebecca."

"Will's a good man," Dennis said, pulling back on the lines as they made a fast turn in the road.

"Is he like you?" Miriam studied the outline of his face in the darkness.

"I don't think so. Brothers usually aren't alike, are they?"

Miriam shrugged, feeling her shoulder rubbing against his. Quickly she pulled away. "I have younger brothers, and they aren't alike."

"And I have no sisters. Are sisters alike?"

"I don't think so."

"I like that," Dennis said, keeping his eyes on the horse, as they made another fast turn.

Miriam swallowed hard, "Your parents weren't Amish, were they?"

"No, did Hannah tell you?"

"*Jah.*"

Dennis laughed. "I suppose she has told you a lot of things about me."

"Oh, I think they like you," Miriam said, feeling her face burning again.

"They're both nice people, and the community has been very blessed by Jake's ministry. I would say there's not one person who would wish someone else had been ordained last year."

"Did you think you would get it?"

"Now that's a strange thing to say. No, but I thought Will might. Rebecca would also have made a good preacher's wife."

"I know. Hannah does too. And I suppose that was a strange question because...you don't really look like a preacher."

"Now what is that supposed to mean?"

"Just...well, I have a hard time imagining you walking around on Sunday morning with your head bowed."

Dennis laughed. "Do you want me looking like that?"

"No, not for a minute."

"Then I suppose it's good I didn't get it—or Will for that matter. He's still talking about leaving the Amish."

"Oh? How serious is he?"

"Fairly serious, I think."

"How about you? You are his brother."

"Do you always ask such serious questions on your first dates?"

"I haven't had very many first dates."

He smiled. "You expect me to believe that? A nice girl like you, charming, witty, in possession of herself. You probably have boys at home lined across the hymn-sing floor to ask you out."

"Maybe I don't want them."

"Well, that would be an answer, I guess."

"So how did you dare ask me on my first Sunday here? You didn't know if I had a boyfriend or not."

"There are ways of finding out."

"Oh, Mr. Detective, are you? And how would you do that—and on such short notice?"

"I had Rebecca find out for me back when I first heard Hannah's sister was coming to Montana. I thought an older sister of Hannah's might be worth looking into. So you see, you're not exactly a stranger to me."

"What if I'm the wild one of the family?"

Dennis laughed, the sound rippling across the night air. "That might be what I want."

"Well, I'm not wild, so I guess you'll have to be disappointed. I'm a decent, ordinary...and even very common person."

He chuckled.

"Don't you believe me?"

"Who said I didn't?"

"You did with your laugh."

"Are you a laugh reader or a mind reader?"

"Would you stop that? It makes me nervous. And what about the girl back there at the singing—the one sitting beside me?"

"What about her?" Dennis turned his head slightly toward her. "You really know how to ask the questions."

"Well, she was looking at you as if she hoped you'd pay her some attention."

"We used to be engaged," Dennis said, staring out into the night.

Miriam's hands flew upward, one hitting the side of the buggy door, the other grabbing his hand and pulling back on the lines. "Dennis Riley, let me off this buggy this minute. I'm walking home on my own two feet."

"It's a long way home."

"I don't care!" Miriam felt the strength of his arm as she pulled back again, now using both hands. And then she felt the slight shaking in the darkness. "You're laughing!" she shrieked. "How can you laugh about such an awful thing? And here I thought you were a decent man. Wait until I tell Hannah this."

"Hush," Dennis said. "Control yourself. I was only kidding."

"You were what?" Miriam asked, holding completely still, her hands still on his arm.

"I was teasing. I've never taken any girl home since I moved here."

"But you sounded serious."

"And here I thought you were a mind reader."

"You are an awful creature, do you know that?" Miriam responded, jerking her hands back to her lap.

"And I think you're pretty sweet…once a person gets past that temper of yours."

"I don't have a temper!" Miriam stated, staring out the buggy front as Dennis turned into Jake and Hannah's lane.

"That's okay," Dennis said, stroking her arm gently. "I should have let you know me better, I guess, before I started making jokes."

"Tell me," Miriam said, pulling away from him. "And I want to know the truth. Are you planning to leave the Amish with your brother?"

"My, my. You *are* a firebrand."

"Are you?"

"What if I am?"

"Don't tease me, Dennis. I want the truth."

"No," he said. "I have no plans to leave. Does that answer the question well enough?"

"I don't know. I think I'll have to keep my eyes on you."

"And I look forward to that. So do you think we can go inside and talk for awhile without waking up Jake and Hannah?"

"I think so," Miriam said, as Dennis brought the buggy to a stop.

Molly tossed her head, and her sides were heaving.

Nineteen

The next morning Hannah brought two cups of tea into the living room and carefully set them on holders. Miriam sat on the couch staring dreamily out the front window at the bright Monday morning sunlight.

"Surely it wasn't that bad," Hannah said with a short laugh. "I've never seen you like this before."

"That's because I've never met someone like Dennis Riley. And to think that he was right here sitting on this couch with me last night."

"Did he ask to come back?"

"I've been waiting for you to ask that," Miriam said, turning around to face Hannah.

"I didn't want to embarrass you in front of Jake just in case he didn't."

"You had doubts?"

"*Nee*," Hannah said. "I really didn't. When are you going to tell Mom?"

"Maybe I won't and we'll keep this a secret between us until I return home this fall."

"With Betty around?" Hannah replied, laughing. "She's probably writing Mom all about her concerns right now."

"Betty doesn't write letters. Not unless she really *has* to."

"This may be a *has* to," Hannah said, handing a cup of tea to Miriam.

Miriam sipped carefully, a sober look on her face.

"So did you ask him if he'd consider leaving the Amish?"

"Yes, I asked him soon after I got into his buggy."

"You don't waste any time, do you. And?"

"He said that he has no plans to leave, but Will does."

"Will does," Hannah repeated the words as she sat bolt upright, her tea spilling across her dress.

"Oh no," Miriam said, jumping up. "I'll get a washcloth."

"Don't bother," Hannah said, wiping the wetness with the back of her hand. "It's just an old dress."

"Maybe I shouldn't have told you about Will. And maybe Will will change his mind. Or maybe Dennis is wrong," Miriam said, sitting down again.

"No, he's probably right. He's Will's brother, so he should know. But this is exactly what Jake's afraid of. Bishop John wants Jake to support an excommunication against Ben and Sylvia Stoll because of the tent meetings Ben is heading up."

"I don't think you should be telling me about church problems," Miriam said. "You're a minister's wife, so of course you should know these things. But I'm not. And, besides, I don't *want* to know."

"You're my older sister, so it shouldn't do any harm to tell you. And whether you want to know or not isn't important. You need to know these things if Dennis is going to get serious about you."

"Oh Hannah, the Amish always have some sort of church problem going on. Can't you just think of me as your older sister who has been missing out on some of the most wonderful, sweet things in life that I now can have for myself? Why can't I be in love with Dennis without having to worry about church problems?"

"Because life is more than just being in love. You need to grow up a bit and learn that."

"Not yet, I don't. I want to enjoy this feeling while I can. Why didn't you tell me what being in love feels like? This woozy feeling, this brightness of the soul, this fascination with even the smallest change in a man's face, this leap of my heart when he even looks at me. No one told me Hannah, or I would have fallen in love a long time ago."

Hannah laughed. "You do have it bad."

"Not only bad, but I have it *good*. Why, Dennis can even turn my insides into mush. No man should have that much control over me, but there it is. He does and I can't help it."

"Miriam, you only met him a few days ago."

"That doesn't matter. All that matters is that I've fallen in love. It needs no more explanation than that. I told you it would happen, and I've known it would ever since Mom agreed to let me come out here."

"And how does Dennis feel about this. Does he return your love?"

"I think he knew ahead of time it would happen too. When he heard your sister was coming, he asked Rebecca to look into whether I had a boyfriend. That must mean something."

"So that's why Rebecca asked about you. I totally missed that one."

"Well, he did," Miriam said, finishing her tea. "Now, aren't you going to tell me we should stop talking about love and get some work done around here? Betty doesn't want to open the riding stable until next week, so until then I want to be useful."

"Well, there's the garden," Hannah said. "I haven't even touched the weeding in days, and there are cherries I need to can. But those could wait."

"No, let's get to it," Miriam said, rising to her feet. "Just show me where the tools are."

"In the barn," Hannah said, taking the teacups to the kitchen. "I'll be out in a minute."

Rinsing the teacups under the faucet, she set them in the sink to drain, and went out to join Miriam in the barn. Miriam already had the door open and came out with two hoes over her shoulders.

"I found them," Miriam said, heading toward the garden, almost skipping in her haste.

Hannah followed with a knowing smile. Love did change people, but rarely was the transformation so rapid. Miriam was changing in front of her eyes from a skeptical, questioning girl to a woman glowing with love and acceptance.

"I think you should slow down a little," Hannah said, as they moved up the rows of vegetables, carefully taking out the multitude of tiny, sprouting weeds.

"I'm just excited this morning, and actually I'm hoeing as slowly as I can."

"I don't mean the hoeing. I mean Dennis Riley."

"I'm not young anymore," Miriam said, pausing to look at Hannah. "Look at you. Married for a few years already, and with a husband who is a minister. No *bobli* yet, but surely that will change before long."

Hannah hoed silently while Miriam studied her face.

"Hannah, something seems different about you," Miriam said. "You're not…"

Hannah hesitated, pausing with her hoe. "I wasn't going to tell you this until later, when you would see for yourself, but I won't be able to keep it a secret much longer. Besides, I have a doctor's appointment soon, so you'd find out anyway. But don't tell Betty yet…if you can avoid it."

"Oh!" Miriam squealed, rushing over to give Hannah a hug. "You're pregnant! That's wonderful. When is the baby due?"

"In November."

Miriam gasped. "Mom knows, of course. That's what all the secrecy was—about me staying till this fall. I suspected Mom was up to something, but I couldn't figure out what. Why didn't I think of this?"

"It's going to be a boy, I just know it," Hannah said dreamily.

"Oh, and Jake…he must be busting all over with happiness."

"He is," Hannah said.

"And I'll be an aunt," Miriam said. "And Mom and Dad will be grandparents for the first time."

"I still have to reach full term, but I so believe *Da Hah* will grant us the grace for a safe delivery this time."

"You know, this really isn't fair—not in the least bit. I'm the oldest, and I wanted to be the one to give Mom and Dad their first grandchild."

"It's a little late to think about that now. And you were the one who wouldn't date boys."

"But I'm catching up fast," Miriam said, a smile crossing her face. She hoed vigorously up a row of vegetables. "Dennis and I will have a whole cabin full of sons, with a few daughters mixed in for good taste."

Hannah laughed. "You sure go from cold to hot really fast."

"That's because I have never met a boy like Dennis before. Just think what would have happened if I had compromised my high standards and dated some other boy before Dennis. I would have missed all this happiness."

"I'm really glad for you," Hannah said, coming to the end of the row and straightening her back. "Remember, though, that everything has trouble in it—even love."

"Oh, you sound like Mom," Miriam said, ready to start on another row.

"Maybe that's because I will be one soon."

Miriam laughed. "Can you imagine us as mothers? I can't. Not that long ago we were two little girls bouncing on our beds and worried about our school grades. Life changes so quickly."

"Did you ever like someone in school?"

"Not really," Miriam said, starting another row back toward the cabin. "I don't think you did either, except for Sam. What a disaster that would have been!"

"You didn't speak up when I planned to marry him, so don't be too hard on me."

"I guess I figured that's what love was like. I thought you married for duty and obligation. I didn't know it was this sweet."

"But Mom and Dad have a *gut* marriage. What gave you the idea that love was so much work and duty?"

"I don't know," said Miriam, stopping to stare toward the mountain range. "It's so beautiful around here. It's no wonder old and wrong ideas get washed out and cleansed." After a moment, Miriam said, "Hannah, shall I tell you something I shouldn't?"

Before Hannah could answer, Miriam continued, "Well, I'm going to, whether I should or not. Dennis kissed me goodbye last night. Can you believe that?"

"With you, I can believe anything. And I hope it was appropriate."

"As pure as the wind-driven snow," Miriam said, smiling sweetly. "Just a little peck on the cheek but enough to make me nearly pass out. Oh, I can only wonder what it will be like when we are married."

"Even roses have their thorns," Hannah reminded. "So what made you think love was all drudgery and duty?"

"You didn't go home with cousin Malinda a lot, did you?" Miriam said, hoeing rapidly again. "I did during the time I was eight, nine, and maybe ten years old. I often stayed overnight, and their house was always a mess. Malinda's mom made us work the whole time I was there. I don't think we ever had a moment's rest except for the few minutes before we went to bed."

"They were poor. At least that's what Mom used to say. Malinda's dad couldn't manage a nickel let alone a dollar," Hannah commented.

"It was more than that Hannah. We weren't that well off until Dad started working in the factory after we were in our teens. Yet Mom and Dad never looked like they would rather die than live. But Malinda's mom and dad did. It was so sad."

"But why didn't you look to Mom and Dad as an example instead of Malinda's parents?"

"I guess their unhappiness made a big impression on me. And then Mary Hochstetler started calling me Malinda's twin. I don't know, but it took a hold somehow. I figured that would be my lot in life."

"And so you never fell for a boy? Never?"

Miriam laughed, "I didn't want to at first, and then it just didn't happen even when I thought I wanted it to. For a long time I saw my destiny as turning out like Malinda's mom and I rebelled against any boy, even when Mom assured me they were decent marriage material. I didn't want a decent marriage. That sounded so dull."

"What if Dennis turns out to be something you're not expecting? You're going so fast. Maybe Malinda's parents started out in love like the way you feel now."

"Hannah, don't do this to me," Miriam declared. "It's not fair. Unless you know something important about Dennis you're not telling me, something other than your fears about Will leaving the Amish, then I don't want to hear it. Don't spoil this for me."

Hannah hoed silently for awhile and then said, "I don't know of anything other than the possibility Dennis might follow Will in leaving the Amish."

"There was one moment when Dennis gave me a scare," Miriam said. "I saw a girl watching him during the hymn singing, and when I asked him about it, he claimed they used to be engaged. When I got upset, he said he was kidding."

Hannah laughed. "It's not true. As far as I know, anyway."

"Still, it scared me, Hannah. Do you think I'm doomed to a life of misery and drudgery if I marry Dennis?"

"Of course not! Don't be silly. I just don't want you to leave the Amish faith. That would surely bring you misery."

"Oh Hannah, there are far worse things in the world than leaving the Amish," Miriam said, arriving at the end of her row.

"See?" Hannah said. "Now you are scaring me."

Twenty

Mr. Brunson pulled his pickup into Bishop John's lane late on a Saturday afternoon and parked by the barn. Jake had said this was the proper time to call when the week's labors were almost over and the bishop would be relaxing in preparation for a day of rest. He climbed out, careful not to slam the door. The silence of the place hung over him as he walked toward the house. He squared his shoulders and continued.

This was what he wished to do, and these were the proper channels. Mary Keim's love would be worth the effort, and he would spend the end of his days in peace and love. It was the best choice he could make from whichever angle one looked.

Knocking gently on the front door, Mr. Brunson stood back to wait. Quick footsteps came across the hardwood floor, the doorknob turned, and the door swung open.

"Good evening, Mr. Brunson," the bishop's wife greeted him with a smile. "What brings you out tonight?"

"I was wondering if your husband would have time to speak to me on a church matter."

"I'm sure he would," Elizabeth said. "He's in the living room waiting on supper. Why don't you come in?"

"I didn't know what time to come," Mr. Brunson said. "I don't wish to disturb your supper."

"Oh, John doesn't mind," Elizabeth said. "And if it goes too long you can join us."

"Well, thank you," Mr. Brunson said, stepping inside and following Elizabeth into the living room.

124

"Mr. Brunson stopped by," Elizabeth said as Bishop John got to his feet. She took the two young children who were playing on the floor and went into the kitchen.

"I'm sorry about this," Mr. Brunson said, glancing toward the retreating backs. "I sure didn't want to disturb your Saturday afternoon."

"You didn't in the least. The children are used to playing elsewhere when visitors come." John motioned toward the couch. "Please have a seat."

"Thank you," Mr. Brunson said, taking his John Deere cap off and laying it on the floor. Perhaps he should have left it at home, but he still wasn't sure about these things. He could hardly be expected to show up the first time fully dressed in Amish attire.

"So what can I do for you?" John asked, leaning forward on his rocker. "I hope none of our church members have wronged you in some way."

"No," Mr. Brunson laughed. "It's nothing like that."

Bishop John cleared his throat, "Is everything going well at the furniture shop with Jake? He's a decent man, but we are all prone to mistakes. I'm sure Jake would be the first one to admit that."

"Jake and Hannah are an outstanding couple," Mr. Brunson said. "In fact they are most of the reason I'm even here to speak with you."

"Oh," Bishop John said, rocking gently. "Well, that's good to hear."

"I have spoken to Jake about this, and he has advised me to speak with you on the matter."

Bishop John nodded, still rocking slowly.

"I would like to join the Amish church—or make an application, however that's done."

"You want to join the Amish church?" John asked, his rocker stilled.

"If you will accept me, I am willing. I know I am an old man, and perhaps that's too much effort to expend for such little return."

"Age has nothing to do with it. But what has brought this desire up? I know you've lived around the Amish community for many years now. Are you attracted to our way of life, to our teachings perhaps? Has Jake been talking to you about them?"

Mr. Brunson cleared his throat. "I have spoken at length with Jake about this, and I want to be clear that he has advised me to drop the matter. I'm the one who continues pushing the subject because I believe I'm in love with one of your church members. I do appreciate your culture, your people, and in particular Jake and Hannah, but I doubt if that would be enough to motivate me to take this step. The truth is, I would like to ask for the widow Mary Keim's hand in marriage."

Bishop John resumed rocking gently and considered his answer. Finally he replied, "Mr. Brunson, I can't decide things like that. No bishop or minister can. That's a matter of the heart. Is that perhaps what Jake also told you?"

"Well, I'm sure Jake would agree, but that's not really the question. She is Amish, and I am not. So how do I begin a relationship with her unless I become Amish?"

"So you have spoken with her about your feelings? Or has Jake spoken to her on your behalf?" Bishop John asked, his face intent.

"Jake refused to speak to Mary, even though I asked if he would. He didn't think it was right."

"Oh," Bishop John said, the rocker continuing. "I'm glad to hear that. Sometimes our young men can do foolish things, even when they don't intend to."

"Jake is one of the most level-headed men I have ever met," Mr. Brunson said. "And scrupulously honest."

"That is good to hear."

"So what I'm asking is, how do you handle these situations—when an outsider wishes to join your faith?"

"With the intention of marrying one of our members?"

"I would hope so, although I understand there are no guarantees of that happening."

"Mr. Brunson, I've never handled anything quite like this, so I must say I'm caught by surprise. I'm also surprised that Jake hasn't told me anything about this, since it sounds like you have had an ongoing conversation for some time already."

"Jake has been advising me against it, and he had no reason to doubt that I wouldn't follow his advice. It was only this week that I've come to a firm decision to pursue the matter."

Bishop John nodded soberly. "Jake is right. And beyond that, what if you join us and Mary decides she doesn't wish to give her hand in marriage?"

"Then that's a risk I would be taking."

"That's an awful lot of work—learning the language, growing accustomed to our culture, and then baptism. After that you couldn't go back to your present church without risking an excommunication. Is that a risk you are willing to take?"

"For love, yes. And would you deny an old man a chance to love again?" Mr. Brunson asked, meeting Bishop John's eyes. "I don't have that many more years left on this earth."

"I see," Bishop John said. "But are you sure that someone else has not already asked for Mary's hand in marriage?"

"No, I don't know that," Mr. Brunson said. "Are you aware of someone?"

John shook his head, "No, but there are always visitors from other Amish communities coming through. In fact there is a load coming from Iowa next week. And things can happen rather quickly as our own suitors wouldn't need to become members first. I mean, you're looking at a year, perhaps two, before you could be baptized, and then there would be the courtship time beyond that."

"I would still like to try," Mr. Brunson said. "If you have no objections. Because even a chance at Mary's hand in marriage would be a great honor for me."

It took only a few seconds of silence before John said, "Mr. Brunson, I hate to disappoint you this way, but I agree with Jake on this matter. I don't think it's wise for you to join the Amish."

Mr. Brunson cleared his throat. "You're forbidding me to join?"

"I have to think about what is best for all concerned, including Mary Keim. It wouldn't be right for you to join if we all know your real reason. I can't place any of our women in that position. If there is trouble later, then I'm responsible. Mary would be the first to agree with that, regardless of how she feels about you."

Mr. Brunson took a deep breath, "I, of course, do not agree with that analysis. I am more than willing to show my intention to stay Amish by whatever means necessary. I am an old man, and the modern life means little to me while Mary's love would mean the world."

"Then why not move back east and join one of the Amish communities there? You could come back in a few years as a member in good standing, and none of us would have any objections."

"And find Mary taken by some other man?"

"*Jah*, you said there would be a risk, and that is the risk."

"So there is no other way?"

"I could speak with the other ministers, but I doubt it. It sounds as if Jake is telling you the same things as I am, and I can't see the other minister, Mose, saying anything different."

"What if I speak with Mary myself on this matter?"

"You would attempt to lure her away from her faith?"

"No," Mr. Brunson said. "I could tell her of my intentions and why I am moving back east, if that is what you require."

"So Mary knows you that well, that she would notice that you have left?"

"It would be for my benefit, not hers, and she does not know of my interest in her."

"That still leaves us where we started," Bishop John said, rocking slowly. "Mary cannot make any promises to you of any nature."

"You would see to that?"

"*Jah.*"

"I see," Mr. Brunson said, rising to go. "Then it seems I have some more thinking to do."

"You are welcome to stay for supper," Bishop John said. "I'm sure Elizabeth has plenty."

"Thank you," Mr. Brunson said, pulling his cap on his head. "But I think I will be going."

"If you wish to talk more on this, please come back again," Bishop John said. "Our door is always open."

"You don't plan to change your mind, do you?" Mr. Brunson asked, already at the front door.

The two faces of the children peered around the kitchen door opening, looking at him.

John shook his head. "I don't think so."

"Good night then," Mr. Brunson said, opening the front door and stepping outside. He walked across the lawn to his truck.

What an old fool he had been, coming to the bishop with his hat in his hand. He was allowing his feelings for Mary to completely cloud his judgment. He should have gone to Mary a long time ago and professed his love for her and asked for her hand in marriage. She wouldn't turn him down. That same look had been in her eyes that he felt in his heart. She was attracted to him, Amish or not. Inside her beat the same type of heart the Lord God had placed in all human beings.

Carefully he backed out of the driveway and accelerated when he got on the main road.

In a few moments he saw Mary's place coming up, nestled off the road, the white two-story house reflecting the slanting rays of the setting sun. She would be home tonight, and he would stop in, profess his love for her, and ask if she would consider leaving the Amish faith. Was that not a worthy price for love?

Pulling his foot off the gas pedal, Mr. Brunson began to turn in, but before his eyes he saw the innocence of her face, the tenderness of her eyes when she met his, the inner beauty shining through her aged face. He took his foot off the brake and accelerated again. No, he couldn't do it. He loved her desperately, and love would not harm what it adored.

He drove with tears creeping into his eyes, wiping them away with the back of his hand. Not since Bernice and Elsie died had he cried. And apparently tears did about as much good now as they did then.

Turning into the gravel lane he saw the lights come on in Jake and Hannah's cabin. He parked along the edge of the gravel by their home. Pulling his handkerchief out of his pocket he blew his nose. He would stop here. He needed to talk to someone. Though they would disagree with him, they would surely understand.

As he walked onto the front porch, Jake opened the door for him, welcoming him inside with a broad sweep of his arm. Hannah was waiting inside. They had obviously seen him coming.

"Good evening, Hannah," Mr. Brunson said, stepping inside. "Am I disturbing anything?"

"No," Hannah said. "Most certainly not. We're always glad to see you."

"Is your sister still staying here?" Mr. Brunson asked.

"No," Hannah said. "She's at Betty's, settling in, as they plan to open the riding stable on Monday."

"That's good," he said, still standing by the cabin door.

"So what can we do for you?" Jake asked. "Will you come in and sit down for a while?"

"No, I had better not," Mr. Brunson said. Had stopping here been a mistake also? The day was not turning out well at all. "I'm returning home from visiting your bishop," he said with an edge of sadness in his voice.

"*Jah.*" Jake tilted his head.

"I spoke to him about joining the Amish faith…and about Mary Keim."

Jake was silent, waiting.

"He will not approve my joining the church since it is so closely connected to my desire to ask Mary's hand in marriage."

"Did Bishop John see any way in which it could be done?"

"Not unless I move back east and join one of the churches there first—without telling Mary why."

"Oh, this is so hard for you, I can see," Hannah said. "I am so sorry. I wish there was something we could do."

"I don't think there is much that can be done," Jake said. "Other than Bishop John's suggestion. Are you willing to do that?"

"I'm thinking about it," Mr. Brunson said. "Would you pray for me?"

"Most certainly," Jake said. "Prayer is always the best thing we can do."

"I'm so sorry," Hannah repeated, standing up to give Mr. Brunson a hug.

"Well, so am I." Mr. Brunson found his handkerchief and blew his nose before walking out the door.

Twenty-One

Hannah watched Jake's stooped shoulders as he stood by the front window, staring after the fading lights of Mr. Brunson's truck. She walked over to join him, slipping her hand into his arm. He lowered his head to rest gently on hers.

"It's not your fault," she whispered.

"I know. It's just one of those things that no one can change."

"Wouldn't it be nice if you could?"

"Sometimes it seems that way, but really, it's the work of God, and we shouldn't meddle in His affairs."

"But couldn't Bishop John have made an exception? Mr. Brunson is such a nice old man. You know he wouldn't have made trouble for anyone. He would love Mary and care for her as good as any Amish man."

Jake put his arm over her shoulder. "Bishop John did the right thing. And I told Mr. Brunson it wouldn't work, so he can't say that he wasn't warned."

"It's still so sad. I think he really loves her. If only it could work out for both of them."

"It still might," Jake said, sitting down on the couch, and pulling her down after him. "Maybe he'll go back east and join an Amish community there. Then after he comes back, Mr. Brunson can ask Mary for her hand."

Hannah laughed. "Not even a dreamy-eyed girl like myself believes that's going to happen."

"I suppose you're right," Jake sighed. "But our concern right now is what I'm going to tell the bishop tomorrow."

"About what?" Hannah asked, stroking Jake's arm.

"About whether excommunication should be used against Ben and Sylvia."

"You still don't think it's the right thing to do?"

"No, but Bishop John wants it done, and I'm the only minister who disagrees."

"Then I would stick with what you feel."

"But Hannah, do you have any idea what that could mean? If I'm wrong and a lot of our people leave because of the tent meetings, Bishop John will blame me for having been too soft."

"Even so, I want you to do what *you* think is right."

"It could cost us a lot."

"I know. And I have a hard time understanding why I feel this way. For a long time I've been worried about what people think of your decisions. But the truth is that even more important than what people think is that you're my husband and I love you. Part of that love is knowing that you do what you think is right. You're a good man, and a good man stays true to his conscience."

"I just want to be sure," Jake said. "If people leave because we were too easy on Ben and Sylvia, it will bother me too. It's not just what other people think. It's realizing that my decision may result in others leaving the faith."

"Look, Jake," Hannah said, running her hand down his beard and playing with his shirt button. "I don't know how to explain it, but I think you see a lot of bad things happening if excommunication is used. Perhaps things that are a lot worse than losing a few church members. How will you feel if Ben and Sylvia are excommunicated because you give in, and then things turn out badly?"

His fingers touched her face. "I don't know."

Hannah leaned into Jake. "All I know is you should do what is right. Because if you don't do what you think is right this time, it will only be harder the next time."

"But what if I'm wrong?"

"Then you'll be wrong, but I don't think you are. You feel very strongly about this, don't you?"

"I do." Jake stared out the cabin window at the faint starry sky over the barn roof. "This summer will be over before long, and Ben will likely move on with his tent to other places, but if we overreact and use methods that aren't right, the bad taste will linger in people's mouths for a long time. And I couldn't really live with myself if that happens."

"Then there's your answer, Jake."

"But who am I to disagree with Bishop John?"

"You are a minister, Jake. You didn't choose this job; it was given to you by *Da Hah*. Isn't that good enough?"

"You are very sweet," he said, pushing her *kapp* back and running his fingers through her hair. "I'm constantly amazed that I should be a minister. Or, for that matter, your husband. *Da Hah* has given me great favor."

"And don't forget, it's also *Da Hah*'s opinion that you should be a father. And you will be as good a father as you are a minister and a husband. Don't ever forget that, Jake."

"But we lost our first child, and that was partly my fault."

"And mine, but does not *Da Hah* forgive?"

"What's come over you?" Jake asked, searching Hannah's eyes. "Don't you have any fears about this pregnancy?"

"I have them all the time, but I believe we have been given grace, and that you will have a son this fall, Jake. Won't that be wonderful?"

"It will be *very* wonderful," Jake said, pulling her tight against himself. "A son or a daughter will be a delight."

After a few seconds, Hannah wiggled out of his embrace.

"Don't you think it's time you forgot about church things for awhile? I'm going to write Mom this evening. Why don't you write to yours?"

A shadow crossed his face. "You know Mom and Dad have never written back, except for that one short letter Mom wrote early this spring. She didn't say much. What could I have done to offend them?"

"Nothing that I know of. They did come to our wedding, and they were happy then, so I'd keep trying," Hannah said, ruffling his hair.

"I just don't know."

"You can preach so wonderfully; I'm sure your letters will be great too. You have a way with words."

"I'm not going to preach to my parents."

"I didn't mean that," Hannah said, crossing the room to bring him paper and a pen.

"I'll try," Jake smiled weakly as she handed them to him.

"You can write at the desk, and I'll go out to the kitchen."

"Go then," Jake said, waving his hand.

Hannah kissed him and left him sitting on the couch. He might have to think awhile before he thought of what to say, but he would write. And it would be good.

Seating herself at the table in the kitchen Hannah pulled the kerosene lamp closer.

> *Dear Mom,*
>
> *I'm sure Miriam has already written you about her arrival out here, and what all has happened since.*
>
> *Miriam has been such a blessing to everyone since she has arrived. I want to keep her out here forever—and not just until the bobli comes. She is like a breath of sunshine in the middle of the rain, and it is raining out here in the church world.*
>
> *I suppose Miriam has told you all about her newfound love. Dennis Riley is a wonderful boy, I guess. Jake seems to think he's okay and won't be affected by his brother Will's possible decision to leave the church. I can only hope he's right because Miriam has lost her heart and then some to this boy. You ought to see her smile, Mom. I have never seen her like this.*
>
> *Jake is very worried about church matters around here, as are the other ministers. There are Mennonite revival meetings coming to our town this summer, and already they are causing trouble. The bishop wants to use excommunication against Ben and Sylvia Stoll, who left the church last year, as Ben is the one promoting the meetings. Jake doesn't think that's right. I don't know much about such things, but it seems very important to Jake.*
>
> *One thing I do know: I don't want him to agree with Bishop John just to go along. Not if it's that important to Jake. I don't know exactly why, but maybe it has something to do with the bobli coming. How that's possible, I don't know. But it feels like our son should have a father who does what he feels is right.*
>
> *Jake thinks there will be much trouble for us if he doesn't agree with Bishop John on this matter, so maybe you can pray for us. I get a sinking feeling every time I think of Jake having to support*

something he believes is wrong. I know I would still love him, but it seems like there would be less man there to love. Does that make any sense?

I don't want to be selfish with him, Mom, I really don't. I try to give him all the time he needs to do the things in church on Sundays. He doesn't take that much time to study unless he's doing it while he reads his Bible in the evenings. Yet Jake still can preach sermons that bless many people.

You may have to burn this letter if I tell you this, but it's so funny. Betty has hidden Steve's old generator out in the haymow, and she uses it to run her cream separator. I haven't told Jake because I don't want him to wrestle with the issue. He likes Betty, but my guess is he would talk to her or Steve, which would bring it to a stop. I think it's cute that Betty can get away with things like that. I would like to do things like that but lack the courage. Betty wouldn't quite be Betty without pulling off things like that.

Kendra said her dad claims Betty has always done things like this, and that he has given up on changing her. Steve said as long as she doesn't want to leave the Amish, and keeps her electric cream separator out in the barn, then it's her own risk.

Betty might have told you, but in case she hasn't, Kendra is dating Henry, Mary Keim's youngest boy. There's other news on Mary Keim, but I don't think I should write about it. It's sad, but it's not about anything Mary is doing, so don't worry.

I have a doctor's appointment soon with Dr. Lisa. She is the same doctor I used last time, and I remember her saying last year there would be a birthing clinic coming to Libby. I'll have to ask about it. The other option of course is a midwife. They have one that everyone likes. She's a Mennonite and drives in from Bonner's Ferry.

I'm starting to show, Mom, and it's the most awesome feeling. Soon it will be obvious when we go to church that I'm carrying Jake's child. Did you always feel this way with us or does it only happen the first time a mom-to-be gets this close? I hope the feeling comes every time!

I told Jake he needs to write his parents tonight, so that's what he's doing. They haven't had much to do with us since we married. It makes me feel funny sometimes because I think it might be my fault. I can't imagine why that would be though. Did I do something to offend them? But then you wouldn't know unless it's something really obvious. If it's that, surely Betty would have told me about it.

I need to close. It's late and we need our sleep. I think Jake has to preach tomorrow, so I'd better go in and see how his letter is coming along.

> *I love you, Mom.*
> *Your daughter, Hannah*

Folding the paper, Hannah walked into the living room and lightly placed her hands on Jake's shoulders. He had his head bowed over his paper, and his cheeks were wet when she touched his face.

"Jake," she murmured, "what's wrong?"

"Nothing," he whispered, his voice catching. "I was writing the letter, that's all. Do you want to read it?"

"But it's not very long," she said, glancing at the paper.

"It's all I can think to say," he said, placing the page in her hand.

She read silently.

Dear Mom and Dad,

Blessings in the name of the Lord.

Hannah and I are doing well, and the coming bobli is still healthy, for which we are very thankful. Hannah has a doctor's appointment soon, but we expect there will be no complications.

I am writing this letter largely because I am wondering about our relationship. I know that I have not always been the son I should have been when I was growing up. I left home twice without much concern for your feelings on the matter. I hope you don't think this was because of rebellion or because I held anything against you. It was simply a time when I was trying to sort out my thoughts and feelings about things.

Hannah has been a great blessing to me, and I know she holds nothing against either of you, as she hardly knows you. Is there a problem between us? Do you feel like we are ignoring you? If you do feel so, we apologize, as this is not our intention.

I know our child will not be your first grandchild, but it will still be yours. Hannah and I want both of you to feel welcome in our home and feel like this grandchild belongs in the family.

If I have done anything to offend you, please forgive me. Hannah also sends her greetings and hopes you can visit us sometime—or perhaps we can make a trip to Iowa soon.

Your son, Jake

Hannah let the page drop back onto the desktop. "You are so sweet," she whispered. "*Da Hah* knows I don't deserve you."

Twenty-Two

Hannah drove Mosey toward town, slapping the reins repeatedly when he slowed. Why did the horse have to be so slow this morning when she was especially in a hurry? Enough peaches for one cooker full sat in the springhouse waiting to be done after the doctor's appointment. Miriam had offered to help days earlier, but the peaches weren't on the market then, and now Miriam was busy with her duties at the stable.

Pulling in Betty's driveway, Hannah slowed down to wait for two riders who were slowly walking their horses toward the trail. Miriam stood beside the barn, watching until they disappeared into the trees. Turning toward the buggy, she approached at a fast walk as Hannah climbed down.

"Good morning!" Hannah said. "I hope I didn't disturb your riders."

"Of course you didn't," Miriam said, smiling broadly. "The horses are really good about vehicles pulling in, although it does disturb the riders' nerves at times. They must think all horses spook for the slightest reason."

"So are you having any other problems with the riders or the horses? I haven't heard much since you moved over here."

Miriam glanced toward the house. "It's not the riders or the horses. I can handle those. It's the looks from Betty I get when I bring Dennis home on Sunday evenings. It sends chills up and down my spine."

Hannah laughed. "You're still welcome to use our cabin for your dates. Jake and I can sit in the spare bedroom."

Miriam smiled. "I think Betty's *finally* getting a little used to Dennis, so we will hope for the best. I don't really want to inconvenience you and Jake anymore than I already have."

"It wouldn't be a bother, really. Betty does need to learn not to meddle."

"Like that's going to happen. Didn't she interfere with you and Jake when you were dating?"

"*Jah*, but it wasn't *all* her fault."

"All I hear from Betty is how dangerous it can be to marry a man who wants to leave the church. How we only have one chance at marriage so we can't afford to mess it up. She points at Rebecca as her example, and I must say that is a good point, but I can't stop loving the man. I just can't, Hannah. And he's not leaving the church. I asked him again Sunday night and he said he wasn't. Dennis said he never plans to, regardless of what his brother might do."

"Do you believe him? I mean, Dennis could just be saying so."

"You don't know Dennis like I do," Miriam said. "He's so honest, so open about his beliefs, so quick to defend the faith, and he's *gut* for me, Hannah."

"And handsome."

"Oh Hannah, quit saying that. I want to marry him. I really do. I'd say yes today if he asked me."

"I knew you had fallen pretty hard, but shouldn't you take things a little slower?"

"At least you don't sound totally like Betty. I don't know if I could stand it, if you were as strong against Dennis as Betty is."

"Maybe I should be, maybe I'm not thinking in your best interests."

"Don't say that," Miriam pleaded. "Please don't say that. You are being the most wonderful sister possible, and one Betty in the family is enough, thank you very much."

Hannah laughed. "What has Mom said about all this? Have you heard from her? I wrote some time ago but haven't gotten a letter back yet."

"I received a letter this morning," Miriam said. "It wasn't an okay, but it wasn't a no either."

"Maybe you should let me read the letter. My judgment isn't as clouded as yours."

"I guess my judgment probably *is* clouded," Miriam agreed as she pulled the letter out of her dress pocket. "But Dennis is so wonderful. Oh Hannah, I can't lose him. I just *can't*!"

"If it's *Da Hah*'s will, then you won't, and I think there's a big test coming up to show you what Dennis is made of. Are your eyes still open enough to see?"

"You mean the Mennonite tent meetings?" Miriam asked as she handed Hannah the letter.

"*Jah*, that's what I mean. And I hope you're not thinking about going with Dennis if he changes his mind and wants to go."

"I wouldn't," Miriam said, turning her eyes to the ground. "Not even if it would tear out my heart, and smash all my dreams into tiny, tiny pieces. I'm not leaving the church."

"You wouldn't leave for love?"

"What is love if you don't see eye-to-eye on matters of faith?"

"Those are awfully brave words. Are you sure you could tell Dennis no?"

"I don't know," Miriam said, grabbing Hannah's arm. "I know what my head tells me, but the man has stolen my heart—all of it. I don't know how I would ever get it back again."

"There have been broken hearts before," Hannah said, pulling the letter out of the envelope.

"Not like mine, and not in the shadows of these beautiful mountains. Do you think *Da Hah* would be so cruel, Hannah, to allow me to see such wonder and beauty, and then take it all away again? I look into Dennis's eyes, Hannah, and I want to die if I can't be his wife someday. I just couldn't even stay here in Montana if..." Miriam wiped away a tear.

"Come now," Hannah said, holding the letter tightly in her fingers as she gave Miriam a quick hug with her other hand. "We must not borrow trouble from tomorrow, and trouble that might never come anyway. *Da Hah* will always give grace to bear whatever trials He gives us."

"That doesn't make me feel any better," Miriam said, wiping her cheek with the back of her hand. "But I know it's true, so I will be brave."

"You don't have to pretend," Hannah said. "*Da Hah* understands when we cry."

"I'll never get over Dennis, if I lose him. I'll just be an old maid forever. After him, there could never be another man for me."

"Let's see what Mom has to say," Hannah said, opening the single page.

> *Dear Miriam,*
>
> *I hope this still finds you well and enjoying your job. I know Hannah loved it a lot when she worked for Betty those two summers. I was sure you would have the same reaction, but it's still good to hear the report.*

We are all as well as can be expected with the winter flu bug thankfully a thing of the past. At least one would hope so, as I haven't heard much for sometime now. Spring took a hold around here early, and summer is already with us. We had our first really warm day, and the garden plants are growing like weeds. Not that the weeds aren't also growing, but we can pull those.

I had all the children out last night, including Isaac, who did little but grumble, but the boy can pull weeds faster than anyone I know. Roy even helped after supper, and we got through the entire garden, which was a big relief off my mind.

I also received a letter from Hannah, but haven't had time to answer it. I thought yours was more important, especially after receiving the letter from Betty. Who is this Dennis boy you're dating, Miriam? Is he a heathen? Of course I'm teasing, but Betty does sound quite worried. She also said that Hannah shares her fears.

If this is true, Miriam, then you should really proceed with much caution. I know you've never lost your heart to a man before, and that you are a little older than some. Perhaps this is why you have fallen extra hard—or maybe it's for the reason you think.

I know that Betty gets excited about things. Sometimes more than what she should. I haven't forgotten how she got things muddled up with Jake and Hannah, but I didn't do too well on that situation myself. So perhaps this time we can keep our heads on and find a better path without the embarrassment Hannah went through. I certainly don't want another daughter walking out on her wedding day. And not just walking out, but walking out just before she said her vows. I thought I would melt right into the floor from embarrassment, and Roy was ready to use the switch on one little girl if she hadn't been so big by then.

So take things easy, is all I can say, and don't lose your head. Ask Hannah what she thinks, as she and Jake have very level heads.

> With much love,
> Mom

"Well?" Miriam asked as Hannah raised her head from the page. "What do you think?"

"She still hasn't forgotten my wedding fiasco," Hannah said.

"That's not surprising. Who could forget that? You were a mess that day and had been for weeks. Yet you were too stubborn to admit your mistake until the last minute. At least you can be thankful you had enough sense then."

"I just couldn't do it," Hannah said. "I couldn't say the words. I couldn't even nod my head yes because I knew the bishop would have taken even that."

"Just be thankful you didn't marry Sam. That's all I can say. Even though it was embarrassing for all of us. I remember thinking I'd never get a boy after that. Not if they knew I was the sister of a girl who walked out on her wedding."

"I'm sorry I was so stupid. And I'll never stop being sorry—as if that will do much good."

"Sam was a nice boy, really. And you would have made a perfect farmer's wife."

"Perhaps better than a preacher's wife."

"Come now, you're a jewel of a preacher's wife. I was just teasing."

"I know," Hannah said. "Well, the time is passing. I expect I'd better get going to the doctor's office."

"Has something happened yet?"

"No, not as far as I know."

"I'm praying for you," Miriam said, touching Hannah's shoulder. "I think this is going to be a very special summer for all of us."

"Thank you," Hannah whispered. "I hope you're right."

"Hannah!" Betty shouted from the house, throwing open the front door, and hurrying across the lawn. "How long have you been out here, and why haven't you told me? There's so much going on all the time, I don't pay attention to people coming and going anymore."

"Good morning!" Hannah answered. "Miriam and I were just catching up on the news."

"I hope you weren't giving her any comfort with that Dennis fellow. If I had anything to say about it, I'd chase him right back to Idaho where he came from."

"Don't you think that's a little hard on him?" Hannah said. "Everyone deserves a chance."

"I say the fellow is up to no good, stealing your sister's heart like that, and all the time having plans to smash her heart to pieces when the summer is over."

"Maybe he loves her as much as Miriam loves him?" Hannah suggested.

Betty snorted. "Why don't you go tell Rebecca that. She could give you an earful on what it's like living with a man who plans to leave the faith."

"I've never heard Rebecca complain," Hannah said. "And Miriam also understands the danger, I'm sure. Don't you, Miriam?"

Miriam grunted something under her breath.

"I hope she does," Betty said. "And I hope your Jake understands how serious a thing he has undertaken. Standing up to the bishop like that. Not many young preachers would dare do such a thing."

"How did you find out?" Hannah asked.

"You know how such things get around. You can't keep it a secret. So is Jake planning to change his mind?"

"I will leave that up to Jake," Hannah said. "But we really shouldn't be discussing church things. It won't improve the situation in the least."

"It sure doesn't do much good leaving it up to the men," Betty said. "They can make a mighty big mess of things, is all I can say."

Twenty-Three

Hannah turned onto the blacktop road, leaning out of the buggy to wave at Betty and Miriam as they stood by the barn. How wonderful it was to have Miriam here, even if it meant Betty was riled up over Dennis. Betty was usually upset over something or other anyway. Besides, Betty would eventually get over it—unless Dennis really was of the same mind as his brother Will, and planned to leave the Amish.

If that happened, it would break Miriam's heart. What would her sister do? Return to Indiana in bitterness, the memory of her summer in Montana forever tainted by regret and disappointment?

"Please, Lord," Hannah whispered, "don't let Miriam's heart be broken. And save us from this threat of the Mennonites. Help Jake do the right thing. If he's wrong, help him be brave enough to change his mind before it's too late."

If Jake changed his mind, that would mean Ben and Sylvia would be immediately placed in the ban. That would certainly simplify things. Anyone who would think of attending the meetings would know they were under the threat of similar actions. And no Amish person would visit a revival meeting under such a cloud...right?

Hannah urged Mosey on again. Betty didn't have a clock in the barn, but Hannah knew she must have used up most of her spare time by now. Dr. Lisa had always been on time last year, and she probably wouldn't look kindly on patients arriving late. The *bobli* was the most important thing at the moment, and thoughts of church matters must be pushed aside. Jake could handle them anyway.

Approaching the outskirts of Libby, Hannah pulled back so hard on the reins that Mosey slid to a complete halt. Behind her an *Englisha* vehicle screeched its tires and then passed her, blasting his horn, the driver obviously upset. Hannah's eyes were on the open field, where men scurried around driving stakes into the ground and laying out a large piece of canvas. Over two large poles at the entrance was a huge banner that read *Old-Fashioned Tent Revival,* and in smaller letters beneath, *Welcome, one and all.*

Pulling in her breath, Hannah slapped the reins. Mosey jumped so hard the buggy jerked forward. The Mennonite tent revival was really coming, and *Da Hah* had chosen not to intervene. Did He have any idea of the damage that might be done to their lives? Surely He did, and still He deemed to allow it. The will of *Da Hah* must be submitted to, and He would give the grace necessary for the temptation. Jake would notice the tent on his way home. He would need to be comforted tonight, but then perhaps he would comfort her. He was that kind of man.

Pulling into the parking lot at Dr. Lisa's office, Hannah got out and tied Mosey to the hitching post. It was nice of Dr. Lisa to supply a hitching post for her Amish clientele. She appreciated their needs, contrary to the Mennonites, who sought to profit from the Amish. Let the Mennonites raise their own young people, instead of stealing them ready-made from hard-working, praying Amish parents, who wanted only the right thing for their families.

Hannah pushed the bitter thoughts away as she walked quickly toward Dr. Lisa's waiting room door and entered.

"Good morning," the receptionist, a jolly looking middle-aged woman, said. "Are you here for an appointment?"

"Yes, Hannah Byler to see Dr. Lisa," Hannah said, signing her name on the paper.

It felt *gut* to say Byler after her name. There wasn't much opportunity among the Amish. And the name felt like Jake, like his strong arms around her when he comforted her, like the smell of his beard when she nestled on his shoulder. She carried his *bobli* now, who would also be a Byler. They would call the child something wonderful and strong like Jake, only it wouldn't be Jake *Junior.* It would be something equally *gut,* and they would know the right name when the time came.

"The nurse will take you in now," the receptionist said with another smile, motioning toward a white-clad young lady.

"I'm Sally," the nurse said. "If you'll come with me, we'll get your lab work done, and Dr. Lisa will see you after that."

Hannah followed the young woman, feeling the pound of her heart and the flood of memories. This was where she had come the last time. This was where the awful news had been delivered.

As they entered the exam room, Sally asked, "Is there something wrong? You seem nervous."

"No, not really," Hannah said. "Just memories I guess. I lost my previous baby…"

"Oh, of course. I saw on your chart that you miscarried last year. I'm so sorry. I'm sure you'll do fine this time."

"I hope so," Hannah said, forcing a smile as she sat down. "I have been praying really hard."

"Then you should be okay," Sally said, fastening the blood pressure strap on Hannah's arm.

Hannah felt the pressure of the strap tighten on her arm and caught sight of the bouncing needle on the gauge. Would this be the first of bad news again? Would alarm soon show on the nurse's face? Would Dr. Lisa come in later, her face long and sober?

"One twenty over eighty," Sally said cheerfully. "Looks like we're off to a good start."

"That's *gut* to hear."

"Have you had any extra stress lately?"

"*Jah,*" Hannah said. Though what it was had best be kept quiet.

"You should try to keep the stress levels down, which means the readings could even be better than what they are. So let's take your blood, and Dr. Lisa will be right in."

Hannah flinched at the sting of the needle, watching the little canister fill with the bright-red fluid from her vein. Somewhere within her, the unborn child was receiving that same blood and building his own at the same time. How wonderful were the ways of *Da Hah*. Jake had read the Scripture one Sunday where King David wrote about being fearfully and wonderfully made.

"There!" Sally said, dabbing the needle prick with cotton and slipping on a small bandage. "Fold your arm for a minute, and everything will be fine."

Hannah kept her arm bent, as Sally left the room with her vial of blood. Minutes passed before the door opened again to show the cheerful face of Dr. Lisa.

"Well, well," Dr. Lisa said. "If it's not Hannah Byler back again. I'm really glad to see you. Some couples who miscarry aren't quite up to trying again so soon."

"Both Jake and I want a baby very much," Hannah said.

"That's the spirit," Dr. Lisa said, preparing to start her examination. "Have you decided yet whether you will be using a midwife? I know you Amish like to use the midwives, but I do have a nice birthing clinic that's operational now. You might want to consider it."

"I'll ask Jake, but I don't think he'll care either way."

"Then it's up to you," Dr. Lisa said, "which is how it should be. Are all your Amish men so agreeable?"

"Mostly," Hannah said, smiling. "But Jake is special, of course."

"I'm sure he is," Dr. Lisa said. "So will it be a boy or a girl? I can put you on the ultrasound and find out."

"No," Hannah said quickly. "I don't want to know."

"Really?"

"*Jah*, I want the birth to be a surprise like it used to be for my mom."

"Okay, whatever you want, but if there are complications, I'll need to look. I guess I don't have to tell you though."

"That's fine. Are there complications?" Hannah asked, her eyes searching Dr. Lisa's face.

"None that I can find. I'll take a look at the blood test and be back in a minute. You can go ahead and get dressed."

Hannah stared at the closed door. It was so *gut* to feel the peace flooding her heart. That must be the grace of God because Dr. Lisa had said there could be complications even though there were none obvious at the moment. She took a deep breath. Her *bobli* would be okay. He was in the hands of *Da Hah*. What to do about the midwife could be decided later. Dr. Lisa would show her the birthing room when it was time. Hannah sat upright on the examining table. It would take time to notify the midwife, if that was what Jake and she decided. And the midwife might have a very busy schedule. She stepped down from the table and quickly got dressed.

The door opened again, admitting a calm-faced Dr. Lisa.

"Everything's fine, Hannah," Dr. Lisa said. "And I see no reason why it shouldn't stay so."

"What about a due date?" Hannah asked. "I was thinking the end of November or so."

"I think you're about right," Dr. Lisa said. "But I don't need to tell you that babies have minds of their own. We understand that and will work accordingly."

"Then I'd better have you show me the birthing room," Hannah said. "I think I need to make up my mind about the midwife."

"Sure," Dr. Lisa said. "The nurse can take you to the back of the clinic. I hope you like what you see. We try to take good care of our patients and the babies they bring into the world."

"I'm sure you do," Hannah said, standing and following Dr. Lisa into the hallway.

"Wait a minute here," Dr. Lisa said, disappearing around the corner. She was back quickly with Sally in tow.

"Here I am again," Sally said. "Dr. Lisa tells me you want to see the birthing room."

"If it's not too much bother."

"Not in the least. Come, I'll show you."

"You take care now," Dr. Lisa said, patting Hannah on the shoulder.

"Thank you," Hannah said before following Sally down the long hallway. Toward the back, Sally held open a door, motioning for Hannah to go first. Stepping into a spacious open room, Hannah paused to look around.

"It's quite homey," Sally said, standing beside her. "Dr. Lisa wanted an outdoor atmosphere, so she went all out with the shrubs and small trees. I told her she'd soon have a forest growing in here. All we lack is a little river."

"And wild animals," Hannah said with a laugh. "No bears?"

"Bears. Now that's funny. No, there certainly aren't any bears in here—unless you count the husbands. They can get a little bearish at times, but we have a room for them if they get out of hand."

"Oh," Hannah laughed. "Do you really?"

"No, actually I was teasing. We want the husbands to stay with their wives and supply all the support they can. There is a Lamaze class most of the couples take, and they arrive well-prepared, believe me."

"What's a Lamaze class?"

"It's where an instructor walks the couples through the pregnancy and birthing time, teaching breathing and relaxation methods they can use when their time comes."

"I can't imagine Jake doing that."

"Oh, most husbands get used to the idea, although it's not for everyone, I suppose. And over there are the post delivery rooms, two of them at present on either side of the birthing room. We want you to feel comfortable during and after the birth."

"I see," Hannah said, glancing into the rooms. Plants were placed in each corner of the room, with smaller ones in front.

"It's nice, isn't it?" Sally said moments later, leading the way back to the front of the building.

"It's very outdoorsy," Hannah said, taking a deep breath. "I'll have to think about this."

"Take your time," Sally said, motioning with her hand toward the front desk. "The receptionist will have your bill, Mrs. Byler, and make your next appointment."

"Thanks," Hannah said, walking to the front and waiting until the receptionist glanced up.

"That will be one hundred seventy-five dollars for your first visit," she said.

"Okay," Hannah said, writing out the check. Thankfully there was plenty of money in the checking account, but this was still a lot. Jake wouldn't object, and neither would she. Any money they spent on their children would be well worth it and then some.

"Thank you," the receptionist said, taking the check. "And your next appointment will be in six weeks. Same time?"

"*Jah*," Hannah said. "That will be just fine."

Twenty-Four

Hannah listened for the sound of Jake's buggy wheels in the driveway, glancing frequently out the kitchen window. The line of canned peaches stood on the counter, cooling in the late-day breeze. Jake wasn't usually late, but there were plenty of reasons he could have been detained. A customer might have come in at the last minute, or he might have needed to go over the work schedule with Mr. Brunson. With the way work was picking up, either option was possible. But Jake would be home soon.

Placing the potatoes and meat back into the oven, Hannah added a piece of wood to the stove and closed the vents a little. Walking into the living room, she glanced out the front window as Mr. Brunson's pickup truck rattled past in a small cloud of dust. He glanced toward the house but didn't wave. *So Jake's delay isn't Mr. Brunson,* Hannah thought.

Walking back to the desk, she sat down and picked up the mail. She laid the copy of *The Budget* aside, her eyes drawn to the letter addressed to Jake. It had to be from his mother, but why hadn't she addressed it to Jake *and* Hannah Byler? *Jah, Jake is her son, but I'm his wife.*

Likely it meant nothing, as Jake had written to his mom, and there was no need to imagine things on top of whatever feelings might already be between Jake and his parents. It could be anything. Farmers got busy with their work, and Jake came from a large family. Considering he'd asked his parents if there was some kind of problem between their families, perhaps this letter would shed light on the subject.

Why not open the letter and see what Jake's mom wrote? Hannah debated the idea. *Would Jake care? Hardly—and he will share the letter with me anyway*. Hannah picked up the letter and then laid it back down again. There was nothing to gain from reading it now. She glanced back into the kitchen and then over at the living room clock. If Jake didn't come soon, something would have to be done about the food.

Hannah paused, listened again, and raced back to the window. *Jah*, it was Jake coming up the lane, pushing his horse hard. She ran out on the porch and then toward the barn as he pulled up there.

"Well," Jake said, as Hannah greeted him with a hug, "what a welcome. I take it there's good news?"

"Really good news. Everything is going well with the baby."

"That *is* good news!" Jake said with a big smile. "Soon you'll be a mother—and a wonderful one at that."

"And you a wonderful dad."

"I'm sorry about being late," Jake said, unhitching Joel. "I couldn't resist and stopped to talk with Ben Stoll at the meeting site. They were just done setting the tent up."

"I saw them working on it," she said, leading the horse out of the shafts. "So what happened? Did talking to him do any good?"

"No, but I had to try."

"Did he say anything to change your mind about excommunication?"

"Well, I'm even more convinced now that they shouldn't be," Jake said, taking the reins from her hands.

"New reasons that Bishop John will understand?"

"I hope so, but I'll explain when I get through putting Joel in his stall and feeding both horses."

Hannah watched Jake disappear into the barn, his shoulders slumping. He probably didn't even realize it, as dedicated as he was to his duty. Oh why did this have to fall on his head? Yet if *Da Hah* willed this, He must also be willing to give grace. And Jake needed a wife who was strong, not one who complained. A complainer would only make things worse.

Walking quickly back to the cabin, Hannah went into the kitchen and began setting the food on the table. Thankfully it was still warm. Closing the oven door, she sat down at the table and waited. Jake came in through the kitchen doorway, giving her a warm smile before going to the wash basin. She listened to the soft splashes of water, allowing the sound to flow over her. How *gut* it was to have a man in the house, and a man like Jake. The sounds ceased for long moments before his slow steps came toward the table.

"Supper looks wonderful," Jake said, pulling out his chair and sitting down.

"I tried to keep the food warm, as you deserve a hot supper."

"I'm the one who didn't come home on time, and I'll gladly eat your food, hot or cold."

He bowed his head, and she did likewise. When Hannah opened her eyes, Jake still had his head down, faint lines of weariness on his face. She watched him until he looked up and smiled sheepishly.

"I'm just tired, I guess," he said, reaching for the food.

"There's a letter from your mother on the desk."

"Oh!" His face brightened. "What does it say?"

"I didn't open it."

"But you could have."

"Perhaps, but I think you'd better. It was addressed to you only."

"Do you think Mom has something bad to say?"

"Not really. I just wasn't comfortable opening a letter not addressed to me. I don't want to cause problems."

"You don't cause problems. You know that. Mom and Dad probably just have a lot on their minds. I don't think there's anything going on beyond that."

"I hope that's all," Hannah replied.

"I'm sure it is," Jake said, taking large bites of food. "Do you want to hear about my talk with Ben Stoll?"

"Of course. Tell me."

"Ben's not backing down one bit. He still claims that the meetings are not really about the Amish, that they are about reaching the lost and dying in the world."

"So why is he having them *here*? He must know that our community might be tempted to come hear him. Especially since so many people know him."

"That's what I asked him again, and he said that was actually the reason they're beginning here. He said this is his home, and the Bible says we should start preaching in Jerusalem."

"What does that mean?"

"I guess the disciples began preaching in their home area of Jerusalem, and Ben is applying the same principle. Or so he thinks."

"And what do you think?"

"That he's after us."

"So do I."

"He asked us to attend again, Hannah. Ben said that if we don't, it will be a sign to him that we're close-minded and unwilling to entertain any ideas other than Amish ones."

"But I don't think it's close-minded to say we're happy being Amish and don't want to leave."

"I don't either."

"With how you preach, Jake, even Bishop John said the Mennonite churches would snap you right up if you showed any interest."

"Well, not quite in those words," Jake said, laughing. "But you don't have to worry. We're not leaving the Amish."

"Then we're not going to the tent meetings, are we?"

Jake chewed slowly, his eyes on his plate.

When he didn't answer, Hannah said, "We can't, Jake. First, what would Bishop John say? And what about me? How could I stand going to a Mennonite tent meeting? I've never been to such a thing in my life. What if they deceive us just by getting us to walk in the tent door?"

Jake smiled. "I don't think they're *that* deceiving. And I really don't know if we should go. I'm still thinking about it. It's just that Ben got under my skin."

"Then you shouldn't talk to him anymore. You don't have to prove anything to Ben or Sylvia. You know what you believe, and so do I."

"I know, but now you see why I don't think an excommunication would help. It would just make Ben even more sure that we're acting out of fear. He might even get bolder than what he is now."

"I sure hope Bishop John agrees with you."

"So do I," Jake said. "But we'll cross that bridge when we come to it."

"I still think you're right," she said, stroking his hand.

When they had finished eating, Jake rose, leaned over to kiss Hannah on the forehead, and then carried his plate to the counter.

"Come, I'll clean up the kitchen later," Hannah said. "You have a letter from your mother to read."

Leading him by the hand, Hannah took Jake to the hickory desk and then turned to go back into the kitchen.

"Wait!" Jake held up his hand. "Let's read the letter together."

"Okay." Hannah turned around to lean on his shoulder as he opened the letter.

Dear Jake,

Greetings in Christian love. We received your letter, and I am finally sitting down to answer it. It was good to hear from you, Jake, and please don't think that we want hard feelings between us. You don't have to apologize, as I'm sure it lays as much on our part as on yours. We haven't done much to talk with you or to address our concerns. And perhaps this is not the place for it, but since you have written, I am assuming it is okay to share our concern now rather than later.

When you left for Montana before you were married, our highest desire was that you stay in the Amish faith. I'm sure you were aware of that, and you seemed to respect that desire. We were then overjoyed to hear that you had made contact with an Amish church and had begun to settle down. When Hannah came along, we again saw no reason to be unhappy or to withhold our approval.

But since then, and especially since your ordination, some matters of grave concern came to our attention. I don't know if it was your ordination or perhaps something else that got us thinking about this, but the calling of a minister is a great and heavy one, Jake. It is the highest duty which our people can be called to. I'm sure you know this. Our faith is an old faith, having stood the test of time for over five hundred years. It is the task of an Amish minister not only to sustain and to promote the spiritual well-being of each and every member, but to sustain the well-being of the faith.

Jake, we love you, and will always love you and Hannah. Any grandchild you give us will be welcomed into the family, as all the others have been. But it is the matter of our faith that takes first place even above family. Surely you know this and have been taught this by your bishop if we failed to do so. Now that you are a minister, this is even more important. You must not let even family come before your duty to your faith.

It has been reported to us from very reliable sources that the Amish community to which you belong believes in proclaiming the certainty of their salvation with God. If we are wrong, then please tell us, but as you know that is not how our community believes. Nor is this the faith of many of the old Amish communities.

It breaks our hearts, Jake, that apparently some of our Amish communities are leaving the old paths, and joining in with such a proud way of thinking. The salvation of a man's soul belongs only to God, and only He can know if we will make it home. To say otherwise—that a man can tell God that He must save him, that we can know what only God can know, is a grievous error taught by the very churches who used to persecute us.

You are a minister, Jake, so you know what's in the Scriptures, how a man is saved by hope, and how hope that is seen is not hope at all. Surely you can see that? If people start saying they are saved, then there's no longer any need to hope. That's an awful state to be in. How will it be when they come up to the judgment seat of God, and He's expecting them to still have hope in their hearts? But some won't have any because they think they're already saved. What will happen to them?

As you can see, our hearts are troubled, and I suppose that's what you picked up. I sure hope this hasn't troubled Hannah, as we think she is a gut wife for you. We couldn't have found anyone better, which makes things all the harder to understand.

The faith is the most important thing, Jake. It must be preserved against all the temptations of the world, and against all the false teachings of those churches that would lure us into the world. Our fear is that this is just one step toward liberalism, and we so don't want our children or our grandchildren going down that path.

I hope I haven't said too much, Jake.

Please tell Hannah hello for us, and may you keep hope alive in your heart.

Your mom, Ida Byler

"Oh Jake," Hannah said, wrapping her arm around his shoulders. "This is so awful. I don't want trouble with your parents."

"So this is what the problem is," Jake said, leaning back in his chair. "I should have thought of this."

Twenty-Five

Mr. Brunson fidgeted with his early supper, pushing the plate of half-eaten food across the table. Time was rolling by, and his heart still hurt. Slowly he rose to his feet and walked over to the front window, pausing to look out over the spread of the valley below. Why couldn't he get his mind off Mary Keim? If joining the Amish here in Montana would have been an option, it might make sense, but going back to Indiana as Bishop John suggested was out of the question. Even for love there were limits. Perhaps the young could afford to be reckless, but he was not a youngster anymore.

Did he dare knock on Mary Keim's door and ask her if she would join *his* faith? No doubt her smile would disappear in a hurry and be replaced with what would be an enduring distrust...or worse, hostility. That would be too great a sorrow. At least now he could speak with her in passing and entertain the faint hope that God would perform a miracle.

But did he believe that? Certainly God performed special graces for others, but would He perform one for an old man whose heart had been captured by an Amish widow? It was highly unlikely. There were many other things in the world that cried out with greater urgency for God's attention.

Tonight was the first night of the Mennonite tent revival. Perhaps that was something he could do. Weren't the Mennonites some sort of cousins with the Amish? Perhaps attending the meetings would give him a new perspective on Amish ways. Jake had seemed mighty upset about the meetings, but that was because he expected his religious community to lose members.

Mr. Brunson glanced at his watch and quickly went into the bedroom to change into his Sunday suit. Driving down the lane, he glanced at Jake and Hannah's cabin. Everything looked quiet. Were Jake and Hannah at the meetings? Mr. Brunson laughed at the thought. That would be like asking if Daniel had willingly gone into the lions' den.

Turning right on the main road, Mr. Brunson passed Steve and Betty's place. Hannah's sister Miriam was walking in from the barn, and he honked his horn and waved. She flung up her arm in response, a big smile on her face. Now there was a sweet girl. It must run in Hannah's family, although most of the Amish were nice. Bishop John had been nice even as he turned down his heartfelt request. That was the problem. What did one do with nice people, even when they weren't cooperative?

The first sight of the tent brought his foot off the gas pedal. He slowed down to make the turn into the field. His pickup bounced across the uneven ground, coming to a halt beside the other vehicles. There was no sign of a parking attendant, and already the faint sounds of singing were coming from the tent. Apparently he was a little late or the meetings were starting early.

Opening his truck door and getting out, Mr. Brunson glanced around. As he closed the door, he noticed there were no signs of buggies in the field but across the parking lot in the mall two horses with buggies were tied to light posts. A smile spread across his face. Would this be the way the Amish arrived, hiding their buggies in plain sight but not on the tent grounds?

Ducking into the tent, an usher met him with a firm handshake and showed him to one of the seats halfway back. Apparently attendance was not very heavy. He nodded at the older couple beside him. They looked familiar, so he must have seen them around town. At least other *Englisha* people were here, so he wouldn't stand out in the group of Mennonites who had come from Kalispell to support the revival effort. He looked around without craning his neck. There seemed to be no signs of any Amish.

The song came to an end, and the song leader announced another number, adjusting the pitch. With the first note, the whole congregation joined in, filling the tent with vibrant music. At least the Mennonites knew how to sing, and they spoke in English, an improvement over the Amish services that were conducted in German.

Perhaps he should try to join the Mennonites and attempt to lure Mary Keim into joining them. Jake and Bishop John would be greatly upset with him, but surely they wouldn't miss one widow too much. But would Mary want to join the Mennonites? Would it be right to disturb her faith for his selfish reasons? And on what grounds could he even be assured of success? She might very well laugh at the idea or, worse, show her displeasure.

Mr. Brunson shifted on his seat. This had all been a very bad idea. He glanced around to distract himself, catching a glimpse of Will and Rebecca with their small children seated on the other side of the tent. Why hadn't he seen them before? Apparently one of the buggies across the road belonged to them. Jake would be upset tomorrow, but at least he had nothing to do with it. But to what Amish person did the *other* buggy belong?

The song was ending, and Mr. Brunson pulled his eyes away from Will and Rebecca. The song leader gave one last wave of his hand before taking his seat in the front row.

Almost at once a young man came up and gave a brief testimony of finding salvation through the evangelist's previous meeting in a neighboring county. That was followed by two more such testimonies. Then a man got up and walked to the pulpit. He carried his Bible with him and had a grim look on his face. Obviously this was the evangelist, and he seemed ready to launch into a fiery sermon.

Mr. Brunson smiled. Let the man preach. It would be good to hear fire-and-brimstone preaching again. Not since his youth in summer camp meetings had he heard much passion in a preacher's voice.

"Good evening," the evangelist began. "If you will open your Bibles to Luke chapter three, verse three, I would like to speak on my message tonight that is called 'The Conditions for Revival.'"

Mr. Brunson heard the rustle of Bibles opening all around him. He glanced at the older couple on his right. The man shrugged and Mr. Brunson smiled. He was not the only one who hadn't brought a Bible to the meeting. Apparently the Mennonites in attendance knew to bring theirs. Across the tent Will looked to be in the same state, glancing around nervously. But Will might be nervous because he wasn't supposed to be at the tent meeting. Rebecca was looking at the floor. The poor woman. She looked like she had no desire to be here.

A heavy burden settled on Mr. Brunson's heart. Was this what all Amish women thought of Mennonites and Mennonite revival meetings? If so, Mary Keim would never consent to becoming one.

Forcing himself to listen, Mr. Brunson turned toward the speaker. The evangelist had already stirred up a fiery passion just from reading the selected verse.

"John the Baptist went forth preaching repentance, and now the church of our day thinks they have found a better way to experience revival. They have cut out repentance preaching. When all the time this is still one of the conditions God uses to bring revival. A man or a woman must repent of their sins."

Mr. Brunson glanced around again. Then, shaken by what he thought he saw, he sat forward, hardly daring to breath. Was he really seeing what he was seeing? In front of him a Mennonite lady had risen to her feet, taking her small child outside. Between the gap, his view was unhindered of the bench in front of her and of an older, obviously Amish woman. It almost looked like it could be…of all people, Mary Keim! Surely he was seeing things.

Desperately Mr. Brunson shook his head, forcing his eyes back to the evangelist.

"Any man who refuses to repent," the man was thundering, "is a man or a woman who will not experience the revival of God. We must be open to correcting our ways. We must not think we know it all, no matter how long we have lived or what we have been taught. God is drawing near to us in these meetings, and He wants us to be open to correction and to a fresh direction from His voice."

Mr. Brunson brought his eyes back slowly, letting them settle on the familiar head. It *had* to be Mary Keim, the tendrils of hair peeping under her head covering were unmistakable. But what was Mary doing at a Mennonite revival meeting? Was she here with friends or visiting relatives? Was she acquainted with the evangelist who was now pulling out a white handkerchief to wipe his face?

"Revival is not renewal," the man said, barely whispering now. "Much of the church wants to be renewed but not revived. Renewal is like rebooting your computer, but you only work with the information you have. Revival is receiving fresh data from God and changing your life accordingly."

Mr. Brunson watched the back of Mary Keim's neck, his heart pounding. Jake had said nothing about any of the Amish people being allowed to attend the meetings because of relatives. Mary must be here for her own reasons, whatever they were. *If it really is Mary Keim…*

Doubt flooded him. It was not possible. Mary would not attend a Mennonite revival meeting. She was too decent, too righteous a woman, too obedient to the faith to defy the edicts of her church leaders. Soon the woman would turn her head, and he would see she was a stranger.

"Who will repent tonight?" the evangelist thundered. "Who will come to the altar and ask God to give him fresh revelation on what is the will of God and what you can do to obey Him?"

From his side vision Mr. Brunson saw the woman returning with her child. Soon his view would be blocked again. He would wait until the service was over to find out for sure. He *must* know. If Mary were here, and there was a chance to speak with her, there would be no leaving until he had done it.

The woman with the child was at the end of the aisle, and people turned their knees to allow her to pass. Mr. Brunson kept his eyes on the gap.

"Turn," he said to himself. "Turn your head just a little."

In a quick motion, at the last minute, the white head covering turned upward with a smile, and Mr. Brunson could see the full side of her face. It *was* Mary! There was no doubt. The next thirty minutes were torture as he alternated trying to pay attention to the evangelist and mentally rehearsing what he could say to Mary after the meeting.

When the evangelist finally wore down, he opened the altar area by saying, "Let everyone come down here in front who wishes to experience the revival of God. Come and give your heart to what God is speaking today. Come!"

Mr. Brunson's thoughts were jerked away from Mary as he noticed across the tent that Will Riley got to his feet and walked forward to kneel.

"God be praised," the evangelist said. "There is at least one man here who wishes to make his life right with God. Now let more come as I pray with him."

The evangelist stepped down from the platform to whisper into Will's ear with a hand on his shoulder. Rebecca broke out into loud wails as a hush settled over the tent. Two women, apparently Mennonites, approached

Rebecca from either side and draped their arms over her shoulders in support. Slowly the sobs lessened.

For the next several minutes a few others came forward. Again the evangelist greeted each one and apparently took a moment to pray for some needs mentioned. Mr. Brunson noticed that all who went forward after Will were *Englisha*. That would be a relief to Jake, no doubt.

"Now are there more people who wish to come?" the evangelist asked as Will walked soberly back to join his wife. The two women nodded to him and left as he sat down beside Rebecca. Her loud sobs resumed, and Will pulled her into a tight embrace.

"Perhaps we can have a song," the evangelist said, and the song leader jumped to his feet to lead a rousing rendition of "God Be with You Till We Meet Again."

Will walked out with Rebecca before the song was over, holding his arm around his wife's waist, their three children tagging along behind. Mr. Brunson watched them cross the open field and walk into the parking lot, where Will helped Rebecca climb into the buggy.

Obviously trouble had come to Amish country. Mr. Brunson's heart pounded as the service concluded and Mary rose to quickly walk across the field to her buggy.

Twenty-Six

Mary Keim's quick steps were taking her rapidly across the grassy field, while Mr. Brunson stood at the edge of the small crowd beneath the tent awning trying to catch up with her. But from where he stood, the people were thick, and by now it would be hard to reach her without running. That would surely draw unwanted attention to them both.

"Good evening, sir," the evangelist said, interrupting his thoughts and sticking out his hand.

"Good evening," Mr. Brunson said, watching Mary out of the corner of his eye as she reached her buggy. Perhaps if he made a dash for it he could still cut her off at the road. But that would be unseemly and others would be watching.

"I'm glad you came out," the evangelist said. "Byron Mast is my name. And yours, sir?"

"Norman Brunson," he said. "I live back up the mountains a bit."

"Oh, Mr. Brunson. Yes," the evangelist said with a smile. "Ben Stoll told me about you. You're a very interesting character."

"Really?"

"Oh, not in that way," the evangelist said with a laugh. "As in a nice gentleman, and I understand you live close to one of the Amish preachers."

"I do," Mr. Brunson said. "Hannah and Jake are a very nice couple."

"So I've heard. I was hoping they would come out tonight. Ben said he thinks he's almost persuaded Jake to attend the meetings."

Mr. Brunson chuckled, a pained look crossing his face as he glanced toward the road where Mary Keim's buggy raced past. Why was the woman driving so fast? Had she been sorely offended by the meeting? Had there been any reason to read hope into her attendance?

"Do I take it you think Jake's not coming?" the evangelist asked.

"I think I'd leave the Amish alone," Mr. Brunson said, his eyes following Mary's buggy out to the main road. "It looked to me like there was at least one here tonight who left a bit upset."

"Oh," the evangelist said, following Mr. Brunson's gaze to Mary's retreating buggy. "That's regrettable. We're not here to upset people. We're here to help straighten people's lives out, but sometimes it tends to get a little messy before all is said and done."

Mr. Brunson was silent, his eyes on the now-empty road and staring off into the distance.

"Do you know the Amish lady?" The evangelist turned toward where Mary's buggy had last been seen.

Mr. Brunson nodded. "I buy eggs from her, and I thought it strange that she was here tonight."

"Perhaps she's looking out for the good of her soul."

Mr. Brunson swallowed hard. "These are pretty solid Christian people from what I've seen, and I've lived among them for over ten years."

"I suppose some of them are," the evangelist said. "But we all have issues in our lives that need to be straightened out from time to time."

When Mr. Brunson didn't reply, the evangelist said, "Again, I thank you for coming. I must greet some of the others as well." And with that, the man was gone.

Now what was he supposed to do? Mary Keim had left, and he had not been able to speak with her. Tonight had turned out to be possibly the only grounds for him to have the kind of conversation he desired with the lady. Now that had been squandered because he'd been ashamed to run across an open field in front of a crowd of people he didn't even know. Mr. Brunson took a deep breath. No, it wasn't just that. He had been afraid of making things worse for Mary. Wasn't that the truth? It was and so he had nothing to be ashamed of. Mary would likely have enough to answer for when Bishop John inquired after her attendance tonight. How much harder it would be with a story circulating that she had been speaking with an *Englisha* man while here.

Slowly Mr. Brunson walked back to his pickup truck. He got in, started the motor, and drove up the blacktop road past Steve and Betty's place. Gas lights burned in the downstairs windows, but the yard was dark and empty. No doubt the family was gathered in the living room, enjoying each other's company, catching up on the day's events. All of which was something he would never get to experience again.

Bernice had been that kind of woman, even though their lives had been much busier than the Amish lived. She had found time to make supper at least one night a week. On Saturdays they had the day to themselves, traveling on short trips into the surrounding countryside of Boston or taking a jaunt on a rented pontoon boat if the waves weren't too rough. Now Bernice was gone, and God had seen fit to stir love in his heart again. Was it all to be in vain? Was that how God worked?

Slowing down for the graveled lane back into the mountains, Mr. Brunson suddenly pulled his foot off the brake pedal and hit the gas pedal instead. Determination flashed over his face. Tonight was the night to walk through the door that had been opened or it might never be opened again. Mary might slam her front door when he knocked, but he would always know that he had tried, that he had taken every opportunity offered him. Wasn't it amazing that Mary had attended the meeting tonight? Yes, it surely was, and love needed to be pursued, no matter how it might appear to anyone else.

Minutes later, as he approached Mary's house, he wavered...but only briefly. Would he face rejection in moments? Could he bear it?

Yes, it had to be tonight. He had to know. He pulled slowly into her driveway and parked to the side of the house. He stepped outside quietly and closed the truck door with a soft whoosh. Still, the sound was way too loud for the stillness of the farm. No noises of running motors came from anywhere—no hum of electric lines—only the soft grunts of the animals in the barnyard and the rustle of the wind in the grass.

The porch floor squeaked under his foot as he approached the front door, and the swing moved gently in the night air, groaning as if in pain. Would Mary even answer if she had a chance to see who had arrived?

He knocked and waited for long moments. He knocked again. Soft footsteps sounded, and the door cracked open.

"Oh, Mr. Brunson!" Mary said, not opening the door any further.

"Yes," Mr. Brunson said. "I hope I haven't startled you."

"A little," Mary said. "But in a *gut* way. I hadn't quite dared hope that you would follow."

"Follow?" Mr. Brunson said.

"Oh," Mary said, her eyes darkened in the shadow of the door. "I didn't mean to imply anything, Mr. Brunson. I wasn't being inappropriate."

"Mrs. Keim, I'm curious. Why did you attend the tent meeting tonight, if I may ask?"

Mary hesitated. "It's not appropriate to say, so I would rather not tell."

"But aren't your people forbidden to attend the meetings?"

"*Jah*, but I went anyway because my heart wanted to go. Perhaps I was too forward in obeying my heart."

Mr. Brunson took a deep breath, "I must say, Mary, that I don't talk your talk very well, so none of this is making much sense. But I really would like to know why you attended the meeting tonight. Could it possibly have anything to do with me?"

Mary was silent. An owl hooted softly in the trees. Finally Mary spoke. "It has everything to do with you. And even now I'm sure Bishop John will have much to say about it."

"You went because of me?"

"*Jah*. I asked *Da Hah* for a sign that my heart was not leading me astray, and He gave me one. You were there tonight. That is why I am speaking to you now instead of asking you to leave."

"So is it possible you know that I went to speak with Bishop John about asking for your hand in marriage?"

"*Jah*. Didn't you know that I knew?"

Mr. Brunson laid his hand on the side of the house, leaning against it. "How would I know that you knew, Mary? I spoke to the Bishop in private."

"Oh, he didn't tell me," Mary said quickly. "So please don't be angry with Bishop John. In fact I don't know how the person who told me got the information, but our people have few secrets. You must understand that."

"I see. Would it be all right if I came inside to talk about this? I think I need to sit down."

Mary laughed, the soft sound tinkling in the darkness. "Of course, Mr. Brunson. I don't have much to offer, and the chickens haven't laid any eggs yet tonight." She opened the door wider and he entered. She shut the door and led him into the dining room.

Mr. Brunson searched her face in the light of the kerosene lamp. "So you knew why I stopped by to buy eggs so often?"

"One man can never eat so many eggs, Mr. Brunson. Not even if he eats them in cakes, pies, and for breakfast."

"But I did," Mr. Brunson said, sitting down on the chair she offered him. "Not one of them was wasted."

"Did your dog enjoy scrambled eggs?"

Mr. Brunson laughed. "No, I ate them myself. I'm not that kind of man."

"I know you're not," Mary said, gently touching his shoulder. "I especially knew when you went to the Bishop and asked his permission to join the church. Were you really serious about that?"

"Yes, I was, and I still am."

"But you wouldn't go out to Indiana and follow the Bishop's advice?"

"No, there are limits to what a man can do, and that was one of them. And there was no guarantee that you would still be available when I returned. I'm also getting old. I know that I love you, Mary. So what am I supposed to do about that?"

"I think you are doing quite well about that," Mary quipped. "That's why I decided to do my part. Isn't that what a wife—even a future wife—is supposed to do? Help pull her share of the load?"

Mr. Brunson let out a breath in astonishment. "Mrs. Keim, I hardly know what to say. I certainly wasn't expecting any help from you. It's not your place at all."

Mary laughed. "You sure do speak like a man—always wanting to be in charge and doing all the work. Well, the Lord didn't quite leave things like that, now did He? He made the woman for a helpmeet, and that's what I always tried to be to Bert while he was alive."

"So you took it upon yourself to attend the meeting. But I still don't understand."

"'It will be a sign,' I told myself. 'If I attend the meeting on the first night, and you also do, then perhaps it's possible between us.'"

"You would base so much on so little?"

"It's not little to me, Mr. Brunson. I know we are a simple people, but when we talk to the Lord it is a big matter to us."

"I'm sorry, I didn't mean it like that. But would you leave the Amish then?"

"Not to be *Englisha*," Mary answered. "But would you consider joining the Mennonites? You were offering to join the Amish, and this should be much easier."

"But what about you and leaving the Amish faith?"

"I'm not that young anymore, Mr. Brunson. My children are mostly raised, except the youngest, Henry. He's dating Betty's girl. He will be fine."

"Mrs. Keim…Mary…I can't tell you…" Tears formed in the man's eyes. "If I seem startled it's because of the suddenness of it all. I never expected this of you. And to think I almost didn't go to the tent meeting tonight!"

"*Da Hah* has His mysterious ways." Mary laughed. "I'm glad you came!"

"So where do we go from here?" Mr. Brunson asked. "And please call me Norman."

"Norman's a *gut* name and almost Amish."

"Does that make you feel better about this?"

Mary smiled, the light of the kerosene lamp softening her face. "I would have accepted whatever name you had."

"Then how do we proceed, Mary?" Mr. Brunson asked, taking both her hands in his. "May I stop by the house and see you, perhaps during the daytime? Or should it only be at night?"

"Always in a rush just like a man," Mary said, laughing and pulling her hands out of his.

"Well, I am old, and there seems to be a lot of things to do."

"You're not that old. Perhaps you should begin by looking into joining the Mennonites, and I can do the same. We could start doing that by attending the rest of the meetings. Would that be okay with you?"

"Okay? It would be lovely."

"Then that's decided."

Mr. Brunson reached across the table, taking both of her hands again, "I really think this will work out between us, Mary. I know we come from worlds apart, and that we have both been married before, but I feel a great love for you. I've grown weary and crusty from living by myself, so you'll have to soften me up again. This church thing seems so big, but we must not let it separate us. Are you willing to try, to give us a chance?"

"Is that a marriage proposal, Norman?"

"It is—given with very clumsy words, I'm afraid."

"They are fine words, Norman, and my answer is *jah* if we can both make it work with the Mennonites."

"We will make it work," Mr. Brunson said, squeezing her hands tightly. Oh how he wanted to kiss her! But what did the Amish allow in these situations? Who knew, and besides, enough chances had already been taken for one night.

"I will see you tomorrow night," Mr. Brunson said, getting to his feet. "Do you want me to pick you up?"

"No," Mary said, with a smile. "I think it would be best if I drive down in my buggy."

Twenty-Seven

Jake ate his supper slowly as Hannah watched his face.

"I made pecan pie today," Hannah said. "Especially for you."

He smiled weakly, briefly meeting her eyes.

"It's the Mennonite revival meetings, isn't it?" Hannah asked, cutting a piece of pie and sliding it onto his plate. "Perhaps you'll feel better after eating this."

"Thanks," Jake said, trying to smile again. "But it will take more than pecan pie."

"I know—but maybe for a few moments you'll feel better."

"Mr. Brunson is acting mighty strange. He wouldn't say much when he stopped in at the shop today, but his face was glowing."

"Do you think he went to the meeting last night?"

"I don't know," Jake said, cutting into the pie with his fork.

"Do you like the pie?" Hannah asked, leaning closer to him as he took a bite.

"You know I love it. You make the best pecan pie in the world. Even Mom can't make pecan pie like you can."

"I don't think you should ever tell her that, but you can sure tell me."

They ate in silence until Hannah added, "Speaking of your mom, shouldn't you write her back about her concerns?"

"I would if I knew what to say, but I don't."

"She'd probably appreciate anything. That was quite a long letter she wrote."

"What would you write to your mom if she sent you a letter like that?"

"Mom wouldn't write a letter like that, and I'm not a man."

Hannah reached over to rub Jake's shoulder, "So what do you think Mr. Brunson is doing?"

"I'm certain he's up to something with Mary Keim, although I can't think what it could be."

"You don't think he's been to speak with her?"

"I wouldn't know how or what *gut* it would do."

"Maybe he's spoken with her about going back East to join the Amish."

Jake shook his head. "There's the business to take care of, and Mr. Brunson wouldn't defy Bishop John like that. He might be in love with Mary, but he's still an honorable man."

"Then perhaps you've been imagining things. Maybe he just had a *gut* day and was feeling well."

"I hope that's all it is," Jake said, getting up from the table. "But Ben Stoll stopped by the shop today, and I know he's up to something. He wanted to talk about us attending the meetings and wouldn't give me a straight answer when I asked if any of our people had been there for the first one."

"I'm so sorry for all the trouble," Hannah said, giving Jake a quick hug. "But you are going to be a father soon. Just think about that instead of dwelling on church worries."

"You're right, of course. What would I do without you?"

"You wouldn't be in this trouble if it weren't for me," Hannah said, meeting his eyes. "They wouldn't have voted you into the ministry as a single man."

Jake tenderly wiped a tear from her cheek. "You are the most wonderful thing that has ever happened to me. I love you very much, Hannah."

"Thank you. I needed to hear that." Hannah lifted her face for a long kiss. "I love you too. Now, I better go clean up the kitchen."

"Maybe I should help you tonight?"

"No, you have enough on your mind already."

Jake released her with a smile and left for the living room, taking the gas lantern with him. Hannah lit the kerosene lamp and set it on top of the stove mantel. By its soft flickering light she heated the water, washed the dishes, and wiped them dry...all the while thinking of how Jake was bearing up under the load. He was holding up well considering all the pressures on him. Was there more she could do for him? Not likely, other than what she had already done—keep the house in *gut* order, prepare his supper, and give him the love and support he needed.

Thankfully Jake gave plenty of love back. It would be awful if he didn't, and they had to go through this time bickering with each other as some couples did. He was such a *gut* man for her...and so wise. Which likely meant that Jake's instincts were correct, and that Mr. Brunson was up to something with Mary, but what could it be? Would Mr. Brunson go behind their backs and lure Mary out into the *English* world? Surely he wouldn't.

Perhaps she should go speak with Mr. Brunson tomorrow, but would that be wise? It was hard to tell.

Drying the last dish, Hannah opened the cupboard door, transferring the plates onto the shelves. Taking the kerosene lamp with her into the living room, she found Jake busy writing at the desk.

She gave him a soft smile. "Writing to your mother after all?"

"*Jah.* I just finished. Do you want to read it?"

"I like to read anything you write," Hannah said, taking the paper from his hand.

Setting the kerosene lamp on the desk, Hannah walked over to the couch, and sat down to read.

> *Dear Mom and Dad,*
>
> *Christian greetings of love. I received your letter and am very glad you shared your concerns with us. I had no idea this belief had become a problem nor was I aware of anything being taught differently here under Bishop John than what I had been used to growing up. We rarely talked about such things.*
>
> *Please accept my apologies if we believe something you hold to be in error. I will try to look into this later, but I have not had the time yet. We are in the middle of so many things right now, and I hope you can have patience with us.*
>
> *There are Mennonite revival meetings going on in the community, which are of great concern to us. I'm afraid it may involve some of our church members.*

Hannah paused reading as a buggy rattled up the lane and turned into the driveway. She looked toward Jake, who had stood up.

"Are you expecting anyone?" Hannah asked.

"No. Maybe it's Betty coming to borrow something or Miriam for an evening visit."

"I'm going to finish the letter quickly," Hannah said, glancing back down at the page.

> *Hannah is doing well with the baby, and we are looking forward*
> *to the birth later this year. I hope you can come visit then if that*
> *is at all possible.*
>
> > *With much love,*
> > *your son, Jake*

"It's a *gut* letter," Hannah said, handing the paper to him.

Jake's hand stayed limp at his side, his eyes staring out of the window. "It's Bishop John and Minister Mose Chupp, and they haven't brought their wives along."

Hannah gasped, hanging on to Jake's arm as he moved slowly toward the door.

"You had better go into the kitchen," Jake said. "You can hear what they say from there."

Hannah nodded, her heart pounding. "What have we done?" she whispered.

"I don't know," Jake said. "Quick, go into the kitchen."

"I'm staying with you," Hannah said, letting go of Jake's arm and sitting on the couch.

"No," Jake said, but the men were already on the porch. Opening the door, Jake stepped aside as they entered, their faces solemn. They removed their hats, laying them on the floor just inside the cabin door.

"I'm sorry to disturb your evening like this," Bishop John said, "but something very urgent has come up."

Hannah rose and motioned with her hand toward the couch. The two men sat down slowly, glancing at her. She turned and fled to the kitchen, pulling out a chair from the table and sitting down in the darkness. The low murmur of their voices rose clearly from the living room.

"I apologize again for this unplanned visit," Bishop John said. "But this matter needs to be dealt with at once."

"What has happened?" Jake asked.

"Someone said that you planned to attend the Mennonite meetings this week," Bishop John said. "Is this true?"

Hannah almost jumped to her feet but forced herself to stay in her chair.

"No," Jake said. "We have no such plans. And even if I wanted to go, Hannah would have strong objections."

"We had hoped it was you who would have the strong objections," Mose said.

"I do have them," Jake said. "It's not Hannah who's holding me back."

"That's *gut* to hear," Bishop John said. "But we still have great concerns about these meetings. Are you aware that our people are attending the meetings?"

"No," Jake replied, "I am not."

"Well they have," Bishop John said. "Will and Rebecca attended, as well as Mary Keim."

"Mary Keim?" Jake echoed.

Hannah rose this time.

"*Jah*, I'm sorry to say it's true," Bishop John said. "We have not yet had time to speak with Mary about the matter. Will, we suspected had a desire to join the Mennonites. It's up to Rebecca now whether she will go with him or not. How we will handle the situation if she doesn't is uncertain at this point. I really wish you had agreed to the excommunication of Ben and Sylvia, Jake. It would make things so much easier now."

"I still don't think it is the right course," Jake said. "This is not an excommunication offense."

"Are you sure you don't have Mennonite sympathies?" Mose asked. "This matter has us very concerned."

"If I have them, I'm not aware," Jake said.

"Then perhaps this will show us where you stand on things, Jake," Bishop John said. "Mose and I have decided that we do need to proceed on the excommunication and that a vote needs to be taken this Sunday. Since you profess to have no sympathies for Ben Stoll, surely you can understand our point of view."

"I can," Jake said. "But I still don't think it would be wise."

"This may help," Bishop John said. "I had hoped I wouldn't need to show this to you—that I would be able to convince you on the merits alone, but I see that you do not trust your fellow ministers very far."

Hannah listened in the silence, and Jake said nothing. Carefully she peeked around the corner of the kitchen door. Bishop John had a letter in his hand and was holding it out to Jake, who wasn't taking it.

"You can read it out loud," Jake finally said. "It might be better that way."

"As you wish," Bishop John said. "This is from Bishop Wengerd in Northern Indiana, whom I wrote to for advice. This is what he says:

> Dear Brethren. My heart also goes out in grief over the situation you have described to me. Thankfully the Mennonites around here are more respectful of our beliefs and stay in their own churches for the most part. Since the brother and sister who have left your church are not following this standard practice, I do believe that there might be grounds for excommunication, as it has been our experience that it is not wise to ignore such challenges to our faith. I hope this helps, and that the rest of the ministry and the council of the church can come to an agreement on this matter.

"What do you think about that?" Mose asked when Bishop John had finished reading.

Twenty-Eight

Hannah paced the kitchen floor. What had Jake done wrong that he deserved this late-night visit? Jake would now be disturbed for the rest of the evening and be unable to sleep till late. He worked hard enough already at the furniture shop.

Her knee hit the back of a chair and tipped it over, and it went clattering across the floor. Hannah held her breath, but the murmur of voices continued in the living room. Finding a spine of the chair with her outstretched fingers, Hannah carefully set it upright. What were they doing to Jake? Would he give in to Bishop John's demands?

Turning toward the kitchen opening, Hannah stood behind the sill and listened again.

"This is a very serious matter," Mose was saying. "We cannot proceed without unity among the ministry. Surely you know that."

"I do," Jake said.

"Doesn't what Bishop Wengerd says mean anything to you?" Bishop John asked.

"It does," Jake said. "But it's also just another opinion. We really have no solid tradition to go on. From what I have read of the forefathers, they were very hesitant to excommunicate members who stayed within the Anabaptist churches."

"But Ben and Sylvia have defied us," Bishop John said. "They aren't acting like family at all. They are moving in to take church members away from us."

"*Jah,*" Mose said, nodding soberly. "That is very true, and I think you

176

should give Bishop Wengerd's opinion a lot of weight. He is, after all, an older bishop, full of the wisdom age brings to the ministry."

"And I am a young minister," Jake said. "I didn't choose this calling, it was placed upon me, and now I must give an answer to *Da Hah* for what I decide. I cannot just go by what others are saying."

Hannah peeked around the corner. Bishop John was shaking his head, his hands clasped in front of him. Mose opened his mouth, his words coming out in a plea.

"You are taking way too much upon yourself, Jake. We are just ministers. It's up to the bishop to lead the church. If John wants Ben and Sylvia excommunicated, then the matter should proceed to a vote in the church."

"Then let it proceed," Jake said. "I am in agreement with that."

"I'm not sure that's the same thing," Mose said.

"It's *gut* enough," Bishop John said, holding up his hand. "I will take the responsibility upon myself for this matter. I will tell the church it's my idea, and that you two are not standing in the way. Is that *gut* enough, Jake?"

Hannah held her breath, as Jake hung his head.

"It's *gut* enough," Jake finally said. "As long as you do not tell them I support the excommunication."

"Then we have unity," Bishop John said. "It's not as *gut* as I had hoped for, but it's close enough. We will have a members' meeting immediately after the service on Sunday, where I will read Bishop Wengerd's letter to the church, and we will take the vote."

"Surely it will pass," Mose said. "I cannot see why it wouldn't."

"I would hope so," Bishop John said. "In the meantime we have a lot of work to do. The two of you need to visit both Will and Rebecca and Mary Keim and find out what their plans are. Don't take your wives with you. I want this to stay between us for now."

"What about the voting?" Mose asked. "How are going to get a vote of unity from those who are already attending the meetings?"

"They will be disqualified from voting," Bishop John said. "That should be easy for everyone to understand."

"I should think so," Mose said. "Since they have already shown where their sympathies lie."

"What about you?" Bishop John asked, looking at Jake.

"I will not stand in your way," Jake said. "I guess it would be hard to expect a clear vote from someone who has already attended the meetings."

"Then it's decided," Bishop John said, getting to his feet. "Now let's get back home, Mose, to our families and not take up any more of this young couple's evening. *Da Hah* knows we have already disturbed them enough."

"It is the work of the church and must be done," Mose said, following Bishop John to the door. They both bent over to pick up their hats and pulled them on their heads. Hannah stayed where she was while Jake shut the door behind them and watched until the faint outline of the buggy had disappeared into the shadows of the night. Jake went into the kitchen and found her sobbing, her head on the table.

"I'm so sorry about this," Jake said, setting the kerosene lamp on the table and sitting down beside her. He ran his hand over her face.

"It's not your fault," she sobbed. "You didn't have anything to do with it."

"I guess it's like Mose said. It's the work of the church."

"It's horrible, horrible work," Hannah said, breaking out in fresh tears. "I can't stand this anymore."

Jake pulled her tight against his chest, removing her *kapp*, and gently taking out her hair pins. He ran his fingers through her hair, pushing the long strands over her shoulder and down to her waist.

"There, there," Jake said. "We still love each other. Nothing has changed that."

"It feels changed," she cried into his chest. "Everything feels changed."

"Do you think I backed down?" Jake asked. "That they got me to change my mind against my will?"

"Well, who wouldn't have?" Hannah asked, searching his face in the flickering light of the kerosene lamp.

"I wasn't backing down," Jake said. "I was just trying to keep the peace. Bishop John still has to get the vote passed."

"You know he will," Hannah said. "And then all those people will be excommunicated. Even Mary Keim will be."

"Not if she doesn't go back to the meetings again or gives a church confession."

"It's all too awful to think about," Hannah said, burying her face in Jake's arms. "I wish you weren't a minister."

"That can't be helped," Jake said, stroking her hair. "You are very beautiful. Do you know that?"

"How can you say that now?" Hannah asked, looking up at him.

"Because I love you," Jake said. "And we will have to be very brave."

"But I'm *not* very brave," Hannah said.

"But you will try to be, I know you will," Jake said.

Hannah jerked her head upright as the faint sound of buggy wheels drifted in from the driveway.

"There's someone coming, and I don't have my *kapp* on," Hannah said, gasping.

"I doubt if it's the ministers again," Jake said, stepping out into the living room. Hannah raced past him, her hair trailing over her shoulders, her *kapp* clutched in her hands.

Finding a match, Hannah lit the kerosene lamp in the bedroom, setting the light beside the mirror and quickly working on her hair. Who would be coming at this hour of the night, and what would they think if she wasn't out in the living room with Jake? Would they think she had already gone to bed?

Pulling on her *kapp*, she brushed the last strand of hair in place and ran out of the bedroom, slowing down as she approached the living room. Taking a moment to catch her breath, Hannah stepped out into the light. No one was around, but Jake's faint form was visible through the front window, standing on the porch.

Was Jake speaking with someone? Had the ministers come back for some final rebuke they didn't want her to hear? Tears stung her eyes as Hannah opened the cabin door. Whoever it was, this time they would have to speak to Jake in front of her.

Jake was staring out toward the barn, waiting, as she stepped up beside him. A faint form appeared out of the darkness.

"Miriam," Hannah gasped. "What are you doing out tonight? And at this hour?"

"It's still early for Indiana people," Miriam said, laughing, the sound tinkling like music across the grass. "And what's wrong with you two? You look like you're seeing a ghost."

"Well, you're not a ghost," Jake said. "So why don't you come on in the house?"

"*Jah*," Hannah said, grabbing her arm. "It's so *gut* to see you."

Miriam laughed again, "I think I'll have to come over more often for a welcome like this. At least someone likes me."

"Are you having troubles?" Jake asked, while he held the cabin door open.

"Lots of them," Miriam said. "But nothing the two of you can't solve."

"Ah," Jake said, "so now we are miracle workers."

"I think you are," Miriam said. "I was cheered up just by driving in the lane."

"It's always *gut* to lighten the soul," Jake said, following the two women inside.

"We do need it," Hannah said, pulling Miriam down on the couch beside her. "Do tell me that you come with good news?"

"First, tell me things are well with you two. I passed Bishop John and Mose Chupp on the main road, but surely they wouldn't be bearers of any bad news."

Hannah glanced at Jake, who didn't say anything.

"Oh," Miriam said. "You are a minister, you don't need to tell me more than that. I don't want to be involved anyway. All I want is to enjoy the great gift of love which *Da Hah* has given me and to never think of another day arriving without it."

"I take it Dennis is still seeing you?" Jake said with a wry smile.

"That's wonderful news," Hannah said. "So I take it that Dennis isn't going to the Mennonite revival meetings? That's even better news."

"No, Dennis isn't going," Miriam said. "He loves me too much for that."

"Is that the only reason he's not going?" Jake asked. "His brother Will attended with his family. At least that's what we've heard."

"It doesn't make any difference," Miriam said. "How many times do I have to say that Dennis is not like his brother? He's wonderful, sweet, and so in love with me."

"That's what they say—love is blind," Jake said. "Still, I think I'd be a little careful if I were you."

"Oh, what do you know?" Miriam said with a twinkle in her eye. "You married Hannah with your eyes closed."

"I did not," Jake said, laughing softly. "They were wide open."

"That's what you say, but I know better," Miriam said. "You would have followed her to the end of the world. I saw that doggy look in your eyes at the wedding. People might think you're this great preacher, but I saw you when you were just a little boy and so in love."

Jake laughed. "I see I didn't fool you, but that still doesn't change the situation with Dennis. He isn't a very safe choice for marriage."

"Then I'm tired of safe choices," Miriam said. "I'm tired of safe Indiana, safe hymn singings, safe boys who are so boring they bring me to tears. I've found what I wanted out here in Montana, and unless Dennis is the one who throws me back home, I'm not going back without him. In fact, I'll be perfectly happy living in these mountains for the rest of my life."

"Sounds like the girl knows her mind," Jake said. "But you've been warned."

"Maybe you should listen to Jake," Hannah said. "He knows what he's talking about."

"Both of you are way ahead of yourselves. I haven't even said what I came to ask," Miriam said. "Can I at least get that out of my mouth before you give me this big lecture?"

"Sorry," Hannah said. "We weren't trying to lecture you, were we, Jake."

"No," Jake said, grunting. "Just warning."

Miriam continued, "It's like this. Betty is making more and more of a fit about me seeing Dennis. I think these tent meetings are really disturbing her world, and I hate to bring Dennis home to the house while Betty is in such a bad mood. Could I please use your living room for a few Sunday evenings until these meetings blow over?"

"I don't know why not," Hannah said, glancing at Jake.

"Sure," he said, with a smile. "It's not like we aren't in enough trouble already."

"Oh, you are both such dears," Miriam said, jumping to her feet. "I just had to know that tonight yet before I could get a wink of sleep."

Twenty-Nine

Jake drove his buggy into Mose Chupp's driveway on Saturday evening, pulling to a stop by the barn and waiting. It was still early, but they needed plenty of time. Perhaps if things didn't go too badly, they might even be able to make both stops tonight. Another evening next week would simply be too much. Hannah was already in tears when he left the house. Wearily he settled back into the buggy seat as Mose opened the front door and came quickly down the walk.

"Good evening," Jake said, as Mose climbed in.

"Good evening," Mose replied, nodding. "It's not a *gut* night, is it?"

"No, it isn't," Jake said. "But Bishop John wants answers, and I guess this is the only way to get them."

"The work of the Lord is often hard," Mose said. "And we must bear the load as true servants of the most high God."

"Yes, I suppose so," Jake said. "But Hannah is much troubled tonight, and it grieves me greatly."

"The women are the weaker vessel," Mose said. "And especially so when they are young."

"You forget that I am young," Jake said, turning out of the driveway onto the main road.

"*Jah*, one does forget such things, but both of you seem much older than your years. I suppose it is the grace of God given for what is needed."

Jake slapped the reins and said "Get-up" to Joel. "I don't like how much stress this is placing on Hannah. She's already lost one baby, and we don't want to go through that again."

"There will be grace given," Mose said, nodding his head soberly. "Of that we can always be sure."

"I still don't like it," Jake said. "And this had better be over with soon."

Mose glanced sharply at him. "You're not thinking of rebelling against Bishop John, are you?"

"Of course not," Jake said. "But still, I'm very short on patience tonight."

"It could get worse before it gets better," Mose said. "But still we must bear the burden. Yes, as you say, you are young, but don't allow yourself to be overcome with the rashness of youth. You are already pushing the limit with Bishop John. I think he's being very lenient with you, considering the circumstances. Some of the older bishops would have you up for discipline already."

"I know," Jake said. "But it still wouldn't be right. I am obligated to give my honest opinion."

"I think that's what Bishop John likes about you," Mose said, settling back into his seat. "You are honest. I suppose you could have left for the Mennonites already if you had wanted to."

"Why do you and Bishop John think I would want to join the Mennonites?"

"Ben Stoll sure went out of his way to try and pull you into these meetings. I guess we could ask the same thing about why Ben might think such a thing of you."

"I don't know," Jake said, slapping the reins again as his horse moved forward. "I'm just tired of the subject. I'm tired of thinking of this mess. I'm tired of being the one who disagrees with Bishop John. I'm tired of the whole thing. I didn't sign up for this. Hannah and I wanted nothing more than a peaceful life here in the valley, and look what it's gotten us. And now my second child is threatened by all this."

"Is Hannah not doing well?" Mose asked. "I didn't know things were that serious. Perhaps Clara could visit her, maybe help out with the housework. Is that what's causing the problem?"

"No," Jake said. "It's the church problems, that's all. And I don't think either of us can take much more, so we'd better get this done tonight, even if it goes late."

"Hannah's sister Miriam is here," Mose said. "Can she help out? And isn't Hannah seeing a doctor?"

"*Jah*," Jake said. "And Dr. Lisa gave a *gut* report on the last visit, and Hannah has another appointment soon. But I'm still concerned."

"Then you should trust in *Da Hah*," Mose said. "He will see you through this. He will see all of us through this."

"Yes, that's true," Jake said. "Whose place are we going to first?"

"I think Will and Rebecca's," Mose said. "That might be the easy one, and we can see if we still have time left afterward."

"I don't think any of them will be easy," Jake said. "I don't think losing people to the Mennonites is ever easy."

"No," Mose said. "But why are you so sure we have lost them? Have they spoken to you already?"

"Of course not," Jake said, turning into Will and Rebecca's driveway. "I would have told you or Bishop John if they had. Can't anyone trust me anymore?"

"I would say Bishop John is placing quite a lot of trust in you by sending you out on this mission tonight."

"Then perhaps it would be nice to not be trusted so much," Jake said, pulling to a stop by the hitching post.

"You must not say such things," Mose said, climbing down from the buggy.

"I know, and I'm sorry," Jake said as he tied Joel. "And now let's hope Will and Rebecca are home or we will have to come back another night."

"They're home," Mose said, leading the way up the graveled sidewalk. "I just saw their children's faces peeking out of the front window."

Jake followed soberly behind him and waited while Mose knocked on the front door. Moments later, Will opened the door halfway, standing with his hand on the knob.

"Good evening," Will said, not moving.

"Good evening," Mose said. "Is it okay if we come inside? We have a church matter we wish to speak with you and Rebecca about."

"Yes, I expected as much," Will said. "And why did Bishop John not come himself?"

"We are not here to argue," Mose said. "We just need to know what your plans are."

"Well, come on in," Will said, stepping aside. "I don't think this should take long. I'm leaving the Amish church. Does that answer your question?"

Mose took off his hat, and Jake did the same. Stepping across the threshold, Mose glanced around quickly. There was no sign of Rebecca or the children.

Is Will keeping them out of sight on purpose? Jake wondered. *Or is Rebecca simply unwilling to speak with us?*

"We still need to speak with you about it," Mose said. "Perhaps you could explain yourself a little better. We'd also like to speak with Rebecca."

"I don't think she wants to speak with you," Will said. "At least that's what she told me."

"I think it would be best if she told us that herself," Mose said, standing in the middle of the kitchen floor. Jake shifted on his feet beside him.

"Then take a seat on the couch," Will said, waving his hand toward the living room. "I will find Rebecca."

Jake sat down beside Mose, keeping his eyes turned toward the floor. Hannah's weeping face rose in his mind. They should have brought along their wives. It would have made things so much easier, but Bishop John had insisted they leave them at home.

A door slammed in the house and Jake jumped. Moments later Will reappeared with Rebecca behind him, wiping her eyes with a white handkerchief. She did not look at them as Will led her to the other couch. They both sat down.

"I'm sorry that we have to speak with you," Mose said, clearing his throat. "But it's necessary that we hear from you how you're feeling."

"I'm not feeling very well," Rebecca whispered.

"Have you been with Will to all the tent meetings this week?" Mose asked.

"*Jah,*" Rebecca said.

"And what are your feelings on the matter? Will tells us he is leaving for the Mennonites."

"This is how we can find peace in our home," Rebecca said, tears springing to her eyes. "There seems to be no other way."

"So it is Will who wants to leave and not you?" Mose asked, his eyes moving to Will.

"It is," Rebecca said. "He is my husband, and I have borne his children, and I love him."

"This is a serious matter," Mose said. "It could involve the church direction your children and your grandchildren take. Have you thought about that?"

"I have," Rebecca said, wiping her eyes again. "But I'm tired of thinking about it. Will is not happy in the Amish church. He has wanted to leave for an *Englisha* church for some time now. I cannot give my word to such a thing, and I would stay behind with the children if necessary, but the Mennonites are another matter. Such a move should not warrant excommunication. At least there is that hope."

Mose turned to Will. "Is this the basis on which to make a church move? Your wife is obviously not in agreement with your decision."

"You can think of me what you wish," Will said. "But I must do what I think is best."

"And you think it is best to take your wife and children out into the world?" Mose asked.

"Perhaps it's the world to you," Will said. "But it's where I came from. I was still a small boy when my parents joined the Mennonites, and then I moved on to the Amish. I guess I made a mistake, and my parents were right all along."

"Are your parents still Mennonites?" Mose asked.

Will nodded.

"His father and mother were down to visit this week," Rebecca said, her voice stronger now. "It's what helped me make up my mind."

"Is your father involved in these revival meetings?" Mose asked. "Surely he would not make church trouble for his son?"

"No," Rebecca said, shaking her head. "It is not like that at all. Will's parents are wonderful people. They wouldn't try to take us away from the Amish church, but just seeing his dad talk with Will about spiritual things—like they haven't in a long time, helped me become comfortable with the idea."

"And they couldn't talk about spiritual things before?" Mose asked.

"I don't know about Will's brother, Dennis," Rebecca said. "But there always seemed to be a strain between Will and his father."

"I was the one who took Dennis to the Amish," Will said. "I said some harsh things to Dad before we left."

"Does Dennis feel the same way you do?" Jake asked, leaning forward.

"No," Will said, laughing. "That's the funny part about this. Dennis doesn't follow me around anymore, so I guess he's grown up."

"Has Dennis been to any of the meetings?"

"We haven't seen anyone there but Mary Keim," Rebecca said. "And Will has promised me he won't try to lure any of the community members to do what we're doing."

"That's *gut*," Mose said. "But we also must tell you that Bishop John is planning on taking a vote this Sunday on excommunicating Ben and Sylvia Stoll. He feels that Ben has made a point of coming into the community to cause trouble and needs to be dealt with."

"Oh!" Rebecca gasped, her hands covering her face. "What then does this mean for us? We can't be excommunicated, Will, we absolutely *can't*."

"That's what I needed to warn you about," Mose said. "Anyone who attends the meetings after that will also be in danger of church discipline."

Will wrapped his arms around Rebecca's shoulder, pulling her close to him. "Don't cry, dear," he whispered. Then turning to Mose he said, "Then we won't be attending any more meetings. That should solve the problem, shouldn't it? But it won't solve the problem of us leaving the church. We can still find a Mennonite church to join. That surely won't bring us the threat of excommunication. Perhaps my parents' church if nothing else, but I must say I am very troubled over this threat. I'm surprised, Jake, that you would give your word to such an outrageous move."

Mose jumped to his feet, "I'm so sorry to hear that you're leaving the community, but there is nothing we can do about that now. We do need to stop this problem of the revival meetings, and that is what the vote is about on Sunday."

"Can't you wait another week?" Rebecca asked, her voice a plea. "There's only one more week of meetings, and no one else is attending that we know of."

"But there could be more who wish to attend," Mose said. "So we can't take the chance, and Bishop John desires it. So, again, we are sorry that you are leaving the church."

"Perhaps it is time for you to go," Will said, leading the way to the front door. He held it open and Mose and Jake walked out into the gathering dusk.

Thirty

Jake drove out of Will and Rebecca's driveway, turning north on the main road. The horse held back, shaking its head till Jake hollered, "Come on, now, Joel."

Silence settled over the buggy as they rode in the falling twilight.

"You could have helped out more back there," Mose said. "I didn't have to do all the talking."

"You did okay. I didn't know what to say anyway."

"Church work is hard," Mose said. "But it needs to be done. The vineyard of the Lord grows weeds just like any other garden and needs tending."

"I wish Will and Rebecca weren't leaving, but I also wish Bishop John wouldn't take the vote on Sunday. It's just going to make things worse."

"Like any of us can change all that. Some things weren't meant to be changed."

"What do you think is going to happen when the vote passes on Sunday?"

Mose shifted on the buggy seat, "I suppose things will get better. I certainly don't think they will get any worse. People usually stay away from what they fear."

"I hope you're right," Jake said, turning in at Mary Keim's lane. "But I still wish we didn't have to use fear to keep people away from the meetings."

"You're young," Mose said, chuckling. "You'll get wiser on these subjects as you age. Especially once you have children. Fear is a necessary part of life."

"That's strange," Jake said as they drove down the dark lane. "I think that's Mr. Brunson's truck parked beside Mary's house."

"I wouldn't know," Mose said.

Jake pulled up to the barn and climbed down from the buggy.

"It *is* Mr. Brunson's truck," Jake said. "He buys eggs from Mary, but why would he be buying eggs at this time of the evening?"

"I wouldn't worry about your Mr. Brunson," Mose said. "The Mennonites are the ones who worry me. If they're not here, maybe we still have a chance with Mary. We can't go back to Bishop John with two failures."

"I hope you're right," Jake said, finishing the knot on the tie rope and following Mose toward the house. A dim light shone out of the front window, with a brighter light beaming from an upstairs window.

"I can't imagine Mary already being in bed," Mose said. "Not with this truck parked in the yard."

"I don't think you can see the living room from the front of the house," Jake said. "If Mary has visitors, they would be back there."

Mose knocked, waited, ready to knock again when quick footsteps came from inside. Mary opened the front door, a wide smile on her face.

"Mose and Jake. What a surprise. I certainly wasn't expecting you tonight. Mr. Brunson was getting ready to leave anyway."

"Mr. Brunson is visiting?" Mose asked. "Why would an *Englisha* man be visiting in your house, Mary? And at this hour of the night?"

Mary showed a slight smile and then said, "I suppose the explaining might as well start sooner than later. *Da Hah* is doing wonderful things in our lives, and I will be glad to tell you about them."

"But Mr. Brunson is here," Mose said, still standing at the front door.

"Oh, he's leaving," Mary said. "I told him to wait until I had said hello and explained a little."

"Explained?" Mose said. "How can it be explained?"

"She said Mr. Brunson was visiting," Jake whispered, but Mose still didn't move.

"Mr. Brunson is here to see me—like the young people see each other on Sunday night," Mary said. "I don't know what better way to say it, Mose."

"But you knew we were coming," Mose said. "Clara said she sent word both to you and Will and Rebecca."

"Yes, I did know. And that's why I'm home tonight and not at the meeting. But it's still not a reason to hide what's happening. We are doing nothing to be ashamed of, Mose. Now do you want to talk about it out here, or can we sit down in the living room?"

Mose nodded, moving slowly toward the back of the house with Mary leading the way.

"This is Mr. Brunson," Mary said, motioning with her hand. "And these are two of our ministers, Mose and Jake. They have come to talk with me about the church."

"Glad to met you," Mr. Brunson said, getting to his feet and offering his hand to Mose. "Of course I know Jake quite well, but I've never seen him in ministerial action."

No one laughed, and Jake cleared his throat.

"Well," Mary said, smiling nervously, "please take a seat. Mr. Brunson was just going."

"Perhaps I should stay, Mary," Mr. Brunson said. "Don't you think so?"

"Thanks," Mary said, smiling gently at him, "but I think it's best if I have this conversation with Mose and Jake by myself."

"I would be glad to stay," Mr. Brunson said, still hesitating.

"I'll be okay. I'll speak with you later."

"Okay. Whatever you wish. I'll see you tomorrow night then at the regular time.

Mary nodded as she followed Mr. Brunson to the front door.

Mose glanced at Jake. "Did you know about any of this?"

"No," Jake whispered back. "The last thing I heard was Mr. Brunson's meeting with Bishop John."

"You two don't have to whisper," Mary said, stepping back into the living room. "Like I said, I have nothing to hide. It's just that things have been happening so fast, and when Clara sent word that you would be coming tonight I figured things could be explained then."

Mose cleared his throat. "So why is this Mr. Brunson, an *Englisha* man, in your house? Thankfully your son Henry is upstairs—or so I assume."

"He is," Mary said, taking her seat again. "But I would have had Mr. Brunson over anyway. He's a Christian man and wouldn't act unseemly in any way. Didn't he have enough decency to speak with Bishop John about his feelings before he ever spoke with me?"

"I'm not disagreeing with that," Mose said. "But it's about how things look, and this looks very out of order. You're a member of the church, and you have an *Englisha* man in the house."

Mary folded her hands. "I guess I am getting a little carried away,

Mose. So perhaps you can tell me how I can best handle this situation with Mr. Brunson."

"You should at least wait until he has joined an Amish group like Bishop John advised before you invite him into your house," Mose said.

"I'm afraid that's not going to happen," Mary said. "Mr. Brunson is planning to join the Mennonite church, and I have also decided to join. So what could we do, Mose, that would make things easier for everyone concerned?"

"Just like that?" Mose asked, not hiding his shock. "You'd just up and leave the faith you were raised in. How can you do that, Mary?"

"It wasn't an easy decision," Mary said. "But I do love the man, and *Da Hah* seems to be in this."

"How do you know that?" Mose asked.

"I asked *Da Hah* for a sign," Mary said. "Maybe it doesn't seem like much to you, but to me it seemed like it would take a lot to accomplish it. I decided that if I attended the first night of the tent meetings, and Mr. Brunson also attended, then I would be open to meeting him halfway—that is if he agrees to join the Mennonites. I had already heard that Norman was willing to join our Amish community if Bishop John had allowed it."

"But that so-called sign is such a flimsy thing to base such an important decision on," Mose said, throwing his hands into the air. "It's very possible that Mr. Brunson had already planned to attend the meetings and you just fell into his plans."

"Perhaps Jake would know whether Mr. Brunson had planned to attend," Mary said. "Did he speak to you about it, Jake?"

Jake shook his head. "Mr. Brunson never talked about the Mennonites or the meetings, although he did seem to be considering Bishop John's suggestion that he move East and join the Amish there."

"There you have it, Mose," Mary said. "Does that satisfy you?"

"No," Mose said. "I still think it's all a big mistake, and one that you will live to regret. You know that marriage is a serious thing before *Da Hah*, and that it's for life. Mr. Brunson comes from a faith that divorces freely when things get rough."

"I have thought of that," Mary said. "And that would be an awful thing to have happen, but I can't think that Mr. Brunson would be divorcing me. He's not that young anymore, and he's joining the Mennonites."

Mose cleared his throat, "I think I should tell you this, Mary. We are taking a vote on excommunicating Ben and Sylvia Stoll because of what they are doing to this community. If that vote passes—as I surely think it will—then anyone who attends the meetings will also be in danger of church discipline."

Mary considered this for a moment and then asked, "You agreed to this, Jake?"

"It's Bishop John's wish," Jake said, looking down. "And I have consented to support him."

"But excommunication is an awful thing," Mary said. "I had hoped it wouldn't come to this."

"This is how seriously Bishop John takes this matter," Mose said. "And my advice would be that you reconsider your plans to join the Mennonites."

"But Mr. Brunson and I already have plans to attend all of the meetings next week. It's quite important that we do, and we have a scheduled meeting with the evangelist on Wednesday night. He's going to introduce us to the pastor of the church in Kalispell."

"I'm very sorry to hear that," Mose said, getting to his feet. "I guess your plans will have to change because I'm quite sure you don't want to be excommunicated, do you, Mary?"

"Of course I don't," Mary said, following them to the door. "But I also can't break my plans with Mr. Brunson. It's an important part of what *Da Hah* is doing for us. Can't Bishop John understand that? Perhaps he would if you tell him."

"Look, Mary," Mose said, pausing on the front porch. Jake waited at the bottom of the steps. "It's not that we're trying to be hard or cruel. Surely you know that, Mary. It's the church we're thinking of. We have feelings too, Mary, and they hurt when church members just up and throw away so much of their lives for something that won't satisfy anyway."

"I can't turn back from Mr. Brunson now," Mary said, her hand on the doorknob. "I do love him."

"But, Mary," Mose said, stepping closer to her. "Think about what you are doing. And now there's the excommunication to think of. I've known you most of my life. And Bert, we grew up together as boys living on farms next to each other. What do you think he would say about this? What would he think about his widow marrying an *Englisha* man?

What's happened to you, Mary? You're acting like some starry-eyed young girl who has lost her senses."

Mary was silent. And then she said, "I will agree to think about this. I can't be excommunicated. That would be too awful."

"There, that's more like the Mary I know," Mose said, putting out his hand to touch her arm. "I'm sure you will come to the right decision. All you have to do is come to church tomorrow instead of going to those meetings, and I will take it as a sign you're willing to make things right with the church. I'm sure Bishop John will be more than understanding"

"I can't promise anything," Mary said.

"Good night then," Mose said. "We will be praying for you."

"Good night," Mary said, her voice cracking with sadness as the men walked across the grass to Jake's buggy.

Thirty-One

Jake turned sharply at the main road, bouncing through the ditch as he let the reins out. Joel dashed forward. Mose was hanging on tightly to the side of the buggy door.

"You don't have to take out your frustrations on me," Mose said. "I know it was hard talking with Mary—although again, you didn't help out much. You could have said more."

"It's probably a *gut* thing I didn't speak more," Jake said. "Or I would have said some things I shouldn't have."

"I thought you were on our side," Mose said. "Remember you told Bishop John he had your support."

"Don't you have a little feeling for Mary? What is she supposed to do now?"

"I think maybe you've gotten a little too close to this situation, Jake. I know that you and Hannah care a lot for Mary, and Mr. Brunson is your employer, isn't he?"

"I work for him, but what has that got to do with it?"

"Perhaps more than you think. I think we should go speak with Bishop John now."

"But it's past nine already, and we have a meeting tomorrow morning at church."

"That may not be enough time to untangle this mess, and I don't think Bishop John should stay in the dark about what we've found out."

"Then you can go after I drop you off. I really need to get back to Hannah. I'm sure she's worried enough already."

"She's an Amish woman. She'll understand what ministers have to do. If we don't get back by midnight, I'm sure Bishop John will send Elizabeth over with news of what's holding you up."

"I don't like any of this," Jake said, but he turned left at the crossroads in the direction of Bishop John's. "And it won't do any *gut* to talk about things. I'm not changing my mind. Excommunication is wrong in this case."

"You are awful stubborn for a young man," Mose said. "Was your father like this?"

"Leave my father out of this," Jake said. "I think we all come from a stubborn people, if I remember correctly."

Mose laughed, "You read too much, Jake, but I suppose it's true. Our forefathers were Swiss farmers, willing to stand up to the religious people of their day. That took some natural stubbornness."

"Their issues were much clearer than this situation," Jake said, pulling into Bishop John's lane. "That would be easier than excommunicating widows who fall in love."

"The world and the flesh haven't changed, Jake," Mose said, climbing down the buggy step. "They have just taken different forms to tempt us. Falling in love doesn't change that."

Jake tied his horse and followed Mose up the walk to the front door. Bishop John opened the door before they arrived, his head framed in the lantern light, his face and beard hidden in the dark.

"You must have bad news," Bishop John said, his voice soft in the late night air.

"*Jah*," Mose said. "Will and Rebecca are leaving for sure, and Mary is already well along in her relationship with Mr. Brunson. She had him visiting tonight before we got there, and they both plan to join the Mennonites."

"Did Mr. Brunson come to this solution at Mary's invitation?" Bishop John asked.

"She's claims he didn't," Mose said. "Rather Mary said it was *Da Hah* who led them both to attend the meetings on the first night. She took it as some sort of a sign."

"Then things are worse than we thought," Bishop John said. "And, Jake, where do you stand after your visits? Surely you see what must be done."

Jake cleared his throat, "Nothing I heard tonight has caused me to change my mind."

"I think we need to talk about where we go from here," Mose said.

"Perhaps," Bishop John said. "But the night is late already and the mind of man can only handle so much bad news. My heart is stirred deeply, and I don't wish my emotions to cloud my spirit. *Da Hah* says in His Scriptures that the wrath of man does not work the righteousness of God. Let us sleep and pray on this. We can speak of it tomorrow morning at church."

"Good night then," Mose said, stepping back down the porch steps. Jake followed him back to the buggy and they climbed in.

"It was *gut* that we told him," Jake said, as he let the lines out. "And I'm glad Bishop John didn't want to discuss it tonight. I really need to get back to Hannah. She will be worried enough the way it is."

Mose laughed. "It's funny that you're agreeing with the Bishop for once. I hope you feel the same way tomorrow. You know that John could really use your support for the vote."

"Bishop John is a wise man, but I haven't changed my mind."

Mose sighed deeply. "I can still remember not that long ago, Jake, when you came to us from working up in those mountains. I guess we could have made a lot of trouble for you. Think about that. You know that one word from Bishop John back to your bishop in Iowa would have stirred up a hornet's nest, as they say. Don't you think it's time you returned the favor?"

"These are matters of the heart," Jake said, turning the buggy into Mose's lane. "How can I say I agree when I don't? You can see already how much trouble this has stirred up. We will be the laughingstock of all the Mennonite world if we excommunicate Ben and Sylvia. They will know why we've done so, and they will use it against us. I can hear Ben running his mouth already."

"I guess that's not for us to decide," Mose said, climbing down from the buggy. "But I still think you should support John tomorrow."

"I'll support him," Jake said, keeping a firm grip on the reins.

"That may not be enough," Mose said. "People are going to see through that. At least that's my opinion. What we need is a firm and united front. So think about it, Jake. Okay?"

"I haven't changed my mind."

Mose forced a laugh. "You *are* a stubborn one. Well, good night then. I hope Hannah isn't too worried."

"Good night," Jake said, turning the buggy around. He avoided the ditch and turned on his buggy lights once he was on the main road. In the stillness of the night he rode, thinking and listening to the horse's hooves on the pavement.

Would Hannah be in tears when he arrived back at the cabin? There had been plenty of reason for her feeling of apprehension. Who would have thought that Mary Keim and Mr. Brunson were up to the things they were? Technically neither had done anything wrong yet, but that would all change tomorrow when Bishop John excommunicated Ben and Sylvia. That action would send an unmistakable signal to the rest of the community.

Jake held the lines in one hand and wiped his face with the other. Should he perhaps support Bishop John fully, lest a real split in the church happen if the members found out there was disagreement in the ministry?

The horse's pace quickened as Jake turned up the graveled lane. He leaned out of the buggy at the first incline, looking toward the cabin, but he could see nothing. Had Hannah given up on him and gone to bed? Perhaps that would be best instead of waiting up and worrying.

Faint clouds scurried across the moonless sky, and the dark outlines of the mountains on the horizon were drawn by the twinkling stars. Jake settled wearily back into the buggy seat. Would Hannah want him to wake her with the heavy news he had to share? Or should he wait until morning? Hopefully he could unhitch the horse, quietly slip into the house, and crawl into bed without waking her. She needed her rest now more than ever with the *bobli* coming. This church stress certainly wasn't needed. Yet neither of them had asked for this burden, nor could they control its outcome.

A light from the cabin window caught his eye. Hannah was still up—or perhaps she had fallen asleep on the couch. Still, she would be there when he walked in the front door.

Quickly Jake unhitched, leading Joel into the barn. He whinnied loudly at the sight of Mosey. Jake closed the stall door behind him, shoveling a small scoop of oats into the feed box. The horse had done its duty tonight and deserved a little extra. Had he done *his* duty? That was the question. Mostly he had ridden along in the buggy and listened to Mose.

He pushed the barn door shut behind him, glancing briefly at the starry sky. From the looks of things, the weather would clear off overnight. Now if this church trouble would only blow away this easily. But church troubles rarely do.

Hannah opened the cabin door when Jake walked up onto the porch. She wrapped her arms around his neck.

"Oh, Jake," she said. "You didn't come back for so long. I was worried. And I made your favorite chocolate cake."

"You didn't have to wait up for me," Jake whispered. "You need your sleep, and I can eat the cake tomorrow."

"But I wanted to wait up. And I want to know how things went."

"I really don't want to talk about it," Jake said, leading Hannah inside with one hand and shutting the cabin door with the other. The kerosene lamp burned on the desk, throwing soft shadows on her face. Jake gently ran his fingers over her lips.

"It must be awful news then," Hannah said, grabbing his fingers in hers. "And it won't go away by not talking about it."

"I suppose not," Jake said, allowing Hannah to pull him down on the couch.

"So what happened?"

Jake spoke in measured tones, tracing the evening's events and conversations.

"I'm afraid I didn't do very well," he said, staring at the lamp on the desk. "Mostly I just listened and rode along."

"But you're the younger minister. You shouldn't blame yourself."

"I don't know, but something just doesn't seem right. And I can't quite put my finger on it."

"But it's wonderful news that Mary and Mr. Brunson are getting together. Don't you think so?"

"I guess that's the problem. I *do* think so, but I don't think we're supposed to feel that way."

"Lot's of Amish people join the Mennonites in Indiana. They do so all the time, and no one says much about it."

"Do you want to join them?" Jake asked, finding Hannah's face in the semidarkness.

"Jake, of course not. You're an Amish minister. We can't leave."

"What if I weren't? Would you want to join then?"

"Jake, I can't believe you're asking this. Is it because *you* want to join?"

Jake stared into the flickering flame of the kerosene lamp.

"Jake," Hannah said, pulling on his arm, "surely you don't want to join, do you?"

"No," Jake replied, still staring at the lamp. "I just want to get away from the trouble we're in." He stood and paced the floor. "Tomorrow I will have to make a decision. There can be no more riding on the fence. I'll either have to give my full support to Bishop John or hold it back. I can't do it halfway. The people will figure out we're not in unity and the situation will get worse."

"But you can't go against Bishop John. Not on something like this."

"Then what am I supposed to do, Hannah? I can't support what he is doing. He's only making the conflict worse, but he can't see it—and I can't change his mind."

"But if Will and Rebecca leave and Mary leaves, and nothing is done, we're likely to lose more members. If they're not disciplined for attending these meetings, others might attend and we'd lose even more people. That's what Bishop John must think and, Jake, he's probably right."

"*Jah*, but such a vote as drastic as excommunication is likely to drive a wedge between all of us, splitting the church for sure. That will be a whole lot worse than losing a few members."

"But you're not the bishop, Jake. John is. This probably weighs more on him than it does on you. He doesn't want to be responsible for losing members because he didn't do what he could, when he could."

"Maybe so," Jake said, sitting back down. "But I can't bring myself to give my word to what Bishop John is doing tomorrow."

"And if you don't support him, you know what could happen, don't you? He could call in other bishops to discipline *you*."

"I know," Jake said, taking Hannah's hands in his. "And if I stick by my conscience and that should happen, will you still love me?"

"You know I will," Hannah said, wrapping her arms around Jake. "I will always love you."

Thirty-Two

Hannah tossed in bed. It had to be a dream. The whole world was moving about. Gasping for breath, she was running in the dim moonlight with looming mountains surrounding her. Tall forms of trees raced past her like watchmen in the night. Had they found some wrong in her? Was she being judged for sins yet unknown?

Heart pounding, Hannah came to a halt. Running was getting her nowhere. Panic mounted in her chest. The cabin had to be somewhere close by. It was only a moment ago that Jake had fallen asleep beside her. Had she stepped outside the cabin for some reason and gotten lost?

Dimly through the trees Hannah saw the log walls of a cabin appearing ghostly in the moonlight. Ah, the first sign of home and Jake's comforting arms. Running again, she approached the wall and reached out for the rough texture of the logs. She leaned against them, absorbing their comforting sturdiness. Slowly Hannah moved to the corner of the cabin, searching in the darkness for the familiar front door and for signs of Jake. But would he be outside looking for her?

But there was no front porch. This was not their cabin. Who lived here? Would they rush out at any moment and confront her? Taking a deep breath Hannah pushed away from the cabin walls, catching a glimpse of something familiar out of the corner of her eye. She had been here before, but when?

In silence, Hannah made her way slowly to the front door. This was the cabin where Jake used to live when he worked for the Forest Service spotting fires. Did someone else live here now? Surely she would be able to explain her presence to whoever might be inside. Jake used to say lost people were helped by the men who worked in the mountains.

Carefully Hannah approached the front door of the cabin. It stood open, the slight wind off the mountains blowing freely inside.

"Jake!" she whispered. "Are you here?"

Hannah peered inside. There was nothing to see, and she had no light. Was this a dream? Touching the side of the doorframe, Hannah felt the rough wood. It sure had the feel of a real log cabin.

Perhaps if she went inside and waited Jake would find her in the morning. He would know, wouldn't he—where she was? This had been his cabin, and somehow he would make the connection. Yet how strange this is. She shouldn't be here, let alone be lost in the mountains. Stepping inside, Hannah paused as movement came from the shadows. Someone else was here.

"Hello..." she whispered. "I'm lost."

The answer was a low growl that filled the room. With dread Hannah turned and rushed outside. She stumbled as her dress caught on something. With a cry, she fell forward, breaking her fall with her hands, feeling the slap of bushes on her face as she slid.

A loud rumble rose from the cabin door, and Hannah rolled over to hide her face in her hands. It would be better not to look. Perhaps if she played dead the pursuing animal would leave her alone. Shuffling paws came across the ground, and Hannah peeked through her fingers. The moonlight played on the huge creature's fur as it approached, his drooling jaw moving slightly.

Sharp pangs ran through her body as Hannah stood to run. But her legs wouldn't move. Pushing with all her strength and reaching with her arms toward the open air, Hannah screamed, "Jake!"

Something grabbed her shoulder, shaking her, and she screamed again.

"Hannah! Hannah! What's wrong?" Jake's voice asked. "Are you dreaming?"

Her eyes flew open, taking in the moonlit room. "It was a bear, a grizzly! It was after me."

"It was a dream," Jake said, pulling her close to him. "There is no grizzly here."

"It came back," Hannah said. "It's outside the cabin."

"No," Jake said. "You were dreaming."

"The *bobli*," Hannah whispered. "I'm going to lose the *bobli* again. That's what the dream was about."

Jake sat up straight in bed. "Surely not! Is something happening now? Do we need to go to the hospital?"

Hannah ran her hand across her stomach, feeling the growing roundness under her fingers. The child moved, and the pangs from the dream drifted away.

"The *bobli*'s still okay," she said. "But I'm scared Jake. I was lost in the mountains, and I found the cabin where you lived when you worked for the Forest Service. There was no one there but the grizzly, and it came after me."

"Come," Jake comforted, taking Hannah in his arms. "It was a bad dream. It didn't mean anything."

"What's going to happen to us, Jake?"

"I don't know," he said. "But *Da Hah* will take care of us. Now, go back to sleep." With that he kissed her.

"If I can stop dreaming," she said, moving over to her side of the bed.

Jake sighed and touched her arm for a moment. Then came the even sound of his breathing.

Trembling, Hannah waited. Did she dare fall asleep again? Would there be another bear or some other fear to haunt the night? Climbing out of bed slowly, she approached the cabin window. The moon, which hung low in the western sky, had gone behind the clouds. Dawn couldn't be far away, and with it would come the Sunday morning service and the vote against Ben and Sylvia—and all that would surely follow.

Hannah shivered. Bishop John was no bear. No doubt her mind was playing tricks, overplaying the happenings from yesterday. Jake was a *gut* man, and he would know how to handle Bishop John.

Still, sleep was far away, and there was no sense tossing in bed. Jake would only be disturbed, and he needed his rest for the day ahead. Slowly Hannah tiptoed out of the bedroom into the living room. Finding the desk, she struck a match, and lit the kerosene lamp.

The light flickered against the cabin window. Hannah carried the lamp with her and walked into the kitchen, hunger stirring at the sight of the chocolate cake on the counter. She set the lamp on the table and removed the plastic cover on the cake and admired the uncut swirl of frosting. Would Jake mind if she ate a piece? Chocolate cake wasn't usually her thing, but the craving was strong. She ran her hand over her stomach again. It must be the *bobli* causing these strange longings. Perhaps Jake's baby liked the same things he did.

Hannah cut herself a large piece and sat down to eat. My, it was delicious. Jake would notice the missing piece in the morning, but she would explain. She needed to calm her nerves from the nightmare—and from her concern about the voting, now only hours away. What if Bishop John stood up in church and condemned Jake for his convictions?

Wearily Hannah finished the last bite of cake, scraping frosting from the side of the plate and licking the spoon. She realized she should get back to bed. She needed to be fully rested for the stressful day ahead.

Walking quietly Hannah returned to the bedroom. She paused to study Jake's sleeping face. How handsome he looked. Hannah trembled suddenly at the thought. She and Jake must not become proud. Even when she gave him a son, and he grew up to sit beside Jake on the preacher's bench on Sunday morning, they must remain humble people. Even when they had a dozen children someday, who were all grown up and still in the faith, they must not become proud. God threw proud beings out of heaven.

Tomorrow Jake would face Bishop John and say what he felt he must say, no matter what. She would be there, trembling on the church bench, fearing the worst, but knowing she must trust that it would all turn out right. Even if Bishop John got up and spoke words of rebuke to Jake, they must bear the burden. Was that not the sign of truly humble people? Speaking back was what the devil did.

"Jake," she whispered as she climbed back into bed, looking over to his sleeping face. "My sweet, dear Jake. I love you so much."

Thirty-Three

Hannah awoke with a start, turning quickly in bed. Jake was already up, his place beside her empty. Quickly she dressed. Jake would be hungry by now. Already the sun was up, and this Sunday morning especially Jake needed his breakfast on time.

Half running out the bedroom door, Hannah slowed down at the sight of Jake sitting on the living room couch reading his Bible.

"I'm sorry I overslept," she said, trying to smile.

"It's not late or I would have awakened you. Do you remember your nightmare?"

"Bears, but I'd rather forget that dream. I'll get breakfast. It won't be long."

"*Jah*, I could use some. I'll harness the horse while you get breakfast."

"Do you have to preach today?"

"I don't know. It's my turn for the main sermon, but after Bishop John gets done chewing me out I may never get to preach again."

"Will it be that bad? I was hoping my fears were just in my dreams. Something that would go away once the sun came up."

"*Da Hah* will take care of us," Jake said, smiling weakly as he put his Bible down and stood up. He opened the door and went outside.

Hannah watched through the window as Jake walked to the barn. His shoulders had a stoop this morning. Jake was way too young for that. Not even a father yet and such burdens. It wasn't right.

With a sigh Hannah turned away and walked to the kitchen. On the table the chocolate cake sat with a large missing piece cut from one side. Pushing the pan to one side, Hannah started the fire in the old woodstove, taking a quick walk out to the springhouse for eggs and bacon. The air was cool with the mountains shrouded in fog. Loud bumps and bangs came from the direction of the barn.

Hannah paused to listen. The horses must be feeling *gut* this morning. Jake would know enough not to feed them oats. The last thing they needed was a too fast ride to church with them all landing in a ditch from a spooked horse. The bear dream from last night had been scare enough for one day.

Returning to the cabin, Hannah added another piece of wood to the stove and prepared breakfast. Jake came in before she was done and took his seat at the kitchen table.

"Hey, who ate the chocolate cake?" Jake asked with a chuckle.

"I did. The craving came over me in the middle of the night, and I couldn't help myself."

"It must be the *bobli*. Is everything still okay?"

"I think so. I haven't noticed anything wrong."

Jake stared out of the kitchen window as Hannah finished the bacon and eggs. She set the bread and butter on the table. Wiping her hands on a towel, she sat down beside Jake. Together they bowed their heads in silent prayer. After the prayer, Jake ate slowly, seemingly lost in thought, and Hannah stayed quiet. He had enough on his mind without her chatter.

Finishing his food, Jake pushed back and waited until Hannah was done before bowing his head again in prayer. In the stillness of the house, Hannah held her breath. It would have felt *gut* to hear Jake pray out loud, but he said nothing.

"We'd better get ready soon," Jake said as he got up from his chair and took his plate to the sink.

"I'll do the dishes and be right in," Hannah said, hurrying to clear the rest of the table.

"Perhaps I can scrub the bacon pan," Jake said while giving Hannah a soft smile. "You still look a little sleepy."

"If you keep on babying me, I'll fall asleep on my feet," Hannah replied, attempting a laugh. "But a little help would be nice."

Jake partially filled the sink with hot water from the stove top and began scrubbing the pan vigorously. Hannah paused to watch him for a moment. His arms were so strong! How quickly the pan became clean.

"Thanks," Hannah whispered when he was done. "I can finish now."

Silently Jake disappeared into the living room, his footsteps fading away toward their bedroom. With the last clean plate placed in the cupboard, Hannah joined him. Jake already had his white Sunday shirt and black pants on. He was reaching for his suit coat in the closet. He slipped it on, gave Hannah an unexpected kiss on the cheek, and went out into the living room.

Hannah relaxed a bit as she changed into her clothes. There really was nothing to be afraid of, was there? Jake was still his friendly, smiling self this morning, albeit a bit pensive, and he was the one who had to face Bishop John and Minister Mose.

When she was ready, Hannah found Jake sitting on the couch reading his Bible again. He stood when she walked in, moved toward the door, and picked up his black hat. Hannah followed him outside and waited beside the buggy while he brought Mosey from the barn. She lifted the shafts for him and fastened the tug on her side.

Jake threw the lines into the buggy, and waited while Hannah climbed in. With a quick pull on the side of the buggy, Jake came up the step and settled into the seat beside her, taking up the lines.

"Get-up," Jake said, slapping the reins gently against Mosey's back.

Mosey started slowly, turning toward the main road. Jake urged him on faster when they reached the blacktop, and the rhythmic sound of his hooves on the pavement increased.

"Are we late?" Hannah asked.

Jake pulled out his pocket watch. "No, but I guess I'm hurrying because I'm a bit nervous."

"I think I'm more than nervous," Hannah said. "I'm a wreck."

"You sure don't look it. You look wonderful and composed."

"Maybe on the outside, but then so do you."

"I guess we don't know how to deal with stress very well."

"I don't think I want to know," Hannah said, pulling out her handkerchief and blowing her nose. "Church didn't use to be like this."

"I know," Jake said, reaching around her shoulders and giving her a tight hug. "But I guess we have to be brave."

Hannah nodded and Jake pulled his arm back to grip the lines with both hands. Ahead of them the farmhouse where church was being held came into view, the line of parked buggies already forming behind the barn.

"I thought we weren't late," Jake said with a quick laugh. "But it looks like half the church is here already."

"Perhaps they're all nervous too," Hannah said, leaning forward on the seat.

"I hope not," Jake said as he turned into the driveway and pulled to a stop beside the walk. "I'll see you later," he said, as Hannah pulled her bonnet strings tight.

"*Jah*," she said, climbing down the buggy steps.

The buggy jerked forward, and Hannah lowered her head as she started up the walks. Why were her cheeks burning this morning? Jake had done nothing wrong, and the line of men out by the barn weren't staring at her. None of them knew about Jake's trouble with Bishop John—or did they?

Betty's smiling face greeted Hannah just inside the washroom door, "Oh, it's so *gut* to see you this morning."

"Where's Miriam?" Hannah asked, undoing her bonnet strings.

"I don't know," Betty said. "I saw her earlier this morning. It sure seems like everyone's early today. Is there some big secret going on?"

Hannah hung her head and didn't answer.

"Oh my, there is," Betty said, taking Hannah's bonnet and laying it on the table. "But honestly, I can't see how there can be too much trouble with Jake around. Jake has always been such a blessing and has such a level head. Jake will take care of it."

Hannah kept her head down and moved slowly toward the kitchen door. Betty would keep talking until she told her what was going on, and that couldn't happen this morning. It would be *gut* to have someone like Betty to tell. Betty would gather her in a hug and understand as only family can.

"You really should tell me about it," Betty said, holding onto Hannah's arm. "There's no one around at the moment."

"I can't," Hannah whispered. "And you'll find out soon enough."

"Oh no!" Betty said. "Has Dennis decided to join the Mennonites? Is that what it is? I can't believe it has come to this, Hannah, but I've been worried ever since Miriam told me you agreed to let her have her dates at your place on Sunday evenings. I think you should have taken a stand on the issue. Miriam is playing with fire, and you know what the Good Book says about people who take burning coals into their bosom. They get singed *gut* and hard. That Dennis and his brother are nothing but trouble. They have been nothing but trouble since the day they came down from Idaho."

"We really have to go on in," Hannah urged. Hopefully no one was listening on the other side of the door.

Behind them the washroom door opened and Betty jumped. Bishop John's wife came in, her face looking pained, but she smiled gently at them.

"Good morning," Hannah said. It wouldn't look proper to rush off just when Elizabeth walked in, as if she and Betty had been having a forbidden conversation.

"I was just telling Hannah," Betty said, her voice still a whisper, "about all the trouble I've been having with Miriam and that awful Dennis Riley. I'm sure he's just turning on the charm until he has an Amish girl firmly in his clutches. That's when he'll make a beeline straight for the Mennonites or who knows where else with his poor wife and children in tow. I say that relationship needs to be stopped before it's too late."

"Oh, I don't know," Elizabeth said, taking off her bonnet. "Dennis seems like a nice boy."

"That's how they *all* are," Betty said, leaning in closer. "They're charmers, those Riley boys, not to mention how good-looking they are. That's the problem with men who are handsome. It goes to their heads, and it puts thoughts into a girl's head that normally wouldn't be there. Look at poor Miriam and how she has lost all the sensibleness she used to have."

"I think it will all work out for the best," Elizabeth said with a smile. "We just have to trust *Da Hah* to help us."

"*Jah*, but I believe in helping out where I can," Betty said. "I just can't understand why no one but me is concerned about the situation."

"*Da Hah* works in His own time and ways," Elizabeth said, leading the way through the kitchen door. As Hannah trailed Elizabeth she heard Betty's footsteps coming. Betty's mind must be in an awful twirl, but it couldn't be helped. At the moment the situation before them simply couldn't be explained.

Slowly Hannah followed Elizabeth around the circle of women, shaking hands. Miriam was at the end of the line, a bright smile on her face.

She leaned closer to Hannah and whispered, "I can't wait till tonight. It's going to be wonderful."

Hannah tried to smile. Hopefully Miriam wouldn't sense her nervousness. Soon enough Miriam too would know that grave trouble had arrived among them. Soon they all would know, and they would look at her from the corner of their eyes. Jake, the new minister, they would think, had grown a big head and was standing up to his bishop.

Thirty-Four

Jake raised his eyes as the song leader led out, drawing the syllables into soaring notes that lingered in the corners of the house. With a blast of sound a hundred voices joined in, singing in unison. Bishop John slowly rose to his feet, followed by Minister Mose. His heart pounding, Jake forced himself to stand, keeping his head down, as they moved up the stairs toward the bedroom for the morning ministers' conference.

Not that long ago he was the one leading out in the singing, sitting comfortably among the men on a Sunday morning. Why had *Da Hah* chosen to change his position in the church? Briefly his eyes caught Hannah's face among the women. It was drawn and pale. He quickly looked away again. Hannah was suffering enough without catching a glimpse of the fear in his eyes.

She had been doing exceptionally well this morning, considering everything. Her dream had been frightening last night, but he had remained strong. It would only make matters worse if he gave in to his fears. In the end they would make it through this with *Da Hah*'s help.

Bishop John paused at the door of the bedroom before opening it, and Jake almost bumped into Minister Mose as he did the same. Jake caught himself just in time and waited until Mose moved on. Inside the room, three chairs were already lined up against the wall, and the bed was moved to one side. Not all hosts were this considerate of their needs, but it helped this morning with the tension so strong. Below them the song leader launched into another line of the song, holding the notes an extra few seconds before the congregation joined in.

Jake's chair scraped on the hardwood floor as he sat down.

Bishop John cleared his throat. "I trust we've all rested well," he said with a faint smile. "I know I managed to get some sleep even with all the thinking I was doing." He paused and then asked, "Has anything changed with you men since last night?"

Jake waited for long moments before glancing at Minister Mose's face. He was the oldest and supposed to go first. To Jake's surprise, the look on Mose's face was even more tense than his was.

Bishop John must have noticed it too. Finally he said to Mose, "I take it there has been something on your part. Have you turned against me too?"

"Ah," Mose said. "It's not what you think. I don't know how to begin. The truth is, old Menno Troyer came to visit me last night after I arrived home."

When he said nothing more, Bishop John prompted him. "Yes, go on."

"I would rather not tell you what he said."

"Old Menno," Bishop John said. "Now I've heard everything. Surely he's not joining the Mennonites."

Mose laughed nervously, "No, but he did have some things to say. Somehow he found out about your plans today, and he said he's voting against excommunication. He wanted me to warn you."

"Why didn't he come to me then?"

"I guess he didn't come to this conclusion till late, and he didn't want to drive all the way up to your place."

"I see," Bishop John said. "Does he know anything about Jake's objections?"

"No," Mose said. "He didn't seem to, but I didn't ask."

"Have you been telling things around, Jake?" Bishop John asked, turning in his chair. "Trying to drum up support for your position?"

Jake shook his head, his throat in a knot.

"Things do get around," Mose said. "I'm not surprised at that, but I was surprised that Menno would be opposed."

"Did he say why?" Bishop John asked.

"*Jah.* He said we're overreacting and would live to regret the decision. Also that he was afraid we will lose more people if we go ahead with this. He said that back East where he comes from, the church would never do anything like this."

"He comes from Holmes County," Bishop John said.

"They take quite a liberal approach to joining the Mennonites in Ohio," Mose said. "So maybe that's where he gets his thinking."

"Did you tell Menno about Bishop Wengerd's letter?" Bishop John asked.

"No," Mose said. "I thought there were already enough people talking, and I didn't know how you'd feel about that."

"You are a wise man," Bishop John said. "But this still leaves the question open as to what we should do. I don't think we can survive the vote if Menno doesn't support us."

"You were going to read Bishop Wengerd's letter to the church," Mose said. "Do you think that will change Menno's mind?"

Bishop John grimaced. "I doubt it. He's more stubborn than Jake here, and that's saying a lot."

"Then you'll have to change your mind," Mose said. "There's really no other way out of this."

"There would be if Jake will support me," Bishop John said. "What do you say to that, Jake? Has the night's rest changed your mind?"

"I'm afraid not," Jake said, keeping his eyes turned toward the floor. "I don't know what else to do. I think we'll be making things worse if we start excommunicating people over this situation."

"And what do you think, Mose?" Bishop John asked.

"Old Menno can make a lot of trouble for us," Mose said. "I think that's the real reason he didn't come to you. He's expecting you not to back down, and it would look better for him if he hadn't been talking to you beforehand."

"Probably," Bishop John said. "But I still wish he would have come to me. I'll have to talk to him after church. So what should we do?"

"I don't know," Mose said. "This is a hard one."

"Yes, it is," Bishop John said, stroking his beard and staring at the floor. "I guess I'll have to be man enough to admit I'm whipped. What do you say, Jake? Do you think I am?"

"I hope you will do what you think is best," Jake said, not looking up.

"I see," Bishop John said. "So we will see what that all leads to. In the meantime, let's still have a meeting after church with the members. I'll warn them again about the dangers at the tent meetings, but that's about all we can do, I guess."

"I think so," Mose said, shifting on his chair. "I sure hope we don't end up losing more people."

"I'll make the warning as hard as I can, and perhaps the two of you can join in. Jake will even support that. Won't you, Jake?"

"*Jah,*" Jake said. "I can support that."

"How *fully* can you support it?" Mose asked, glancing sideways at him.

"I don't know what you mean," Jake countered.

"I mean after last night, I'm wondering if you don't have some sympathies for the Mennonites yourself."

"If I did, I would leave," Jake said. "And I'm not leaving."

"That doesn't sound all that encouraging," Bishop John said. "Could you perhaps make that a little stronger? Especially since I want you to have the main sermon today. I'd like to hear about your reasons for not joining the Mennonites."

"I don't know what to say," Jake said. "I can't imagine being anything else but Amish. I mean, I don't want to be anything but Amish."

"Does Hannah have anything to do with your decision?" Mose asked. "I know she comes from a very stable family and is committed to the Amish life. Is that what's holding you here?"

"Why would I want to leave, and what does Hannah have to do with it?" Jake asked, sitting upright.

"Not many Amish preachers can preach like you do," Mose said. "I'm sure the Mennonites would welcome you with open arms. Didn't Ben Stoll go out of his way to speak with you about the tent meetings?"

"He did," Jake said. "But that has not caused me to leave the Amish."

"I'm glad to hear that," Bishop John said. "And let's not start fighting among ourselves. *Da Hah* knows we have enough troubles already. If Jake says he's with us, then that's *gut* enough for me. I want him to have the main sermon today, and you, Mose, will open up. I think it's your turn."

"*Jah,*" Mose said, "it is."

"Then we're agreed," Bishop John said, getting to his feet. "Let's get back down to the church meeting before they think we've climbed out the bedroom window and gone home."

Mose laughed, but Jake kept his head down as he stood up. How was he supposed to preach the sermon when he was so distrusted? How was he to prove himself with such an accusation hanging over his head?

Bishop John walked out the door, the stair treads squeaking on the his way down. The singing stopped by the time Jake reached the bottom. Carefully he looked across the faces of the women, but he failed to catch Hannah's eye. Another look might draw attention, and perhaps she wouldn't have understood the emotions in his eyes anyway.

Jake lowered himself onto the hard bench and clasped his hands as Minister Mose got to his feet.

"Dearly beloved, brothers and sisters in the Lord," Mose began. "We all know that the Day of the Lord draws ever nearer and that the enemy is out and about like a roaring lion seeking whom he may deceive and devour. We have been warned by *Da Hah* Himself and have no one to blame but ourselves if we are deceived."

Jake shifted on the bench. If there were some way he could see Hannah, he might try a little smile in her direction. Perhaps that would relieve her tension over what she thought was coming. That there would be no vote was *gut* news to share with her. His eyes gazed over the area of women's benches where she had been sitting, but he couldn't see her.

"How can we say that we serve God when we have one eye on the world?" Mose was saying. "Each day the temptations are all around us, and if we do not guard against them, the enemy can plant his seeds in our hearts that one day will grow into weeds no one can pull out."

Bishop John was nodding as Mose continued, and Jake tried to relax. What in the world was he supposed to preach on when his turn came? Mose was doing the warning, and plenty of it. Should more be done? It would be a safe subject even if he was repeating the words. What would convince Bishop John that he had no intentions of leaving the Amish? Not much, once such thoughts were planted and had taken root. Hopefully he wouldn't say anything that would make things worse. The question was, what would make things worse?

Mose wrapped up his thoughts and sat down.

"Now let us pray," Bishop John said and a rustling of sound spread through the house. Closing with the Lord's prayer, Bishop John rose to his feet, and everyone remained standing while he read Scripture. A few of the younger boys shuffled sideways through the tight aisle between the benches to go outside for a short break.

Bishop John closed the Bible, and with the sound of the people seating themselves, Jake walked slowly forward to where Mose had been standing. He took a deep breath and began.

"May the grace of our Lord and Savior Jesus Christ be with us today. We are all unworthy servants at best, who seek to follow in the footsteps of One who has gone before us. The writer to the Hebrews said that we are surrounded by so great a cloud of witnesses, and we are. Many have gone before us in this journey to heaven and have left us with great examples to follow.

"I am reminded this morning of our forefathers who now more than five hundred years ago endured fire, sword, drowning, hunger, separation from their families—all to leave us a heritage worthy of the name of the Lord. They did not think of themselves as better than others nor did they hold themselves up as worthy of the high calling of the gospel.

"Yet in their humility *Da Hah* chose to use them to raise the standard of Christianity higher than it had been for many generations. They were the ones who were willing to sacrifice all so that the true gospel of the apostles and prophets could be restored."

Jake clasped his hands, and paced slowly back and forth. Bishop John was nodding his head. Mose wasn't looking at him, but it didn't really matter as long as Bishop John was happy.

He paused in the silence and then paced again as he spoke again. "Our forefathers were reformers in their day. They followed in the footsteps of men like Martin Luther and Zwingli, but they wanted to go further than those men desired to go. Our fathers believed that the church should take no part in the state government and that oaths should not be taken in loyalty to anything. That no man needed to swear to make his word believable. That instead our words ought to be believed by virtue of the manner in which we live our lives.

"And they believed that Luther and Zwingli went too far in correcting the doctrines of the Catholic Church. That, yes, faith was necessary, and Abraham, as the apostle Paul said in Romans, was justified without the works of the law. Yet this is not the same as saying that Abraham was justified by faith alone.

"The apostle James writing his own letter says clearly that a man is not justified by faith alone, but that faith without works is dead. So our forefathers spoke out against the ungodly lives of the church people around them. They believed that infant baptism was not enough to save a person, but that men needed to repent of their sins, that they needed to live holy lives, and walk in the fear of *Da Hah*. For this they were persecuted, pursued across most of Europe, and called rebaptizers, and every other evil name their accusers could think of.

"Finally God opened a way for them to come to this country and to live in peace from those who so hated them. Today it is our calling and duty to uphold the great traditions we have received from these men and to be thankful that we are even counted worthy of the task."

Jake slowed down, taking a deep breath. Out of the corner of his eye he saw that Bishop John was still nodding. So he must not have said anything out of order. Emboldened, he continued for another thirty minutes, adding to what he had already said and quoting what related Scriptures he could remember.

For a moment he caught sight of Hannah's worried face. Oh, if he could only stop and speak with her, but that was not allowed.

Eventually, Jake said, "I will now close. And I ask for testimony on what has been said. Will Bishop John, Mose, and Menno express themselves? And may God's blessing be on what they say."

Jake sat down, and waited for Bishop John to begin.

Thirty-Five

Hannah searched through the stack of bonnets on the table. Jake would soon be waiting for her. He had left the house with his head bowed a few minutes earlier. It was all so confusing. What had happened? Had there been a confrontation between him and Bishop John? Was that why there had been no vote on excommunication? Sure, Bishop John had been firm enough with his warnings, but that was to be expected. And now where was her bonnet?

"I've been waiting for a chance to speak with you," Betty said, bustling out of the kitchen doorway. "You still look so worried, and nothing bad happened today, so I can't figure it out."

"I guess I just thought something bad was going to happen...but it didn't," Hannah said, continuing her search.

"Well, that just shows how wrong a person can be," Betty said. "You ought to hear Steve when he starts reminding me of all the times I'm wrong on my predictions. I suppose Jake will have the same story for you this afternoon."

"I don't think so," Hannah said. "He was the one who told me."

"Jake?" Betty asked. "That's hard to believe, but I guess men can be wrong too. It's hard to imagine Jake being wrong though, what with the sermon he gave today. In all my life, I must say, I haven't heard such preaching, and from such a young man. I know Bishop John was just sitting there happy right down to the bottom of his Sunday shoes. He must be so glad to have such a *gut* minister who can help him so handily."

"I don't know about that," Hannah said. "But Jake will be waiting for me. He left the house awhile ago, and I can't find my bonnet."

"Oh," Betty said, reaching into the pile. "Well, here it is. You must be really distracted today."

"I guess I am," Hannah said, trying to smile.

"It's the baby, isn't it?" Betty said, taking Hannah's arm. "Is it serious? You're surely not going to lose the *bobli* again? Have you been to see the doctor lately?"

"I'm going this week," Hannah said. "But I don't think that's the problem."

"Trouble comes when we least expect it. You shouldn't let down your guard, Hannah, even when the doctors tell us everything is going well."

"I'm going more by what I feel, even if the doctor tells me everything's okay. I haven't forgotten the last time."

"Why don't you stop by this week on your way to the doctor's?" Betty asked, her face brightening. "It would be so great to see you, and we could talk for longer without being interrupted."

"I'd like that," Hannah said, slipping her bonnet over her head, and moving toward the door. "But I really have to be going. Jake's waiting."

"Remember that I don't approve of Miriam's doings tonight, but I'm turning a blind eye," Betty said, following Hannah through the wash-room. "You take care now."

"I'll tell her," Hannah said, laughing softly. "But I don't think she will listen."

"I don't think so either," Betty said. "So I guess we have to live with the girl, even if she messes up her life. What a shame that will be, and what is an even greater shame is that it will happen in Montana under my roof. Your mom will never forgive me."

"We made it through my problems," Hannah said over her shoulder.

Betty smiled and waved.

When Hannah came around the corner of the house, Jake was already waiting at the end of the walks. Mosey's head was hanging down almost to the ground. Hannah pulled herself up the buggy step and settled in beside Jake. It was so *gut* to sit beside him again, and she pulled his arm tightly against her side.

"I won't be able to drive like that," he said, slapping the reins with his free arm.

"What happened, Jake? Please tell me before I pass out. It's only been Betty's wild chatter that's been keeping my mind off you."

"I guess *Da Hah* chose to have mercy on me," Jake said, turning Mosey left onto the blacktop road.

"You'll have to tell me more than that."

"Old Menno Troyer visited Mose late last night. He had apparently heard about the upcoming vote and objected to it. Bishop John didn't want to proceed with him opposed."

"Just like that and it was over?"

"Not really," Jake said, urging Mosey on. "It's never over that easily, but I think Bishop John liked my sermon today, so that's *gut*."

"Who wouldn't?" Hannah said, pulling on his arm again. Jake laughed and put his arm around her shoulder.

"Mose wanted to know if I was only staying Amish because you were opposed to us joining the Mennonites," Jake said, glancing sideways at her.

"Surely you straightened him out on that," Hannah said, nestling against him.

"I tried but there's only so much a person can do. I don't think good sermons are helping much either."

"Then preach bad ones. I don't care. Maybe Betty would stop gushing about them."

Jake laughed again, the sound filling the buggy.

"It's *gut* to hear you laugh," Hannah said, looking up at Jake's face. "I thought we'd never laugh again."

"I know. Even I was afraid this time. I suppose troubles will come back again, like they always do, but they seem gone for right now."

"I know," Hannah said, taking a deep breath. "I think we need to enjoy ourselves a little. Do you want to go back for the hymn sing tonight?"

Jake looked at her. "You must think we're still young."

"Well, we are. We don't even have our first *bobli* yet."

"It won't be long now," Jake said, as he turned into their lane. "You've started to show."

"I know. I've stopped serving tables on Sundays. It doesn't seem in order."

"But you look okay," Jake said, pulling up to the barn.

Hannah smiled as she climbed down and helped him unhitch. She waited by the buggy while he led Mosey into the barn. Taking his hand when he returned, she walked with him toward the cabin.

"My, my," Jake said. "You really must think we're still young. Holding hands and all."

"Well, it's about time we held hands again, don't you think? And what about going to the hymn singing tonight? Will you take me?"

"Why not!" Jake exclaimed, holding the cabin door open for her. "And what about popcorn this afternoon like the old folks do? And then we'll go to the hymn sing."

"I have the food made for tonight, so that's not a problem."

"Food made? What's going on tonight that requires food?" Jake asked, sitting on the couch with a long sigh. "Visitors?"

"Miriam's coming over with Dennis for her date."

"Oh yes, I forgot about that."

"We'll patch things up with Betty later. What's important now is that Miriam has a decent, relaxed place to have her dates."

Jake sighed. "I'll leave such things to you. I have enough troubles without worrying about dates. Just bring me the popcorn, and I'll be happy."

"You could help me. It's not easy making popcorn on a woodstove."

Jake jumped up from the couch and followed Hannah into the kitchen. "For a woman who once blew up her kitchen, you've come a long way," Jake said.

"You shouldn't bring up my past. It's not nice. Even Betty knows that."

"I know." Jake struck a match and lit the kindling in the firebox. "And it's high time I build that new cabin and get a gas stove for you—and a refrigerator. I think we can afford it now."

"I see you still know how to light a fire."

"So you think I've forgotten? That would be really nasty—making my wife work with a woodstove I didn't know how to light."

"I like my woodstove, and the new cabin can wait until after the baby comes. Really it can, Jake."

"I'm at least getting the foundation in this fall yet," Jake said, adding more wood to the fire. "I'm determined. That way the new home might get done by early next summer, since we don't have as many nice days to work with around here like they do in the East."

"It's okay with me," Hannah said, pouring a cup of popcorn into the popcorn maker. "What will it be like?"

"It'll be really nice," Jake said, waving his hands around in description. "I don't know exactly how big, but there's a dealer up near Kalispell. I might write to him for plans. Do you have any suggestions on what you want?"

"Kalispell," Hannah said, shivering. "Isn't that where the Mennonite church is that Ben and Sylvia Stoll attend?"

"*Jah*, but let's not think about church things today, even if it's Sunday. I feel like I've been doing church work all week."

"But the tent meetings are going on all week yet, aren't they?"

"*Jah*, but I don't want to think about that either."

"Do you think we'll lose more people—other than Will and Rebecca and Mary?"

"I hope not, but can we talk about something else? Please?"

"*Jah*, of course," Hannah said, smiling gently. "I guess I'm still a little strung out. My nerves will settle down before long."

Hannah moved the popcorn maker over the glowing oven lid.

"Think about our cabin," Jake whispered in her ear, holding his hands over hers on the handle.

"I'll blow up my kitchen again with you helping this way," she said, laughing softly.

"Only the popcorn maker will blow up, and then we'll have soft white kernels all over the place. How bad can that be?"

"So which one of us is going to turn the handle?"

"I think I will," Jake said, pushing her fingers out of the way. "Maybe the kitchen won't blow up that way."

"You're awfully full of yourself," she said into his beard.

"So tell me about the cabin," he whispered back, slowly turning the handle.

"I want the cabin to be big," she said. "Full and roomy on the inside, with great soaring cathedral ceilings in the main room."

"That doesn't sound very Amish."

"I know. That's why it's going to be big but decent. There's going to be lots of room for our children. And an upstairs loft with bedrooms and a bath."

"That sounds plain to me."

"Isn't that what we are?"

"*Jah*, but I want something nice for you."

"A refrigerator and a gas stove will be plenty, Jake. And really we don't have to do anything. I'm happy here. Perfectly happy here. Don't I have you?"

"And soon our *bobli*."

"*Jah*, and isn't that enough?"

"I'm still building the cabin. This one is way too small."

"Maybe Bishop John was right?"

"Bishop John?" he said as the popcorn began pinging against the metal popper.

"He said you are very stubborn."

Thirty-Six

Hannah hitched Mosey to the buggy, pausing as the sound of Mr. Brunson's truck came down the graveled lane. She waited, wondering if Mr. Brunson would stop in and speak with her—or was he uncomfortable now that his relationship with Mary had turned serious?

As Mr. Brunson came into view, Hannah waved. Mr. Brunson waved back, slowing down a little. Hannah caught sight of his face. He looked happy, but he didn't stop.

Climbing into the buggy, Hannah guided Mosey down the lane and turned toward Libby at the blacktop road. Great fluffy clouds filled the skyline above the mountain range, diluting the raggedness of the peaks. The clouds were moving slowly to the south. They glided along as if pushed by the hand of *Da Hah*, although the science book in school had said wind currents were responsible for cloud movements. Was *Da Hah* perhaps like that? Hiding His hand behind the natural things of the world?

Hannah sighed. Was He trying to move Jake and her in some direction with the events of the past weeks? If He was, they didn't seem to be moving much. Trying to survive was more like it. If old Menno Troyer hadn't spoken up, who knows what action Bishop John might have taken against Jake. Yet Bishop John had a kind heart, didn't he? Maybe he would have come to the same conclusion on his own.

Mosey shook his head, as the tugs tightened on the slight uphill climb past Betty's place. Hannah almost pulled back on the lines. No one was working at the barn, but it was still early. Should she stop in? But the conversation might take longer than she had time for. The questions would have to wait until after the appointment with Dr. Lisa. Had any new people from the community been attending the tent meetings this week? Jake hadn't been told of any, but that didn't mean anything. Betty likely would hear of it first.

Hannah drove on thinking how Jake had been burdened all week, even with the *gut* news from Sunday. Hannah tightened the reins as the tent came into view, its canvas sides moving slowly in the wind. Did *Da Hah* also move with His hand behind those flimsy walls? Had Mary done the right thing in agreeing to join the Mennonites, even if she was in love with Mr. Brunson?

Perhaps things looked differently once one was older, but still that would be an awful big change to make. Mosey turned his head to look at the tent, staring for long moments.

"They'll be gone soon," Hannah said out loud. "Really soon, and I can't wait. Jake has already suffered enough."

Mosey shook his head, turning to look at the other side of the road.

"I know," Hannah said. "I can't stand the sight of the tent either. I wish they had never come here, but they did, and now we all have to deal with the mess."

Hannah jumped at the loud honking of an automobile horn behind her buggy and jerked back on the reins. Mosey slowed down, but didn't come to a stop. With a loud roar of the engine, a dark blue pickup swung around the buggy, the young teenage boy who was driving waving wildly. He turned around briefly to look back, a big smirk on his face. Hannah took a deep breath as she turned into Dr. Lisa's parking lot and pulled her horse to a stop. She sat for a long moment in the buggy without moving. Was it true what her people said? That the Mennonites were simply a step out into the world? Would Mary Keim and Will and Rebecca Riley end up among the *Englisha*? Were their young folks slated for the fate of the rude young boy who roared past buggies and considered it a great joke?

"It must never happen to us," she whispered as she climbed down and tied Mosey securely to the light post. "Jake and I have to raise our children to fear *Da Hah* and to walk in holiness. Please help us, God. Protect us from the evils of this world."

Pressing her arms tightly around her swollen body, Hannah walked across the parking lot and up the steps into Dr. Lisa's office.

"Good morning," the receptionist said brightly. "How are you today?"

"Okay," Hannah said, smiling weakly.

"You look a little peaked."

"I'm okay," Hannah said, taking a seat as the receptionist looked skeptically at her.

Nurse Sally came bustling up the hall, and Hannah turned toward her. Perhaps Sally would take her back in right away, out from under the receptionist's scrutiny.

"Good morning, Hannah," Sally said cheerfully. "Are we ready to go back?"

"*Jah*," Hannah said, quickly getting to her feet.

The receptionist was still watching her as Sally led her down the hall. Did she really look that awful? Or was the kindly middle-aged lady simply allowing her motherly concern to get the best of her? Perhaps she had a daughter whose pregnancy had ended badly. Hannah shivered at the thought.

"Are you cold?" Sally asked.

"No," Hannah said. "I'm fine."

"I guess we'll see," Sally said, taking her temperature quickly.

"I'm just a little tired," Hannah said. "Maybe that's why I'm looking peaked."

"Pregnancies can do that," Sally said, lifting Hannah's arm to strap on the blood pressure gauge, then pumping in air until the strap bit into Hannah's arm.

"How is it?" Hannah asked as Sally wrote down the numbers.

"It's up a little, but we'll see what Dr. Lisa has to say. Come with me, and we'll get you ready."

Moments later Sally disappeared, and Hannah stared at the white wall as she waited. It was so different here, as it should be. This was a doctor's office where bodies were nurtured and cared for. But the cabin at home was also what it should be, a place where the love between her and Jake could grow. A place of comfort, of shelter from the world, and a place where their children would be safe.

The door opened and Dr. Lisa came in.

"How are you doing, Hannah?" she asked, picking up the chart Sally had left.

"Fine, I think," Hannah said, forcing a smile.

"Your blood pressure is up," Dr. Lisa said, taking Hannah's hand. "Are you still under a lot of stress?"

"I guess," Hannah said, taking a deep breath. Dr. Lisa might as well know. "There's been a lot of church things going on."

"I see," Dr. Lisa said. "Are you worried about this pregnancy?"

"Sometimes," Hannah said. "But not really. I think this one will be okay."

Dr. Lisa smiled. "That's a good way to look at it. Have you thought more about using our birthing room?"

"*Jah*," Hannah said. "And I appreciate the offer but I'd like to have the baby at home. It's the way it should be. It's not that your room isn't nice—it certainly is. I'm sure it fits the needs perfectly of most people."

"Does Jake agree with you on this?"

"I haven't told him yet."

"Well, you can always change your mind later. I try to be flexible, but I think you should contact the midwife soon. They sometimes have their schedules filled up. The woman's name is Mattie Esh. The receptionist will give you Mattie's card on your way out."

Hannah nodded and repeated the name.

"So that's settled then," Dr. Lisa said, stepping back from the table. "And everything else looks fine. I would say we have a nice, healthy baby coming along."

"Thanks," Hannah said. "I hope I haven't offended you with my decision not to use the birthing room."

"Not at all," Dr. Lisa said. "But let my office know at once if you should change your mind or if Mattie has any problems. I would much rather know sooner then after the problem has gotten out of hand."

"I promise," Hannah said. "And thank you so much."

"The receptionist will take care of you then, and you should be okay," Dr. Lisa said, closing the door behind her.

Hannah refastened her clothes and walked down the empty hall to the front desk.

"All ready to go?" the receptionist asked.

"*Jah*," Hannah said, taking out the checkbook.

"Was everything okay?" the receptionist asked, handing her the bill.

"My blood pressure was a little high," Hannah said, writing out the check. "But nothing serious."

"Oh, that's good to hear."

"*Jah*, it is," Hannah said, passing the check over the counter.

"So when will you be in next?" the receptionist asked, rising to her feet. "Let me ask Dr. Lisa because it doesn't say anything on your chart. Or did she tell you?"

"No," Hannah said. "I have plans to use the midwife now. Dr. Lisa said that should be okay unless complications come up. She said you'd give me her card."

"Yes, certainly," she said as she reached for a small stack of cards near her phone. "And Dr. Lisa did tell you to call us if there are any problems?"

"*Jah*, I promised her I would." Hannah tucked the card in her pocket.

"Don't forget then," the receptionist said.

"I won't," Hannah said as she left. Mosey turned his head to look at her and whinnied when she got closer.

"I made the right decision, I know I did," Hannah whispered as she untied Mosey and climbed into the buggy. "I want to have the *bobli* at home, the way it's supposed to be."

Guiding Mosey back into the street, Hannah settled back into the buggy seat. "Please God," she whispered, her eyes sweeping the range of the Cabinet Mountains, "Let the *bobli* be okay. He can grow up here in this wonderful land, and Jake will be such a wonderful father for him."

An *Englisha* car came from out of town, slowing down when it drew closer. Hannah pulled the buggy over toward the shoulder as the vehicle passed, its occupants looking back at Hannah, obviously amused. At least they had no objections to slowing down for Amish buggies. Perhaps they were from out of town and were surprised to see Amish in Montana. At least they weren't like the tourists back home in Indiana, who sometimes stopped to take pictures of Amish buggies. That was another *gut* reason to live out here in the West.

As she approached the site of the tent, the canvas sides still swayed in the wind. Ben Stoll's tent. At least it was his doing that it was here. So happy had she been in her thoughts about the *bobli*, she had forgotten about the Mennonite revival meetings. Would Ben see that it returned next year to claim more converts?

"Don't let it happen, God," she whispered. "We need a place to raise our family in peace. Jake doesn't deserve another summer like he's been through. Can You please change Ben Stoll's heart, and send him some-where else with his missionary zeal?"

Hannah sighed as the fluffy clouds moved across the ridges of the mountains.

"But not our will, but Yours be done," she whispered. "If You see fit to allow another trial like this next year, please give Jake and me the strength to bear it. We are not strong of ourselves, but we ask that You give us Your strength, and give Jake the wisdom to make the right decision if Bishop John wants to excommunicate Ben again. And please don't leave us alone. We so want to do what is pleasing to You."

Thirty-Seven

Hannah pulled right at Betty's driveway. Mosey tossed his head and wanted to turn the other way, but she finally responded to the steady pull.

"You'll get home to your barn soon enough," Hannah remarked, pulling up to the hitching rack. The barn door stood open, but there was no sign of Miriam. Hannah climbed down and tied Mosey to the post. He hung his head wearily and Hannah laughed. "You haven't been on a long trip, so stop acting so lazy."

Mosey jerked his head up and Hannah jumped as the screen door of the house slammed and Betty approached. "I've been waiting all morning for you to stop in, Hannah. How did the doctor's visit go?"

"Fine."

"Oh, it's so *gut* to see you again," Betty said, giving Hannah a big hug.

"I just saw you on Sunday," Hannah reminded with a laugh.

"But with all that's been going on, it seems like longer."

"I know," Hannah said, her face darkening. "Have you heard of any more of our people going to Ben's tent revival?"

"No," Betty said, her voice full of relief. "Not one single person! And that's not everything…but maybe I shouldn't be telling you this."

"Then maybe you shouldn't," Hannah said. "I don't think I can handle any more bad news."

"It's not like that," Betty said, her smile never dimming. "This is *gut* news. Ben Stoll is upset that no more Amish have come. Can you believe that?"

229

"That *is* good news. I was sure hoping no one else would go."

Betty glanced around, as if someone could be listening. "Ben has somehow found out about Jake's opposition to the excommunication thing."

"Oh no. I wonder how?" Hannah asked.

"I don't know, but I imagine this will make Jake look good to Bishop John."

"Because Ben found out about it?"

"No, silly, because Ben is blaming Jake for his failure to get more Amish people. For myself, I think the man had dreams in his head of being a minister. Maybe even of starting up a Mennonite church right in this area with the members he would steal from our community being his first converts."

"I don't understand."

"Because now even Will is upset with Ben. I can't believe that I am the first person to tell you this *gut* news. I thought for sure you had already heard."

"Look," Hannah said, taking Betty by the arm, "why would Ben blame Jake for his failure?"

"Because Jake was the one who opposed the excommunication, that's why."

"I still don't understand."

"See, Ben had his hopes set on the excommunication going through. He was planning to make a big deal out of it at the tent meetings. He even had plans to go door-to-door to all the Amish people and tell them how wrong Bishop John was. It was going to be his big chance to bring in many more from the community."

"But it wouldn't have worked. You wouldn't have left, would you?"

"No, of course not, but some of the others might have if Ben was able to convince them that excommunication was too harsh. At least that's what Ben was hoping for."

"Who told you all this?"

"Rebecca," Betty whispered. "Ben went by Will and Rebecca's one night after one of the meetings and blew off a head of steam to Will about it. But now don't you tell anyone I said so."

Hannah smiled. "So now I can be really glad Jake stood by what he believed. Although it was really old Menno Troyer who should be thanked.

He's the one who said he wouldn't vote for the excommunication and thus changed Bishop John's mind."

"But it all wouldn't have happened without Jake. So don't go saying Jake's part wasn't important. I know we're not supposed to be proud of our husbands, but this was a really important thing. And Rebecca also said Ben is leaving the area for good next week."

"But will he come back next year?"

"I don't think so. Not since Will told him he's changed his mind about joining the Mennonite church Ben wants to start up. Will said after having Jake as his minister and listening to Ben sound off, he could never sit on Sunday mornings listening to Ben preach."

"Oh, but that's an awful thing to say."

"I don't think so," Betty said. "Ben had it coming to him for what he's put this community through."

"But we have to still love Ben."

"I do," Betty said weakly. "It will just be easier to love him once he and Sylvia are back in Kalispell for good."

"What are Will and Rebecca planning to do?"

"It looks like they're still going Mennonite, but just not here. It wouldn't surprise me if Will took Rebecca back to Idaho where his parents are."

"That would be too bad. Maybe he'll change his mind?"

"Well, if he does, that would be a job for Jake."

"Maybe if we pray," Hannah said, looking toward the Cabinet Mountain range. The fluffy clouds were still there, sweeping across the ridges.

"This one will take more than prayer," Betty said. Then she looked away and said, "Well, speaking of changing minds, I guess this is the time for me to admit that maybe I was wrong about Dennis."

"Well, that *is* a change of mind."

"*Jah*, it is. I can say now that I'm convinced that Dennis is a *gut* man, even though I'm still not so sure about Will. So there, I've said it. Beyond that I'm not responsible for the girl's wild plans, nor am I responsible for what will happen when your mother finds out. It wouldn't surprise me if we heard her scream all the way from Indiana."

"What is Miriam planning to do?"

"I'm not saying," Betty said, firmly placing her hand on her mouth. "There are some things that even *I* can't say."

"So where is Miriam?" Hannah asked, glancing around. "I didn't see her in the barn."

"She's riding back by the river this morning—since we don't have any people stopping by. I told her she needs to spend some time *thinking*, but I don't think it will change her mind. She has a harebrained idea."

"When will she be back?"

"I don't know," Betty said. "She's been gone awhile."

"Then you have to tell me what she's planning to do. Is it something awful? It can't be joining the Mennonites. You said there aren't any more of our people attending the meetings."

"I'm not saying. You'll just have to wait until Miriam comes back and ask her."

"I can ride out to meet her," Hannah said, starting to move toward the barn.

"Not in your condition, you're not," Betty said, taking Hannah's arm. "I'm not going to allow it. If something would happen, I'd never forgive myself."

"But I know how to ride. I've ridden since I was a little girl."

"You're staying here, and there's simply no question about that."

"Then I'll walk out to meet her." Hannah said, taking a few quick steps.

"Hannah Byler, I declare! You are as stubborn as your sister," Betty said with a sigh. "Oh, all right. If you insist, I'll help you get the horse ready. But if you fall off, I'll blame myself for the rest of my living days."

"Well, you could tell me what Miriam is up to, then I wouldn't have to go."

"No, I won't do that. I suppose you'll be okay if you take the mare. She's gentle."

"Okay," Hannah said. She waited while Betty went to the barn for the horse.

When Betty returned with the saddled horse, she helped Hannah pull herself up on the mare. Mosey whinnied loudly in objection.

"You just stay here and behave yourself," Hannah told him. "I'll be back before long."

At the trail's head, Betty let go, and the mare trotted quickly toward the river.

"Now, don't you go too fast," Betty hollered after Hannah, and she turned to wave.

What on earth is Miriam up to? Hannah wondered. Betty said it was *gut* news, but news that would still upset their mother. With a quick kick against the mare's side, Hannah urged the horse into a gallop. The soft gurgle of the river reached her ears long before she saw the water through the trees. Perhaps Miriam was already on her way back, and she wouldn't have to ride far. Hannah pulled back on the reins when she reached the bank and looked north where the trail followed the river. There was no sign of Miriam or her horse.

Quickly Hannah moved on, falling into the soft roll of the mare's movements. She was an easy horse to ride, as were all of Betty's horses. It was a requirement in her business. Stopping at the next rise, Hannah still didn't see Miriam. Here the mountain range could be seen on all sides, and Hannah slowed to study the beauty around her.

She had brought Jake here before they had spoken of their love for each other. They had ridden along this river and laughed at the joy of each other's company, even though it was forbidden then to speak of their feelings. How mixed up she had been, and how close she had come to making the biggest mistake of her life. Was Miriam about to do likewise?

Betty's reassurances were small comfort. Hadn't Betty's idea of the right man for her been Sam? *Jah, it had.* Betty had a wonderful heart, but she wasn't always on the right track with her feelings. Had she talked Miriam into something she shouldn't be doing, like she had done with Sam and her?

Urging the horse on, Hannah moved along the riverbank, keeping the reins taut in case there was trouble. Surely she could keep her balance even with a stumble, but there was no sense in taking any chances.

Coming over the next ridge, Hannah caught sight of Miriam ahead, seated on the best horse Betty had—a beautiful gelding with a golden-brown coat ending in white stockings on both front legs.

"Miriam," Hannah yelled, but Miriam continued looking toward the northern range of the distant mountains.

At a fast trot, Hannah went down into a slight dip in the trail, riding up the other side with the mare's sure feet never missing a beat.

"Miriam," she called again.

This time Miriam turned and waved, but didn't move her horse. Hannah approached, finally coming to a stop beside her sister.

"What are you doing out here?" Miriam asked, turning around again.

"Looking for you and wanting to hear this great secret Betty says you have."

"I'm glad she didn't tell you," Miriam said, her eyes back on the mountain range. "Although I expect it must have been hard for Betty to keep such *gut* news from spilling out."

"So what exactly are you up to? If you don't tell me soon, I'll scream."

"How did your doctor's appointment go?" Miriam asked with a straight face.

"Fine," Hannah said. "Tell me. *Now!*"

"I'm glad to hear that," Miriam said. "It would have been awful to hear bad news from the doctor on the morning your sister tells you of the biggest, the best, the most wonderful news she has ever had to share in all her life."

"Just say it," Hannah said, leaning forward over the mare's slim neck.

"I've had to spend all week convincing Betty," Miriam said. "That woman is the limit. It would be easier to convince a porcupine to take in its quills than for that woman to change her mind. If you ever say a doubtful word about this in her presence, then I'm sure she'll flip right back and you'll have undone my hard work. So you have been warned."

"Miriam," Hannah said, "I have work to do at home. Get to it."

"I know," Miriam said, a look of sheer joy filling her face. "And so do all of us. Dennis and I are getting married early this fall. Right here in Montana. Betty has agreed to have the wedding at her place."

Thirty-Eight

Hannah was setting the table as the sound of Jake's buggy came up the lane. She paused to listen for a long moment before turning back to the cabinet drawer for the forks and spoons. Jake was home. Would he have news to share? Maybe. With the way things were going, Mr. Brunson might have stopped by the shop and announced his wedding plans!

Sliding the potato and meat plates out of the oven, Hannah placed them on the table on hot pads. Jake hadn't had a meat-and-potato supper all week, and he deserved it more often. He might think she was celebrating once she told him Miriam's news, but the supper preparations had been started early in the morning even before she knew about Miriam and Dennis's plans.

Walking to the cabin door, Hannah waited until Jake was on the porch before she stepped out and wrapped her arms around him in a big hug.

"Well, this is a nice welcome! Good news, perhaps?" he asked, holding her at arm's length.

"Yes," Hannah whispered. "*Gut* news all day and then some. I don't know if I can handle anymore…if you happen to have some."

"The only news I have is a letter from my mom."

Hannah glanced up at his face. "I hadn't thought of that. Surely your mom wouldn't send bad news after your nice letter to her."

"No," Jake said, "probably not. I haven't read it yet, but she would not send bad news, I'm sure. But you should be full of news about your doctor appointment. Did it go well?"

"Yes, everything is fine and on schedule. No problems at all. Now, come eat your supper. It shouldn't get cold. We can read the letter afterward."

Jake said, "There *is* some other good news. I brought home the plans for the new log house."

"*Gut.* Then we'll look at the plans too—after we've eaten."

"I hope you like them," Jake said as Hannah took off his hat and laid it by the front door.

"I'm sure I will. Now come," Hannah said, leading him by the hand.

Silently Jake sat down at the table and bowed his head in prayer. Hannah held her breath as Jake prayed out loud.

"Great God in heaven, the Maker of all the world, we humble ourselves tonight in Your presence, giving You thanks first of all for Your Son Jesus, and for the grace You bestow upon us each and every day. We are especially thankful for the news that Hannah has received at the doctor today. That our child is still healthy, and that Your will still is that he should be born and bring joy and happiness to our home."

Hannah found Jake's hand under the table, squeezing it as he continued praying. When he was finished, she lifted her face to his, making no attempt to hide her wet cheeks. "Thank you," Hannah whispered, "for caring enough to give thanks for the *bobli.*"

"You and the child mean a lot to me."

"And now you really must eat," Hannah said through her tears. She dished a large helping of potatoes onto Jake's plate.

"You shouldn't spoil me, even if I'm starved," Jake teased.

Hannah waited until he had dipped the gravy onto his potatoes before she took potatoes for herself.

"There is more news besides the baby," she said softly. "A lot more *gut* news."

Jake glanced questioningly in her direction.

"Betty claims there have been no more of our people attending the meetings and that Ben is discouraged. She doesn't think he'll be back again next year."

"That is *gut* news, and I suppose Betty has her information correct. I haven't been told anything by Bishop John."

"She is usually right, at least on such things. She's not always right on some others, like who should marry whom."

"You've never forgotten that, have you?"

"It's not just us. She was also wrong about Miriam. Dennis asked Miriam to marry him on Sunday night right here in our living room. Miriam said yes!"

Alarm filled Jake's eyes, his spoon stopping halfway to his mouth.

"Dennis is not leaving the Amish, if that's what you're thinking," Hannah said. "In fact, he was very impressed with Bishop John's decision not to excommunicate Ben and Sylvia Stoll. I think that's what pushed Dennis to make a commitment and ask Miriam to marry him."

"That is *gut* news. Bishop John made a wise decision."

"You played your part," Hannah said, squeezing his arm.

"It was all by the grace given from *Da Hah*," Jake said. "We must not take credit for ourselves."

"I know," Hannah said, rubbing his arm.

"I think you ought to eat your supper," Jake said.

Hannah turned back to her plate with a smile.

"Perhaps I should since Miriam and Betty are coming over later to talk about the wedding. Is that okay?"

"I'd like to show you the prints for the new cabin before they come."

"Then the dishes can wait," Hannah said.

A few minutes later Jake had finished and Hannah took her last bite. "While I clear the table, why don't you bring in the plans from the buggy, and if Miriam and Betty show up before I get to the dishes, they can help with the dishes while we talk."

"That sounds like a *gut* idea," Jake said. He went out to get the plans while Hannah quickly cleared the table. When she heard him come in again, she joined him in the living room. Jake was seated on the couch staring at several white sheets of paper spread out in front of him on the floor.

"You haven't opened the letter from your mom yet," Hannah reminded, sitting down beside him.

Jake smiled at her. "Let me show you these first. Look at this."

Hannah followed the point of his finger as he traced the outline of the proposed log house. "Do you think it will be large enough?"

"I suppose it depends on how many children we're having," Hannah said, leaning tightly against him.

"Only *Da Hah* knows that, but we can plan for a dozen."

"I think we'd better take them one at a time," Hannah said, trying to make sense of the plans before her. "How do I tell what size the house is? It looks huge on paper."

"It's just a simple design," Jake pointed again. "Nothing fancy at all. Just a house with a rectangular shape, but I think inside we can take the stairs up to the loft with a landing in between which will add a nice touch." Jake turned the page, revealing details of the first floor. "When you walk in, there will be a large living room with a high ceiling. There will also be a large bedroom and two smaller rooms besides the kitchen on the first floor. The upstairs will have four rooms, two on each side of the stairs."

Hannah drew in her breath, "It sounds awfully big. What will we do with so much room when we get old and are all by ourselves?"

"We'll worry about that when it happens. For now we can shut off the upper level until our family grows. So what do you think?"

"If you like it, then so do I. But you know I really am happy right where we are."

"I know—and I'm thankful for that. In fact, that may allow us to move a little slower than I had thought at first. Perhaps I could put the foundation in this fall, and then get the logs up early next summer."

"Or the next," Hannah said.

"Once you see the logs going up, you'll want to move in right away."

Outside, the rattle of buggy wheels on gravel turned both of their heads.

"Miriam and Betty," Hannah said. "And we haven't read the letter from your mom yet."

"I can read it while you women plan the wedding," Jake said, getting up. "I'd better go out and help them unhitch."

"They'll just tie up," Hannah said, glancing out the window. "I don't think they're staying that long."

Jake laughed. "Remember who's here and why—Betty and Miriam and you to plan a wedding."

"Then I'll shoo them out of the house when it gets too late," Hannah said, opening the door.

Betty was coming up the walk at a fast pace with Miriam close behind. "I couldn't *wait* to come," Betty said. "I already started planning things on the way over, but Miriam made me quit, and now I feel like I'm going to explode."

"I wish Mom were here to be part of this," Hannah said, holding the door open for them.

"I do too," Miriam said. "But we can't do anything about that."

"Good evening, Jake," Betty said, glancing at the prints lying on the floor. "Did we interrupt something?"

"Not really," Jake said. "Hannah and I were looking at plans for our new house."

"Then we can wait a little while," Betty said. "I'd love to see what you're planning to build."

"Ah, no—not now," Hannah interrupted. "We'd better start planning the wedding. And I still have the dishes to do."

"Then we'll help while we talk," Betty said, marching resolutely toward the kitchen. Miriam shrugged her shoulders and followed. Hannah gave Jake a quick smile and whispered, "I want to see your letter after they leave."

Betty was already pouring hot water from the pot on the stove. She said over her shoulder, "You really have to get a gas water heater for your new house, Hannah. I hope Jake has that on his list of improvements."

"I'm sure he does," Hannah said with a laugh. "But I don't mind things as they are. I guess I've gotten used to it."

"Well that's all fine and dandy," Betty said, adding soap. "But if we don't get busy with these plans, we'll have a wedding only half put together. Hannah, your wedding should serve as an example of what *not* to do. It was close to a wreck, and we had plenty of warning for that. Can't you Miller girls get your minds together in a way that causes less planning grief?"

"It's not my fault," Miriam giggled. "How can you plan the meeting of the man of your dreams?"

"Well, it's just not very sensible," Betty said. "And you've caused me almost as much heartburn as Hannah did. And believe me, I thought she was the limit with her disaster with Sam. Walking out on a wedding. You're surely not planning to do that, are you, Miriam? Because if you are, I'm going home right now and not putting in one more lick of work."

"No one *plans* to walk out on a wedding," Hannah corrected. "Now be quiet before Jake hears us. We're supposed to be talking about Miriam's wedding."

"Just reminding us all of what happened in the past," Betty said, washing the plates. "That's the only way we'll keep a level head on ourselves, and even then it might be hard."

"So what about Mom?" Miriam asked, rinsing the first plate and drying it. "I've already written her, but I didn't go into details about what I'm expecting of her."

"If she shows up for the wedding, you ought to be thankful," Betty said.

Miriam laughed. "I don't think it's that bad."

"Don't worry," Hannah joined in. "Mom will tell us soon enough what she wants to do. If we get our plans together on this end, she can decide when to come out to help."

"I want the wedding to be in Betty's barn, near the same spot where Hannah had hers," Miriam said. "I still haven't forgotten how wonderful that was."

"We could at least have it in the house instead of the barn," Betty said.

"No, I want the wedding in the barn with the horses I've learned to love. I want the barn doors open so I can see the mountains when we say our vows. Oh, Hannah, I can't thank you enough for coming to this wonderful place and giving me the chance to meet such a wonderful man."

"You'd better get the stars out of your eyes," Betty said. "It can turn cold here in the early fall, and that barn door will need to be shut tight. That's why I say we squeeze everyone into the house and be done with it."

"I won't have it," Miriam said, shaking her head. "We have to take the chance, even if it turns cold."

"You're stubborn enough, I see," Betty said. "Just like your sister. Well, let's start with the planning then. I want names of all the table waiters, so we can contact them right away. That is unless you're using the young people from around here."

Miriam wrinkled her brow, "Dennis said he doesn't care, and we can't use most of his family anyway. That's sad, but it's just the way it is."

"Stop the moaning," Betty said, sitting down at the kitchen table. "Bring me a pen and paper, Hannah. We're going to start on the list of who you find acceptable."

Hannah retrieved the paper from the living room desk, pausing to give Jake another quick smile. He was seated on the couch, his mom's letter in his hand, a soft look on his face. "*Gut* news?" she asked.

He nodded. "They're coming for a visit."

Thirty-Nine

Hannah and Jake stood waiting at the Greyhound bus station in Libby, with Mosey hitched to the surrey borrowed from Betty. Hannah's heart was racing as she glanced nervously down the road toward the south.

"What is your mom going to say about me? She wrote you a nice letter, but she didn't mention anything about me."

"Mom has nothing against you," Jake said, leaning against the buggy wheel. "The only problem she ever raised about us was our church's belief in the assurance of salvation."

"She probably thinks I led you into that belief," Hannah said with another quick look down the road.

"Perhaps we can get that straightened out while they're here," Jake said. "I don't want to lecture them, but if they ask, I can answer their questions."

"Please don't say anything," Hannah said, taking his arm. "I so want this stay to be a pleasant one for them. This is their first visit since the wedding, and I want them to feel welcome here. I want them to want to come back. Especially since they will soon have a grandchild here."

Jake stared off toward the mountains in the distance. "How fast things change. It's seems not that long ago I got off the bus here as a confused Amish boy, not sure where I was going to end up. *Da Hah* must have had His eye on me even when I was unaware of it."

"Of course He did. Oh, here comes the bus! I'm so nervous I could break out in a cold sweat."

"Mom always liked you," Jake assured her.

"Did she tell you so?"

"Not in so many words, but I can tell. Come, let's meet them."

Jake took Hannah's hand and led her across the parking lot toward the bus as it bounced in from the main road and came to a stop with a deep roar of its engine.

Hannah let go of Jake's hand and clasped her hands tightly.

"Are you cold?" Jake asked.

"No, just scared out of my wits."

The door of the bus opened and *Englisha* streamed out. Hannah tried to catch a glimpse of black hats and bonnets through the bus windows and thought she saw something.

"Here they come!" Jake stepped forward, taking Hannah with him. "Mom!" Jake said, shaking her hand.

Hannah clung to his arm, forcing herself to step forward and shake Ida Byler's hand.

"Hannah," Jake's mom said, taking Hannah in her arms. "My, you are far along already. I guess I knew that, but seeing you makes it all the more real!"

Jake shook his dad's hand. "It's not something we've kept a secret from you."

"I guess seeing for myself is different from hearing about it," Ida repeated. "And I am so glad we could finally come to visit you. I told Uriah we had to come before the baby did because you'll soon be knee-deep in diapers and won't have time for two old people like us."

"You know we always have time for you, Mom," Jake said. "So did you have a good trip?"

"Really *gut*," Uriah said, stroking his long, white beard. "I must say these mountains make me feel young again. One forgets such beauty when one becomes old."

"You were out here for the wedding," Ida reminded. "You remember that, don't you?"

"Of course. I used to come hunting in these mountains too. Way back before I was married."

"Really?" Hannah said. "Jake did some hunting last year."

Jake's dad smiled. "Perhaps Jake can take me hunting for a day if there's enough time."

"I didn't know you used to hunt here," Jake said. "But I'm afraid the hunting season isn't for another month or so. Maybe you can come back then?"

Ida laughed. "No, we're not coming back for an old man to go tramping about the mountains and getting himself killed. We've come to see our family."

"Well," Uriah said. "I guess that takes care of my hunting plans."

"I guess it does. Well, let's get your luggage, and we can head to the cabin," Jake said, walking to the side of the bus. His dad followed, pointing out two suitcases stacked in the luggage compartment.

"I hope these fit in the buggy," Uriah said with a smile. "I told Mom not to pack so much, but she thinks we're going to visit the wilderness."

"Just ignore Uriah," Ida said, coming up to stand beside Hannah. "We'll be perfectly fine. I know about your cabin, and Jake's stinginess with modern things. I do think gas is allowed in your church, isn't it? But it's like Jake to try and save money. Hannah, you should have complained to him about those things a long time ago."

"Oh, but I like our cabin," Hannah said quickly. "And I don't mind heating water on the woodstove. I hope it won't bother you too much."

"We grew up poor," Ida said. "And it won't hurt us to live a little lower for one weekend."

"You make things sound terrible at their place," Uriah said as they reached the buggy.

"I didn't mean to," Ida said. "But it was you who brought up the subject."

"That's okay, Dad," Jake said. "I know I'm stingy, but I do have plans to build something better for Hannah soon. She deserves a nicer place."

"I'm sure she does," Ida said. "And is this your buggy?"

"No," Jake said. "We haven't purchased a surrey yet. This is borrowed from Betty, Hannah's aunt. It's their old one, and they said we could use it while you were visiting."

Jake's dad laughed as he climbed in, "And here I thought it might be another example of Jake's stinginess. Because when you do buy one, son, you really better get something in better shape than this one."

"I will, Dad, when the time comes."

"It looks like the time's not that far away," Uriah said, with a glance to Hannah in the backseat.

"We can still drive the two single buggies for awhile," Jake said. "Even after the baby arrives."

"I suppose so," Uriah said, settling in as Jake waited for the highway to clear before turning Mosey onto it.

"Are you seeing a midwife or a doctor by now?" Ida asked as Jake gently slapped the reins on Mosey's back.

"*Jah*, a midwife," Hannah said. "I was seeing a doctor, but I've settled for a midwife for the delivery. Her name is Mattie Esh, and she came down the other week for our first visit. I liked her. Although Jake hasn't met her yet."

"Then all is going well?"

"Mattie thought so, and I checked out fine on my last visit to Dr. Lisa. She will also be available if something goes wrong. I guess they work together well—the midwife and Dr. Lisa."

"Well, you certainly look okay," Ida said with approval as silence settled over the buggy, broken only by the steady beats of Mosey's hooves on the pavement.

After a few moments Hannah glanced out of the side door and stiffened as they approached the now open field.

Ida's gaze followed Hannah's. "Is this where they had those horrible tent meetings?"

Hannah nodded.

"It even killed the grass," Ida said, leaning out of the buggy for a better look.

"The tent sat there for almost a whole month," Hannah said. "But I guess the worst is over now."

"Did you lose a lot of people?"

"One family and a widow."

"Isn't that just awful?" Ida said. "Even one person lost to the world is a great tragedy."

"It is," Hannah said. "But it could have been worse. My sister Miriam's boyfriend didn't leave, even though his brother did. That had us worried."

"You don't think he's staying Amish just to get her? And then leave later? They do that sometimes, you know."

"I don't think so," Hannah said. "Dennis doesn't seem to be that type of man."

"I hope not," Ida said. "But you can't be too careful about such things.

Once they get the knot tied, men can get mighty strange ideas into their heads. But the worst thing is when they decide to get up and leave the church. I guess there's not much a woman can do in such situations."

"Rebecca is pretty broken up about their move," Hannah said. "That's Will Riley's wife, the young couple who's leaving."

"Is there a Mennonite church around here?"

"No. They're moving back to Idaho where Will's parents live. We expect them to go anytime now."

"Are they still coming to church?"

"So far, but Mary Keim, the widow, has already left for Kalispell. Her son is keeping the farm. He's the one who's dating my aunt Betty's daughter."

"Then the feelings can't be too bad among the community people. That's *gut* to hear."

"*Jah*, it is, and Jake had a lot to do with that."

"Jake did?" Ida said "Did he throw his support behind the bishop like he's supposed to?"

Hannah winced. "They did come to an agreement finally, but Jake's wisdom and conscience helped out a lot."

"I'm glad to hear that," Ida sighed. "I worry about Jake sometimes. He's always been the strange one of the children, and then he was ordained at such a young age. I wish it hadn't come so soon, but who can judge the ways of *Da Hah*?"

"I think he's been wonderful," Hannah replied. "He sure has been wonderful for me. I couldn't ask for a better husband."

Ida patted Hannah on her arm. "Then I shouldn't be telling my fears to you, as I suppose all mothers worry about their children."

"I'm going to try not to," Hannah said. "But I suppose it's going to be hard."

"Especially when they get older, and start running with the young folks. That's when it gets really hard."

"Jake said all of your family turned out okay, so you must have done something right."

"Only with grace from *Da Hah* did all turn out okay," Ida said. "It certainly can't be done any other way. And it seems like it takes more with each generation, but maybe that's just because I'm getting older."

"That's Betty's place there," Hannah said, motioning as they drove by. "My sister Miriam has been staying there all summer."

"Oh, that's the farm where your wedding was held. I thought it looked familiar."

Uriah turned around in the front seat. "What are you two women chattering about back there?"

"That's where Jake and Hannah's wedding was held," Ida said, pointing to the ranch. "Hannah's aunt Betty's place."

"Oh," Uriah turned around again. "It looks like a nice place."

Ida smiled at Hannah, taking her hand in hers. "I'm so glad Jake found such a *gut* wife. It does my old heart good to see him so happy."

"He's wonderful," Hannah said, feeling her face grow warm. *Now why on earth am I getting embarrassed about Jake? I'm married to him, after all.*

"And one who stands by him in the *faith*," Ida said, letting go of Hannah's hand. "That's something I wanted for all of my children. It's hard enough to live life the way it needs to be lived without a life's partner pulling the other way."

"I wouldn't want anything else for Jake," Hannah said. "I hope you know that."

Ida nodded, "But it's *gut* to hear you say that."

The next several minutes passed in silence and then Hannah said, "We're almost home."

Jake pulled back on half the reins and with a rattle of gravel they turned up the road toward the cabin.

Ida was looking out of the window toward the mountains ahead of them. "Do you ever get used to such beauty all around you?"

"I haven't yet," Hannah said.

"They look a little scary though," Ida said soberly. "I think one weekend will be enough for me."

"I don't think Jake will ever want to live anywhere else."

"I heard that," Jake said, not turning around in the front seat.

"Well, I don't think you would," Hannah said. "You love it out here, don't you?"

"It's much better than the flat country in Iowa, that's for sure," Jake said.

Uriah laughed heartily. "I can see your point, but I'll take farming country any day. I like working in the open fields without high hills looking down on you all day."

"There's our cabin, Mom," Jake said, slowing Mosey down to a walk. "And Mr. Brunson—the man we've told you about—lives up the road a bit further."

"Well, it looks cozy," Ida said. "But it could be a little bigger, that's for sure."

"I'm ahead of you on that," Jake said. "The plans for our new house are in the living room right now."

"We'll want to look at them," Ida asserted.

"They're very nice," Hannah said. "I didn't tell Jake exactly what I wanted, and he still came pretty close to what I would have chosen."

With a jerk Mosey came to a stop by the barn. Uriah jumped down. Hannah climbed out on her side, waiting behind the buggy until Ida joined her. Together they walked toward the cabin while the men unhitched the horse.

Forty

By the time the Sunday meeting was over and the four Bylers were settled back in the cabin after church, the rays of the warm afternoon sun were shining brightly through the front cabin window.

The weekend visit had been short, Hanna thought as she walked into the living room with heaping bowls of fluffy white popcorn for Jake and Uriah. Behind her Ida followed with freshly squeezed lemonade made with cold water from the spring. Hannah gave Uriah a bowl, and he took it with a big smile on his face. "Now is this as *gut* as Iowa popcorn?" he asked.

"I don't know," Hannah said as Ida passed him a cup of lemonade. "I guess you'll have to taste it and see."

Uriah took a long sip, a satisfied look spreading across his face, "At least that's *gut* stuff. The taste must come from your spring water because the lemons looked the same to me."

"Now you see why I don't mind the lack of a refrigerator."

"I do see," Uriah said. "I think I'd like to move out here myself. I'd love to live with a spring in my backyard. What do you think, Ida? Will you join me?"

"Stop talking such nonsense!" Ida said, returning from the kitchen with two more glasses. "You are a farm boy at heart, and nothing is going to change that."

Uriah laughed. "I think I could get used to this country after only my second time here, and that's saying a lot."

"Well, it *is* a nice community," Ida said. "Now you sit down, Hannah, and I'll get our popcorn bowls."

"And bring the big bowl back with you," Uriah called to Ida's retreating back. "This is as *gut* as Iowa popcorn."

"So what did you think of the people you met today, Dad?" Jake asked while slowly eating his popcorn.

"Your Mom and I had a long talk with Bishop John. He had only *gut* things to say about you, and I can't say how happy that makes both of us."

"Jake is a wonderful preacher," Hannah said, not looking at Jake as he shook his head.

"Sometimes that's not *gut* though," Uriah said. "But I was glad we got to hear you preach today, son. I didn't hear anything I disagreed with."

Jake nodded but said nothing. Hannah thought he seemed a little nervous today, and this explained it.

"You still did good," Hannah whispered, reaching over to squeeze Jake's hand.

A grateful smile played on his face.

"Did I hear you tell them we talked with Bishop John?" Ida asked, coming in with the popcorn bowls.

"*Jah,*" Uriah said, nodding.

"Did you tell Jake about what we asked him?"

Uriah took another handful of popcorn and before eating it said, "No, and perhaps we shouldn't even bring this up with Jake. He's not responsible for church doctrine. Surely you know that."

"No, he's not," Ida said, "but it sounds like he has a lot of influence around here, and I already wrote to him about it, so it's not like he doesn't know how we feel. And I'd really like to know how Jake explains this assurance of salvation that Bishop John claims we can have."

"Mom, you know it's not my place to instruct you and Dad," Jake said. "I'd rather you asked Bishop John your questions."

"Then we'll not count it as instructions," Ida said. "Let's just hear you explain this thing. How can we know *Da Hah*'s mind when it comes to our salvation?"

"Mom, please," Jake said, his hand on his bowl of popcorn.

"Someone just drove in," Uriah said, his voice low.

Jake jumped to his feet. "It's Mr. Brunson. I wonder what he wants on a Sunday afternoon?"

"I still want my question answered," Ida said. "But I can wait until the man leaves."

"I should think so," Uriah said as Jake went to open the door.

"Am I intruding?" Mr. Brunson's voice reached the inside of the cabin.

"Not at all," Jake said. "My parents are here. Why don't you come in and meet them?"

"I'd like that," Mr. Brunson said, stepping inside. "I so enjoyed meeting Hannah's parents last year."

"This is my mom," Jake said, "Ida Byler. And my dad, Uriah. This is only their second time visiting Montana, and Dad already wants to move here."

"Then they can have my place," Mr. Brunson said, shaking their hands. "How are you folks? It's great to meet you. Hannah and Jake have been such good friends during the time they've lived here. I can't tell you what great people they are."

"That's good to hear," Uriah said. "The Lord wishes all of us to have a good testimony to those who are without."

Mr. Brunson laughed. "I don't think I'll be on the outside much longer."

"Oh," Uriah raised his eyebrows. "Are you thinking of joining the Amish?"

"Please have a seat, Mr. Brunson," Jake said, offering him his chair.

"I really can't stay long," Mr. Brunson said. "But thanks anyway."

Hannah held her breath, watching Mr. Brunson's face, waiting for his answer to Uriah's question.

"Well, it's like this. I *almost* got to join the Amish," Mr. Brunson replied. "But the good bishop turned me down. Not that I have any hard feelings, as the Lord worked things out splendidly between Mary and me."

"Mary?" Ida gasped. "Is that the Mary who left the church? The widow? You have doings with her?"

Mr. Brunson paused. "I guess Jake and Hannah haven't told you?"

Jake shook his head slightly.

"I didn't mean for Jake and Hannah to keep this a secret," Mr. Brunson said. "Or is this one of those Amish ways I haven't learned about yet?"

"We just didn't come across the subject," Jake said.

"I guess you know that we work together at the furniture shop," Mr. Brunson said, glancing at Uriah, who nodded.

"Mary's leaving has been hard on all of us," Jake said, clearing his throat.

"I imagine so," Mr. Brunson said. "I guess that means I have a lot of explaining to do."

Uriah cleared his throat loudly, "Do I understand you correctly that you are taking one of the Amish women out to the *Englisha* world?"

"No," Mr. Brunson said. "I am joining the Mennonite church with her."

"I see," Uriah said. "That's a little better, but is that something a man of your obvious character should be doing? Aren't there women in your world who could be your wife?"

"Uriah," Ida gasped. "Please don't speak such words."

"It's okay," Mr. Brunson said, a look of joy crossing his face. "Mary has been a gift from the Lord as certainly as my first wife, Bernice, was. Not since her passing have I felt such love for a woman."

"But this Mary is Amish," Ida said, shifting slightly in her chair.

"I must say it looked impossible," Mr. Brunson said, the joy still glowing on his face. "But the Lord worked things out okay. Let's just say I'm one happy man in my old age."

"Well, then, we wouldn't want to speak against such a thing," Uriah said. "And anyway, this is a local church matter."

"Jake has been wonderful to work with," Mr. Brunson said. "But I really don't want to interfere with your afternoon any longer than I already have. Mary has been wanting me to stop by and tell you the news, but I haven't gotten around to it. I could have said something to Jake at the shop, but I wanted to speak with both of you, Hannah and Jake."

"*Jah*?" Hannah said, leaning forward on her chair. "Good news?"

"We've set the wedding date for next month, and I'll be moving to Kalispell to be with her. We've already found a place and are closing on it next week. Mary said she wants to send you a wedding invitation, but she doesn't wish to make things more uncomfortable for you than they already are."

"I'd love to attend," Hannah said, catching a glimpse of the look on Ida's face. "But of course we can't, so tell Mary I wish her all the best with her new life. She is such a *gut* woman."

"Yes, she surely is," Mr. Brunson said. "Now, I really must be going." Turning to Uriah and Ida, he said, "You two have a safe trip back home, and the offer still stands about my place."

"I don't think we're moving to Montana," Ida said quickly. "Uriah is very much a farm boy."

"He looks like a farm boy," Mr. Brunson said, glancing back as he opened the cabin door. "Sorry again to interrupt your Sunday afternoon."

Jake followed him outside, and their voices rose and fell as they continued to talk on the porch.

"An interesting character, that man is," Uriah said, resuming his popcorn eating.

"But he stole an Amish woman," Ida said. "That might be interesting, but it's not very nice."

"I think Mary was quite willing," Hannah said. "She went to the tent meetings on her own, and they met up there. That's the story at least, and I guess they think it is *Da Hah*'s doings—His way of getting them together."

"People deceive themselves in all kinds of ways," Ida said. "It sounds unlikely to me."

"Ah, let the old people enjoy each other," Uriah said. "At least Mary's not leaving the Amish for the *Englisha* world."

"Is that what you're going to say when one of our children leaves for the Mennonites?" Ida asked, an edge in her voice.

"I didn't say it wasn't a serious matter," Uriah said. "But it's a local church matter here, not anything we have a say in."

As Jake entered, Ida said, "Now, I want an answer to my question. Don't think I've forgotten about it. Sit back down and start talking."

"You could at least remind Jake what the question is," Uriah said. "He's probably forgotten."

Jake shook his head. "I remember. And I don't know that I understand everything, but I did think of something the other day that might help."

"I want you to explain the verse in Romans," Ida said. "Where the apostle says we are saved by hope, but hope that is seen is not hope. For how can we continue to hope for what we already have?"

"*Jah*," Uriah said, nodding solemnly. "That's a hard question, and one that I've never seen the answer to. It seems to me that if we can know we are saved, then there is no more reason to hope for it."

"Don't you think Christ has brought salvation to us?" Jake asked.

"That's what the bishop tells us," Uriah said. "But if He has then we don't need to hope for it."

"It's best not to make the Scriptures say what they don't say," Ida said. "I think the apostle wrote very clearly in Romans, and there is no way around what he says."

Jake countered, "But Jesus said that the Spirit of the Lord was upon Him to preach the gospel to the poor, to heal the brokenhearted, to deliver the captives, to give sight to the blind, and to set at liberty those who are bruised. Doesn't that sound like salvation has come?"

"*Jah*," Uriah said, stroking his beard. "But I do not like to set a Scripture against another Scripture like two bulls fighting each other. The apostle said what he said."

"I'd say it's pretty plain," Ida added.

"I hope you don't think me out of my place," Jake said, his face pained. "But perhaps you're not understanding properly what the apostle is speaking of."

"I don't see how it could be better said. We are saved by hope," Uriah said, taking a deep breath.

"But what is being saved?" Jake asked. "I think the apostle said what it was a few verses earlier, and it's not the spirit, it's the body. When Christ came, He brought us spiritual salvation, but our body isn't saved yet. If it would be, we never would get sick or have temptations anymore. That is what is saved by hope someday."

"He talks like a Mennonite," Ida said. "Jake, who has been filling your head with these thoughts?"

"I wasn't trying to instruct you, Mom, or you either, Dad, but you asked the question."

"*Jah*, it does say that," Uriah said, still stroking his beard. "But I have always thought this was a very dangerous doctrine."

"Then don't go falling for it," Ida said, getting up to refill his lemonade glass. "Now that I've heard your answer—if that is indeed your answer— maybe it's time we talked about something else."

"Since we're leaving tomorrow you'd better start talking fast," Uriah said with a smile. "That is unless you plan to move back here with me. That Mr. Brunson has offered us the sale of his place."

"If I didn't know you were teasing I'd leave right now," Ida said, then softened by adding, "But I have to admit Montana is a wonderful place to live."

Forty-One

Hannah remembered that the hardest part of carrying a baby was the waiting. Even with the first pregnancy and the tragedy of losing the baby, she had learned that patience was very much part of the process.

The few weeks since Jake's parents had visited had flown by with little to set the days apart. Now that her time was drawing closer, Hannah's waiting seemed all the harder.

The late morning found Hannah waiting by the front window of the cabin, glancing repeatedly down the graveled lane toward the road. If the midwife didn't come soon, there wouldn't be time to get to the bus station in Libby before her mother's arrival. Seeing Mattie yesterday would have fit her schedule much better, but the midwife said in her letter that today was the only day she could come.

Hannah glanced around the small cabin. It was spotlessly clean. She had tried to keep it that way since Jake's parents had been here. Yesterday's quick cleaning was all that had been necessary to keep it in good order. At least there was much to be thankful for—a clean house. Things could have turned out quite badly with Ida and Uriah's visit, but it hadn't. Jake's parents had left on the bus with big smiles on their faces, and Jake seemed much happier now whenever he talked about them.

A small cloud of dust rose in the distance, and Hannah went out on the porch and waited.

The midwife's car came to a halt at the end of the walk, and the woman got out of the car with her large bag.

"I'm not late, am I?" Mattie asked.

"Not really," Hannah said making sure she smiled. "It's just that I have to meet my mom at the bus station at noon. I think I can still make it."

"Oh my, how rushed everything is these days. It seems like I can't keep up anymore. But it's wonderful that your mother is coming to visit. She's a bit early for the baby though. You're not quite ready yet."

"She's coming for my sister Miriam's wedding in two weeks."

Mattie raised her eyebrows. "Well, in your condition I hope you're not having a big part in it or anything."

Hannah laughed. "No, not if Jake has anything to say about it. He's quite worried about me, so I suppose I'll sit and watch everyone else do all the fussing around."

"Has the stress been getting to you?"

"Not really. Not the wedding anyway. Jake's parents were here for a visit. That was stressful enough, but we made it."

"Ah, the in-laws, well, sit down on the couch so I can look you over."

Hannah lowered herself down slowly. "I'm glad his parents came. I really am. They're wonderful people, and Jake needed to talk some things through with them."

"Then we'll count it a blessing in disguise. How's your eating coming along? Any change in appetite?"

"No, not really, unless it's *less* of an appetite. Nothing much fits down there. I think it's going to be a big boy."

The midwife laughed. "Did Dr. Lisa ever do an ultrasound?"

"No, it's just been my guess from the way the *bobli's* carrying on."

"They can get a little rowdy, both boys and the girls, so that doesn't tell us much. Are you still comfortable having the birth at home? It's your first time, after all."

"I think so. Dr. Lisa said we could contact her if necessary. You're not expecting any problems with the birth are you?"

"No," Mattie said. "Everything looks as it should. I'd like to leave you some herbal tea though. It's not a miracle worker of course, but it can help prepare your body for the hard work ahead."

"I'm glad our child will be born in the cabin."

"Idealistic, are you?" Mattie said with a grin. "My guess is the stars in your eyes will grow dim once the contractions start. Childbirth is no picnic."

"I'll be ready. In fact, I *am* ready."

"You'll be fine, Hannah. The baby's still turned right, seems healthy, and has a steady heartbeat. You don't have any excess swelling in your feet."

"Just in the middle section," Hannah said, laughing. "I must say it feels *gut* though, in a strange way. It reminds me that I'm bringing a child into the world."

"Yes, it's a great privilege to bear a child, and a home birth is the best, if the Lord so wills. But we must not tempt Him with our foolishness."

"I'll try not to. I'll be honest with how I feel."

"Just be sure you don't overdo it with all the community activities. Perhaps your mom will calm things down for you while she's here."

"She will only do me *gut*. I know that much."

"Do you want me to help with hitching up the horse for your trip into town?" Mattie offered as she put her instruments into her bag.

"Jake already has Mosey's harness on, but thanks."

"I'll see you soon then."

Hannah nodded and followed Mattie outside. She waved goodbye, and then walked to the barn and pushed open the barn door. Mosey stretched his nose out to nuzzle her hand.

"I didn't bring anything, silly boy. We have to go to town today. Mom's coming. Isn't that just too wonderful to be true?"

Mosey flicked his ears forward and stared out the barn door.

"Come," Hannah said, untying the rope from the stable door. "We have to go. We might already be late."

Leading the horse outside, she held the shafts up with one hand, swinging the horse in with the other. The maneuver left her gasping for air.

"I don't think I can do this much longer," Hannah admitted with a laugh. "At least not until after the baby comes. I don't think you'll mind if you get to stay home for awhile."

With the tugs fastened and the lines thrown in the front, Hannah climbed in, taking a moment to settle comfortably on the buggy seat.

"Get-up," she called to Mosey and slapped the reins. He jerked his head and took off at a slow trot. At the end of the lane, Hannah held him at a stop until the highway was clear.

As she passed Betty's place, Hannah slowed down. There were no *Englisha* vehicles parked in the barnyard, so Miriam must not be busy with the horses. Should she stop and ask Miriam to come along? No, even if Miriam wanted to go along there really wasn't room for all three of them and her mom's luggage. Changing to Betty's surrey wasn't an option. Her mother's bus might be pulling into the depot any moment. She clucked to Mosey to increase his pace again.

Behind her Hannah heard her sister's voice call her name above the beat of Mosey's hooves. She turned to look back and saw Miriam standing on Betty's front porch waving at her. Quickly, Hannah pulled back on the reins, bringing Mosey to a sliding stop. The horse shook his head and lowered it in disgust.

"Sorry," Hannah said. "But I think Miriam does want to go along."

"Hannah!" Miriam's voice reached across the lawn, and Hannah leaned out of the buggy door. Miriam came racing toward her, tying her bonnet's strings as she came.

"Miriam, I don't know if we have room for you and for Mom and her luggage."

"We'll throw it on top," Miriam said as she quickly climbed in. "We're closed today. I had to insist, and I don't care what Betty says about it. We can't keep up this pace with Mom coming. At least *I* can't keep up this pace with the wedding so close and so much to do. It's my wedding, and I only get one in my lifetime. At least I hope there's only one."

"Is Betty trying to squeeze the last riding fee out of the summer?"

"You could say that, and it's gone on long enough. I've made plenty of money to pay for my room and board, and lots besides that. Betty has no reason to complain."

"Sounds like it's a good thing Mom is coming. You and Betty might drive each other out of the house before the wedding." Hannah snapped the reins a bit to get Mosey started again.

"I can always come up to your place."

Hannah glanced sideways at Miriam.

"I'm just teasing. Betty gets on my nerves, but she's letting me use her barn for the wedding, and for that I will always be grateful."

"What if the weather turns cold? Will you move the wedding inside then?"

"No," Miriam said. "We're having it in the barn even if the snow's flying, which it won't be because it's my wedding day. Betty's been trying to scare me half to death with her predictions of an early winter, but

I'm having none of it. *Da Hah* brought me out here by His mighty hand and is giving me a wonderful man in Dennis. Why would He make it snow on my wedding day?"

"I don't know. *Da Hah* doesn't always explain Himself."

"Now *you're* trying to scare me."

"No, I'm not. But I do agree that it's not likely to snow. Jake said there's talk among the long-term locals of an Indian summer. I suppose they know more about the subject then Betty does."

"There," Miriam sighed deeply, settling back into the seat. "I knew you'd make me feel better. And when I see Mom, I'll be floating above the clouds."

"So is everything going well with you and Dennis?"

"Of course it is," Miriam sat up straight. "What do you mean? Have you heard anything?"

"How would I hear anything that you don't already know? Don't be silly."

Miriam sighed deeply. "I can't imagine Dennis ever doing anything wrong. He's so wonderful."

Hannah laughed. "You do have your head in the clouds."

"I know. I've had it there ever since I came to Montana."

"I hope you haven't forgotten the real reason you came," Hannah said, glancing at Miriam.

"Nope, I haven't," Miriam said with a smile.

"Would you take care of the baby if he came next week before the wedding?"

"What!" Miriam shouted so loudly that Mosey jumped forward and Hannah clutched the reins. "The baby's coming that soon?"

"You don't have to scare the wits out of me," Hannah said, bringing Mosey back to his usual lazy trot. "No, he's not coming that soon. I was teasing."

"Hannah, are you *sure* you're teasing?" Miriam searched Hannah's eyes. "Did the midwife tell you something this morning?"

"Oh, so you do remember I was seeing the midwife?"

"Hannah, stop this! Yes, I do remember. Are you all right?"

"Yes, of course I am. And so is the baby."

Miriam leaned back in her seat. "And is Jake still being nice to you?"

Hannah laughed. "Of course he is."

"Oh, Hannah," Miriam groaned. "I want you to promise me you won't have the baby until *after* the wedding. And I promise you I'll take very *gut* care of your baby. I'll kiss him every day and then some."

Hannah laughed again. "I can't promise you that!"

Miriam glanced ahead as they neared the depot. "Do you suppose that is Mom's bus up ahead?"

"It is!" Hannah gasped, slapping the reins so hard that Mosey lunged ahead. They rattled across the parking lot and pulled up beside the bus with a flourish. Their mother was standing beside it with two other passengers, her suitcase by her side, a happy smile on her face.

"What have we here?" she asked as Miriam and Hannah climbed down from the buggy and ran up to her, leaving Mosey standing with the reins limp across his back.

"Oh Mom!" both young women said together, wrapping their mom on each side with a hug.

"My, my," Kathy said. "What a welcome! And you come flying in the parking lot like I'm the Queen of Sheba."

"You are," Hannah said. "And it's so *gut* to see you."

"And you too," Kathy said. "How are things going for you, Miriam? I assume the wedding is still on?"

"Don't start that, Mom," Miriam said. "Betty and Hannah have already been giving me fits. Dennis is the most wonderful, handsome, godly man I have ever met."

"It sounds like you have it bad," Kathy said with a smile.

"What did Dad say about you coming two weeks early?" Hannah asked, taking her mom by the arm and leading her toward the buggy.

"He's fine with it. He'll be coming out with the van load next week," Kathy said. "So how is the baby?"

"I just had a meeting with the midwife this morning, and everything's fine. Isn't that wonderful?"

"It is," Kathy said. "You'd better get me to Betty's place quickly. I'm sure the poor woman is half sick with worry from all the work that needs to be done."

"She's almost in bed," Miriam said, walking up with her mother's suitcase.

"You don't say! Hannah, drive that old horse of yours as fast as you can."

"I'm just teasing, Mom," Miriam admitted. "Just relax. Everything is under control."

Forty-Two

Hannah walked toward the kitchen to check out the noise that had awakened her. The sun was not yet up and bright moonlight streamed in through the front window of the cabin, illuminating the living room. Hannah held her hand to her forehead, now throbbing with the warning of a coming headache.

When she arrived in the kitchen, she saw Jake at the woodstove. "What are you doing in my kitchen?" she asked as she plopped into a chair, her hand still on her forehead.

"You've been working yourself way too hard, and I decided to fix breakfast," Jake said, puttering over a pan on the stove. For some reason he looked older this morning—wiser and disgustingly cheerful.

"You haven't fixed breakfast since your bachelor days." Hannah groaned. "And who knows how it tasted then?" she added.

Jake smiled broadly, stirring the pot of oatmeal. "Then sample my fare, dear lady, and tell me you detest my sweet offerings."

"Something has gone to your head," Hannah said as Jake dipped out a bowl of oatmeal and set it in front of her.

"Perhaps it's love that's gone to my head—on the day of Miriam's wedding," Jake said. "Now eat while I fix the toast."

"I could eat three eggs, if you can make them."

"Coming right up!" Jake said without turning around. "That sounds more like it."

"What's the weather like? If we have snow Miriam will be so disappointed."

Jake didn't even glance out the window. "I was outside an hour ago, and I'd say Montana has a beautiful Indian summer day prepared especially for your sister's wedding."

"That's a relief!" Hannah said, taking a second bite of oatmeal and feeling her headache slipping away.

"How are you doing?" Jake asked, turning from the stove.

"I'll be okay, I guess. You'd better watch the eggs. Don't let them burn. I'm really hungry."

"I can make eggs with my eyes closed," Jake said, still looking at her—now with a frown. "Hey, you don't look so good. Do you think the *bobli* is coming today?"

"Not on the day of Miriam's wedding. He wouldn't dare."

"No, I didn't think so. I'm just trying to cheer you up because you really do look tired."

"I don't have time to be tired. Not today."

"Then the eggs will help," Jake said. A minute later he slid them onto Hannah's plate and bent over to kiss her on the cheek.

"We'll have to leave soon," Hannah said, accepting his kiss.

"*Jah*, so let's eat. I'm starved." Jake brought his already full plate over and sat down at the table. They bowed their heads in silent prayer. Hannah finished her eggs before Jake was done and left for the bedroom to change. Jake finished his breakfast, quickly washed the few dishes, and then went out and hitched Mosey to the buggy. He tied him up at the hitching post before he came back in. Minutes later he had his white shirt on and his new black suit jacket slipped over his broad shoulders.

"There," he said. "Now we're ready to leave."

"You look handsome enough to get married today yourself," Hannah said playfully as they left the bedroom.

Jake laughed and turned around to give Hannah a careful hug, "And you look like you are a happily married woman. That makes me feel very *gut*."

Hannah held his hand as they walked out the cabin door, "I expect this will be my last time out before the baby comes." She groaned and hugged her bulging waist.

Jake helped her into the buggy and then untied Mosey. He climbed in and softly said "Get-up" to get Mosey on the way.

"At least we don't have far to go," Jake said. "The wedding could be at the other end of the community."

"Do you think Mary and Mr. Brunson will be there?"

"Miriam invited them, didn't she?"

"*Jah*, but Mary might not want to come if she thinks it will make people uncomfortable."

"I'm sure she's welcome."

"I hope she feels so, and it would be so *gut* to see her again."

As Betty's place came into view, Jake said, "It looks like we're early. There are only a few buggies here."

At the front door, Betty's oldest daughter Kendra opened it with her boyfriend, Henry Keim, standing behind her.

"Good morning," Kendra said as Jake and Hannah came up the walk. "It's such wonderful weather. Miriam is nearly sick with happiness."

Henry grinned broadly over Kendra's shoulder.

"Is your mom coming?" Hannah asked Henry.

He nodded.

"I'm so glad," Hannah said. "I was hoping she'd come."

"Miriam's upstairs with your mom," Kendra said. "I'll go tell her you're here. She's had her wedding dress on since five o'clock. Mom told her it was much too early, but Miriam was too excited to listen."

Before Kendra could go, the stair door opened. Hannah drew in her breath as Miriam stepped down, followed by their mom. Miriam's dark-blue dress seemed to float out from the stairs.

"Well, what do you think?" their mom asked, stepping off to the side.

"Oh my!" Hannah said. "It turned out so lovely. It's as wonderful as it could be."

"And the weather," Miriam said, beaming. "Can you believe such a wonderful gift from *Da Hah*? And to think I once thought I'd never get married."

"Things do change," their mom said. "Now be careful. You'd better come in and sit in the bedroom until it's time to go out."

"What about me?" Dennis said from the living room door, a big grin on his face.

"You look okay," Kathy said, running her eyes up and down his new black suit. "Just don't make too much noise."

"Mom," Miriam said, going to stand beside Dennis, her eyes shining, "I'm keeping him with me."

"Then sit on the couch and just wait," Kathy said, guiding them both toward the living room.

"I wonder if my wedding will be like this," Kendra said. And then she slowly turned red as she caught Henry's eye. "I didn't mean anything by that."

"I know," Henry said, taking her hand. "But I'm sure our wedding will be just as *gut*, I promise you."

A deep blush spread up Kendra's neck.

Hannah left them gazing into each other's eyes. It wasn't that long ago when Jake would have made her turn just as red if he had said something like that.

The next hour was filled with last-minute details, with Betty and Kathy scurrying from the kitchen to the barn and back to the living room. Finally, the time came when Betty came in and said, "More people are starting to arrive. Dennis's cousin and his girlfriend had better not be late. We can't start until all of the bridal party is here."

"Betty, they're just now arriving," Miriam whispered in excitement, having stood up to watch out the living room window.

Betty sighed. "Will I *ever* be glad when this day is over!"

A few minutes later Betty once again dashed into the living room with an announcement. "It's time! The preachers have already started walking in."

Kathy jumped up and said, "Okay, now line up and start walking."

"And no one fall down going across the lawn!" Betty added. "Steve mowed it yesterday, so there's no excuse."

With that, the wedding party followed as Betty and Kathy led the way to the barn.

"It is a lovely day, isn't it?" Kathy quietly said to Betty, who nodded. People were watching them already, turning their heads to see the bridal couple, who stopped just outside the barn door while the others went in. Kathy motioned Hannah toward her seat. With a grateful sigh, Hannah sat down and slowly glanced around.

Jake was sitting on the ministers' bench. Her dad and Steve sat straight across from them, her dad with a slight grin on his face. Steve was looking around hurriedly, as if looking for any cobwebs on the barn beams that might have been missed. Everything had been whitewashed last week and then swept out again last night. Hannah's aching arms testified to her efforts on behalf of a clean barn floor.

To Hannah's left she caught the eye of Mary Keim, who smiled and looked quite plain in her Amish dress. She must have decided to forgo her new Mennonite clothing out of respect for Miriam. Mary had always been careful about the feelings of others, so her modest dress was no surprise.

A soft sound of moving cloth on hard benches swept through the crowd, as everyone turned to watch as Dennis's cousin and his girlfriend came into the barn. Dennis and Miriam were next, with Kendra and Henry following behind. From her outside seat, Hannah didn't have to crane her neck to see that Miriam looked radiantly happy.

Dennis's cousin and girlfriend took their places in the middle of the six designated chairs set up across from each other, waiting until the others were in place. Then together the six sat down in perfect unison. Hannah smiled. It was a wedding just like Miriam had wanted. At her wedding, one of Jake's brothers had sat down too quickly, but she hadn't cared.

With a loud voice, the song leader gave out the first number, and the singing began. The preachers got up and walked toward the house with Miriam and Dennis following behind. Hannah watched them go, holding her breath. Miriam had been quite confident that no one would fall down on the lawn, but if someone *was* to fall down, that was the place.

The line disappeared into the house with no mishaps, and Hannah breathed easier. They would soon be back from the last-minute marriage instructions, and shortly thereafter they would be man and wife. It was strange to think of Miriam as a married woman, but then perhaps Miriam had thought the same thing about her. Well, if things turned out as well for Dennis and Miriam as they had for her and Jake, they would be fine.

The singing rose and fell, echoing off the barn ceiling. Eventually Dennis and Miriam appeared again, followed ten minutes later by the line of ministers. Jake got up to speak first and told the familiar story of Abraham sending his servant to look for Isaac's wife. Hannah listened to the rise and fall of Jake's voice, feeling the joy it brought her. He was her husband, even if he was a preacher, and soon she would do for him what no one else in the community could do. She would have his *bobli*. They would be a family, just Jake and her and the *bobli*. In the years ahead, if *Da Hah* willed, many more children would follow.

Jake concluded his remarks and sat down. Minister Mose asked everyone to stand as he read the Scriptures. Bishop John had the main sermon, lasting over an hour, in which time the joy on Miriam's face kept increasing. Hannah thought Miriam looked ready to cry when Bishop John asked her and Dennis to come forward and join hands.

Hannah didn't move on the hard bench until the questions had been asked, answered, and Bishop John said they were now man and wife in the eyes of *Da Hah* and man. Nothing but death could ever part them.

When the last song was sung, the bridal party stood, and Dennis led the way into the house. Hannah followed with Kathy and Betty.

As they entered the living room, Miriam gave all of them big hugs, holding Hannah the longest.

"None of this would have happened without you," Miriam whispered into her sister's ear.

"Shhh…," Hannah whispered back. "It was but *Da Hah*'s grace. That's all."

"The men are setting up the benches now and the corner table is ready," Betty announced. "We're taking the food out right away. Dennis and Miriam need to go first…so let's go."

Dennis took Miriam's hand and led her back out the kitchen door and across the lawn.

"They are such a wonderful couple," Kathy said.

"I know," Betty agreed. "But don't go telling them. It would go to their heads."

Forty-Three

Hannah tossed and turned in bed. She was swimming in a great lake. All around her huge waves came rushing in, washing over her head, leaving her gasping for air. Around her stomach a giant creature had grabbed her and was squeezing at regular intervals until she cried out in agony.

"Hannah, Hannah!"

Jake's soft voice seemed to come from a great distance. She awoke to his hand gently shaking her shoulder in the darkness. Hannah clutched his arm, wiping her hand across her wet forehead.

"You were dreaming," Jake said. "Is everything okay?"

"I don't know." Hannah groaned as pain crept across her body again. After a moment she said, "I think the *bobli*'s coming!"

"The *bobli*!" Jake leaped out of bed and groped for his clothing. "They don't come quickly, do they?"

Something clattered across the darkened floor. Silence followed until Jake lit a match with a soft scratch and transferred the flame to the kerosene lamp. Dim light flickered on the bedroom walls of the cabin, and Jake's anxious face came into focus.

"You know what to do," Hannah said. "Go call Mattie from Mr. Brunson's cabin. Mary left us the key above the sink. Then let Betty and Miriam know."

"Okay," Jake said. "But should I disturb Betty and Miriam in the middle of the night like this?"

"*Jah*," Hannah said. "Betty said she wanted to know, and Miriam said she would come whatever the hour. It was her idea, and she wants to be here. I was so hoping it wouldn't happen at nighttime."

"How close are you?" Jake asked, already at the bedroom door.

"You'd better hurry!" Hannah groaned.

Jake's running feet faded away followed by another crash. Moments later the front door opened with a creak and slammed shut. Hannah lay listening, trying to breathe slowly. The pain was dull now but waiting like a phantom in her body, ready to leap out of the shadows again.

"Please help me, God," she whispered. "I'm all alone now…and yet I know You are with me."

The pain came again, and Hannah clutched her hands tightly together. It seemed harder this time, and very close to the last stab. Dimly in the distance she heard the sound of Jake's driving horse galloping toward Mr. Brunson's cabin.

Surely Jake would be able to get in. He had the key, and Mary said they were keeping the phone connected until Hannah's baby came.

Would Mattie be able to drive down in time? She was only an hour away, so surely she could. Mattie had said confidently that she had never been late for a birth. Hannah watched the flickering light of the kerosene lamp on the cabin walls for long moments and then climbed out of bed. Walking was *gut*, wasn't it? And it might calm her fears.

After pacing for a few minutes, Hannah stopped at the bedroom window and looked out over the starry sweep of the night sky. It was so clear tonight, almost as if one could see straight into the heavens. Was *Da Hah* near? *Jah*, He was. Had he not been with them over these past few months?

With a faint rattle on the gravel, Jake's buggy came down from Mr. Brunson's cabin, driving fast, his lower lights on, his form dimly visible inside the darkened conveyance. He didn't stop but continued on to Betty's. He must have been successful in reaching the midwife or he would have stopped in to tell her.

Hannah watched until the buggy disappeared on the main road. Another spasm of pain gripped her. Clasping her hands over her swollen stomach, she bent over the bed until the pain passed. She straightened and collected herself, pushing the fallen strands of hair away from her face. She walked out to the living room, taking the kerosene lamp with her. Its light threw wild shadows on the wall, flickering across the rocking chair and Jake's little desk in the corner. Hannah paused, a smile creeping across her face. The moment of the *bobli*'s arrival had finally come. The next few hours might be filled with pain and agony, but *Da Hah* was with her, Jake loved her, and they would soon be a complete family—something no one could ever take away from them. Not even death could completely erase what *Da Hah* had done.

Standing at the living room window, Hannah looked out across the darkened landscape to the mountains, their ridges outlined by the stars. How beautiful they were tonight. They had seen her fears, but they had also seen her love.

The spasm caught her by surprise, and Hannah cried out, the sound echoing off the cabin walls. She clutched the edge of the rocker, holding on until it passed.

"Dear God, help me," she prayed. "Help me be strong. Help me be worthy of Jake's love and the wonderful *bobli* You are about to give us."

Hannah slowly let go of the rocker and walked into the kitchen. The light of the kerosene lamp reached just inside the doorway, revealing a bowl lying on the floor. So this was what Jake knocked over in his rush to find the key to Mr. Brunson's cabin. She awkwardly bent over to pick up the bowl and return it to the counter. Tomorrow it could be put in its rightful place. Tonight more important things were at hand.

Returning to the bedroom, Hannah lay down and gave up the idea of more walking. The spasms seemed to be coming quicker, and she clutched the bed quilt through them, trying not to cry out.

It seemed like ages before the faint sound of buggy wheels came up the driveway again. So Jake must have made it to Betty's and was returning, but it was Mattie she really needed.

The cabin door creaked on its hinges and quick steps came toward the bedroom. *It's not Jake's tread, so it must be Betty's,* Hannah noted.

With a great bustle of energy her aunt burst in. "My, my!" Betty said. "A *bobli* on the way and the midwife nowhere in sight. What is wrong with that woman? I do declare, you can't depend on anyone anymore."

"Where's Jake?" Hannah asked, attempting a smile.

"He drove on to let Miriam know. Why, I don't understand. There's nothing the girl can do tonight anyway, and she might as well stay home with her husband."

"Miriam wanted to know," Hannah groaned.

"I declare," Betty said again, taking Hannah's hand. "Now tell me, how are you doing. Are the pains coming strong yet?"

Hannah nodded.

"Oh my!" Betty said, letting go of Hannah's hand. "This baby is going to come before the midwife gets here, I just know it. Now I'm here and don't know what on earth to do for you. I suppose I shouldn't have come, as useless as I am at a time like this."

"I'm glad you came."

"You need a midwife, not me."

"She'll be here before long."

"I hope so," Betty said. "This is nerve-wracking." She jumped up to look out the window. When she saw nothing, she returned to the side of Hannah's bed. When Hannah yelped in pain, Betty ran to the window again, but the gravel lane was empty.

Finally Hannah said, "I think I heard something in the lane."

Betty walked quickly over to the window.

"It's Jake's buggy, and I see car lights behind it."

"Is Miriam with him?"

"I can't see, but you should be worrying about whether it's the midwife."

"It couldn't be anyone else."

"I'll be right back," Betty said, disappearing with the kerosene lamp.

Hannah waited in the darkness, trying to breathe deeply. She heard the cabin door open just as the pain started again, blocking out everything else. Betty came rushing back in followed by Miriam and the midwife. Jake's head appeared briefly in the bedroom doorway.

"Out, out!" Betty hollered at Jake. "This is no place for men. You'll just get in the way, and we already have three women in here."

"But it's my *bobli*!" Jake said, not moving.

"I said *out*!" Betty took his hand firmly and lead him back to the living room couch. "Now sit," she said. "We'll let you know when the baby's here."

After a brief look at Hannah's progress, Mattie said, "It'll be awhile yet. Miriam, why don't you sit with Hannah on the other side of the bed. Maybe that will help keep her mind occupied."

"There's nothing that will keep my mind occupied right now," Hannah said through clenched teeth.

"It will soon be over," the midwife said. "And you will remember this no more, like the Good Book says."

"That's right," Betty said from the doorway. "I forgot my pain as soon as my babies came, so keep your spirits up."

"What about Jake?" Hannah asked.

"He's not coming in here," Betty said. "It's not decent, and he can't handle it."

The midwife laughed softly. "I think it should be up to Hannah whether she wants Jake present. Do you want him in here, Hannah?"

"I don't know," Hannah said as the pain came again.

"That's all the answer I need," Betty said. "He's not coming in, and let's hear no more about it."

"I'm here," Miriam whispered from the other side of the bed, holding her sister's hand.

Hannah turned her head to smile weakly at her.

The minutes settled into an hour of pain…then a second hour passed with only brief respites in between contractions. Hannah saw Jake's face frequently at the bedroom door, but Betty always pounced on him with vigor.

"At least tell him what's going on," Hannah whispered.

"We are telling him, dear," Mattie said. "There's nothing going on. We're just waiting."

"Is there a problem?" Hannah asked.

"No," the midwife said. "Everything's fine, and it will be time soon. It looks to me like you will have a dawn baby."

"Dr. Lisa said we could call her if we need to," Hannah reminded her.

"I know," Mattie said. "And I would call if there were any danger, but there isn't. Just take courage. It won't be long now."

"I want him to come now!" Hannah said.

"So you still think it's a boy?" Mattie asked.

"*Jah*," Hannah said. "It's got to be a boy. Jake needs a boy."

"I think Jake will be happy either way," Mattie replied.

"He'd better be," Betty said. "Or I'll whack him over the head myself."

After another brief look at Hannah, Mattie said, "I think it's about time. In a few minutes, I'll tell you to push and when I do, that's your signal to give it all you've got. And then when I tell you to relax, you can stop pushing until I say push again. Are you ready?"

Hannah nodded as vigorously as she could muster while Betty watched nervously by the door and Miriam clutched Hannah's hand.

Several minutes later, with the first light of day sneaking over the mountain peaks, Hannah lay back on her pillow listening to the silence of the room. Miriam still had her hand in a firm grip. Betty and Mattie's forms moved rapidly about at the foot of the bed.

"Why isn't he crying?" Hannah whispered to Miriam.

"I don't know," Miriam said, squeezing her sister's hand.

Hannah tried to sit up, but she couldn't find the strength.

Miriam stroked her hand, a worried look on her face. Hannah struggled to rise again just as a piercing cry rent the room, followed by Miriam's sigh of relief.

"Is it...?" Hannah began.

"It's a boy!" Mattie said. "How did you know?"

Hannah didn't answer, letting her body go limp on the bed. The tears of joy came.

"There, there," the midwife's voice roused her as she wrapped the baby and then carefully placed him beside Hannah with the words, "I think this little fellow wants his mother."

Hannah turned toward the baby, emotion overflowing. "Tell Jake to come," she said.

Betty grunted from the foot of the bed but promptly bustled out. Moments later she returned with Jake following hesitantly.

"Come!" Hannah said, raising the baby blanket slightly. "I have something for you."

Jake moved slowly, coming to stand with his hands on the bed, his eyes on Hannah.

"Are you okay?" Jake asked.

Hannah nodded and Jake's eyes turned to the baby.

"Hold him," Hannah said. "And see what you want to call him."

"It's a boy?" he said, a broad smile spreading over his face. He lifted the baby carefully, cradling him tightly to his chest. The light of the dawn played on Jake's face and beard as he studied the baby.

"David," Jake said finally, turning to Hannah. "We will call him David, for he is a very special child. Do you like that?"

"*Jah*," Hannah said. "David is a *gut* name."

"Now let's get you out of here," Betty said, pulling on Jake's sleeve. "I don't care if you are a preacher. Hannah needs her rest."

Hannah watched as Jake's eyes lingered on the baby's face as he gently slid little David back onto the bed.

"You are wonderful," Jake said, turning to brush his hand across Hannah's forehead.

"That's enough," Betty snapped. "I said out of here, and out of here it will be."

Hannah laughed softly, joy filling every fiber of her being.

Forty-Four

Hannah lay on the couch looking out through the cabin window with baby David cradled in her arms. Miriam was cleaning up the breakfast dishes in the kitchen, her buggy still parked in front of the barn. Jake was home today, waving his arms around out in the open field as he directed the *Englisha* backhoe driver who was digging the footers for their new log home.

"Can I get you anything?" Miriam asked, her face appearing in the kitchen doorway.

"No. I just had to get out of bed and on my feet a little."

"Don't overdo it. It's not even been a week yet," Miriam said as she disappeared again.

Hannah's gaze fell to baby David's face, still wrinkled, but filling out more each day. He struggled to open his eyes, squinting up at her face and flexing the fingers on one hand. Soft black hair covered his head, reaching almost to his ears.

Hannah held her breath in awe. He was so perfect, so breakable, and yet so boyish—and all hers and Jake's. Tears welled up in her eyes as unspeakable joy rose up inside of her. How could *Da Hah* make something so wonderful? He had, but how was it possible?

"You're all mine," Hannah whispered. "And Jake's, but especially mine."

Would there be more children? Hopefully, but there would never be another moment like this one, when she held her first child in her arms. "I can't believe you're finally here," Hannah said, running her fingers over his soft cheeks. David opened his mouth, trying to follow the flow of motion across his skin. His eyes focused, blinking slowly, and then drifted off again.

"Do you want a glass of orange juice?" Miriam asked from the kitchen door.

Hannah nodded but said nothing.

"Is something wrong?" Miriam asked, noticing the tears spilling down her sister's cheeks.

Hannah shook her head. "No, I'm just enjoying David and watching his dad work outside."

"But you're crying."

"It's my first baby, Miriam. Of course I'm crying. You'll cry too."

"Oh, Hannah, he's so cute. David is truly the most wonderful baby I've ever seen."

"You have to say that. You're his aunt," Hannah said with a weak laugh.

"No, I mean it. He has to be the most wonderful baby ever born."

"Whatever you say," Hannah said, brushing the tears away. She glanced out the window at Jake. He had paused and was looking toward the main road. What he saw, Hannah couldn't see, but most likely it was a delivery of job materials.

Miriam handed Hannah the orange juice and asked, "Do you want anything else?"

Hannah laughed. "Let me think about it. I'm not used to being served hand and foot."

"Well, relax and enjoy it. Before long you'll be on your feet and back to work as hard as ever."

"I suppose you should go home soon," Hannah said. "It really worries me that you're away from Dennis so long. I mean, I know you promised me, but you haven't been married that long."

"Kendra's coming over to be with you tonight," Miriam said. "Betty insisted and I accepted because I miss Dennis. But I promise I'll be back bright and early tomorrow morning. Even before the sun comes up."

"I'm not complaining. I feel very pampered and spoiled."

"Look who's here!" Miriam said, pointing out the window. "Mr. Brunson and Mary. They must have come to see the baby."

"Oh, Miriam," Hannah gasped. "I don't look decent, and I don't have my head covering on. Do something quick. I wasn't expecting visitors."

"Relax," Miriam ordered, removing a shawl from the hall closet and draping it over Hannah's shoulders. "That's all you need. You look fine."

Hannah clutched the shawl with both hands, balancing David on her knees as Miriam went to open the door. Mary came rushing inside with Mr. Brunson right behind her. He took his green John Deere cap off, his face grinning from ear to ear.

"Well, what have we here?" Mr. Brunson's voice boomed. "A baby I do declare, and a Byler baby at that."

Mary bent down to give Hannah a hug. "I was so glad to hear that everything went well. Were you able to use the phone okay?"

"*Jah*," Hannah said. "Jake got the call through just fine. Thank you so much."

"Motherhood is so wonderful, isn't it?" Mary said, turning to coo at baby David. "What sweet little things they are."

"*Jah*," Hannah said. "He couldn't be any sweeter."

"A right handsome fellow," Mr. Brunson said, standing sideways over the couch to get a better view. "And I can see Jake all over him, so I'd say he's off to a good start."

Hannah ran her hand lightly over her son's hair.

"Has he been sleeping well?" Mary asked.

Hannah nodded, not trusting her voice.

"Well," Mr. Brunson boomed. "I think I've seen the baby, so I'll go out to see Jake, if you ladies don't mind."

"Thanks for coming," Hannah said, wiping a tear from her cheek. "It's so good to see both of you."

"You too. Take care now, you hear?" Mr. Brunson said and then disappeared out the door.

"Mary, may I get you a glass of orange juice?" Miriam asked.

"Sure," Mary said, taking a seat at the other end of the couch. "That would be wonderful."

"I'll be right back." Miriam jumped up and headed into the kitchen.

"So how have things been going?" Mary asked, reaching over to pick up David from Hannah's lap. Carefully she cradled the baby, laughing softly in his face. David opened his mouth and slowly waved one hand aimlessly.

"I think he likes you," Hannah said with a smile.

"I sure hope so!" Mary said as Miriam brought in the glass of orange juice, setting it beside the couch within Mary's reach.

"And how about you, Hannah? How are *you* doing?" Mary asked.

"I'm tired all the time and want to sleep, but hopefully that's normal."

"It's very normal, but it won't be long now before you're back up and full of energy," Mary encouraged.

"How are you and Mr. Brunson doing?" Hannah asked.

"Hannah, it's just wonderful! We're enjoying each other to the fullest. Sometimes it's hard for me to believe that *Da Hah* allowed it to happen again—that I found another wonderful man, but He did."

"We sure miss Mr. Brunson. It gets kind of lonesome around here."

"I can imagine that," Mary said, laughing. "We're trying to sell the place, but no success yet."

"There's no chance of the two of you moving back?"

"No, I'm afraid not," Mary said. "We couldn't drive over the mountains to church every Sunday."

"Then you'll have to visit more often."

"I would love that. I'm sure it won't be hard to talk Norman into it."

After a few minutes more of visiting, Mary stood and said, "You're tired and visitors should know when to leave. You need rest." With that, she handed David back to Hannah and said, "Dear, you take care of yourself." She bent over and gave Hannah another hug.

"I will," Hannah said, her eyes on baby David as his feet moved under the blanket. As the door closed behind Mary, Hannah teared up again. She turned to Miriam and said, "I can't seem to stop crying."

"At least they're happy tears," Miriam said.

Hannah looked out the window and saw Mr. Brunson and Jake shaking hands goodbye while Mary waited at the edge of the field. When Mr. Brunson turned to leave, Jake looked toward the cabin. He stood still for a moment, his eyes on Hannah. He smiled and waved. She could feel his love reach her across the distance.

"Tears of joy, yes. That's what they are," Hannah said, her eyes still on Jake.

Miriam placed a hand on Hannah's shoulder, and when she glanced up, Hannah noticed tears on Miriam's cheeks.

"Now *you're* crying!" Hannah exclaimed.

"*Jah*, but they're tears of joy too."

"We've both gone silly," Hannah said with a laugh.

"I know," Miriam said, wiping her eyes. "It's all Montana's fault, really, don't you think?"

About Jerry Eicher...

As a boy, **Jerry Eicher** spent eight years in Honduras, where his grandfather helped found an Amish community outreach. As an adult, Jerry taught for two terms in parochial Amish and Mennonite schools in Ohio and Illinois. He has been involved in church renewal for fourteen years and has preached in churches and conducted weekend meetings of in-depth Bible teaching. Jerry lives with his wife, Tina, and their four children in Virginia.

The Little Valley Trilogy

A Wedding Quilt for Ella

Ella Yoder's wedding with Aden Wengerd and the building of their dream house is set for June. But when Aden is suddenly taken from her, Ella begins to doubt God's love.

When her family pressures her to marry the new young bishop, Ella asks for six months to heal from Aden's death. Meanwhile, Aden's brother, Daniel, helps Ella build her dream house based on a drawing by her sister, Clara, that is incorporated into Ella's wedding quilt.

Can healing come through a house...a quilt...a community?

Ella's Wish

Ella Yoder has moved into her dream home. In the stillness of the great house, Ella ponders her options. How is she to survive on her own? Will she ever get over Aden? What will happen to her?

Two would-be suitors soon make their intentions known, but Ella is unsure of her feelings. As she agrees to take care of Preacher Stutzman's three motherless girls, Ella's heart is touched by their love for her. Could their affection be the answer to Ella's quest? Can God speak through the love of children?

You'll fall in love with Ella and hope with her for the love and happiness she seeks.

Coming August 2011, book 3: *Ella Finds Love Again.*

The Adams County Trilogy

Rebecca's Promise, Rebecca's Return, and *Rebecca's Choice*

Rebecca's Promise

Rebecca Keim has just declared her love to John Miller and agreed to become his wife. But she's haunted by her schoolgirl memories of a long-ago love—a promise made and a ring given. Is that memory a fantasy that will destroy the beautiful present...or is it real?

When Rebecca's mother sends her back to the old home community in Milroy to be with her aunt during and after her childbirth, Rebecca determines to find answers that will resolve her conflicted feelings. Faith, love, and tradition all play a part in Rebecca's destiny.

Rebecca's Return

Rebecca returns to Wheat Ridge determined to make her relationship with John Miller work. But in her absence, he has become suspicious of her. When John is badly injured, their relationship hangs in the balance.

Rebecca goes back to Milroy to aid her seriously ill Aunt Leona. While there, Rebecca visits the old covered bridge over the Flatrock River...a place of memories and a long-ago promise.

Where will Rebecca find happiness? In Wheat Ridge with John? Or should she stake her future on a memory that persists...and the ring she's never forgotten? What is God's perfect will?

Rebecca's Choice

Rebecca Keim and John Miller are engaged and looking forward to married life. But when Rebecca returns to her hometown to attend a beloved teacher's funeral, John receives a mysterious letter accusing her of marrying him for money. Fighting his past jealousies, John tries to ignore the accusation.

When Rebecca is named sole heir to her teacher's three farms, she is shocked by the condition—she must marry an Amish man. When John confronts Rebecca, she proclaims her innocence. Then Rachel Byler, the rightful heir, arrives and seeks vengance by revealing secrets that have the entire community reeling.